CAPTURE
OR
KILL

NOVELS BY VINCE FLYNN

AND BY KYLE MILLS

VINCE FLYNN

CAPTURE OR KILL

A MITCH RAPP NOVEL
BY DON BENTLEY

EMILY BESTLER BOOKS

ATRIA

New York   London   Toronto   Sydney   New Delhi

EMILY
BESTLER
BOOKS

ATRIA

An Imprint of Simon & Schuster, LLC
1230 Avenue of the Americas
New York, NY 10020

First Emily Bestler Books/Atria Books hardcover edition September 2024

EMILY BESTLER BOOKS/ATRIA BOOKS and colophon are trademarks of Simon & Schuster, LLC

Simon & Schuster: Celebrating 100 Years of Publishing in 2024

For information about special discounts for bulk purchases, please contact Simon & Schuster Special Sales at 1-866-506-1949 or business@simonandschuster.com.

The Simon & Schuster Speakers Bureau can bring authors to your live event. For more information or to book an event, contact the Simon & Schuster Speakers Bureau at 1-866-248-3049 or visit our website at www.simonspeakers.com.

Manufactured in the United States of America

1   3   5   7   9   10   8   6   4   2

Library of Congress Cataloging-in-Publication Data has been applied for.

ISBN 978-1-6680-4583-1
ISBN 978-1-6680-4586-2 (ebook)

To Vince—thank you for Mitch Rapp.
I hope this book makes you proud.

CAPTURE
OR
KILL

PROLOGUE

T HE demonstration was a bit dramatic for Azad Ashani's taste.

Then again, he was surrounded by dramatic people.

In a setting that was markedly at odds with the confidence displayed by the Quds Force operatives in charge of the demonstration, Ashani stood at the edge of a granite cliff overlooking a sprawling valley. The night was gentle in comparison to the day's brutal heat, and even though it hadn't rained in weeks, Ashani thought he could taste a hint of moisture in the air.

Or perhaps that was just wishful thinking.

In Ashani's opinion, this entire gathering was held together by naivete, misplaced hope, and blind vengeance.

A cough racked his thin frame.

Turning, he spat a wad of phlegm onto the rocky soil. Though the demonstration's fiery culmination still flickered from the rocks rimming the base of the cliff, the flames were much too far away to illuminate the color of his saliva.

No matter.

Ashani knew its hue all the same.

Red.

It was always red.

Withdrawing a red handkerchief from his pocket, Ashani ran the soft fabric over his cracked lips. He'd done an admirable job of hiding his symptoms thus far, but those days were quickly coming to an end. Ashani might be a master spy, but he was no magician. Sooner or later, he would experience a coughing fit in the wrong company, or the doctor he'd sworn to secrecy would whisper in the wrong ears, or the cocktail of medications masking his symptoms would cease to be effective. One way or another, the disease devouring his innards would make its presence known.

He was standing at the edge of a precipice in more ways than one.

"What is this madness?"

The question, though whispered, was not one that he could afford to ignore.

Ashani was in his late fifties, with a slim build and average stature. Though not physically imposing, he still inspired fear. As head of his nation's Ministry of Intelligence, or MOIS, Ashani led an organization with a bloody history. Conversation ceased at Ashani's appearance. Those who saw him on the street often crossed to the other side of the road.

But a man in his position had enemies.

Ashani had begun his career as a paramilitary officer, and he was a veteran of the Iran-Iraq War. He no longer had an operator's muscled build, but there was a hardness to him. A sharp edge that even age and the ravages of his illness couldn't entirely dull. For the most part, his adversaries were external to the organization he led.

For the most part.

But a knife thrust wasn't any less deadly just because it came from a trusted lieutenant rather than a barbarian at the gates.

"I think the choice of venue is . . . inspired," Ashani said.

His questioner snorted.

Ashani had served in the MOIS his entire life, rising to the rank of "minister" half a dozen years ago. Even so, the man standing next to Ashani was a mystery. True power in the Islamic Republic of Iran rested not with the nation's president or any of the popularly elected officials who exercised pseudo governing authority in the parliament. These offices were just for show. A mechanism to convince the populace that they actually had a degree of say in the manner in which their nation was run.

They did not.

True power resided in just one body—the Guardian Council.

This conclave of twelve men consisted of six Shia clerics and six lawyers. The Supreme Leader, a cleric named Ali Hoseini-Nassiri, reigned over the council. This arrangement meant that the Islamic Republic of Iran was governed according to the whims of an eighty-year-old Shia imam. An elderly theocrat whose last remaining earthly wish was to witness the apocalyptic battle that would bring about the return of the fabled Twelfth Imam. Ashani did not think that the combination of a dictator fixated on leaving a legacy of blood and ashes and a cadre of sycophants singularly focused on providing him with the means to do so was a harbinger of good fortune for the nation he loved.

But he was not foolish enough to say this to the man standing next to him.

The man in question, Darian Moradi, was a relative newcomer to the MOIS. Prior to his appointment as Ashani's deputy a month earlier, the young cleric hadn't held an official position in government. Instead, he'd served as the adjutant to a ranking member of the Guardian Council.

A cleric who could very well be Iran's next Supreme Leader.

Unlike Hoseini-Nassiri, Moradi's boss seemed less focused on the never-ending quest to destroy Iran's Jewish neighbor and more on stabilizing the regime through normalization with the rest of the world.

This made Moradi's question both interesting and dangerous.

"Inspired by the magnificent vista?" Moradi said. "Or the giant man-made sinkhole?"

Ashani stood on the eastern side of the plateau. Behind him, the mountain continued skyward. The drivable trail that led from the mountain's base ended at the plateau, becoming a rocky path passable only to donkeys or goats. The plateau's other occupants were gathered at the western side of the terrain feature about seventy meters distant. Their jubilant voices carried across the open ground as they gestured toward the flames licking the metallic wreckage strewn across the valley floor.

No doubt the venue was chosen in part to showcase the clear night.

In part.

There were plenty of places in Iran that offered a commanding view of the sky along with the requisite room needed to catch large chunks of smoldering aluminum and plastic as they fell to the earth. The decision to hold the demonstration here undoubtedly had much to do with what had once been concealed beneath tons of cement and steel on the valley floor.

But agreeing and voicing that agreement were two different things.

Ashani eyed his companion.

At first glance, Moradi was nothing remarkable. His beard was the prescribed length, his circular turban sparkling white, and his gray *qabaa* robe elegantly tailored. Though he was ostensibly Ashani's second-in-command, the cleric clearly maintained an open line of communication with his former boss. Even so, Moradi was respectful to Ashani and did not flaunt his obvious political connections. His thin frame showed none of the corpulence often associated with Iran's ruling elite, and his short stature was not aided by platform shoes. Most importantly, the dark eyes present behind his clear framed glasses were sharp and thoughtful.

The eyes of someone who saw much but spoke little.

In their admittedly limited interactions, Ashani had yet to put the man in a box. Moradi asked intelligent questions, did not trade on his former boss's influence, and wasn't prone to ravings meant to demonstrate his religious fervor. He reminded Ashani of a particularly keen aide-de-camp. This was a man with whom it would be easy to let down one's guard.

Which was why Ashani intended to do the opposite.

"It is a very nice evening," Ashani allowed.

This was true.

April and May were two of the more pleasant months in Isfahan. The bitter cold of winter was a thing of the past and the spring rain briefly returned life to the desert. Only two weeks ago, Ashani would have needed a thick coat and gloves to survive the brutal winds that buffeted the cliff face, but tonight the temperature hovered around 18 degrees Celsius and the breeze felt gentle and warm.

"You are a cautious one," Moradi said with a chuckle. "Willing to discuss the weather but no words for the sea of flashing red lights?"

The red lights in question winked from atop the type of portable barriers that normally heralded a stretch of road marred by construction. But the constellation of crimson beacons blinking from the valley floor had a different purpose. Ashani was not a civil engineer, but he didn't believe anything would be built upon the concrete cairn the barriers ringed in this lifetime.

Or even the next.

The barriers were meant to prevent the unwary from venturing too close to a radioactive cavern. A cavern that had once contained the centrifuges and feeder reactor that were critical to Iran's nuclear weapons program. Billons of dollars lay beneath the rubble.

Billions the Islamic Republic of Iran did not have.

Ashani sighed.

This was the second time the cleric had brought up the elephant in the room.

"What happened here was a tragedy," Ashani said.

"How many died?"

Ashani turned from his contemplation of the massive crater to find the little cleric's eyes on him. This time no merriment shone from their depths.

"Too many," Ashani said.

"You were almost one of them."

Moradi's response seemed more statement than question, but Ashani knew he still owed the cleric an answer.

"Yes."

"What do you think about the disaster?" Moradi said.

"The loss of life was tragic," Ashani said. "The perpetrators should be brought to justice."

"Yes, yes," Moradi said, waving away Ashani's answer. "You are suitably outraged, and we must swear vengeance on the Americans, the Jews, the Kurds, or whoever sabotaged our supposedly impenetrable nuclear weapons research facility. I will save us both the trouble and pretend that you regurgitated the appropriate rhetoric, but you've misunderstood my question. I want to know what you think about the site's purpose—the development of an atomic bomb."

This time Ashani didn't have to fake his reaction.

Though the two men were standing apart from the huddle of figures gathered at the cliff's edge, Ashani still couldn't believe what he'd just heard. Belief in the necessity of the Iranian nuclear weapons program was canonical in its fervor. Tens of billions had been spent on the effort, and the ensuing international sanctions had crippled Iran's economy. Even so, continued adherence to this strategy wasn't given any more thought than questioning why water was wet.

It simply was.

Moradi might as well have been asking Ashani if he believed that Muhammad was Allah's prophet. Ashani hoped for a coughing fit or some other excuse not to speak. A burst of laughter echoed from the group of men clustered at the far side of the bluff.

Fools.

They were all fools.

A gaggle of clerics from the Guardian Council in their formal robes, the vice president of Iran in his Western-style suit, and the man who'd conceived this plot—a Quds Force colonel.

Originally brought into existence by the first Supreme Leader with the goal of safeguarding the resistance, Quds Force had become a nation within a nation. Ashani often thought of them as akin to the Nazis' feared Schutzstaffel, or SS. Operatives answerable only to the Supreme Leader himself. That these fanatics were responsible for tonight's demonstration and the scheme it supposedly validated came as no surprise.

That Iran's ruling class was considering their plan was.

While Moradi's former boss was not in attendance, tonight's gathering included power brokers from across the Iranian government. This event was indicative of a seismic shift in Iran's approach to the West. A shift Ashani suspected would prove to be the undoing of the nation he loved.

Where did that leave him?

"What I think about the program is immaterial," Ashani said, choosing his words carefully. "I do not make policy decisions. I serve the Islamic Republic of Iran and the Supreme Leader Ali Hoseini-Nassiri."

"Of course you do," Moradi said with a smirk, "but what about the operation the Quds Force operatives are proposing? If you were the Supreme Leader's advisor, would you counsel that such a venture was wise?"

Ashani would not.

Yes, what the Quds Force imagined had a chance of working, and yes, even he had to admit that their operational planning was impressive. But as the concrete tomb at the base of the cliff could attest, grand schemes often led to grand failures. The flames consuming the downed aircraft's wreckage looked more like a funeral pyre than a victory bonfire.

"If the Supreme Leader desired my thoughts, I would provide them," Ashani said, locking eyes with the cleric, "but my words would be for him alone."

Moradi held his gaze for an uncomfortably long time before slowly turning away. As a career intelligence officer, Ashani prided himself on his ability to read people, but he couldn't tell what the cleric was thinking.

"This is madness," Moradi said, whispering the words. "Absolute madness. And no one can stop it."

Moradi strode away before Ashani could reply, which was just as well, since he wasn't sure how he would have responded. Yes, this was madness. If the Quds Force plot succeeded, there was a very real chance the Middle East would be plunged into a regional war. If it failed, the radioactive cavern at the cliff's base would look like a playground in comparison to what the Americans would do to his country.

Ashani was in violent agreement with Moradi on the cleric's first point.

Not the second.

There was someone who could stop this rush to madness. A man who terrified Ashani in a way that even the disease consuming him did not. Sometimes survival required a willingness to do the unthinkable. Ashani was a dead man, but perhaps his wife and daughters didn't need to share his fate.

It was time to make a deal with the devil.

A devil known as *Malikul Mawt*.

The Angel of Death.

CHAPTER 1

"I'm taking this chair."

The muscular Pakistani man grabbed the chair in question and dragged it across AstroTurf-coated concrete to the far side of the patio. He didn't wait for a reply from the table's occupant. The Pakistani's companion, a pretty brunette, frowned at her date's boorish behavior. Though the sun had long since set and the evening's unseasonably muggy air settled on the shoulders of her robin-egg blue *shalwar kameez* like a thick cotton blanket, she still shivered.

Sunrise Café was a trendy spot, and its outdoor courtyard was much in demand. The patio was populated by white wicker tables and matching chairs adorned with plush red cushions. Potted plants surrounded the seating area and hung from wooden adornments while cooling electric fans provided a semblance of a breeze.

The breeze had not caused the woman's shiver.

Something about the slim man seated alone at the far side of the café gave her pause. Though there was nothing about his manner to suggest that he'd understood what her boyfriend had said, or taken offense at her date's rude actions, the woman could not shake her sense of unease.

The man had an olive complexion and thick, black hair that had begun to gray at the temples. He could have passed for a half a dozen nationalities, but his expensive linen slacks, tailored sport coat, and silk dress shirt worn open at the collar had a European flair. He hadn't so much as looked up from his paper during the earlier interaction, but as if he could feel her gaze, he did so now.

The woman swallowed.

Though the man's face bore no malice, his eyes made her stomach tremble. The black orbs stared through her, and she shivered a second time.

"Sorry," the woman said, mouthing the word.

The man gazed at her for a beat longer.

Then, he slowly nodded.

"Sorry for what?" her date said. "Him? He's nothing."

The woman smiled at her companion as he settled into his chair. "I'm sure you're right," she said.

Her boyfriend was not right.

The man had gone back to his paper and a sense of calm settled over the patio, though the woman couldn't help but think that it was the calm before a storm.

Mitch Rapp was accustomed to being underestimated.

To be fair, Rapp made a practice of appearing as something other than he was. This was not so much because he was embarrassed about his vocation as that what he did for a living wasn't often discussed in polite company.

Rapp was a professional killer.

"FAIRBANKS confirmed. I say again, FAIRBANKS confirmed, over."

Rapp fought the urge to grind his teeth at the radio transmission, choosing instead to vent his frustration on his espresso. Selecting the unsuspecting spoon lying adjacent to the ceramic cup, he stirred the dark contents with an altogether unnecessary vigor.

Rapp knew that the man currently making his way down School

Road toward Sunrise Café had been given the CIA code name FAIR-
BANKS. He knew that the Pakistani businessman owned homes on
three continents. Rapp knew that he walked with an altered gait because
of a cricket injury that had occurred at age twelve, that his hook nose
curved slightly to the left, and that his right cheek sported a trio of
pockmarks courtesy of a bout of measles.

Pockmarks that formed a precise isosceles triangle.

Rapp also knew that FAIRBANKS was a shitbag of the first order.

He knew all this because Rapp had been hunting FAIRBANKS for
the better part of five years and, after finding him, had personally
pitched this operation to Irene Kennedy, the director of the Central Intelligence Agency and Rapp's boss. Rapp no more needed a CIA analyst
who was watching FAIRBANKS's route of travel from miles away, courtesy of a clandestine camera to verify the businessman's identity, than he
needed help picking out his own mother from across the kitchen table.

But the voice was whispering in his ear all the same.

With a final stir of the swirling liquid, Rapp tapped the spoon on
the edge of his cup before setting the utensil on the saucer's edge. The
silverware's placement was perfect, exactly ninety degrees from the cup
and without a drop of liquid to foul the white tablecloth or the precisely
folded newspaper lying to the cup's left. This level of attention to detail
was not because he suffered from obsessive-compulsive disorder or because he had a particular penchant for table manners.

No, his current behavior was driven by something else.

His legend.

While his features and polyglot ability permitted Rapp to pass for a
number of nationalities, the Bordeaux-colored passport in his sport
coat pocket proclaimed him a proud citizen of the République française
and he intended to behave as such. Rapp was well traveled enough to
know that not every French businessman was a caricature of the anal,
self-absorbed Frog lampooned by American popular culture, but the
stereotype existed for a reason. For the most part, people saw what they
expected to see, and when the events of the next few moments were

over, Rapp fervently hoped that his fellow Islamabad diners remembered a meticulous Frenchman occupying the table closest to the pedestrian path.

If they remembered anything at all.

"IRONMAN, please confirm you received our last transmission, over."

On the pretext of scratching an itch, Rapp sent an index finger deep into his ear canal and removed a tiny flesh-colored receiver. He ruffled his paper to distract any wandering eyes even as he deposited the pea-size bit of electronics into his coffee, where it promptly sank from sight. Though he knew his actions would necessitate a sit-down with Irene when he returned stateside, Rapp already felt better.

The same could not be said of his earpiece.

An operational team was sometimes merited, but this was not the case tonight. Rapp had begun his CIA employment by working as a singleton. A lone killer. He hadn't worked alone because he was some sort of antisocial vigilante. Rapp operated solo because he was good.

Very good.

The kind of good in which additional operational support tended to become a hindrance rather than a help. Saddling Rapp with extra shooters when he didn't need them was the equivalent of teaming Kobe Bryant with players from a local high school. Unless Rapp picked his teammates, the other operatives just got in the way.

And he had not picked this team.

As if summoned by his thoughts, his burner phone vibrated.

Rapp reached into his pocket and powered down the device.

While he considered the earpiece gracing the bottom of his coffee cup extraneous, the same could not be said of his phone. There was a difference between being headstrong and acting foolishly. In roughly three minutes, Rapp intended to rid the earth of a particularly vile human being, and he had no intention of following his prey into the afterlife. To escape, Rapp would need the burner phone, so he permitted the device's continued presence, but he did not need the distraction poised by whoever was currently texting him.

A car pulled up to the curb on Rapp's left.

He allowed his gaze to settle on the vehicle with the same casual interest that might be displayed by any of the café's patrons.

Rapp's interest was not casual.

FAIRBANKS did not owe his survival to good fortune. While Rapp had been in the field long enough to understand the role that luck played in any operation, this alone was not enough to keep a man safe from a predator with Rapp's abilities.

FAIRBANKS was still alive because he'd had help.

Help of the kind only a nation-state could provide.

By killing FAIRBANKS, Mitch intended to send the government who had aided and abetted his evil an unambiguous message—the old rules no longer applied. Nearly a decade after nineteen jihadis had perpetrated the worst attack on American soil since Pearl Harbor, the war on terror had reached an inflection point. The Islamic Republic of Pakistan could either help the United States track down and eliminate terrorists or suffer the consequences.

A blunt message to be delivered by a blunt-force object.

The car door opened, and a man exited.

But not just any man.

Colonel Dariush Ruyintan stood not more than a stone's throw from Rapp's table.

Though Rapp was a veteran of countless clandestine operations, the sight of Ruyintan rocked him to his core. The Iranian Quds Force expeditionary commander had more American blood on his hands than any single individual save perhaps Osama bin Laden himself. He had funded the work into explosively formed penetrators and had masterminded the ratlines through which the devices had poured into Iraq from Iran. Though the US troop surge had stabilized Iraq and saved the war, Ruyintan had been the one who'd made it necessary. The intelligence officer had been so successful at countering American anti-insurgency efforts that Irene had lobbied to replace the head of Al Qaeda with Ruyintan as the number one counterterrorism target.

The CIA director hadn't won that battle, but she'd had a pointed conversation with her top counterterrorism operative all the same. If Rapp ever found himself able to eliminate the Iranian, he was to do so. Fate had just served up the opportunity of a lifetime, but there was a problem.

Rapp already had someone else to kill.

CHAPTER 2

T HE Iranian colonel entered the café's outdoor seating area in a
scrum of bodies.

Rapp eyed the protective detail with the disdain a well-heeled
Frenchman would show a cluster of suit-clad ruffians who had deigned
to interrupt his final espresso of the night. But underneath Rapp's disgusted expression, he was evaluating the men with an assassin's practiced eyes.

The detail was good.

Though Rapp rated Iranian Quds Force members only slightly
higher than the black scorpion he'd mashed into his hotel room floor
this morning, he did not allow his derision for who they were and what
they believed to influence his assessment of their martial capabilities.

Only fools and dead men underestimated Iranians.

Mitch was neither.

The protective detail flowed across the open patio like an ocean wave
cresting a sand castle. The six men were dressed in business formal—
suits, lace-up shoes, and dress shirts open at the collar. The suits were
high-quality, and the jackets were worn unbuttoned.

The bodies beneath were lean and hard.

Rapp had been killing men long enough to recognize the difference between protective details that used bulk to deter would-be attackers and those who relied on training. Thick-necked, muscle-bound 'roid-heads might dissuade drunk frat boys in a college bar, but they were ineffective against professionals.

By comparison, Ruyintan's detail looked like a pack of hyenas.

The men didn't attempt to intimidate through sheer physicality. Instead, their cold eyes and blank expressions did the talking. The two lead bodyguards swept past Rapp and continued into the café proper. The remaining four boxed Ruyintan as he ambled up the cobblestone sidewalk leading from the street to the café's synthetic-turf-covered patio.

Rapp watched the procession long enough to make eye contact with the colonel before returning his gaze to his newspaper. The Iranian's show of force was impressive, but Rapp's legend proclaimed him a businessman who helped interested parties navigate tiresome regulations. The kind of regulations meant to curb the sale of illegal firearms.

Men with guns weren't exactly a novelty.

"*Pardonnez-moi, monsieur, aidez-moi, s'il vous plait?*"

The Iranian bodyguard spoke in accented but understandable French. His lean build mirrored that of his companions, but his shoulders were heavier and chest broader. A middleweight surrounded by welterweights. He had a pugilist's flattened nose, and his misshapen knuckles were crisscrossed with scars. His foot placement suggested boxing, but his cauliflower ears pointed toward a passion for wrestling. Either way, this was not a man to be taken lightly. The bodyguard stood a respectful distance from Mitch, but his posture suggested the question was not rhetorical.

Rapp decided to put this theory to the test.

"*Non,*" Mitch said, turning the page on his newspaper as he spoke. His semi-slouch radiated a disinterest that was starkly at odds with the tendrils of tension tightening his stomach. FAIRBANKS was nothing if not punctual. In just seconds, the Pakistani businessman would be rounding the corner, no doubt eagerly anticipating a nightcap at his favorite coffee shop.

Rapp had endured more oversight during the planning phase of this sanctioned assassination than the last dozen combined. As evidenced by the clandestine camera array and the voice that had been formerly whispering in his ear, killing a scumbag on the streets of an ally's capital city was not an insignificant act.

Even toward an ally as fickle as Pakistan.

Sending a message was all well and good, but doing so effectively required a certain subtlety. Rapp was the first to admit that the word *subtle* was not a descriptor often applied to him, but in this case he agreed with the strategy. FAIRBANKS needed to die in a manner that left no misunderstanding as to the cause of his demise while still throwing enough doubt on the identity of the perpetrators to allow the Pakistani government to express public outrage while privately realizing they'd been given an ultimatum.

This message would be infinitely harder to send if the Iranian's guard dogs ran Mitch out of the café. Ruyintan mounted the café's steps and strode across the AstroTurf. But rather than heading for the coffee shop's welcoming front door, the Iranian angled left.

Toward Rapp's table.

CHAPTER 3

"Excuse me, sir," Ruyintan said. "Do you mind if I join you?"

Rapp did mind.

Besides the fact that he could see FAIRBANKS's gray-streaked hair as he meandered down the street to his left, Rapp had a thing about sharing tables with Iranian colonels.

But Ruyintan wasn't one to take no for an answer.

Before Rapp could reply, the Quds Force operative appropriated a chair from a nearby table and sat. That the chair had only moments before held the same muscular Pakistani man who'd originally stolen it from Rapp seemed of little concern to the Iranian. Two of the colonel's bodyguards emerged from the café and helpfully explained to the enraged musclehead that his latte would taste much better if he chose to finish it inside the café.

The Iranians' persuasive words seemed to calm him.

Or maybe it was sight of pistols bulging from shoulder holsters.

Either way, the man stormed into the café, and his date got up from her seat and meekly followed. As the pretty woman drew even with Rapp, she graced him with a tentative smile and then disappeared inside.

When it came to women or chairs, there really was no accounting for taste.

A second pair of guards positioned themselves to either side of Mitch's shoulders and the final pair faced the road.

"Sorry," Mitch said, ignoring the skin-crawling feeling that adversaries in his blind spot always produced, "but I'm expecting someone."

"Not just someone," Ruyintan said. "You are waiting for a certain Pakistani businessman. He thinks he's meeting Monsieur Dubois to discuss a rather sizable acquisition. But that isn't so, is it? You might have a maroon passport, but the Republic is not the land of your birth any more than French is your native tongue. Your given name is actually *Saeed. Farid Saeed.*"

Ruyintan had been speaking in French until he'd arrived at the final sentence. Those words had been rendered in Arabic, perhaps to give the nom de guerre the emphasis it deserved.

Not much surprised Mitch.

This did.

Mitch returned the colonel's gaze.

The Iranian was both as Rapp expected him to be in person and different. Ruyintan's appearance basically tracked the dossier photos the CIA had compiled on the Quds Force expeditionary commander over the years. Though he was dressed in the same Western-style business casual attire of his men, it was clear that Ruyintan was not some boardroom banker.

Or at least it was clear to Rapp.

Ruyintan's coal-colored hair was sprinkled with gray and stylishly cut. His obligatory beard was trimmed close to the skin and his TV-ready face was that of a politician rather than a warrior. But a closer look at the wrinkles around his eyes and the sun marks on his forehead suggested that this was the visage of a man who'd spent the majority of his life outdoors.

And not the sort of outdoors associated with a country club's golf course.

As the faint pucker on his right cheekbone could attest, Ruyintan led his troops from the front lines, not a cushy command post in Tehran. Though the blemish could have been attributed to childhood acne, Rapp knew the mark's true source—a 5.56mm round.

An *American* 5.56mm round.

Ruyintan had sustained the wound in Fallujah, Iraq, when a Marine rifleman's shot had cratered the stucco wall next to him rather than his skull. The metal fragments had just missed the colonel's eye. Rapp had wondered on more than one occasion how many US lives might have been saved if the Marine's aim had been true, but it was Ruyintan's presence rather than his appearance that surprised Rapp the most. The air surrounding the Quds Force commander seemed charged with electricity. As if the Iranian were a lightning bolt poised to strike. Though he'd encountered them sparingly, Rapp had met such men before.

Dangerous men.

Ruyintan had begun the conversation in a manner meant to startle Rapp, which meant that he had an expected fraction of a second to decide how to respond. Maybe up to an entire second if he pushed his luck. For most people, a single second wasn't much time.

Rapp wasn't most people.

In the time required to draw a breath, Rapp ran through several potential courses of action. In his left breast pocket, Rapp carried a pen that, when triggered in a very specific manner, emitted 5 ccs of slow-acting neurotoxin. Since FAIRBANKS traveled with bodyguards, Rapp had expected to be frisked prior to their sit-down. As such, he was not carrying his customary Glock and suppressor, but even a man with Rapp's abilities did not prowl the streets of Islamabad unarmed.

A knife featuring a four-inch ceramic blade and a 3-D printed hilt formed the latching mechanism on Rapp's belt. The weapon would never win an award for sexiest killing implement, but it was custom-made for Rapp's hand, easily concealed, and couldn't be discovered by a metal detector. Rapp was confident that he could end Ruyintan's life before one of his bodyguards intervened. What happened next would be a bit of a free-for-all, but Mitch liked his odds.

Even so, he did not give in to his homicidal urge.

Yet.

Over the course of their years working together, Rapp had grudgingly come around to Irene's way of thinking when it came to the big fish. The men who ordered foot soldiers into harm's way should be afforded the same opportunity to meet Allah as their underlings.

But sometimes, there was a benefit in delaying their departure.

Small fish were a dime a dozen. Big fish, on other hand, could serve as bait for an even larger catch. So rather than shove the dull end of his teaspoon through the Iranian's right eyeball, Rapp decided to do something even more shocking.

Talk.

"What do you want?" Rapp said.

Following the Iranian's lead, Rapp asked the question in Arabic, but unlike the Quds Force officer's Persian-accented vowels and consonants, Mitch's had an Iraqi flavor. In a turn of events that had delighted Stan Hurley and flummoxed agency linguists, Rapp spoke Arabic with a pronounced Iraqi accent.

A Mosul accent, to be precise.

Some people were born to compose symphonies or solve mathematical equations.

Mitch was created to hunt his nation's enemies.

"I want to propose a way that our two organizations can achieve a common goal," Ruyintan said.

The cloud of gray hair representing FAIRBANKS paused at the café's entrance.

Then he continued down the sidewalk.

Rapp kept his outward expression blank, but inside he seethed.

His meeting with the Pakistani businessman had been the result of months of intelligence work. Untold resources had been dedicated to finding the man, developing a pattern of life, constructing an interdiction plan, and moving the required assets into place. And this was to say nothing of the hoops Rapp had to jump through to get this killing sanctioned. All told, the operation easily represented a year of Rapp's life, and that year was now vanishing down an Islamabad side street.

Rapp was livid.

Farid Saeed was not.

Rapp had spent years perfecting the Saeed persona. A former officer in Saddam's army turned illicit businessman. Most former Iraqi army officers chose one of two paths: criminality or terrorism. As members of the Baath party, the soldiers were Sunni in a Shia-majority country and quickly found themselves targets of Iranian-sponsored militias on the lookout for a little payback after years of suppression under the Iraqi strongman's rule. With a choice between starvation or execution, it wasn't hard to understand why these former soldiers rarely became upstanding members of the Iraqi community.

Farid Saeed was no exception.

"What goal?" Rapp said.

Rapp was genuinely interested in the Iranian's answer.

The Saeed legend had been developed to provide Mitch with the freedom to move across the Islamic crescent without attracting attention. Rapp was not a traditional case officer. His efforts were dedicated to hunting men, not converting them to CIA assets. As such, he hadn't tried to use his bona fides to penetrate terrorist organizations or recruit informants. That he'd come to the attention of Iranian intelligence was not surprising, but the fact that he was known by name by one of the Quds Force's most dangerous operatives was an unforeseen but not necessarily unwelcome development.

Regardless of what the Iranian said next, Rapp was certain he'd have a ready reply.

"The goal of killing Americans in Afghanistan," Ruyintan said.

Or perhaps not.

CHAPTER 4

MITCH Rapp did not commemorate his successes with notches on his pistol grip.

He might have begun his life as a paramilitary officer in no small part as revenge for the deaths of his fiancée and the two hundred and sixty-nine other innocents who'd perished after a Libyan terrorist had planted a bomb on Pan Am Flight 103, but that was then. Rapp had long since transitioned from killing as an emotional salve to killing as a way of life. Assassinating his nation's enemies was a job that needed to be done, and he was uniquely suited to do it.

End of story.

Or at least Rapp wanted to believe this was the case.

But sometimes he wasn't so sure. At this moment, he wanted to reach across the table, snare the preening Iranian in a cross-collar choke, and squeeze his throat's soft tissue until the Quds Force officer's eyes bulged.

Instead, Rapp asked the obvious question.

"How?" Rapp said.

A smile lit the Iranian's face.

"You see?" Ruyintan said. "Even adversaries can find common cause when it comes to killing Americans. Tell your organization that we have something that can change the course of the war in Afghanistan. Something that will be as impactful there as our improvised explosive devices were in your country."

When it came to impulse control, Rapp was something of a savant, but this shitbag was putting even his legendary skills to the test. Rapp had visited the military's burn center at Fort Sam Houston in Texas. He'd seen the results of Ruyintan's handiwork up close. Amputations were horrific, but disfigurements caused by the molten slugs generated by the Iranian's explosively formed penetrators, or EFPs, were in a class all their own. He'd spent time with a CIA colleague who'd sustained third-degree burns over 50 percent of her body after an EFP had detonated beneath her vehicle.

Her face had been rendered unrecognizable.

A cross-collar choke was too good for Ruyintan.

Instead, Rapp envisioned a spear hand to the throat to get the colonel's attention, followed by blunt-force trauma to his cranium. When it came to payback, nothing beat a good old-fashioned head-bashing. Strategic intelligence was all well and good, but sometimes the instinctive response that came with spotting a cockroach was the correct one—smash its crunchy body into the floor.

Rapp would get the pertinent information from this Quds Force murderer.

Then he would kill him.

"What something?" Rapp said.

The Iranian's smile grew wider even as he shook his head. "I've always found deeds preferable to words. In light of the history of mistrust between our organizations, I propose a show of good faith instead. A demonstration."

"What kind of demonstration?" Rapp said.

"An unmistakable one. Within the hour, I expect our handiwork to be the topic of discussion on every Western news channel."

The part of Rapp's mind dedicated to battlefield calculus did the operational math. Six bodyguards, but only two of the minders had their attention focused on the table. Two-to-one odds were not great, but Rapp had done more with less.

Could he kill Ruyintan before the Iranian's minders intervened?

Yes.

Would he be able to extricate himself afterward?

Probably, but the ensuing mayhem wouldn't be pretty.

Unfortunately, killing Ruyintan was no longer Rapp's primary concern. The peacock was being deliberately cagey. While Rapp could wring the details from the Quds Force operative if given enough time, Rapp needed the man alive and in a mostly functioning state in order to conduct a proper interrogation. This precondition took assassinating the Iranian outright off the table.

Time to change the equation.

With an exaggerated look at his Rolex, Rapp got to his feet.

"Where are you going?" Ruyintan said.

The Iranian's Cheshire cat grin was gone, replaced by another expression.

Worry.

"You've already made me miss one appointment," Rapp said. "I don't intend to miss another."

For a moment, the Iranian's mask dropped.

Though Rapp had never met Ruyintan before, the face now staring back at him was one he recognized.

The face of a killer.

Then, the fake smile returned.

"Fine," Ruyintan said. "I will tell you what is about to happen, but take care with the information."

"I understand the concept of operational security," Rapp said, still standing.

"Of course you do," Ruyintan said, "but you mistake my meaning. The details I'm about to provide are known to no one outside my organization. No one. This means it will be very easy to isolate the leak should what I tell you become more widely publicized."

Ruyintan's hard expression left no doubts about how he intended to deal with such a leak, but Farid Saeed wasn't a man who was easily intimidated.

This was a trait Rapp happened to share with his fictional persona.

"You came to me," Rapp said.

"I did," the Iranian said, "but at the moment I'm having trouble remembering why."

Rapp made as if to slide around the table, but stopped when Ruyintan held up his hand.

"Just south of the Spin Ghar mountains," Ruyintan said. "Pakistan."

Rapp hesitated.

"Now that I have your attention," Ruyintan said, "sit."

Rapp slowly settled back into his chair.

Though outwardly he gave no sign, his heart was racing.

The Spin Ghar mountains were part of the rugged terrain that delineated Afghanistan's southern border with Pakistan. More importantly, the mountain range was known for the Battle of Tora Bora—the ill-fated American attempt to capture bin Laden in the closing months of 2001. The area presented no shortage of targets for the special operators responsible for decapitating the terrorist organizations that called the area home.

"You want specifics?" Ruyintan said. "At this moment, a flight of American helicopters is ferrying a team of commandos toward what they believe is an unsuspecting high-value target. The operation won't go quite as planned."

"I need more than that," Rapp said.

"No, you don't. Watch the news, then talk to your organization. If you're interested in brokering a deal, call this number."

Ruyintan withdrew something from his pocket and tossed it at Rapp.

A business card fluttered through the air before coming to rest on the table. A series of digits were written in black ink across the bottom of the card stock in an engineer's precise hand. According to his dossier, the Iranian had earned a postgraduate degree from the prestigious Moscow Engineering Physics Institute.

Ruyintan hadn't just flooded Iraq with EFPs.

He'd helped design the weapons.

Rapp picked up the card, turning it in his fingers.

"Excellent choice," Ruyintan said, getting to his feet. "You will find that I make a much better friend than enemy."

The thinly veiled threat should have struck Rapp as cliché.

It did not.

CHAPTER 5

VICINITY OF THE SPIN GHAR MOUNTAINS
AFGHANISTAN-PAKISTAN BORDER

CAPTAIN Mark Andess Garner watched the world slide by in a series of green-tinged images.

Though night-vision technology had come a long way since his father had carried a clunky starlight scope while patrolling the jungles of Vietnam, the grainy picture still seemed otherworldly. On nights like this, the two-dimensional rendering was more reminiscent of a video game than an actual operation.

But there was nothing make-believe about what Mark was going to attempt.

He leaned into the wind, straining against the harness securing him to the troop bench bolted to the MH-6 Little Bird helicopter's exterior. The small aircraft didn't top out much faster than a high-end sports car, but there was no getting around the exposed feeling riding into combat this way engendered.

Even so, Mark preferred this method of travel to a Chinook.

While considerably faster, the larger helicopter's interior was claustrophobic. Though to be fair, this probably had more to do with the fact that Mark and his fellow Rangers regularly stuffed the aircraft to the breaking point. A 160th pilot had once famously remarked that there was always room for one more Ranger.

Mark, and men like him, had been putting this thesis to the test ever since.

"Havok 6, this is Spooky 23. YUENGLING is ICE. I say again, YUENGLING is ICE. Transitioning to SHINER, over."

"Spooky 23, this is Havok 6," Mark said after keying his radio, "copy ICE. Gold and Blue elements are ninety seconds out from SHINER, over."

The MH-6 banked left as Mark spoke, the egg-shaped helicopter dropping in altitude as the warrant officer at the controls dipped into the draw that would lead the bird to YUENGLING. Mark was pretty good at orienteering, but the Night Stalker's ability to precisely navigate while hurtling through the air at treetop level was impressive. Mark could easily identify the rounded green mass that would soon resolve into a rocky outcropping, but the terrain rushing by below the helicopter's skids still resembled an ocean of green.

Fortunately, Spooky 23 was the call sign belonging to an AC-130J Ghostrider. In addition to bringing a frightening amount of firepower to the fight, the four-engine gunship sported an impressive optics package capable of sundering the dark Afghan night. If the AC-130 said that Mark's landing zone was clear, it probably was.

Either way, Mark was going to find out for sure in just under sixty seconds.

"Havok 6, this is Desperado 7. We are phase line QUEEN. I say again, Desperado 7 is phase line QUEEN, over."

"Desperado 7, Havok 6," Mark said. "Copy phase line QUEEN. Call MELLENCAMP, over."

"This is Desperado 7. Roger all."

The laminated topographical map depicting the operational graphics hand-drawn with a grease pencil was still stuffed into one of the pouches on his tactical vest, but Mark didn't need to consult it. His company had been rehearsing this hit for the last three days. As the company commander, Mark had memorized the concept of the operation long ago. Tonight, he and his eighty Rangers were conducting a mission he'd lobbied for since arriving in-country three months previously.

The compound they were hitting belonged to a high-ranking member of the Hizb-i-Islami Gulbuddin network, or HIG. As with many of the jihadi splinter groups that infested Afghanistan, the HIG was hard to describe. It had been the recipient of substantial funds from Pakistan and Saudi Arabia during the 1980s fight against the Soviet Union's invasion of Afghanistan. Now the HIG was part criminal organization, part jihadi group, and part quasi-political party. Though everyone agreed that he had American blood on his hands, the HIG leader residing in the compound had been permitted to continue to consume oxygen for just one reason.

Politics.

The man's compound was located on the far side of an invisible line delineating Afghanistan and Pakistan. That the area's inhabitants didn't recognize such a border was immaterial. The terrorist compound was in Pakistan and was therefore untouchable.

Until tonight.

As a small-town boy from State Road, North Carolina, Mark was not much on politics. He'd chosen to attend the United States Military Academy at West Point and earn a commission in the Army out of a sense of patriotism and planned to return to his rural hometown once his Afghanistan tour of duty, and his company command, were complete.

If he never had to deal with a three-letter agency again, it would be too soon.

But Mark didn't have to be a politico to understand that the recent string of terrorist attacks across the American heartland had changed the calculus of Washington's decision-makers. The president had decided to unleash the hounds, which meant that terrorists who were once considered out of reach were safe no longer. Whether this reflected a global change in policy or just a temporary reprieve was immaterial. Mark and his band of merry marauders had been given the green light, and he intended to hit the gas pedal.

"Havok 6, this is Desperado 7, we have a maintenance issue on one of the trucks. Combat power is now five vehicles. I say again, five vehicles."

"Desperado 7, this is Havok 6," Mark said. "Roger all. Continue the mission, over."

Doug Peluso, the Green Beret who went by the call sign of Desperado 7, replied with two clicks of his radio. Operation IRON FIST had been Mark's brainchild, but an undertaking of this magnitude still needed buy-in from multiple overlapping entities. While Mark might not have a future in politics, he had learned long ago that one of the easiest ways to secure buy-in was to offer another organization a seat at the operational table.

Case in point, the Green Beret detachment from Operational Detachment Alpha, or ODA, 535 were not part of Mark's chain of command, but they owned the battle space where the target compound was located. Rather than engage in a protracted and unfruitful turf war over who would command and control IRON FIST, Mark had done something rather novel—he'd offered Desperado 7 a piece of the pie.

The grizzled team sergeant had instantly accepted. Doug and his twelve-man ODA, along with a contingent of Afghan National Army commandos, were now riding toward the objective in six Hilux pickup trucks. That the six trucks now equaled five was an inconvenience, but not a game changer. Mark had more than enough organic combat power in the two platoons carried in the helicopters hurtling toward the compound. The Green Berets and their Afghan allies would provide the outer cordon while Mark's Rangers conducted the assault.

The target compound was nestled in the northern end of a bowl created by the intersection between a north–south running draw and an east–west running ridgeline. A single unimproved road provided vehicular access to the compound. The ridgelines to the rear of the compound were riddled with goat trails that undoubtedly allowed foot traffic to come and go without being seen, but progress would be slow going and easily visible by the loitering AC-130.

At least that was the plan.

But as Desperado 7's radio call had just demonstrated, plans had a way of changing. Phase line QUEEN depicted the turnoff from the hard-ball road east of the compound that bridged the distance between several of the small villages dotting the Pakistan-Afghanistan border. Though not exactly an interstate highway, the road saw enough traffic that the six-vehicle Green Beret convoy wouldn't attract much attention. But once the trucks made the turn from QUEEN onto the dirt-and-gravel path leading to the compound, this would no longer be true. The operation's high-value target, or HVT, had grown to enjoy the protection his location in Pakistan offered him, but that didn't mean he was compla-cent. Watchers working for the HIG thug no doubt lined the foothills flanking the road.

But that was okay.

In about ninety seconds, the HVT was going to have his hands full.

As if hearing Mark's thoughts, the Little Bird flared as the pilot brought the aircraft in for a rushed but steady landing. The Rangers seated next to Mark were off the troop bench and moving forward in a crouch before the helicopter had even fully settled. Mark hit the quick release on his seat belt and followed, his mind on the multiple radio calls echoing through his Peltor earmuffs as his feet carried him for-ward. As per their reputation, the Night Stalkers had deposited him precisely on target and exactly on time. Judging by the radio chatter, the helicopters containing the assault team were also adhering to the opera-tional schedule.

Mark removed a thermal spotting scope from his assault pack, ex-tended the tripod, planted it in the rocky soil, and panned the device to his right. The six Rangers who had exited the helicopter with him were also busy, but they knew their jobs and needed no handholding from Mark. His RTO, or radio telephone operator, was already expanding a concave satellite antenna while the two-man sniper team were survey-ing likely targets and completing their range cards.

Chris Jancosko, a Marine field artillery officer serving an exchange tour with the Rangers, was verifying radio communication with the indirect fire assets that would be supporting the assault. The final two Rangers in Mark's element disappeared into the brush to the northwest of the rock outcropping to establish a security position.

"Havok 6, this is Havok 16. We are release point inbound, over."

Mark swung his scope to the left until the target compound swam into view. He'd selected the rock outcropping as his command post because the elevated position offered him an unobstructed view of YUENGLING while still affording a defensible position for his small command team.

Though the circling AC-130 was much better equipped to decide whether the compound was ICE or CHERRY, as commander, the final determination was Mark's. His Rangers were about to rain down hellfire and brimstone on the enemy based on his orders. Mark owed it to them to personally check the terrain for enemy fighters before clearing the assaulters onto the objective.

Other than its size, the compound wasn't that different from others that dotted the landscape. The ten-foot-high walls were constructed of mud brick and stood four feet thick. The bricks had baked to concrete hardness by years of exposure to the unrelenting Afghanistan sun and scouring wind that howled down the valley. Covered guard towers flanked the compound's steel gate. One position held a DShK heavy machine gun while the second had space for a pair of guards.

Neither tower was occupied.

"Havok 16," Mark said, using the call sign of his senior platoon leader, Jeff Mishler, "this is Havok 6. I confirm that YUENGLING is ICE. No enemy in sight. You are cleared to the objective, over."

"Havok 6, this is Havok 16, roger that. Gig 'em, sir."

Mark smiled.

As a graduate of Texas A&M, Jeff sought to work the university's signature phrase into nearly every conversation. While Jeff's response wasn't proper radio protocol, Mark made an exception for his hard-charging senior platoon leader. The Ranger Regiment did not attract shrinking violets or wallflowers.

Panning his optic back to the right, Mark centered the scope on the gap in the ridgeline where he expected the helicopters carrying Jeff and the rest of the assaulters to appear. Mark loved being a Ranger, but he'd had to adjust to the role of company commander. As a platoon leader, Mark had swept across the objective with his men, often just behind the breaching team.

As commander, Mark's role differed. His job was to command and control the fight rather than lead it. This was why he was on a rock out-cropping almost a thousand meters west of the objective instead of rid-ing in a Chinook alongside his Rangers. Mark's head knew that his ability to coordinate the fight and bring additional combat multipliers like close air support or Chris Jancosko's artillery to bear did far more to support the effort than adding just another rifle to the stack.

Sometimes his heart wasn't so sure.

Mark adjusted the optic's focus as he wondered if the pilots from the 160th Special Operations Aviation Regiment were running late. Then he tweaked the thermal's gain and level, and what he'd mistaken for background scatter resolved into a pair of helicopters. The pilots had elected to approach the compound using nap-of-the-earth flying in the hopes of masking the Chinook's presence for as long as possible. Even so, the pair of helicopters were low even by Night Stalker standards.

The birds' landing gear was almost kissing the gravel road.

The Chinook and trailing Black Hawk thundered up the draw, and Mark felt the pride that only came from leading America's finest war-riors into combat. In seconds, his men would be on the objective, strik-ing a decisive blow against a truly bad man.

Some days Mark couldn't believe he actually got paid to do this job.

"Mark," Chris Jancosko said, grabbing his shoulder, "we might have trouble."

And then there were days when he earned every last cent.

CHAPTER 6

RAPP didn't run.

At least not at first.

While the information Ruyintan had just provided was time-sensitive to Rapp, it would not be for Farid Saeed. Though his muscles felt like coiled springs, Rapp had remained seated for several minutes after the Iranian and his entourage vacated the café. Each second passed with the subtlety of a chiming gong, but Rapp finished skimming the *Telegraph*'s front page before lazily dropping a handful of rupees on the table.

Then, he'd stood, glanced at his watch, and made for the cobblestone street.

Sunrise Café was situated in a cluster of shops that were separated from a collection of residences by School Road. Though the grassy median bisecting the thoroughfare often served as a gathering place for groups of men, the patch was empty tonight. Perhaps because the pedestrians were all on the western side with Rapp, patronizing the restaurants, clothing vendors, and rug stores surrounding the café.

Rapp meandered through several alleys that cut deeper into the urban area heading generally west as two urges battled for primacy. Like a homing pigeon, he could feel FAIRBANKS lurking just out of reach. As expected, the sight of armed men in his favorite café had scared off the businessman, but Rapp still had a reasonably good idea where the terror financier was heading.

After his nightcap, FAIRBANKS habitually closed out the evening at his favorite hookah lounge five blocks away. FAIRBANKS was an enemy combatant, but his weapons were spreadsheets and bank transfers rather than guns or knives. The financier was not an intelligence operative, so his reaction to the commotion at Sunrise Café would be very different than Rapp's. Odds were that he would seek comfort in his routine rather than alter it. Rapp had missed his first opportunity to bring the man to justice, though the secondary option was still there for the taking.

But for the bit of news Ruyintan had just delivered.

At this moment, American special operations forces were flying into an ambush.

If the Iranian was telling the truth.

Rapp could think of many reasons why this might not be the case, chief of them being that this entire overture was nothing but a dangle. The Quds Force officer had been adept enough to suss out Rapp's Saeed persona and track him to a random café in Islamabad. Who was to say that the intelligence operative's penetration hadn't gone a step further? Perhaps the entire point of the meeting was to attempt to determine whether the former Iraqi army officer who was posing as a Frenchman was actually an American CIA operative?

Too many questions and not enough time to answer them.

Rapp angled left, away from the jostling pedestrians, toward a trash-strewn opening between two adjacent buildings. The pockmarked concrete was less alley than a gap in construction between a chocolate store to the left and a bookstore to the right. A dumping ground for refuse and a repository for stagnant rainwater. Rapp reached into his pocket, withdrew his mobile, touched a series of keystrokes to sanitize the call log and contact list, and then tossed the device into the garbage pile overflowing the mouth of the alley.

Cell phone theft was a cottage industry in Islamabad, and he was confident that the mobile wouldn't lie unattended for long. He hadn't detected any overt surveillance, but his meeting with Ruyintan hadn't been a random encounter. Mitch Rapp might still be clean, but Farid Saeed assuredly was not. Until he determined how and why he'd been compromised, tradecraft dictated that his cell needed to go. This made warning the appropriate person about the coming ambush more difficult.

Fortunately, Rapp had a plan.

As did the pair of thugs waiting at the far end of the alley.

CHAPTER 7

THE pair of men did not seem surprised to see Rapp any more than a moray eel lurking in a cave is surprised to see a fat fish swim by. In a series of moves much too choreographed to be spontaneous, the duo edged out of the darkness and flanked Rapp. And just in case their intentions weren't clear, the man to Rapp's left deployed a folding knife with a smooth *whisk* while his partner produced a snub-nosed revolver from the back of his pants. The gunman spoke something unintelligible, and while Rapp's Urdu wasn't anywhere near as good as his Arabic, the command wasn't difficult to intuit.

Give me your money.

For a moment, Rapp considered doing just that.

The men weren't jittery from drugs and didn't seem nervous, suggesting that this was not a crime of opportunity. The alley was a shortcut for a confluence of shops, a hookah bar, and at least one house of ill repute.

The pair weren't here by happenstance.

The thugs were probably under the protection of the Sakhakot gang or one of the other numerous organized crime entities. Entities that had undoubtedly reached an understanding with the ISI, the

Islamabad Police, or both. They were professionals who understood the rules of the road. The occasional beating might be overlooked, but outright murder would be frowned upon. If Rapp handed over the contents of his pockets, he would probably be allowed to pass.

Probably.

But Rapp was in a hurry.

A man needed killing and a piece of intelligence that might save American lives had to reach the right pair of ears. Rapp didn't have time for bullshit and was in no mood to play the role of meek victim.

The two would-be muggers had just rolled snake eyes.

Now it was time to see if they intended to walk away from the table or double down.

"Move."

Rapp gave the command in Arabic and then added his best Urdu translation for good measure. His choice in languages communicated a subtle but unmistakable message—the robbers had miscalculated. The man standing before them spoke Arabic with an Iraqi accent. He was not a tourist or some other easy mark. The thugs had set a trap for a mouse and mistakenly snared a lion. The prudent course of action would be to acknowledge their mistake and move on.

The men were not prudent.

The gunman extended the pistol one-handed and thumbed back the hammer with an ominous *click*. The knifeman turned his wrist, aiming the blade at Rapp's midsection while stepping closer. His placement was perfect. Near enough to lunge but positioned so as not to foul his partner's gunline.

The textbook way to maximize a two-on-one advantage.

Textbook when not facing someone named Rapp.

A competent knife fighter in close was usually more dangerous than a gunman, but in this instance, Rapp's calculus said differently. The gunman's pistol was a double-action revolver, and the hammer was cocked. A minuscule amount of pressure applied to the trigger would send a bullet tearing through Rapp's midsection.

This wouldn't do.

"Okay," Rapp said in Arabic, "okay."

Rapp reached into his pocket, snared his billfold, and offered it to the knifeman with his right hand.

Rapp was not right-handed.

The knifeman stepped closer, extending his hand to accept the wallet. An instant before their fingers touched, Rapp dropped the billfold and lunged. Snaring the knifeman's wrist, Rapp ripped the thug toward him. The unorthodox move accomplished three things: One, the knifeman stumbled forward, obscuring his partner's gunline. Two, the right side of the thug's body now shielded Rapp from the knife in his left hand. Three, the knifeman's elbow joint locked.

The joint did not remain locked.

Rapp brought his dominant left forearm down in a murderous strike, hammering the extended elbow.

The joint ruptured with a wet-sounding *pop*.

The knifeman didn't scream as much as shriek. A high keening sound more reminiscent of beast than man. Releasing the shattered elbow, Mitch fired a short, brutal punch toward the knifeman's throat. He missed the thug's Adam's apple but still connected with his neck. Rapp torqued his hips into the blow, sinking his front two knuckles deep into the man's flesh.

The keening turned to wheezing.

The knifeman's blade clattered off the concrete as he instinctively reached for his throat.

Sometimes a person's instincts saved their life.

Not today.

Using the wobbling man's body for cover, Rapp crouched, scooped up the knife, and flung the blade at the gunman. The weapon smashed against the gunman's chest hilt-first. He flinched and the pistol barked, sending a bullet sparking off concrete. Rapp followed the blade's flight path. He stepped past the still-choking knifeman and caught the second thug's arm as the gunman tried to bring the re-volver onto target. Rapp fired a hook into the man's liver.

He folded in half.

Stripping the pistol from his grasp, Rapp thrust it beneath his jaw and pulled the trigger. A red mist exploded from the back of the man's head. Ignoring the crumpling body, Rapp shifted to the knifeman, catching the man by the back of his shirt as he tried to stumble toward the alley's mouth. In a single, smooth motion, Rapp shoved the revolver into the base of the knifeman's skull and fired.

The thug collapsed.

Rapp paused, taking in his surroundings like a wolf sniffing the wind.

The altercation had been louder than he would have liked, but the revolver's small caliber combined with Rapp's use of contact shots had done much to mask the gun's report.

More importantly, his assailants were dead and he was not.

By Stan Hurley's standards, this constituted success.

Shoving the pistol into the back of his pants, Rapp searched the dead men with quick, efficient motions. He found what he was looking for in the knifeman's front pocket. Extracting a mobile phone, Rapp dialed and held the cell to his ear.

A familiar voice answered on the third ring.

"Hello?"

"It's me," Rapp said. "We have a problem."

CHAPTER 8

"I'M listening," Irene Kennedy said.

Rapp skirted a puddle as he quickened his stride.

Like a dead carcass drawing flies, murder scenes attract attention. Though Islamabad wasn't Vienna, the capital of Pakistan still had an image to maintain. A few months ago, a CIA contractor in Lahore, Pakistan, had killed two armed men who had attempted to rob him. The Pakistanis responded by arresting the American and throwing him in jail.

Rapp had no intention of spending a single minute in a Pakistani prison.

He had unfinished business with FAIRBANKS.

"This line is not secure," Rapp said, "but I've got something time-sensitive."

"Okay."

After almost two decades together, Rapp's relationship with his one-time handler was a bit like marriage. The good kind of marriage. Each person knew who their partner was and who they weren't. Was Irene irritated that Rapp had ditched communications with the Agency team tasked with monitoring the FAIRBANKS hit?

Probably.

Was she surprised?

Probably not.

Rapp's actions would require an explanation, but that would come later. He was still the guy you called to do impossible tasks, and Irene had learned not to second-guess his tactical decisions. If Rapp rang her on an unsecure line with news of a problem, she listened.

Rapp passed through the alley and paused at the far end. A parking lot beckoned, the spaces filled with dinged-up sedans and questionable-looking motor scooters. While this section of Islamabad featured many of the more well-to-do neighborhoods, no motorist escaped the capital city's traffic unscathed.

Rapp eyed the collection of cars, checking for a surveillance or interdiction team.

A high-end jewelry store with the requisite surveillance cameras occupied the far side of the parking lot. A pedestrian area flanked by wooden slat benches and a collection of trees waited to his left while a series of trendy shops stretched to his right in strip mall fashion.

Careful to remain in the shadows, Rapp studied the shops.

Most were brightly lit, but the space two down from where he was standing was vacant. Its exposed storefront was open to the elements like a gap in an otherwise full smile. Piles of brick, a rickety ladder, and rusty scaffolding suggested that the space was being renovated.

Perfect.

"Gimme a sec," Rapp said.

He left the alley and headed right.

After sliding past the darkened windows of a perfume shop, Rapp slunk into the abandoned storefront. He edged past a wheelbarrow, buckets of drywall mud, and piles of trash, seeking the space's darkest corner. The dim lighting revealed what Rapp had hoped to see—a rear exit. Easing the door open, he peered into another dark alley. Unlike the one from which he'd emerged, this one ran north and south. North meant heading back toward School Road, but south led deeper into the sprawling commercial zone composed of shops, restaurants, and the like.

Perfect.

"Okay," Rapp said, easing the door shut. "I have reporting that suggests a US operation in the vicinity of the Spin Ghar mountains has been compromised. Specifically, helicopters loaded with American commandos are en route to hit a compound housing a high-value target as we speak. It's a trap."

Though she hadn't handled assets in years, a good case officer never lost her Farm-trained instincts. Irene might now be the CIA director, but Rapp's update would hit her like a shot of epinephrine.

His update must have prompted a thousand questions.

She only asked one.

"What's the source of your reporting?" Irene said.

Rapp had been expecting this question, but he still wasn't sure how he wanted to answer. While the SIGINT, or signals intelligence, capability of Pakistan's ISI was nowhere near NSA levels, only a fool underestimated his adversary's technological prowess. He was calling on an unsecure line. That he was doing so using a cell he'd liberated from a pair of street thugs via a onetime number designed specifically for agents in duress meant that this discussion should be lost among the millions of other calls flooding Pakistan's cell network. The odds were minuscule that the ISI would be able to isolate a needle from the surrounding digital haystack.

Minuscule but not zero.

"SUNSPOT is the source," Rapp said, giving the code name assigned to Ruyintan.

Silence answered.

Rapp's boss was one of the most intelligent people he knew. Irene Kennedy didn't think three moves ahead. She visualized the entire chess match. She was the yin to his yang. The deliberate and methodical counterpart to his propensity for audacity and violence of action. Irene wasn't prone to emotional outbursts, but Rapp had learned to listen to her silences.

This one spoke volumes.

"Can you describe the interaction?" Irene said.

The warbling of a police siren echoed through the air.

Rapp froze, not daring to breathe until the changing Doppler indicated that the car had passed by. He wasn't superstitious, but anyone who did what he did for a living understood the importance of subliminal cues. The soft whispers from his lizard brain. His predatory instincts were screaming that it was go time.

"SUNSPOT initiated contact," Rapp said.

"Why?" Irene said.

"Not over this line. I've given you all I can. I'll check in later."

"Busy?" Irene said.

"I've got an appointment to keep," Rapp said.

"Understood," Irene said. "Break a leg."

Rapp intended to break several.

CHAPTER 9

"WHAT kind of trouble?" Captain Mark Garner said, eyeing his fire support officer.

"The artillery kind," Chris said. "The battery commander just jumped on the radio to let me know that their authorization to shoot into Pakistan has been pulled. I'm sorry."

Mark was pissed, but not surprised.

American artillerymen were the best in the business, but indirect fire was by nature an inexact science. The first rounds almost never hit the target, which was why an experienced forward observer like Chris Jancosko was a critical arrow in every ground commander's quiver. Should the need arise, Chris would serve as the link between the cannons firing the 155mm high-explosive shells and the target. After the first volley, Chris would walk subsequent rounds onto target by issuing corrections in azimuth and distance via radio to the gunners who were located at a forward operating base twenty kilometers away. This was how artillery worked.

Unfortunately, firing unguided rounds into Pakistan had the military brass more than a little nervous. Authorization had been granted to incorporate indirect fire into the raid during the rehearsal, but Mark had seen the writing on the wall. If anyone in the chain of command developed cold feet, the big guns were out.

And now his premonition had come to fruition.

"It's not your fault," Mark said. "Get on the horn with the AC-130 and make sure they know they're the only game in town. I need them ready to put steel on target."

"Got it," Chris said.

The Marine clicked the transmit button on his radio and began to speak. Mark didn't bother to listen in. Chris had aptly demonstrated his competence over the last three months. The Marine was more than capable of conveying the seriousness of the situation to the orbiting Air Force gunship. In a weird way, Mark felt grateful for the snafu. No mission ever went according to plan. Ever. Now that the gods of war had thrown their obligatory curveball, maybe the rest of the operation would be smooth sailing.

"Sir," Specialist Greg Glass said, "I've got Talon 6 on the line."

Or maybe not.

Talon 6 was the call sign for Lieutenant Colonel Brandon Cates, the commander of 1st Battalion, 75th Ranger Regiment. In other words, Mark's boss. And while Mark got along just fine with Cates, the fact that his boss was tying up the radios seconds before Charlie Company was about to hit the objective was not a good sign.

Taking the offered radio handset from Glass, Mark pressed the push-to-talk button and spoke.

"Talon 6, this is Havok 6 actual," Mark said.

"Roger, Havok, be advised that our OGA liaison has reporting that IRON FIST may be compromised, over."

"Havok 6, this is Havok 16, we are PETTY. I say again, assault element is PETTY."

PETTY was the brevity code signifying that the assault team was thirty seconds from the objective. Catching Greg's eye, Mark nodded. The RTO immediately transmitted a response using the Havok 6 call sign, freeing Mark to stay on the line with Brandon. Mark had been in command for almost a year and his battlefield interactions with his RTO now bordered on telepathy.

"Talon 6, this is Havok 6," Mark said as he panned his thermal sight back to the compound. "Assault elements are Phase Line PETTY and I've confirmed that Objective YUENGLING is ICE. Please advise, over."

This was Mark's way of politely asking his boss what Brandon expected him to do with the turd he'd just dropped in Mark's punch bowl. OGA stood for Other Government Agency, a catch-all term for many of the three-letter agencies that provided intelligence to the JSOC, or Joint Special Operations Command, planners. These were the men and women who supplied Mark's Rangers with the intelligence briefings for many of their missions.

"Havok 6, this is Talon 6. You're the man on the ground. Your call, over."

Mark could have guessed Cate's response. Like most battalion commanders in the storied 75th Ranger Regiment, Brandon had served as a company commander and platoon leader in the organization before eventually returning to command a battalion. He'd earned his spurs during the initial invasion of Afghanistan a decade earlier. Like the good leader that he was, Brandon was deferring the decision to the person with the best situation awareness—Mark.

Mark scoped the compound a final time. The men who wore the regiment's coveted tan beret were three-time volunteers. They did not endure the harrowing selection process because they coveted safety. Since their inception, Rangers had garnered a reputation for going where others wouldn't to do what they couldn't. IRON FIST had required months to approve, weeks to plan, and countless hours to rehearse. The compound's high-value target was not just another Taliban commander. He was a high-ranking HIG member and an integral player in the flow of matériel and men across the porous border.

A second opportunity to capture or kill him might take years to materialize.

If ever.

OGA's assessment that the mission might be compromised was just that. An assessment. In combat as in life, there were few absolutes. If Mark waited for a 100 percent concurrence from the intelligence community before pursuing a target, he'd spend his entire Afghanistan rotation sitting on his thumbs. There was a time to play it safe and a time to be audacious.

This operation fell into the latter category.

"Talon 6, this is Havok 6," Mark said. "We are proceeding to HENLEY, over."

Once again, Greg was listening to Mark with one ear and the assault force with the other. Mark could see his RTO's lips moving as he parroted Mark's instructions to the assault force. Besides serving as the last name for one of the greatest singer/songwriters of his generation, HENLEY also designated the release point, or RP. This was where the two helicopters carrying the Rangers would break formation. The Chinook would deposit the blocking force on the south side of the compound while the trailing Black Hawk would fast-rope the assaulters onto the main residence's roof.

HENLEY was the point of no return.

"Roger that, Havok 6. Good hunting. Talon 6, out."

Mark passed the handset back to Greg in favor of the one that connected him to his platoon leader. He considered passing a warning to Havok 16 but didn't. The assaulters were less than thirty seconds from the objective. Jeff Mishler already had enough to worry about.

Instead, Mark switched to his command internal frequency.

"Stay frosty," Mark said to the Rangers gathered on the hilltop with him. "We just received some concerning intel. If you see anything that looks hinky, don't wait for clearance from me to deal with the threat."

Mark switched frequencies back to the assault net even as his headquarters element acknowledged his instructions. He could hear Chris Jancosko whispering into his lip mike as the fire support officer made final coordination with the Air Force gunship. Two-hundred-pound men kicking in doors looked sexy on TV, but there was a reason why artillery was called the King of Battle. If push came to shove, the AC-130's 105mm howitzer could kill a shit ton of bad guys real quick.

"Havok 6, this is Havok 16, we are HENLEY. I say again, Havok 16 is HENLEY."

Jeff's voice sounded crystal clear in Mark's Peltor headset, but the thundering *whump* from the approaching helicopters made the update extraneous. Aviation was great for speed and covering long distances, but there was nothing covert about a pair of helicopters barreling down a draw toward a box canyon. The rotor noise seemed to be coming from everywhere as the *whump, whump, whump* from the blades reflected off the rock face.

"One Six, this is 6," Mark said, "you are cleared to YUENGLING. I say again, cleared to YUENGLING."

"This is 16, roger all."

Mark zoomed in on the compound. This was the moment of truth. As if on cue, a spherical thermal signature materialized on the southern tower. A human head. The guard tower had been occupied after all. The sentry must have been sleeping out of sight on the tower's floor. The sentry reached for the DShK and Mark was in the middle of calling out a warning when the man's head exploded.

Ranger snipers were on the job.

Mark keyed his radio, preparing to transmit a warning to Jeff, when a bright flash demanded his attention. It took Mark a moment to realize he'd seen the burst of light from his left, unaided eye, not through his scope. The flash had originated from the hillside behind the compound and was now a tiny orange firefly streaking skyward.

No, that wasn't quite true.

The pinprick of light wasn't arcing toward the heavens like a tracer round. It pirouetted midflight, changing from a course aimed at the stars to something much more worrisome.

The helicopters.

CHAPTER 10

MARK mashed down the radio transmit button.

"Havok 16, you are taking fire. Abort, abort, abort."

The garbled reply was cut off midsentence.

One moment the Chinook was thundering down the valley. The next, the pinprick of light detonated just below its number one engine. The bright flash reached Mark an instant before the accompanying thunderclap. The helicopter began a ponderous turn to the left as flames shot the length of the fuselage. Mark's thermal sight rendered the dense, thick smoke pouring from the cabin into harmless shades of white, but he knew the truth.

His Rangers were in trouble.

A second flash erupted from the hillside. The pinprick clawed its way skyward, this time angling toward the Black Hawk. The targeted helicopter dumped flares in an incandescent waterfall while banking to the right, searching for a way out of the kill zone formed by the narrow valley.

Mark slapped Chris Jancosko on the shoulder.

"Suppress that hillside," Mark said.

The fire support officer responded with a thumbs-up since the Marine was already speaking into his lip mike. A heartbeat later, a string of flashbulbs engulfed the hillside as the orbiting AC-130 went to work with its howitzer. The explosions echoed across the valley, uprooting trees and rendering the hillside a series of smoking holes. The Black Hawk thundered untouched over the ridgeline, still trailing flares like a comet's sparkling tail.

The Chinook was a different matter.

The school bus–size helicopter nosed toward the valley floor. Flames engulfed the fuselage, but the aircraft continued its ponderous descent, suggesting that someone was still piloting the bird. Against all odds, the 160th aviators at the controls were bringing the aircraft down in one piece.

Then it slammed into the hillside.

CHAPTER 11

R APP eased out of the exit to the construction space and the night washed over him like a second skin. Though he had and could kill under just about any environmental conditions, night still felt the safest. The darkness slid across his body like a cool breeze. While his intellect understood that modern technology had in large part mitigated the advantages once offered by operating nocturnally, Rapp's predatory instincts weren't so sure. But darkness or not, nothing could hide the fact that Rapp now faced a tough decision.

He followed the alley south, toward the neon-tinged light brightening the passageway's entrance. He paused just short of the swirling pool of pink, green, and red luminescence that marked the way back to civilization. Prior to his scheduled meet with FAIRBANKS, Rapp had reconned the warren of alleys that connected the commercial district, memorizing various routes to and from Sunrise Café as well as other destinations of interest.

Destinations like the hookah bar where FAIRBANKS liked to close out his evenings.

The bar beckoned from the far side of a series of shops that were laid out like a reverse number 7. Rapp was at the northeastern corner of the 7 while the hookah bar anchored the southwestern point. As with the previous strip mall, new construction was interspersed with the existing boutiques, restaurants, and cafés so that almost every other storefront stood empty. A pedestrian walkway of raised cobblestones spiderwebbed across the parking area separating Rapp from the bar and providing access to the assortment of shops.

He studied the hookah bar, considering.

Stan Hurley, Rapp's mentor, had passed along many lessons to his protégé. Truth be told, though Rapp had operated alongside the crusty old field hand for almost twenty years, he still found himself learning from Stan. Besides teaching Rapp how to best kill a man, perhaps the most important thing Hurley had imparted was when not to kill. Specifically, when to temper the bias for action that ordinarily made Rapp so effective at his job. As Stan was wont to say, he hadn't recruited Rapp to be a suicide bomber.

The life of a good guy for the life of a bad guy was never an even trade.

Though he wasn't blown yet, Rapp was keenly aware of the two dead bodies cooling on the crumbling asphalt less than a kilometer away. The hookah bar's bright façade was like a Siren's song. Prudence dictated that Rapp turn left and head south another two blocks toward a strategically parked motor scooter and safety. FAIRBANKS was on borrowed time. Whether Rapp ended his life today, tomorrow, or a week from now wasn't important. Agency analysts had penetrated the web of secrecy shrouding the businessman once. Given enough time and resources, the eggheads should be able do it again.

Should.

With a sigh, Rapp traded the safety of darkness for the neon lights.

He did not turn left.

CHAPTER 12

THE target should never be permitted to dictate the assassin's actions.

Hurley had drilled this truism into Rapp's head. An operative could not allow their feelings for the target to direct how far they pushed the operational window. At least not if the operative wanted to have a career that spanned more than just one kill. An unfavorable tactical situation was still an unfavorable situation whether the assassin's target was Adolf Hitler or Mickey Mouse. Put another way, an assassin could not allow the evilness of the man or woman they were hunting to increase the level of risk they were willing to accept in order to hunt them.

This rule was inviolate.

And then there was FAIRBANKS.

Rapp lengthened his stride as he headed for the hookah bar, neither avoiding the shadows nor seeking them. He tailored his movements to match those of the shoppers milling in front of the storefronts and wandering across the cobblestone path. Irene had authorized this job in part to send a message to the Pakistanis, but there was a difference between a subtle tap on the shoulder and flipping your opponent the bird.

Rapp should know.

He'd done both.

Despite his calm appearance, Rapp's heart began to accelerate. This was not because he enjoyed killing. Rapp was neither a sociopath nor a troubled soul looking for absolution. He dispatched terrorists with the same casual disregard a plumber showed when unclogging a stuck pipe. Killing was Rapp's vocation, nothing more.

But FAIRBANKS was a special case.

Nine years ago, when the war on terror was still new and the depths to which America's adversaries would stoop not fully understood, a brave journalist had traveled to Pakistan to interview a potential source for a story on Al Qaeda.

He'd never returned.

Instead, the journalist had been made to account for twin sins. He was an American, but even more egregious, a Jew. Instead of meeting his source for tea, the journalist was kidnapped off the streets of Karachi in broad daylight, made to release a captivity video, and then decapitated. The journalist's execution was recorded, and the video was distributed on the internet by the jihadis who'd killed him. The journalist's wife had been five months pregnant with their first child at the time of her husband's death.

While FAIRBANKS hadn't been the one to draw the steel blade across the journalist's throat, the businessman's money and connections had made the killing possible. If that had been the end of the ordeal, his actions would have still been more than enough to earn FAIRBANKS a spot on Rapp's list.

It hadn't been.

In recent years, FAIRBANKS had begun to flaunt his connection to the killing to increase his street cred among the jihadi sects. Even worse, he'd begun hinting that the ISI was protecting him from American retribution.

This had been a step too far.

In light of the recent terrorist attacks on American soil, Rapp had been authorized to visit rough justice on FAIRBANKS. While Rapp had no intention of decapitating the man on live television, he wanted to use the businessman's death as a mechanism to send a message of his own.

Not all deaths were created equal.

Rapp reached the parking lot's midpoint.

The large windows framing the hookah bar's entrance offered an unobstructed view of the establishment's brightly lit interior. FAIRBANKS was clearly visible surrounded by his two hulking bodyguards. The businessman was enjoying a booth to himself while the rest of the establishment's occupants kept a respectable distance.

Showtime.

Rapp rolled his shoulders to loosen his muscles as he mentally rehearsed the series of events that would bring FAIRBANKS's time on earth to an end. The pen loaded with neurotoxin still resided in the pocket of his sport coat, but the manner in which he would administer the poison would differ from his original plan.

As would the ensuing fallout from FAIRBANKS's demise.

In the café scenario, Rapp would have met the financier under already established pretenses. The man's death hours later would have been both hideous and directly attributable to poison, but the mechanism for the drug's delivery would have been in question.

Not anymore.

Rapp was about to surprise FAIRBANKS. While he was confident in his ability to diffuse the terrorist's suspicions long enough to clandestinely administer the neurotoxin, Rapp knew that his bodyguards would recall the unexpected encounter and draw the appropriate conclusions. Rapp's face would be remembered, and his description disseminated throughout the jihadi network.

Never a winning proposition for an assassin.

But winning proposition or not, this was the hand that Rapp had been dealt and he intended to play it. If the FAIRBANKS job had been easy, the Agency would have sent someone else to do it. Rapp was here because he was uniquely suited to punch the financier's ticket.

It was just that simple.

Until his phone rang.

CHAPTER 13

For a long moment, Rapp considered not answering.

He wasn't just on the job.

He was moments away from walking into a crowded room to kill a terrorist. Like a fire-and-forget missile, once Rapp was activated, he could not be called back. He had been chosen for the Orion program precisely because his psychological profile showed the sort of independence and critical thinking that a deep-cover operative needed to stalk and kill his prey in a foreign land absent a safety net. Rapp didn't ask permission before he squeezed the trigger. Nor was he subject to the whims of a staff weeny watching the encounter from a thousand miles away.

But the caller was not a staff weeny.

Rapp slowed his stride as he dug the phone from his pocket. He was thirty feet from the front door. Close enough to attract the attention of one of the bodyguards standing post in front of FAIRBANKS's car. Rapp felt the man's attention and used his peripheral vision to evaluate the bodyguard's response.

He was good.

The man reacted to Mitch's approach by clasping his hands in front of his chest. Known as the interview stance, the positioning permitted the bodyguard to block an attack or go hands-on without telegraphing his intent. But even as he prepared for a potential physical confrontation, the man didn't focus on Rapp. Instead, his gaze swept over the assassin and continued past him, marking the dark corners of the square along with Rapp's fellow pedestrians. The guy was well trained, probably ex–special operations. Former soldiers who chose poorly when it came to accepting postmilitary gigs did not get a free pass, but it did change Rapp's calculus.

Slightly.

He pulled out the phone and examined the caller ID, hoping that the call was from someone else.

Anyone else.

Though the corresponding series of digits didn't have the 202 indicative of a Washington, DC, area code, Rapp still recognized their significance. If redialed, the call would probably go to the last remaining public phone in America, but Rapp knew who had actually originated the call.

"*Allo?*" Rapp said, turning his body away from the bodyguard as he spoke.

Rapp wanted to ensure that the bodyguard didn't hear an English reply.

"Your warning was correct," Irene said. "A helicopter full of special operations forces was just shot down. Recovery operations are ongoing, but initial casualty estimates are quite high. The pilots of the trail helicopter said that the aircraft was brought down by a missile. A missile at night. Do you understand?"

Rapp clenched his jaw.

He did understand.

He counted many members of the special operations forces community as colleagues and friends. The operator fraternity was both small and tightly knit. Odds were that his friends had just lost comrades in arms, but that wasn't the worst of it.

A helicopter had been brought down by a shoulder-fired missile at night.

Rapp had spent enough time in Afghanistan and Iraq to understand a helicopter's inherent vulnerability to shoulder-fired missiles. While great advancements had been made in the countermeasures department, the easiest way to mitigate the danger posed by man-portable air-defense systems, or MANPADS, was to fly at night. A shoulder-fired missile used infrared sensors to home in on a helicopter's hot engine, but the sensor's acquisition window was very narrow. To target a helicopter, the gunner first needed to visually identify the aircraft before he could point the missile's seeker head at his desired target and achieve the necessary prelaunch lock-on. The adage that you couldn't kill what you couldn't see was the reason why American aircraft operated indiscriminately once the sun set. The cloak of darkness didn't make helicopters invulnerable, but it did render the threat posed by MANPADS largely moot.

Until tonight.

Rapp had thousands of questions, but now wasn't the time to ask them. An Islamabad police car trimmed in the force's distinctive yellow and blue color scheme approached from the southeast and turned into the parking lot. The vehicle's light bar remained dark, and the cruiser departed after taking a turn around the pedestrian area, but Rapp wasn't mollified. The officers could have been on a normal patrol, or they might have been canvassing the area in response to two dead thugs recently discovered in a trash-strewn alley.

Rapp was on borrowed time.

"*Tamaan*," Rapp said.

Okay.

The call ended.

His noncommittal response hadn't communicated anything specific because further words were unnecessary. Irene understood him better than anyone. She'd passed along her message.

The rest was up to him.

Rapp glanced at the hookah bar. As if he could feel Rapp's gaze, FAIRBANKS shifted in his chair and squinted at the window. The darkness outside combined with the bar's bright interior meant that the businessman most likely couldn't see Rapp.

He probably didn't need to.

Predators had a way of sensing other predators.

Turning his back on FAIRBANKS, Rapp pulled Ruyintan's business card from his pocket. The precise handwriting taunted him. As demonstrations went, shooting down an American helicopter was pretty effective.

Shooting one down under the cover of darkness was a game changer.

The loss of life was tragic, but if the Iranians really had discovered a way to target helicopters at night, the consequences to the American war effort would be devastating. Until the targeting mechanism was better understood, the tons of equipment and personnel that moved across Afghanistan and Iraq by air would be at risk. Getting to the bottom of this took priority over everything.

Even FAIRBANKS.

Rapp punched in the digits from the business card and hit the send button. The phone rang and a familiar voice answered.

"It's Farid," Rapp said in Arabic.

"Do I have your attention now?" Ruyintan said.

"Perhaps."

The Iranian chuckled.

His laugh brought to mind the rasp of snakeskin sliding across old bones.

"I think this technology might be of interest to your friends in Iraq," Ruyintan said, "but what happens next is up to you."

"What do you mean?" Rapp said.

"Further discussions will be held face-to-face."

"Where?" Rapp said.

"The Intercontinental Hotel in Kabul. Tomorrow, seven p.m."

"With you?" Rapp said.

Another raspy chuckle.

"My part in this is done," Ruyintan said. "A coworker will handle things from here."

"Who?"

"Azad Ashani. Do you know him?"

Farid Saeed did not.

Mitch Rapp most certainly did.

CHAPTER 14

IRENE Kennedy stared at her phone, unsure of which number to dial.

This was not because the director of the Central Intelligence Agency was indecisive.

While her deeply analytical mind made her a cautious person, she helmed an organization charged with lying, stealing, and cheating on behalf of the nation it served. In the rough-and-tumble world of espionage, Irene had found that the British Special Air Service's motto of *Who Dares Wins* was a much more apt way of describing how she conducted business than the carpenter's adage of *measure twice and cut once*. But sheer audacity was no substitute for operational planning even when it came to her most willful kinetic operative.

Occasionally, Mitch Rapp even agreed.

Tucking a length of auburn hair behind her ear, Irene put herself in Rapp's shoes.

The best assassin to ever graduate from Stan Hurley's school for wayward boys was not impetuous. That he'd reached middle age in a profession that favored the young spoke to something more than just his physical aptitude for violence. Early in his career, Rapp had evaded both the CIA and the French DGSE and police after an assassination in Paris went wrong thanks to an American traitor. That he'd survived the combined dragnet of one national law enforcement organization and two intelligence services was impressive. That he'd done so while fighting delirium from a gunshot wound sustained during the ambush stretched the telling to near-superhero levels.

Mitch Rapp would not go off half-cocked, but once the man settled on a course of action, he executed it ruthlessly. Irene had learned long ago that she aided Rapp most effectively by acting in a support role rather than attempting to command and control him.

But in order to help Rapp, she first had to understand what he intended to do.

"Irene, do you have a minute?"

Irene looked up from her desk to see Mike Nash standing hesitantly in her doorway.

As always, Irene was struck by the physical semblance between Nash and Mitch. Though he was five years younger and an inch shorter than Rapp, the two could have been siblings. They had same square jaw, muscular build, and overall demeanor. Mike had brown hair to Rapp's black, but until recently the two men had also shared the same brash operator confidence.

This was no longer true of Nash.

Now the former Marine looked like a seven-year-old who'd just been caught playing with his father's power tools. Unfortunately, this stark transformation could also be laid at the feet of Mitch Rapp.

"You're a deputy director now, Mike," Irene said. "I always have a minute for you."

She smiled as she spoke, trying to soften the rebuke.

Mike had spent his entire career in the field and was still coming to terms with the notion that he was part of the head shed. Where before his interactions with the CIA director had usually been buffered by Rapp, Nash was now a member of the Senior Executive Service. The promotion was perhaps the military equivalent of jumping rank from sergeant to general—a transition that was unheard-of outside the context of war.

Then again, the United States was at war even if many of the politicians charged with governing the nation pretended otherwise.

"Right," Nash said, crossing the threshold into Irene's office. "The operations team tagged with monitoring Rapp's meet experienced some technical difficulties."

Nash stared at Irene expectantly, willing her to read between the lines.

Irene knew what her newly minted deputy was driving at, but she refused to take the bait. She understood that the former paramilitary officer felt like a fish out of water and could sympathize with his predicament. Her own transition from agent runner to management hadn't been without the occasional bump in the road, but if Nash intended to be taken seriously by the suits who inhabited Langley's seventh floor, he had to dispense with the timidity and start leading.

"I'm sorry, Mike," Irene said. "You'll have to be more specific."

No smile accompanied her words this time.

"It's Rapp," Nash said with a sigh. "He ended communication with the team."

"How do you know?" Irene said.

"Because the CCTV camera feed we hacked showed him dropping his earpiece into his coffee."

This time Irene suppressed her smile for a different reason.

She loved Rapp like a brother, but he was without a doubt the most stubborn human being she knew. Rapp was never obstinate just to be difficult, but when it came to helming operations, he tolerated no second-guessing. As someone who'd worked alongside the operative for years, Nash should know this.

Or perhaps it was more accurate to say Nash *did* know this and therein lay the problem. During the preoperational brief, Nash had presented a request from the tech team to try out the hacking software and a new low-profile comms system on an active mission.

Rapp's mission.

Irene understood that the ask was partially driven by operational need, but she suspected that the vehemence with which Mike advocated for the request stemmed from a desire to show his new constituency that he wasn't just another knuckle dragger who would automatically defer to his former comrades. Irene appreciated the mindset but thought Nash's approach was poorly executed.

There were missions and then there were *missions*.

Rapp had made his bones stalking targets across Europe. As the times and target sets had changed, he'd made adjustments to his modus operandi and now employed a team of sorts. But this all came with the caveat that once a target package was approved, Rapp had the final say on how the hit was executed. With this in mind, Irene had expected Nash's request to go down in flames.

Here again Rapp had surprised her.

After listening to his friend speak, Rapp had agreed with one large asterisk—as the man on the ground, he reserved the right to terminate surveillance for any reason. It appeared that her top counterterrorism operative had exercised this prerogative shortly before his encounter with Ruyintan.

"Sounds like something you need to take up with Mitch," Irene said.

Nash nodded, his puppy-dog eyes hardening.

When Rapp had first suggested that Nash transition from the clandestine to the white side of the business, Irene had gone along for the ride. On the surface, the proposition killed two birds with one stone. It gave the press, and more importantly the American people, a genuine hero and rallying point for the war on terror. But more importantly, it arrested Nash's noticeable downhill slide and probably saved his marriage. Now, almost two years after the transition, Irene found herself contemplating something she almost never second-guessed.

Her judgment.

"I know, I know," Nash said, his tone contrite, "but I'm still trying to understand how the new organizational chart plays out in real life."

Irene paused.

This was an aspect she hadn't considered. Yes, Nash was Rapp's boss on paper, but anyone who had even a passing relationship with Mitch Rapp knew that no one told the world's best clandestine operative what to do. Nash had a point. It was difficult to exercise your authority if you didn't know where its boundaries actually lay.

She had herself to blame for this lack of clarity.

"I understand," Irene said, "and I appreciate that this is new territory. Going forward, I want you to assume that you and Mitch are peers. Try to work out your differences without my intervention. If that's not possible, I'll play referee. Okay?"

"Sure," Nash said.

"Good," Irene said, "because I need your expertise."

"On what?" Nash said.

"Rapp."

CHAPTER 15

"HOLY shit," Nash said.

Irene wasn't one for the casual use of profanity, but in this case, she agreed with her deputy's assessment. In some ways, Rapp was the equivalent of a stealth bomber. He penetrated the enemy's defenses and serviced targets too well protected for any other weapons system. But with this incredible capability came equally large problems when things went south.

And things had definitely gone south.

"From an operational perspective, you know him better than anyone," Irene said, drawing Nash back into the conversation. "Given what's happened, what will he do next? I need to prep the president and respond to the events in Afghanistan. But first, I need to understand what Mitch is thinking."

The pair were in the seating area of Irene's office. She was a bit of a minimalist, and this was reflected in her office's décor. Rather than the extravagant settings favored by many of her foreign counterparts, Irene made do with one long couch set with its back to her office's window, a rectangular, glass coffee table, and four chairs, two across from the couch and one at each end of the coffee table.

Nothing had changed from the previous discussion besides their location, but Nash's transformation was remarkable. Now that they were discussing operational versus personnel issues, the Marine's confidence had returned. It was this man rather than the mouse who had hesitantly entered her office earlier that Irene needed. The old Nash was still in there. It was Irene's responsibility to draw him out.

"Rapp's course of action is obvious," Nash said. "He'll go to Afghanistan."

"Even if that means losing his shot at FAIRBANKS?" Irene said with a frown.

Nash nodded, seemingly oblivious to his boss's doubt. The Marine's gaze lingered over her shoulder, but Irene doubted Nash was admiring the picture of Tommy on her desk.

His mind was in Pakistan.

"Rapp plays the long game," Nash said. "He got to FAIRBANKS once. He'll be able to get to him again. Rapp will view this as a postponement, not a cancellation. Making his terminal list is the equivalent of a stage-four cancer diagnosis. You're going to die. It's just a question of when."

Irene refrained from commenting on the morbid analogy.

The clandestine service from which Rapp, and until recently Nash, hailed was staffed with hard men and women expected to do hard things. Besides, Nash was right. When it came to snuffing out the enemies of his nation, Rapp was relentless. Irene thought of another analogy that was perhaps better suited to describing an encounter with her top assassin—playing Russian roulette with a bullet loaded in each chamber.

Sometimes miracles happened and people survived cancer.

No one survived Mitch Rapp.

"Besides," Nash said, continuing his thought, "Rapp will see Afghanistan as the priority. FAIRBANKS needs to die, but Ruyintan is on an entirely different level. People who don't know Mitch make the mistake of thinking he's a vigilante. Rapp can certainly hold a grudge, but he's not out for revenge. At least not anymore."

Nash was absolutely correct, and Irene was surprised she hadn't made this connection. Or maybe she had, but the evolution had occurred so slowly that she hadn't dwelt on its ramifications. When she'd started with Rapp, their relationship was conventional, even if its outcome hadn't been. She was the handler and Rapp was her asset. Put another way, Irene was the guidance system to Rapp's smart bomb. While Mitch certainly had the latitude to improvise while operating in the field, he did not make wholesale changes to the mission.

Then.

This was not to say that Rapp had morphed into some sort of loose cannon. He had not, but neither was he just a trained attack dog. Irene had no problem with Rapp exercising operational initiative, but the politicians who oversaw the CIA's clandestine activities often felt differently. This was especially relevant today. Two operations that had the potential to aggravate and embarrass the Pakistanis had just failed to achieve their intended results, one in spectacular fashion. While Rapp viewed the political fallout associated with his personal war on terrorism as only slightly more important than the price of milk, Irene knew differently. Senator Barbara Lonsdale had stuck her neck out for both operations.

This was not an insignificant act.

Senator Lonsdale had once been the opposition party's leading CIA critic, but a series of brutal terrorist attacks in the nation's capital had drastically changed her view of the intelligence organization. Three years before, suicide bombers and gunmen had attacked numerous civilian targets, including a DC eatery that was popular with the political crowd. The list of dead included seven senators and Lonsdale's closest friend and chief of staff, Ralph Wassen.

Almost overnight, Lonsdale went from being a thorn in Irene's side to one of the CIA director's biggest supporters. Even though many in

her political party seemed ready to throw the baby out with the bath-
water, Senator Lonsdale's commitment remained unwavering. While
this bit of courage paled in comparison to the fortitude displayed by the
spies Irene led, it was courage nonetheless.

As her nation's spymistress, Irene accepted that she would be the re-
cipient of political attacks. Attacks often levied by the very men and
women she had taken an oath to serve. That was part of the game. But
just because she was a convenient target didn't mean she had to go quietly
into the night. Senator Lonsdale had put her reputation on the line by
backing the raid on the HIG compound and the hit on FAIRBANKS even
though both would occur on Pakistani soil.

The least Irene could do was return the favor.

If Nash was right about Rapp's intentions, he would put the FAIR-
BANKS operation on hold to focus on the Iranians. She viewed the assassination as delayed, not blown, but her political masters might not
see things the same way. Providing Mitch Rapp room to maneuver was
the best way to salvage both operations while proving to Lonsdale that
her trust had been merited.

"Why Afghanistan?" Irene said.

"Ruyintan must have Quds Force operatives in-country," Nash said.
"That's the only way he could have known about the ambush ahead of
time. The operation took place in the vicinity of the Spin Ghar mountains, which are about fifty kilometers south of Jalalabad Airfield. Rapp
will want to check in with our chief of base in J-Bad as well as the SOF
folks headquartered at FOB Fenty. My money is on him catching the
next flight to Kabul."

"On the Saeed legend?" Irene said.

Nash nodded.

"We spent a long time building it. I didn't understand at the time
why Rapp was so particular about the details. Now I do. I don't know
if he could have articulated it then, but I think Rapp somehow knew
that he'd need a legend capable of withstanding the kind of scrutiny
that would allow him to do more than just waltz into a country and

knock off a few terrorists. I think he was preparing for a deep penetration."

The same thought had occurred to Irene.

Rapp's ability to do what others couldn't went beyond just the physical. Yes, the man seemed born to kill terrorists in the same way in which Eddie Van Halen had been born to play guitar, but it went further than that. Rapp possessed a sort of operational sixth sense that was hard to define and impossible to teach. He was more like a coyote who could spot a hunter's trap than a chess master able to foresee an opponent's strategy. Rapp had probably constructed the Saeed identity for a scenario exactly like this one. Her top operative was doing his part to turn their current setback into a win.

Irene intended to do the same.

"I think you're right," Irene said as she stood. "Send Scott Coleman and his team to J-Bad. I don't know what Rapp has in mind, but I want to make sure we prestage any support he might need."

"Got it," Nash said, getting to his feet. "What about you?"

"I'm wading into the fray too," Irene said.

Nash paused, a look of surprise on his face. "You're deploying to Afghanistan?"

"Worse. The White House."

CHAPTER 16

"**G**OOD afternoon, Teresa," Irene Kennedy said. "I need to see the president."

President Alexander's administrative assistant consulted her computer and frowned. "You're a bit early, Doctor Kennedy. He's still meeting with Ted."

"I understand, but I need to see him. Now."

Irene kept her tone polite, but firm.

"Of course," Teresa said. "Go on in."

Irene smiled her thanks, moved past Teresa's small desk, and opened the door to the world's most famous office. Irene didn't envy the president's assistant. In a town famous for the egos of its residents, Teresa served as the gatekeeper for the planet's most exclusive calendar. Everyone who made it this far was convinced of their own importance and it often fell to Teresa to sort the wheat from the chaff.

Over the years, Irene had made it a point to never abuse the president's standing instructions that she was to be provided with instant access when she requested it. Though she respected President Alexander, he was not the first commander in chief Irene had served and she was not unduly impressed with him or his office. Irene was not a politician, nor did she aspire to become one. This distinction separated her from 99 percent of the people who came to the Oval Office with intentions to curry favor with its occupant.

When Irene said she needed to see Alexander, Teresa waved her through.

But today was different.

Today, Irene almost wished she'd been refused access if only to have a few more moments to gather her thoughts.

This update was going to be a doozy.

Normally, Irene enjoyed her limousine ride from CIA headquarters in Langley, Virginia, to the White House. The SUVs driven by her protective detail employed the usual flashing lights as she traveled, but Irene wasn't sure this actually helped her arrive at her destination any sooner. In a town full of important people, DC motorists weren't always inclined to make way for yet another convoy of unmarked vehicles. Depending on traffic, Irene could usually count on being alone with her thoughts for between twenty and forty-five minutes.

Not today.

No sooner had her driver pulled out of the underground parking lot reserved for her and other select CIA executives than the limousine's secure phone began to chirp. Irene answered and soon had a sense of how the rest of her day would play out. As her car rolled south through the checkpoint granting access to the George Bush Center for Intelligence, as the headquarters campus was officially known, toward the west–east–running Dolley Madison Boulevard, she considered turning around. The president needed to hear the update she'd just received, but more importantly, those words needed to be immediately followed by a plan of action.

A plan Irene didn't have.

Yet.

Addressing her driver, Irene tasked him with doing something he never thought he'd hear the director of the Central Intelligence Agency say—take the long way. After ensuring that he'd correctly understood her request, the long-serving protection detail agent dutifully complied. In what was surely another omen of what was to come, *the long way* added a whopping five minutes to Irene's commute. She had used each second to its utmost, but as Irene strode into the Oval Office, she couldn't help but wish she'd had just a bit more luck.

Like maybe a flat tire.

"Irene—you're early."

Though the words sounded like a statement, Irene knew that President Joshua Alexander was asking a question. A question partly driven by her unexpected appearance and partly because she'd left the Oval Office door glaringly open.

Unsurprisingly, Ted Byrne, Alexander's chief of staff, had not taken the hint.

"What have you got, Irene?" Byrne said.

Byrne had known Alexander since the president was a little tyke and had played high school football for Alexander's father. He was fiercely loyal to his boss, but as was often the case with these types of relationships, he occasionally presumed too much. In this regard, Irene felt Alexander's pain. Half the time, Stan Hurley still saw her as his best friend's pink-beret-wearing little girl rather than his boss.

Perhaps more than half the time.

"This is for the president only, Ted," Irene said. The big man's face reddened, but Irene felt no sympathy for him. She'd given Byrne the chance for a graceful exit. He was the one who'd chosen not to take it.

"Why don't you grab a cup of coffee, Ted?" Alexander said. "I'll circle back with you in a bit."

Joshua Alexander had been born to be president.

Though his forties were wanning, Alexander was still one of the youngest-ever holders of the nation's highest office. A former collegiate football player, Alexander's six-foot-two frame was still a trim one hundred and ninety pounds. He was a handsome man with a full head of sandy brown hair and alert, hazel eyes. But it was his charisma rather than his looks that made Alexander the quintessential politician. When the full force of his attention was directed toward someone it could feel like standing in the middle of a spotlight on an otherwise dark stage.

Byrne huffed a bit as he got to his feet, but Irene knew the chief of staff wasn't mad.

Not really.

That was the effect Joshua Alexander had on people.

A moment later, the door swung shut with a thud, leaving Irene alone with the leader of the free world.

"Let's have it," Alexander said.

"It's CRANKSHAFT, sir," Irene said.

The president eyed Irene for a beat, his upraised eyebrows registering the significance of her statement. Though the words were innocuous-sounding enough, the meaning behind them was not. CRANKSHAFT was the code word corresponding to a special access program her people had been working for years.

A special access program focused on finding Osama bin Laden.

"Give me some good news," Alexander said.

"I'm afraid it's a mixed bag, sir," Irene said. "Our attempt to gather DNA failed."

"Son of a bitch," Alexander said. "What happened?"

Irene knew her boss's frustration was not directed at her.

Not entirely.

Countless pundits had opined on the stress generated by the world's most important job, but after watching the changes wrought on the multiple presidents she'd served, Irene had a different view. The pressure exerted by the presidency really couldn't be put into words. It was a weight in the literal sense of the word.

A burden under which Alexander was beginning to slump.

Though the president's appearance hadn't been ravaged in the manner of many of his predecessors, the presidency had taken a toll in other, less notable ways. He was still charming when the occasion warranted, but Alexander's disposition had taken a more cynical turn. He expected things to go wrong more often than right.

Days like today were the reason.

"Our Pakistani asset was not able to gain access to the compound," Irene said. "He tried to contact the men we believe are CRANKSHAFT's bodyguards and couriers via the phone number our analysts derived. No one answered."

"That's it?" Alexander said. "He didn't even knock on the fucking door?"

Alexander's voice had risen in volume as he spoke so that the last two words had been nearly shouted. The outburst was both rare and revealing. The stress really was getting to him. Or maybe it was more fair to say that it was getting to all of them but for different reasons. Irene stood silently for a moment, allowing the president's anger to wash over her even as she tried to ignore the tightening sensation in her chest.

Alexander was pissed, but she welcomed his frustration.

He'd just opened the conversational door Irene intended to walk through.

"The asset is a doctor, not a CIA officer," Irene said. "We all knew using him this way would be a stretch. From the beginning, his handler said that the asset's motivation was purely financial. I believe her words were something along the lines of *Don't expect too much and you won't be disappointed.*"

Alexander knew that Irene had a photographic memory, which meant that he also probably knew that the phrase she'd just quoted was lifted word for word from the case officer's cable. The Pakistani doctor had been charged with distributing the hepatitis B vaccine to the rural areas surrounding the mountain town of Abbottabad, Pakistan. His recruitment had been rushed and his training minimal. On the surface, the doctor's tasking had been simple—vaccinate the occupants of the imposing compound known among the locals as the Waziristan Haveli, or Waziristan Mansion, due to the thick Waziri accents of its occupants.

But even the simplest of taskings had a way of turning complex.

"So that's it?" Alexander said. "We're done?"

"With this asset, yes," Irene said. "With the compound, no. I think we need to change our approach. Send in someone who isn't afraid to knock on the front door."

"You're talking about a CIA officer," Alexander said with a frown. "We've been over this."

They had been over this.

Numerous times.

At this very moment, a troop of SEAL Team 6 assaulters were training on an exact replica of the Abbottabad compound in a remote area of North Carolina. This was to say nothing of the team of CIA officers conducting round-the-clock surveillance of the Abbottabad compound from a nearby safehouse.

To his credit, Alexander had agreed with each of Irene's requests to escalate toward a raid on the compound, save one. Until he had absolute proof that bin Laden was the lanky man captured by drone footage pacing back and forth across the compound's courtyard while wearing a hat with a large brim that obscured his face, the president did not want an American anywhere near the Waziristan Haveli.

On this point, Alexander refused to budge.

Irene intended to change his mind.

"Yes," Irene said, "I am. This is what my people train for. Let them do their jobs, sir."

Alexander reached for the coffee cup on the corner of his desk, realized that it was empty, and frowned. As delaying tactics went, it wasn't the most subtle, but Irene resisted the urge to fill the silence. She'd made her case for using a CIA officer to conduct a reconnaissance of the compound numerous times. Doing so again would only weaken her position.

Besides, the president hadn't yet said no.

That was progress.

"You said your update was a mixed bag," Alexander said, clasping his hands behind his head as he leaned back in his plush leather chair. "That implies that you've got some good news."

"I do, sir," Irene said.

Irene opened the satchel she was holding and withdrew a folder.

The cover sheet was orange and stamped with a series of acronyms, each meant to spark fear in the heart of the beholder. Irene didn't like taking material at this classification level out of Langley, but in politics, as in the intelligence business, words were cheap. If she was going to convince her boss that years of hard work had finally borne dividends, Irene would need more than just vague assurances.

The collection of papers she handed across the Resolute Desk had that in spades.

"What's this?" Alexander said, reflexively taking the documents.

"Remember the two men who live with their families in the compound?" Irene said.

"The ones you're convinced are couriers for Al Qaeda?

"Not just Al Qaeda," Irene said. "Bin Laden. And I can prove it."

Alexander raised an eyebrow, but he didn't dispute her statement.

This was also progress.

Satisfying the president's exceptionally high standard for what he considered proof of who called the compound home had been a game of back-and-forth for the last two weeks. To his credit, Alexander had authorized the CIA safehouse and given the go-ahead for the SEALs to begin preparations for an eventual assault, but that was as far as he'd been willing to go.

Hopefully, that was about to change.

With a long sigh, the president began to read. Within a few pages, Alexander's eyebrows shot from where they'd been resting above skeptically narrowed eyes to the top of his forehead. The stack of read papers to his left allowed Irene to chart the president's progress through the intelligence report.

He'd arrived at the good stuff.

"It is bin Laden," Alexander said, his chair snapping upright.

The president's words carried a reverence that was at odds with the revulsion etched across his face. It was as if Alexander were afraid that merely speaking the terrorist mastermind's name would cause him to vanish.

Irene nodded. "Our linguists have combed through the text. The speech pattern and sentence construction match other bin Laden fatwas. The level of detail and familiarity with ongoing operations expressed in the communiqué also indicate that the sender is a senior Al Qaeda commander. That message came from bin Laden."

"How did you get it?" Alexander said.

"We've had one of the compound's courier/bodyguards under electronic surveillance for the last several weeks," Irene said. "He practices excellent tradecraft with his cellular devices."

"Explain," Alexander said.

"The courier switches phones randomly and discards them after a single use," Irene said. "He buys his burners from a rotating selection of stores, making interdiction of his hardware extremely difficult."

Extremely difficult was perhaps too charitable a description.

After identifying the potential courier, Irene had dispatched paramilitary officers to Abbottabad with instructions to hack into the man's cell phone. The Al Qaeda operative had proven to be too wily. He never kept his phone active for more than a day and he never bought a replacement at the same store.

"Then how did you get to him?" Alexander said.

"The internet cafés," Irene said. "We were able to crack his phone twice since we've been monitoring the courier, but we found zilch. No hidden files, no texts or calls to numbers of interest, and no emails. Both times we gained access to his cell we got nothing."

The president leaned forward, intrigued. "Maybe he's clean."

Irene shook her head. "His obsession with operational security suggested otherwise. Yes, his phones were absent incriminating data, but his actions said we were on the right track."

"What do you mean?" Alexander said.

"Besides your own, how many telephone numbers can you recite?" Irene said.

"My parents'," the president said. "Maybe a couple of others."

"Any of them cabinet members?" Irene said. "What about the leader of your Secret Service detail?"

Alexander shook his head.

"Exactly," Irene said. "The contacts section of our cell phone serves the purpose that a Rolodex and good old-fashioned memory used to fill. But the courier's phone didn't contain a single name or number. Not one. And even if he had it encrypted on the phone somewhere we couldn't find, he switches devices constantly. No one goes to this much trouble to remain anonymous unless they have something to hide. And this guy did."

"'Did'?" Alexander said.

Irene nodded. "We got our first break when a paramilitary officer tracked him to an internet café. They're part coffee shops, part hangout joints, and depending on the part of town, sometimes a first step in the jihadi recruitment process. They're located all over Abbottabad, but the courier drove to a town ninety miles away instead."

"Did you catch the courier meeting with known Al Qaeda operatives?"

Irene shook her head. "He only used cafés without ties to extremist groups. Like his constantly rotating cell phones, our guy goes out of his way to remain clean."

"Maybe he is."

"The information in that document you're reading says differently," Irene said. "And before you ask, yes, at least one of the email recipients is a known Al Qaeda commander."

The change in President Alexander's expression would have been laughable were not the subject so serious. Irene's boss had what a theater teacher had once termed a rubber face. His hazel eyes and open features could express a wide range of emotions that lent credence to his words.

In the profession of politics, this was an attribute.

In the world of espionage, less so.

"You want to do what, then?" Alexander said. "Send an Agency paramilitary team to take a peek inside the compound?"

Irene shook her head. "Getting a declared team in-country this quickly would attract attention from the Pakistanis. The ISI is an unreliable ally at best. At worst, elements within that intelligence organization are actively working to thwart us. Sending a standard paramilitary team to Islamabad without alerting the ISI is a nonstarter. We need a different approach."

"Rapp?" Alexander said.

Irene shook her head. "I'm afraid Mitch is spoken for."

"How so?" Alexander said.

"He's running down the Iranian connection to the Afghanistan Chinook shootdown," Irene said, raising a hand to forestall the coming flood of questions. "I'll update you in full once I have the complete picture. All I know right now is that Mitch is off the grid and probably on his way to Kabul."

At one time in his presidency, Alexander would have pressed for more details over Irene's objections. Not anymore. After the devastating terrorist attacks on DC and the nearly catastrophic follow-up by the same jihadi cell, the president had changed his way of thinking. When politicians tried to keep Mitch Rapp on a leash, people died. Irene was hoping this wasn't a lesson the president would have to learn twice.

"Then who do you want to send?" Alexander said.

"Two people," Irene said. "I have a NOC who is uniquely suited for this mission, but they will need help."

"What kind of help?"

"A distraction. The best way to keep the ISI from noticing what we're doing is to give them something more interesting to watch."

"Like what?" Alexander said.

"A delegation of spies."

Alexander stared back at her in confusion.

Then, his eyes narrowed.

"You want to make an official visit to Pakistan?" Alexander said. "Now?"

"Not an official visit. Our Pakistani friends are holding a regional security summit. A number of countries are attending, including the Iranians. I think we should go as well."

"I need you here."

"Understood, sir," Irene said. "That's why I'm sending another executive in my stead. Someone who's synonymous with the CIA in the public's mind."

"Who?"

"Mike Nash."

CHAPTER 17

"IT'S done."

Azad Ashani held the secure mobile to his ear as he leaned on his balcony's intricately worked, wrought-iron railing and admired the view. Thirty years ago, he and his wife, Samira, had scraped together every rial to their name in order to make the down payment for this three-bedroom flat. Back then, Farmanieh was not the trendy suburb that it was today, but real estate had still been expensive. Located in the northern outskirts of Tehran, the suburb was full of shady, tree-lined streets, parks, and plenty of quiet neighborhoods. On a clear day, Azad could see the majestic Elburz Mountains, which guarded Tehran from the damps winds that swept south off the Caspian Sea. Best of all, his apartment was only a thirty-minute commute from his office at MOIS headquarters, located just east of Sanaei Street.

Azad had spent the best years of his life in this modest apartment.

Those days were now at an end.

"He agreed?" Ashani said.

"Why do you sound so surprised, my friend?"

The man on the other end of the phone was many things to Ashani.

Fellow intelligence operative, sometimes rival, and potential salvation. The word *friend* did not make Ashani's list.

Even so, there were appearances to maintain.

For now.

"We have both been at this game a very long time," Ashani said. "Only the foolish or inexperienced expect intelligence operations to go as planned. We are neither."

A chuckle that sounded like the rasping of dry bones greeted Ashani's words. Ashani was preparing to continue speaking when a spasm gripped his lungs. Muting the phone midcough, he dug his ever-present handkerchief from his pocket as his chest shuddered. Ashani pressed the cloth to his lips and waited for the bout to run its course. When the fit ended, he returned the crimson square to his pocket.

Ashani didn't bother to check the fabric for blood speckles.

The damp cloth was answer enough.

"That cough doesn't sound good."

"I'm fine," Ashani said. "Just a bit hoarse from allergies."

"I can have one of my men take the meeting in Kabul instead."

"I said I'm fine."

Ashani had meant to be firm, but his response came out angry. Maybe that was just as well. This conversation was on dangerous ground. Showing weakness could doom everything.

Besides, he *was* angry.

Angry at the world.

"I didn't mean to imply otherwise. Both you and the organization you lead are critical to this endeavor. I just wanted to offer my full support. As a partner."

Partner.

Another interesting choice of words.

As with his personal relationship with Colonel Dariush Ruyintan, the professional interactions between the Quds Force and Ashani's MOIS were complicated and often characterized by the internecine backstabbing one might expect from two rival organizations. Ashani thought that *competitor* rather than *partner* more aptly described the interplay between Iran's foreign intelligence service and the expeditionary arm of the Iranian Revolutionary Guard Corps.

But this had been before Ashani had volunteered to take point on a few of the crucial logistical issues plaguing Ruyintan's pending Afghanistan endeavor. The demonstration Ashani had witnessed in Isfahan had served its purpose. At the event's conclusion, the Guardian Council had enthusiastically approved Ruyintan's proposed operation against the Americans. An operation Ashani was determined to thwart. Using the Quds Force colonel to deliver a message to the man Ruyintan believed to be Farid Saeed had been the first step in Ashani's plan.

It would not be the last.

"I understand," Ashani said, trying for a conciliatory tone. "I appreciate your concern, but my ticket to Kabul has already been purchased. As I told the Supreme Leader, I am committed to doing my part."

This time, Ashani didn't have to fake sincerity. He was absolutely committed to doing his part. His part to ensure Ruyintan's Afghanistan operation went down in flames. Better that than the flames that would engulf Iran's refineries, remaining nuclear facilities, and perhaps even Tehran itself. Fire and brimstone would surely be the American response to Ruyintan's madness if the Quds Force commander succeeded.

"All right, then," Ruyintan said, "safe travels. I will see you in Islamabad."

Ruyintan ended the call before Ashani could reply.

This was just as well.

Ashani had no intention of seeing Ruyintan in Islamabad or anywhere else.

Unfortunately, he could no longer shoulder the effort to save himself and his nation alone. Yes, Ashani had convinced Ruyintan to reach out to the man the Quds Force commander thought was a gateway to the Sunni militias actively opposing the Americans in Iraq, but Ashani would need help for what came next. He had to start involving others.

People like the Angel of Death himself, Mitch Rapp, and Ashani's pragmatic new deputy, Darian Moradi.

But these men would not be his only coconspirators.

The most important person to this entire endeavor was still bustling around the kitchen only meters away. Ashani sighed as he drank in the beautiful vista for what might be his final time. The night skyline glittered like precious stones scattered across a canvas of black while the streetlights below cast halos of light through the thick canopies of the oak trees lining the street. The echoes of urban life drifted through the air, providing a soundtrack for Ashani's contemplation.

His flat had two features that made his home an ideal place for a spymaster to seek solace. One, his residence was on the building's top floor. Two, Ashani had the only balcony on his side of the building. These characteristics equated to a modicum of privacy. Privacy that allowed the MOIS minister to engage in confidential conversations outside his apartment and the potential listening devices hidden therein.

Sometimes these conversations were with fellow government employees.

Sometimes they were with his wife.

Turning, Ashani crossed the balcony in three quick slides, opened a sliding door constructed of unusually thick glass, and stuck his head inside.

"Samira, can you come here? We need to talk."

"Of course, my love."

Ashani relished the warmth of Samira's voice.

He only hoped that warmth remained after she heard what he had to say.

CHAPTER 18

NOREEN Ahmed eyed the trembling device with a hatred more suited for an angry rattlesnake than a vibrating cell. In what she regarded as a minor miracle, the buzzing phone hadn't awakened her sleeping husband. When they'd first married ten years ago, Brian would stir if their cat padded across the room.

Today, he slept like the dead.

Working twenty-four-hour shifts as a surgical resident could do that.

Swiping the phone from her nightstand, Noreen eased from her bed, holding the still-pulsating device against her chest. Her legs screamed and her shoulders and arms throbbed, but she managed to hobble across the hardwood floor without making a peep. Her FBI physical fitness test was less than a month away, and she was doubling down on her daily workouts to ensure she was ready.

In a regulation that only made sense to a government bureaucrat, there were no age gates to the FBI's entrance exam. This meant that, at thirty-five, Noreen was expected to achieve the same standards as someone a decade her junior. Rather than dwell on the insanity of this policy, Noreen simply trained harder. In her experience, government regulations rarely made sense.

And Noreen had plenty of experience.

Only after softly closing the door behind her did Noreen consult the screen on her vibrating phone. The number was unlisted, but she recognized the prefix. For a long moment, she thought about not answering. She was on leave, after all.

Terminal leave.

Then, she thumbed the green button.

"Hello?"

"Noreen Ahmed?"

"Who's this?" Noreen said.

Though she had a pretty good idea where the call had originated, the voice was unfamiliar. Even more important, she was on vacation and her employment with her current employer ended in three weeks. She felt little need to be polite. In the lexicon of her soon-to-be-former profession, Noreen was bulletproof.

"This is Deputy Director Mike Nash."

Or perhaps not.

Though the camera on her cell was taped over, Noreen still felt strange talking to a seventh-floor executive while wearing just a black tank top and the skimpy sleep shorts Brian loved. Resisting the urge to grab a sweatshirt from the laundry basket resting on the floor, she padded over to the couch and took a seat next to the orange cat that had been her companion since college.

Tigs was ten pounds overweight, blind in one eye, and hard of hearing, but she seemed to understand Noreen on an empathetic level. No sooner had Noreen crossed her brown legs than Tigs moved into her lap and began to purr.

"Yes, sir," Noreen said, with a look at the bedroom door. "What can I do for you?"

Her benign response still felt like a betrayal.

She'd promised Brian.

Promised.

"I know you're on leave, but I'd like you to please come in," Nash said. "It's urgent."

Noreen's gaze traveled from the accusing bedroom door to the framed picture resting on the end table. She and Brian just after he'd proposed. Then as now, their opposing complexions complemented each other. His alabaster face pressed against her nutmeg cheek. A boy who could trace his heritage back to County Antrim in Northern Ireland had married a girl whose parents hailed from central Pakistan.

Only in America.

The wedding had been a compromise of sorts. A mixture of Muslim and Catholic traditions that had mollified their prospective mothers-in-law while satisfying neither. Noreen had always thought that the biggest threat to their marriage would come from interfamily strife spawned by their very different backgrounds.

She'd been wrong.

"I don't think so," Noreen said.

Tigs vibrated like a tuning fork as she purred her agreement.

"What's that?" Nash said.

"I'm not coming in," Noreen said. "Sir."

She'd paused before adding the honorific, almost not uttering the word. But that wouldn't have been right. Regardless of how things had turned out, the state of her marriage could not be laid solely at her employer's feet. She and Brian were adults responsible for their own choices.

"I see," Nash said.

Noreen expected the conversation to end.

It did not.

"Noreen, can I ask you a question?"

Noreen paused again, trying to spot the trap behind the words.

Mike Nash had served his country in combat as a Marine before transitioning to the Agency as a paramilitary officer. According to the national news, he'd single-handedly stopped an attack on the counterterrorism center. Even though some of the details of what happened that day hadn't been disclosed, Noreen had no doubt that Nash was a hero. The voice on the phone didn't belong to a run-of-the-mill seventh-floor bureaucrat. Noreen might be disillusioned with the CIA and pissed off at what the long hours and frequent deployments had done to her marriage, but she had no cause to make Nash the target of her frustration.

"Sure," Noreen said.

"Do you remember what it felt like the first time you walked across the seal?"

He did not need to specify which seal.

For CIA case officers, there was only one.

In an organization rife with rituals, there was one tradition that was considered inviolable—until a CIA officer graduated from the Farm, he or she was not permitted to walk across the sixteen-foot-diameter granite seal embedded in the lobby floor of the original head-quarters building. This was not so much a rite of passage as an homage to all the clandestine operatives past and present who'd gutted it through the CIA's grueling school for spies at Camp Peary, an old naval training site located near Williamsburg, Virginia. For an organization built on secrecy, there were few ways to recognize the achievements of its most important employees.

Walking across the seal was one of them.

Of course, Noreen remembered the first time she'd strode across the seal after skirting it for so long.

She always would.

"Yes," Noreen said.

"Me too. Want to feel that way again?"

With a final look at the bedroom, she answered.

CHAPTER 19

S COTT Coleman had mixed feelings as he surveyed Forward Operating Base, or FOB, Fenty.

On one hand, he couldn't escape the fact that he was in foreign and mostly hostile territory. Even prior to the events of 9/11, Jalalabad had been an important city. With its proximity to the Pakistan border, large population, and agriculturally favorable climate, Jalalabad has served as the center of gravity for multiple military campaigns from medieval times to the present day.

But you wouldn't know this by the state of the airfield that serviced the city. With a single runway, a decrepit control tower, and a few crumbling buildings, the facility made its austere cousin in downtown Kabul look metropolitan. FOB Fenty had sprung up around the airfield, adding much-needed infrastructure while attempting to modernize the aging facility, but the airport proper still had the look of a one-horse town.

This was not the case.

Located an hour southeast of Bagram Air Base by helicopter, Jalalabad was critical to the American efforts to subdue the Taliban and take control of the rugged mountains and treacherous terrain located in the no-man's-land between Afghanistan and Pakistan. The first military units to occupy the airfield had set up tents and austere living arrangements not far from the runway.

Now the FOB boasted wooden B-huts, showers, and the all-important fully functioning dining facility. While Fenty was still a far cry from the Burger King– and Dairy Queen–equipped Bagram boardwalk, Jalalabad had a feeling of modernity. But as the guard towers, earth-filled Hesco barriers, and triple-strand concertina wire could attest, this was not Club Med. The Americans might be fully in control of the airfield, but the battle space on the far side of the earthen barriers ringing the FOB was another story.

The city's population wasn't as unruly as Kandahar, the birthplace of the Taliban, located almost four hundred miles to the southwest, but they weren't exactly lining the streets with American flags either. The surrounding villages were filled with people who were indifferent to Americans at best and Taliban sympathizers at worst. Nearly ten years after the war on terror had begun in Afghanistan, the infrastructure in Jalalabad might have changed for the better, but Scott couldn't say the same thing about the people.

This sentiment had been validated moments after the C-130 carrying Scott and his team of three operators had landed. As the men were exiting their aircraft, they'd been greeted by a volley of Taliban rocket fire that had sent everyone scrambling for the bunkers.

"Hell of a welcome, don't you think?"

Scott turned from the bunker's tiny window to the speaker.

Will Bentley was the newest member of Coleman's team. The former Force Recon Marine was in his late twenties, and though his six-foot frame was a respectable one hundred and seventy pounds, Will looked like a beanpole next to his companion, the linebacker-sized Joe Maslick. The former Delta Force assaulter was a quiet guy who wasn't much on trash-talking, but he was a close-quarters battle, or CQB, expert and one of Scott's best men.

Little Charlie "Slick" Wicker rounded out the trio.

Slick's diminutive five-foot-six frame was at odds with his more muscular counterparts, but the SEAL Team 6 sniper more than made up for his small stature with his ability to put steel on target from breathtaking distances.

Wicker was the best sniper in the free world.

"I kind of like the Taliban's way of saying hello," Scott said, pitching his voice loud enough for his entire team to hear. "Nothing says you're not in Kansas anymore like watching the jihadis blow the shit out of a volleyball court."

Chuckles greeted his words, but Scott knew the men had received the message. The Taliban's aim had been off, and the rockets had impacted an empty section of the FOB, causing damage but no injuries. They'd been lucky.

This time.

But only a fool relied on luck in a war zone. To be fair, the three men with Coleman weren't exactly combat novices. All had multiple tours of duty in Afghanistan, Iraq, or both under their belts. Though he'd once been the commander of SEAL Team 6, Scott had left active duty long ago, but his work for Rapp had taken him to those same places. When it came to combat, Coleman didn't believe in playing fair. He stacked the deck by only choosing to work with the very best.

These three men more than met that qualification.

"Didn't need a rocket barrage to remind me where I'm at," Maslick said. "The display at the end of the flight line did the trick."

Mas's comment resonated with Scott.

While scrambling for the bunker, the operators had sprinted past a makeshift memorial to the Rangers killed in the recent Chinook shootdown. Seven tan berets rested atop seven rifles thrust muzzle-down into seven pairs of brown desert combat boots. According to scuttlebutt from troops on the C-130, another twelve Rangers had been injured during the crash sequence.

Like most members of the special operations community, Coleman had mixed feelings about the Chinook helicopters he and his fellow SEALs often rode into battle. On the one hand, the aircraft were fast and powerful enough to ascend to the high mountain passes favored by the Taliban. A Chinook's cavernous crew compartment could deliver the same number of special operators in one trip that would require two Black Hawks or multiple MH Little Bird helicopters.

But the flying dump trucks also came with some negatives.

Though the 160th pilots who piloted the enormous aircraft were capable of astounding feats of airmanship, the massive helicopters would never be called nimble. Chinooks were huge targets, and their large passenger capacity often translated into a devastatingly high casualty list when the helicopters were brought down by enemy fire. In Iraq, Chinooks had been banned from flying during the daylight hours because of their propensity to draw enemy missiles. The recent shootdown was even more troubling from a tactical perspective since the aircraft had been brought down when Chinooks were generally considered invincible—at night.

"Do you know any of the casualties?" Coleman said.

Maslick shook his shaggy head.

"Not personally. Before the Unit, I served in Second Bat. All the casualties came from 1st Ranger Battalion, but the community's pretty small. I'm sure my running buddies do."

The all-clear signal indicating that the FOB was no longer under attack echoed down the flight line, saving Coleman from replying. As he led the way out of the bunker's dank confines, a pair of Apache helicopters thundered by overhead. If the gunships were returning to base, Coleman felt fairly confident there was nothing left outside the FOB to shoot. Next to a platoon of frogmen, nobody loved putting steel on target more than Apache pilots.

"What's the plan?" Will said.

That was a great question.

"It's fluid," Coleman said. "Rapp still hasn't surfaced, but I received a text from an Agency analyst while we were on the C-130. They got a hit on Rapp's Farid Saeed persona. He popped up on the manifest for a Kam Air flight from Islamabad into Kabul." Coleman glanced at his Luminox dive watch. The timepiece was Swiss-made and much too expensive for fieldwork, but Coleman was a SEAL. He had an image to maintain. "It should be landing in about an hour."

"We gonna pick him up?" Will said, his confusion evident.

Coleman shook his head. "He's still dark for a reason. My guess is that he'll clear customs in Kabul and run a surveillance detection route. Once he's sure he's clean, Rapp will head for Bagram. From there, he'll either give us a call or catch a flight here."

"The old hurry-up-and-wait drill," Will said.

"Welcome to Team Rapp, kid," Charlie said with a smile.

"I'm gonna wander over to the TOC and see what ops are scheduled for the next twenty-four hours and who we might be able to rope into serving as a quick reactionary force. You guys find somewhere for us to bunk, then zero your weapons and start prepping gear. Questions?"

There were none.

This was not because Coleman's pipe hitters understood the plan. At this point, there wasn't anything that could even loosely be termed a plan, but that was okay. With the exception of Will, this wasn't anyone's first Rapp rodeo. Mitch had a deserved reputation for getting shit done, but no one would term his operations *low-profile*. Even the world's best quarterback couldn't function without the protection of a good offensive line. Before he took his team into the field, Coleman would have a plan, but if experience was any guide, Rapp would end up calling an audible.

Welcome to Team Rapp.

Then again, if Coleman had wanted predictable, he'd still be attaching demolition charges to the rusted supports of some derelict oil rig. Life as the CEO of SEAL Demolition and Salvage Corporation had been lucrative, predictable, and utterly boring. Life with Rapp could be challenging, but there was something that service with the CIA provided that Coleman hadn't found in the civilian world.

Job satisfaction.

Eyeing the collection of B-huts, Coleman selected the one with the most antennas and headed toward it. Someday, Coleman might decide that it was time to take his company totally legitimate again.

Until then, supporting Rapp was his business.

And business was good.

CHAPTER 20

"**A**NYTHING?"

Captain Mark Garner tried to keep his voice unemotional as he asked the question. Judging by the CIA officer's reaction, he hadn't succeeded.

"No," the portly man said, raising his hands in a placating gesture. "I know you're concerned, but we're doing all we can. As soon as we have something, you'll be the first to know."

Mark stared back at the man, Dan, trying to contain his emotions.

Dan was the CIA's chief of base for Jalalabad, and he was responsible for collating all the various intelligence products generated in Regional Command East, an area of Afghanistan that encompassed many of the nation's worst hot spots. He wasn't a shooter by any stretch of the imagination, and his slovenly appearance didn't do much to inspire confidence.

Dan's stringy hair flopped over a mostly bald pate in what might have been the world's worst comb-over. His patchy faux operator beard looked like a Brillo pad, and his ample belly hung over cargo pants that were at least an inch too short. His desk was a mess of papers and crumpled candy wrappers, and an elaborate pour-over coffee rig shared space with a half-eaten bag of gourmet jelly beans.

If this knucklehead was responsible for providing a coherent, actionable picture of what was happening on the ground to Mark's chain of command, it was no wonder they'd been unable to locate Mark's missing Ranger.

Mark had purposefully placed his hands on his hips so that he wouldn't inadvertently clench his fists, but his body still vibrated with equal parts rage and frustration. Though the five or so CIA analysts who shared the B-hut with Dan were pecking away at their laptops, there had been zero intelligence products worth a damn distributed by this fusion cell since the ill-begotten raid on the HIG compound had turned Mark's world upside down.

After hours with no word from the CIA, Mark had decided to pay Dan a visit.

What he'd found hadn't been reassuring.

Rather than address Mark's concerns with anything approaching urgency, Dan seemed to imply that Mark should go back to his side of the compound and leave the intelligence professionals to do their work.

Mark had no intention of doing so.

Almost an entire platoon of his Rangers had been killed or wounded. The dead were beyond Mark's help.

The living were not.

"Look," Mark said, crowding Dan's personal space, "I don't mean to be a dick, but I've got a missing Ranger who's most likely in the hands of Taliban, HIG, or Haqqani thugs. If they get Saxton across the border into Pakistan, the next time we see him it'll be on a jihadi torture video as some black-masked fucker saws his head off. I've got sixty jacked-up pipe hitters waiting to rain down hellfire and brimstone, but we can't do shit until you find us a *goddamn target*."

Despite his best efforts, Mark's voice had grown steadily louder until his last two words had come out at a shout. The previous twelve hours had been the worst of Mark's life. Doug Peluso and his team of

Green Berets and Afghan National Army commandos had been a god-send after the shootdown. Mark's remaining Rangers had hit the compound as planned while Doug and his men had secured the Chinook crash site, provided first aid to the wounded, and begun medevac operations.

This change in plan hadn't come without cost.

Because the Green Berets had deviated from their original tasking to provide the operation's outer cordon, no one had been on squirter control. Mark's assaulters had captured the HIG commander who'd been the raid's objective, but several of the HVT's lieutenants and fighters had escaped into the surrounding mountains.

That wasn't the worst of it.

After the dust cleared on the assault, Mark had learned some terrible news.

One of his Rangers was missing.

The Ranger, Sergeant Fred Saxton, had been part of the element tasked with clearing the compound. Resistance from the compound's defenders had been fierce, and Saxton's Ranger buddy had been shot in the chest during the assault. In the fog of war that accompanied a mass casualty event and an ongoing operation against a determined and well-equipped enemy, no one had realized that Saxton was missing until much too late. The working theory was that Saxton had been surprised while rendering aid to his fallen teammate, overpowered by HIG fighters, and carried away by the fleeing jihadis.

With a start, Mark realized he'd grabbed hold of Dan's desk.

And was shaking it.

Mark folded his arms across his chest, embarrassed about losing his composure. He knew that he was on the ragged edge, but Dan's perceived lack of urgency wasn't helping. Mark's Rangers were still kitted up just feet from the helicopters that would carry them into battle.

Dan was sipping coffee and munching jelly beans.

Something had to give.

"What's going on, *Steve*?"

Mark turned to see someone standing in the doorway to Dan's office.

The CIA operations center was small and reasonably well lit. A pair of flat-screen televisions dominated the far wall while a map board with notes annotated on clear acetate covered the second. The B-hut's windowless interior had the feel of a library, and its CIA occupants could have been university students researching their dissertations.

Dan's desk was located in the corner farthest from the wooden hut's single entrance. His workspace had plywood partitions for walls and a door that opened to the bullpen. Besides the clatter of fingers on keyboards, Mark's conversation with the chief of base was the only thing interrupting the silence, so he was surprised he hadn't heard the visitor enter.

Steve seemed doubly so.

Mark knew that CIA officers frequently used false names when stationed overseas, but it pissed him off that the clandestine operative had used a legend with him. Mark wasn't some asset the chief of base had recruited from a Kabul slum. He was a fellow warfighter. That Dan had chosen not to disclose his true name made Mark even angrier.

"Nothing *Steve* and I can't handle," Mark said. "Or was it Dan, or maybe John Doe? I can't seem to keep you guys straight."

Mark turned his back on the newcomer, already dismissing the man. Sure, he had the untamed look of someone who operated beyond the Hesco barriers and mud brick walls that delineated FOB Fenty from the Wild West that was Afghanistan, but Mark wasn't impressed. Buying loyalty from corrupt warlords with suitcases full of cash wasn't for the faint of heart, but neither was boarding a helicopter to take the fight to the enemy in the dead of night.

Mark did feel a grudging respect for the CIA's Ground Branch operators, but he knew the snake eaters stationed at J-Bad by sight if not name. The olive-skinned man with shaggy black hair and a matching beard might be a step above the slovenly chief of base, but he was not a shooter and was therefore unworthy of Mark's attention.

"Don't take this the wrong way, stud, but I wasn't asking you. What's the story, Steve?"

The way the newcomer so casually dismissed Mark irritated him but also piqued his interest. The man hadn't raised his voice, but he'd asked the question in a manner that expected a response. Judging by how Steve was squirming, the chief of base wasn't keen on providing one.

"Hey, Mitch," Steve said. "Didn't know you were coming."

"Just hopped off a C-130 from Bagram. What'd I miss?"

Mark didn't have to be a body language expert to see that the newcomer made the chief of base nervous. And not the kind of nervous that an unexpected visit from a superior might provoke. This looked more like honest-to-goodness fear.

Maybe this Mitch guy wasn't so bad.

"This is Mark. He's the Ranger CO and one of his guys is unaccounted for—"

"Missing," Mark said, interrupting. "The phrase you're looking for is *missing and presumed captured*, which gets closer to *missing and presumed dead* every second I spend fiddle-fucking around here instead of leading a company of Rangers to find him."

"What's stopping you?" Mitch said.

"Great question," Mark said. "JSOC is gun-shy after losing that Chinook. My chain of command won't authorize a follow-on mission until they understand how a shoulder-fired missile managed to bring down a helicopter at night. They'd also like intel on who might have my Ranger and where he's being held. You know, the sort of intel the CIA's supposed to provide."

Mark had worked with the Agency long enough to know that trying to pit one officer against another was a losing battle. The CIA was an incredibly close-knit entity, and though he was certain they fought behind closed doors just like any other organization, the officers he'd worked with always presented a united front. By stating his frustrations so plainly, Mark had probably just shot himself in the foot. Mitch might have been sympathetic before, but in response to a frontal assault by a knuckle dragger like Mark, he would undoubtedly close ranks with Steve.

"What the fuck, Steve?" Mitch said.

Or maybe not.

"Come on, Mitch," Steve said, looking over Mark's shoulder, "it's not my decision. The chief of station is crawling up my ass. He doesn't want any case officers leaving the wire until we have a better understanding of the current threat assessment."

Mark was not an intelligence officer, but that sentiment made zero sense. Gaining a better understanding of the current threat assessment required case officers to leave the wire. Maybe there was something he didn't understand.

"The chief of station is in Kabul," Mitch said. "You think someone sitting in a bunker one hundred miles away has a better grip on the situation here than you?"

"He's my boss, Mitch," Steve said.

"I swear to God, we're going to lose this war," Mitch said, shaking his head. "If I thought explaining how to do your job was worth the effort, I'd give it a try. Instead, why don't you tell me what you do know, and I'll decide whether to ship your ass back stateside now or offer you a chance to redeem yourself."

"But the chief," Steve sputtered.

"Don't worry about the chief," Mitch said. "If Bill's as fucked-up as you, his ass will be on the seat next to yours on the flight back to Dulles. For the last time, what do you have on this missing Ranger?"

The CIA officer looked like a beached fish gasping for air. His mouth opened and closed, but he didn't speak. Steve's forehead glistened as beads of perspiration ran down his scalp. Opening his mouth for the third time, Steve replied.

"One of our assets provided actionable intelligence on a high-value target who was a key member of the HIG leadership team. We provided that intelligence to JSOC, who tasked Captain Garner and his Rangers with prosecuting the target and—"

"And it was a trap," Mitch said. "I want to talk to the asset. I assume he's hanging by his balls somewhere nearby?"

Steve shook his head. "The asset is no longer in communication with his handler."

"Go round his ass up."

"We . . . uh . . . well . . . we can't seem to find him right now, Mitch."

Mark realized his hands were now balled into fists and he had to make a conscious effort to unclench them. He started toward Steve, but what felt like an iron band gripped his shoulder.

Mitch's hand.

"Let me get this straight," Mitch said. "You sent these Rangers on a hit that turned out to be an ambush and now you've lost the fucker who fed you the bad intel? Holy shit."

While Mark wanted to scream at Steve or beat him senseless, Mitch's question stopped him. Something about the man's cold, emotionless delivery made Mark want to shiver, and he wasn't even the CIA officer's target.

The chief of base wilted. "Mitch, I'm sorry. We—"

"Tell me what you do have," Mitch said. "Now."

"The HVT," Steve said, almost babbling. "We have the HIG leader and some of his men in custody."

"Where?" Mitch said.

"Here."

Mark hadn't known this, but it made sense. The HIG compound his Rangers had hit was only about fifteen minutes from J-Bad by helicopter. Some of the most critically wounded Rangers had been transported to FOB Fenty's medical clinic for stabilization before undertaking the much longer flight to Bagram. Apparently the raid's prisoners were at J-Bad awaiting transfer to Bagram's detention facility.

"That's the first thing you've done right," Rapp said. "Get them ready for transport."

"I'll check the air manifest," Steve said. "I'm sure there's a flight to Bagram later today."

"They're not going by air."

"What do you mean?" Steve said with a puzzled tone.

"I mean we're moving the prisoners by ground."

CHAPTER 21

CONTRARY to popular belief, Rapp did not kill everyone who irritated him.

As he was fond of telling Irene, he could and did practice restraint when the situation merited it. The issue was that he'd become accustomed to solving problems by eliminating people, and the more he had to deal with jackasses like Steve, the more attractive this method of problem-solving became.

This was not to say that Rapp had any intention of killing a fellow American, but he'd be lying if he said the idea of removing Steve from the equation didn't have a certain appeal. Rapp operated in a world in which he was unshackled from the need to seek approval from his superiors once an operation was set in motion. This was because he reported solely to the director of the CIA and possessed neither the inclination nor desire to move into management. As such, Rapp was unincumbered by the second-guessing that plagued the many of his career-minded coworkers.

Rapp was a field man to his core.

He had zero utility at Langley, and he viewed fellow field operatives like the young Ranger commander as kindred spirits. While Rapp wasn't one for recklessly endangering American lives, he believed there was a time to go all in.

Now was that time.

"You want to drive the prisoners to Bagram?" Steve said. "That will take almost five hours."

"Just get them loaded, Steve," Rapp said.

"What about you?" Steve said.

"I'm going for a little hike in the Spin Ghar mountains."

Silence greeted Rapp's reply.

Steve looked at the Ranger commander for help, but Mark didn't seem inclined to speak.

With a sigh, Steve bit the bullet.

"I'm not doubting your abilities, Mitch," Steve said, "but there is zero chance you will get into those mountains unseen. Zero. I just had a Delta Force Troop commander in here trying to figure out how to insert a couple of his long-range reconnaissance teams. He couldn't make it work. That stretch of terrain is one of the most highly trafficked pieces of ground in the region. Goat herders, Taliban, HIG, Al Qaeda, and even the Pakistani army all use those trails. The SEALs, Green Berets, and Ranger Regimental Recon folks have tried putting reconnaissance elements into the mountain passes for years. No one has been able to clandestinely insert a team. No one."

"Couldn't agree more," Rapp said, eyeing the map board. "That's why I'm not gonna try."

Steve shook his head. "I want to get this American back as much as anyone, but a recon in force won't work either. Best case, Saxton's captors smuggle him over the border into Pakistan at the first sign of American vehicles heading for the foothills. Assuming that he isn't there already. Worst case, the jihadis decide the juice isn't worth the squeeze and put a bullet in the Ranger's head. It can't be done."

"Bullshit," Mark said. "My guys went in there once. We can do it again. I just need intelligence and a couple of helicopters."

The young Ranger officer looked ready to knock Steve out, and while the chief of base could probably use a good ass-whupping, Rapp didn't have time to play referee. His meeting with Ashani was in nine hours. He needed take care of this missing-Ranger situation and then catch a fight to Kabul.

"Is Coleman in-country yet?" Rapp said to Steve as he wedged himself between the CIA officer and the angry Ranger.

"Right here, boss."

Rapp turned toward to see Scott Coleman leaning against the B-hut's doorframe. For reasons not entirely clear to Rapp, the SEAL was smiling.

"How long have you been standing there?" Rapp said.

"Long enough."

After Stan Hurley and Irene Kennedy, Scott Coleman was the person Rapp trusted most in the world. The SEAL had been his right-hand man for operations too numerous to count, but Rapp still didn't get the frogman's sense of humor.

"How many shooters did you bring?" Rapp said.

"Three."

Rapp was hoping for more, but he'd make it work. "Get them in here. We need to do a mission brief."

"Will do," Coleman said.

The blond SEAL left without another word.

"What mission?" Steve said.

Ignoring the CIA officer, Rapp turned to Mark. "Do you have any Afghan shooters?"

"I don't," Mark said, shaking his head, "but there's an ODA team on J-Bad that has a company-plus of Afghan Army National Commandos. The team sergeant's name is Doug Peluso. I've worked with him before. He's good shit."

"Get him in here too," Rapp said. "Pronto. We're on the clock."

"On it," Mark said, heading for the door.

"Mitch," Steve said, grabbing Rapp's arm. "Have you heard a word I've said?"

"Every single one, unfortunately," Rapp said. "Now it's your turn to listen. Get Bill on the phone in Kabul. Tell him the shit's about to get real. I'm gonna put together a list of assets and taskings. His job is to provide them, no questions asked. If he has a problem with that, tell him that the next time his phone rings it will be Irene calling to explain that his career in the Central Intelligence Agency is over. Got it?"

"Mitch, you have to believe me," Steve said, his tone pleading, "you will never be able to sneak into that valley. Never."

"I don't plan to sneak in," Rapp said.

"What do you mean?" Steve said.

"I plan to get invited."

CHAPTER 22

SIXTY minutes later, Rapp was bouncing along a pothole-ridden road with his hands manacled.

He knew the restraints were necessary, but he still wasn't happy.

While he couldn't see through the black hood covering his face, Rapp could hear rushing water over the sound of a rumbling V-8 turbo-diesel engine. The spring rains had been exceptionally heavy this year, and the Kabul River was still at flood stage.

The Russian-made Ural-4320 cargo truck Rapp was riding in was the equivalent of the veritable M939 five-ton, which had hauled equipment and troops for the American military for more than thirty years. Like its US counterpart, the Russian version had a large tarp-covered cargo area located behind a small cab. The truck boasted all-wheel drive for its six tires, but even the most surefooted of vehicles were at risk on these roads.

As was the case with most infrastructure projects in Afghanistan, billions of dollars had been allocated toward improving the roads that wound through the mountainous nation. Also par for the course, very little of that money had been used to pave and level roads. If things were progressing according to plan, Rapp's truck was currently heading southwest out of J-Bad in a circuitous route meant to circumvent a few newly erected barriers restricting access to the more direct Jalalabad–Kabul highway. The detour followed the serpentine twists and turns of a tributary of the Kabul River, and the drop-off to the churning water was both steep and barrier-free.

As a former Ironman, Rapp was an excellent swimmer, but it was difficult to swim when your hands were manacled to a chain bolted to the truck's metal frame. And this was assuming Rapp would be in any condition to swim after the truck plunged down the sheer twenty-foot cliff. Three Marines had tragically drowned in this same tributary after their up-armored Humvee had misjudged a turn and toppled down the embankment. Even so, the water's icy clutches weren't Rapp's most pressing concern.

That honor belonged to his fellow passengers.

"Who are you?"

The question was asked in Pashtu by the smelly human being seated on the troop bench to Rapp's left. While Rapp was no stranger to living in the bush, the stench emanating from the prisoner was a doozy even by Taliban standards. The fighter smelled like he'd either rolled in excrement, or a portion of his body was rotting.

Or both.

Although the olfactory experience was less than pleasant, Rapp felt his hope stir at the man's question. He'd arranged to be seated next to the prisoner for this exact reason. Now Rapp needed to take advantage of the opportunity presented to him.

Even if that meant breathing through his mouth for the foreseeable future.

Rapp paused as if weighing how much to reveal.

This was not an unreasonable reaction. The dozen or so fighters sharing the truck bed with Rapp were all manacled and hooded as per standard prisoner transport procedures even though there was nothing standard about this convoy.

But the smelly HIG fighter didn't need to know that.

"Speak Arabic?" Rapp replied in labored and heavily accented Pashtu.

"*Aywa*," the man said.

Of course he did.

Though the fighter dressed and smelled like a run-of-the-mill foot soldier who'd spent far too much time in the company of goats, his appearance was deceiving. Rapp's seatmate was actually the high-value target from the ill-fated raid. Since the HIG commander went by many names, the CIA analysts who'd developed his target package had christened him with the code name CYCLONE.

"I'm a brother from Iraq," Rapp said in Arabic.

"I could tell by your accent," CYCLONE said. "I will call you Abu al-Iraqi, then."

"Who are you?" Rapp said.

This time CYCLONE let the silence build.

Rapp forced himself to relax even as he could feel the seconds tick by. The next part of this engagement was critical. While Rapp wasn't an agent runner per say, he knew a thing or two about handling assets. Ninety-nine percent of the time, Rapp thought that people in the intelligence community erred too much on the side of caution. In a world full of nails, a hammer usually was the best tool.

Not today.

Today Rapp had to try something that was anathema to his usual modus operandi.

Subtlety.

"I am the bearer of bad news, Abu al-Iraqi," CYCLONE said.

"What news?" Rapp said.

CYCLONE snorted. "They are taking us to Parwan Detention Facility. Afghans might run the prison, but only the Americans decide who leaves. I would prepare for a lengthy visit."

"I don't think so," Rapp said.

"You doubt me?" CYCLONE said.

"Not in the least," Rapp said. "I just have no intention of going to prison."

As if on cue, Rapp felt the truck slow.

Then, the world exploded.

CHAPTER 23

T be fair, it wasn't the entire world that exploded.

The thunderclap originated from somewhere outside the truck, but with nothing but cheap canvas standing between Rapp and the concussive blast wave, it sure felt like the world was ending.

Suddenly, shooting started.

For anyone who'd been on the receiving end of either firearm, the chattering of an M4 carbine firing sounded decidedly different from the barking of an AK-47 rifle. The HIG commander seemed to fall into that category.

As did Rapp.

"Brothers are attacking the convoy!" CYCLONE shouted.

"Quiet," Rapp said, leaning closer to the other man. "It's not an attack. It's a rescue."

"How do you—"

"I said *quiet*." Rapp emphasized the command by slamming his shoulder into the HIG commander. "If you want to live, be still."

To his credit, CYCLONE fell silent even as screams echoed around them.

Rapp and his fellow prisoners were secured by a single chain that ran through the manacles binding their wrists. The chain was fastened to eye bolts sunk into the truck's chassis at regular intervals, preventing the captives from moving. As such, just one guard shared the cargo area with them. Though the Afghan was outmanned twelve or more to one, the manacles and black hoods restraining the captives meant that he had nothing to worry about.

From his prisoners, anyway.

An AK-47 sounded to Rapp's right. The report was deafening in such close confines and the muzzle blast buffeted his chest and face. A scream morphed into a gurgle as bullets presumably found their target.

"Here!" Rapp shouted in Arabic. "I'm here."

"What are you doing?" CYCLONE said.

"Leaving," Rapp replied as nimble hands pulled the hood from his face and pressed a key into his fingers.

"Hurry," Rapp's rescuer said, "the Americans are coming."

"Help the brothers," Rapp said. "I'm right behind you."

Rapp worked the handcuff key into the crusty lock, fighting an accumulation of rust, grit, and probably blood. In what should not have been a shock to him, the Afghans in charge of transporting the prisoners hadn't dedicated a lot of time to ensuring the restraints actioned smoothly. Then again, these men were probably not the cream of the crop. The role of prison guard was universally assigned to people who fit a demanding criterion: sick, lame, or lazy.

The key began to turn.

He carefully applied more torque, trying to split the difference between overcoming the debris jamming the locking mechanism and snapping off the key's plastic grip. After a final twist, the manacles opened with an audible *click.*

"*Allahu Akbar,*" Rapp said as he stripped off the restraints and let them clatter to the floor.

Though he had spent more than his fair share of time in restraints of one sort or another, Rapp didn't have to fake his relief. After years of working as a counterterrorism operative, he'd developed a pretty accurate assessment of his abilities. While he wasn't Superman, Rapp had no issue putting himself up against anyone.

As long as his hands were free.

Properly restrained, Rapp was no more dangerous than a cubicle dweller.

Scrambling to his feet, he stepped across CYCLONE, trampling the HIG commander's toes in the process.

"Wait, Abu al-Iraqi," CYCLONE said. "Help me."

Rapp ripped opened the canvas flap at the rear of the truck. A gust of wind stirred the stagnant air, carrying with it the echo of gunfire, screams, and dying men. The breeze combined with the sounds of the battle catalyzed the prisoners. Shouts and pleas for help rang through the cargo area.

"Can't save everyone," Rapp said. "Sorry."

"I am not just a common soldier," CYCLONE said. "I command fighters along the border. Many fighters."

A barrage of automatic weapons sounded from just outside the truck.

"Truly?" Rapp said, yelling to be heard over the din.

"I swear it by Allah," CYCLONE said. "Hizb-i-Islami Gulbuddin. You have heard of it?"

Rapp had certainly heard of the HIG.

"Perhaps," Rapp said.

"I lead the HIG in Pakistan," CYCLONE said. "Free me and my organization will be in your debt."

Letting the tarp fall back into place, Rapp turned to CYCLONE. Ignoring the pleas from other prisoners, he grabbed a handful of the HIG commander's hood and ripped it from his head. "If I help you, you will honor your vow," Rapp said. "I am not a man to be trifled with."

"Of course, Abu al-Iraqi," CYCLONE shouted. "Of course."

Rapp didn't know whether it was the authenticity in his voice or the sound of chattering M4s that did the trick, but the warlord's eyes shone with fervor. The ability to decipher truth from bullshit was a prerequisite in Rapp's world, and his internal lie detector was telling him that CYCLONE was telling the truth.

For now.

Loyalty in this tribal nation couldn't be bought, but it could be rented.

Rapp was about to rent a dump truck's worth.

Grunting, Rapp pulled the warlord forward so that he could get at the man's hands. He was none too gentle, but CYCLONE didn't complain. Once again, Rapp plunged the handcuff key into the grimy lock and twisted, this time with better results. He didn't know whether his success was because he could see the manacles or because the raging gunfight prompted an adrenaline-fueled response of his own and he didn't care.

With a rasp, the restraints opened.

Grabbing the warlord by the back of his neck, Rapp manhandled the scrawny man toward the rear of the truck. Then he slid the canvas out of the way and jumped to the ground. Rapp landed in a crouch, letting his leg muscles cushion the five-foot drop.

His companion wasn't so graceful.

CYCLONE caught his leg on the tailgate and tumbled to the gravel.

Rapp ignored the warlord in favor of searching the ground for a weapon.

He found one.

An AK-47 lay next to the truck's right rear wheel. Rapp grabbed the rifle, ejected the magazine, checked its load, reseated it, and cycled the weapon's bolt. CYCLONE tried to stand, but his dismount from the truck must have been even worse than it looked. The warlord was favoring his ankle.

Badly.

Rapp was moving to help CYCLONE when he caught motion in his peripheral vision. Turning, Rapp saw an American coming around the side of the truck. Releasing the safety, Rapp brought the AK-47 to his shoulder and fired.

The rifle barked, and the American spun to the ground.

Rapp sighted on the limp man's chest, but his crimson-stained shirt didn't move.

Rapp turned back toward the warlord.

"You are very good, Abu al-Iraqi," CYCLONE said.

"We need to get to the Hilux trucks," Rapp said, pointing toward a bend in the road. "My brothers will—"

A giant flash followed by a pair of thunderclaps interrupted Rapp. The explosion echoed from where Rapp had been pointing.

"*Alqarf*," Rapp said.

"I'm assuming those were your trucks?" CYCLONE said.

Rapp didn't reply, but the murderous look he directed at the warlord was probably answer enough.

CYCLONE smiled. "I know this place. Head for the trail leading into the trees over there. Quickly, while the Americans are still occupied."

Rapp turned toward the dirt trail but hesitated.

"Your brothers fought valiantly, but they cannot be saved," CYCLONE said. "Don't dishonor their sacrifice by needlessly martyring yourself. I have people in the next village. Get me to them, and I will repay my debt. With interest."

With an utterance that sounded more like a growl than speech, Rapp dropped his rifle, lifted the warlord into a fireman's carry, and ran for the trail.

CHAPTER 24

Scott Coleman breathed an audible sigh of relief as the two figures disappeared into the woods.

Letting his sling catch his M4 rifle, Coleman withdrew a thermal imager from his chest rig and peered through the eyepiece. As expected, the forest sprang to life in monochrome shades of white and black. What was less expected was the effect the change of spectrums had on the two vanishing men.

The HIG warlord, CYCLONE, was rendered into a recognizable human shape with white "hot" spots depicting his head, hands, and ankles. His torso was drawn in shades of black signifying that the fabric from his clothes was "cold" in comparison with his skin. The thermal sensor's algorithms had stitched together the image based on temperature differentials exactly as expected.

The same could not be said of his companion.

Coleman adjusted the monocle's focus until the image was as clear as the optic could deliver under the current environmental conditions. Then he squeezed the trigger on the sight's handgrip, capturing a series of digital photographs. While Rapp's extremities and exposed skin were also rendered with white pixels, his torso looked different.

Instead of a cold "black" representation that mirrored CYCLONE's image, Rapp's midsection bore a blindingly white capital X. In the visual spectrum, Rapp's clothing looked perfectly ordinary, but under the discrete frequency the thermal imager saw, he was a marked man thanks to the specially designed fibers embedded in his shirt.

"All Chaos elements, this is Chaos 6," Coleman said after keying his radio's transmit button, "Ironman is clear of the objective. I say again, Ironman is clear of the objective."

Coleman listened as his teammates acknowledged the transmission, trying to ignore his thundering heart. Working with Rapp was never boring, but this operation might have been one of the most stressful Coleman had ever undertaken. To win CYCLONE's trust, Rapp had proposed a pseudo rescue attempt that was as audacious as it was dangerous. One misplaced shot, one instance of the wrong weapon being aimed in the wrong direction, and people would die. As if hearing Coleman's thoughts, the American whom Rapp had "killed" with his AK-47 got to his feet.

Will Bentley gathered his M4 and trotted toward Coleman.

This had been the most dangerous part of the rescue, and Coleman had originally slotted himself for Will's role. The magazine of the AK-47 Rapp had fired was loaded with Simunitions, or cartridges containing a paint capsule rather than a projectile at the tip. The weapon had been clearly marked and hand-delivered, but the fog of war wasn't just an expression. In the confusion sure to enfold the ambush/rescue, Coleman visualized countless scenarios in which a rifle with live rounds inadvertently ended up in Rapp's hands.

As the team leader, Coleman thought that he should bear the greatest risk.

His teammates had disagreed.

In a rare argument between team members, Will, Charlie Wicker, and Joe Maslick had all thought Scott should be commanding and controlling the engagement instead. The Green Beret, Doug Peluso, agreed. Coleman knew his men had a point, but his sense of duty wouldn't let him concede it.

So, Rapp had made the decision for him.

Now that the engagement was over, Coleman knew that his teammates had been right. The ambush and subsequent prisoner escape might have been executed flawlessly from CYCLONE's perspective, but things hadn't been so peachy on the other side of the battlefield. Coleman had needed to navigate several last-minute hiccups on the fly, including a potential friendly-fire incident between Doug's Afghan Army National Commandos and the Afghan National Police charged with guarding the prisoners.

Coleman gave a relieved sigh as the knots in his stomach slowly untangled.

The dangerous part was over.

"Chaos 6, this is Grip 13."

"Go for 6," Coleman said.

Grip was the call sign for the Reaper drone drifting through the sky overhead. True to form, Rapp had convinced both the CIA chief of base in Jalalabad and his boss, the chief of station in Kabul, to get religion. The list of taskings and assets Rapp had requested seemed over-the-top even to Scott, but the agency had come through on every ask. The loitering Reaper was exhibit one.

In another stroke of good luck, clear skies had permitted the UAV to fly at an altitude of forty thousand feet. After almost a decade of watching compatriots die in Hellfire missile strikes, the jihadis had learned to listen for the unmistakable buzzing sound made by the drone's engine. But at more than eight miles above the earth, the Reaper's engine noise was lost to the combatants on the ground.

At least that's what Coleman hoped.

"Roger 6. Ironman is looking good, but the rest of you need to get off the X pronto. The explosions woke up the neighborhood. I have several vehicles full of military-aged males heading your way. ETA one zero mikes, over."

Coleman sighed.

Part of him thought that he ought to press his luck and set up an ambush for the approaching forces. In the never-ending skirmishes between the anticoalition forces and NATO, the jihadis had proven to be masterful at adapting their tactics to make use of the ever-changing Western rules of engagement. Lately this had taken the form of a concerted Taliban effort to locate their fighters within villages considered *safe* by the Americans.

This strategy had a twofold effect in that it made it harder to distinguish the jihadis from the villagers while also hampering the Americans' ability to conduct surgical raids against known targets. Any misstep or collateral damage meant a parade of dead women and children laid out for the media. The armed convoy heading toward the ambush site could be Taliban, HIG, Haqqani Network, or even Al Qaeda fighters.

But Scott didn't know that for sure.

This was Afghanistan—a country in which any male over the age of fourteen was permitted to carry an AK-47. With this in mind, it was just as likely that the collection of trucks contained the village's version of a militia—basically a neighborhood watch outfitted Afghan-style. As much as Coleman wanted to leave the bad guys with a few less foot soldiers, it wasn't worth jeopardizing Rapp's mission.

If the last decade was any indication, this war wasn't going away anytime soon.

"Roger that, Grip," Coleman said. "Chaos 6 is pulling off the objective time now. Keep your eyes on Ironman, over."

"Grip copies all. Easy day."

Coleman doubted that very much.

CHAPTER 25

"**S**o that's where we stand, Mr. President. The remaining prisoners have been secured and are safely back at FOB Fenty along with all the American and Afghan assets that participated in the diversion. Any questions, sir?"

Irene turned from the LCD screen showcasing the imagery from the Reaper drone orbiting over the site of the faux ambush to the president.

The Situation Room always felt chilly, and despite the fact that she was wearing a long-sleeved blouse and slacks, Irene still fought the urge to shiver. Between the flat-screen TVs lining the walls, the communications suite that provided a secure connection to anywhere on the globe, the plush leather chairs, polished wood conference table, warm overhead lighting, and even the coffee station, the Situation Room had been designed with the men and women who made the nation's most important decisions in mind. Why the room had to be kept at a temperature more suitable for a meat locker was beyond her.

"No, I think I'm tracking," the president said. "Well done."

Irene didn't become a spy because she craved public affirmation.

Between her mentor and predecessor as CIA director, Thomas Stansfield, her *uncle* Stan Hurley, and her own father, espionage was a family
business. She'd joined the Agency because she loved her country and
believed that working in the clandestine service was the most effective
way to utilize her talents. Now, as the leader of the world's premier intelligence organization, Irene was comfortable in the shadows. If she did
her job, terrorists died in foreign locales far from US shores and the
American people were none the wiser.

That said, receiving an *attagirl* from the one person who actually
knew the lengths to which the men and women Irene had the pleasure
of leading went to in order to ensure that their countrymen could sleep
safely in their beds at night was rewarding. But in this case, Irene took
no joy in the president's pronouncement. While her gaze was centered
on her boss, Irene's peripheral vision was locked on someone else.

General Alton Rex.

"Excuse me, sir, but I have a couple of questions."

If experience was any guide, the military officer's statement was a
bit misleading. The Air Force general's *questions* were really objections
masked in the pretense of ensuring that he understood the plan Irene
had just briefed. In the best of scenarios, the military and the CIA
worked together seamlessly. In the worst, they squabbled over battle
space, mission creep, and access to resources. Irene had served with
several chairmen of the Joint Chiefs of Staff, and while she hadn't always seen eye to eye with her uniformed counterparts, she'd respected
them and their opinions.

Not Rex.

"Of course," President Alexander said. "Go ahead."

"Yes, sir," Rex said with a smile. "I'm just a farm boy from Omaha,
but I'm not sure I understand what we're trying to do here."

Like his perfectly bronzed skin and sparkling white teeth, General
Rex's modest-beginnings shtick was artificial. As the leader of an organization that numbered more than twenty-one thousand people en-
compassing a multitude of races, religions, and creeds, Kennedy did not

draw conclusions about a person based on their upbringing. While her formative years had been spent overseas rather than milking cows, as Rex liked to claim, the general's hardscrabble childhood wouldn't bother her in the least.

Had it been true.

While an expert on dairy farms Kennedy was not, she had a finely tuned bullshit detector, and the Air Force officer registered off the scales. After enduring his farm-boy routine one time too many, Irene had made some quiet inquiries. Turns out that Rex had grown up on a farm in the same manner in which Irene had been crowned Miss Maryland, which was to say not at all. Rex's father had been raised several houses up the road from a dairy farm and had milked cows as a teenager. While Rex had certainly visited the farm on occasion during trips to see his paternal grandparents, he'd never worked there. For reasons known only to him, the general had appropriated his father's experience.

As lies went, Rex's falsehoods weren't exactly treason, but Irene was more concerned with the motivation behind the mistruths than the words themselves. The general deliberately manipulated facts to suit a narrative he'd constructed. As a case officer, Irene made her living through misdirection, but her deceptions targeted the enemies of her country, not the people charged with keeping it safe.

Along with his fake tan, wrinkle-free face, dyed hair, and whitened teeth, Rex's altered background was an attempt to create a better version of himself. A version that might be more attractive to the talent management people who recruited talking heads for cable news programs. Irene could forgive the man his vanity, but she could not tolerate his selfishness. White House staffers were famous for lining up their exit opportunities while still serving in the administration, but in some ways this was to be expected.

Not so for the president's military advisors.

The man charged with counseling the president on all things armed forces–related should be wholly focused on his current job, not a lucrative postmilitary career. But each interaction with Rex seemed to confirm that the general did not share her convictions. Unfortunately, her boss had not arrived at the same conclusion.

Yet.

"What we're trying to do here is save one of your Rangers," Irene said, her delivery deadpan. "The ground force commander's assessment is that the area of operations where Sergeant Saxton is likely being held is too heavily trafficked by enemy combatants to conduct a clandestine reconnaissance. This plan is designed to addresses the military's blind spot."

"By sending a single CIA asset on a suicide mission?" Rex said, slowly shaking his head. "I'm sorry, but I just don't see it."

Irene had weathered many a meeting that hadn't gone her way. Washington's petty politics and the oversize personalities grated on her but paled in comparison to the life-and-death situations her people faced in the field. If listening to blowhards bloviate on topics they didn't understand was Irene's cross to bear, so be it. Her years in management had made Irene something of a savant when it came to her ability to refrain from issuing an oftentimes justified emotional response to the idiocy she so often encountered.

She didn't lose her cool.

Usually.

"I apologize if I'm misunderstanding your point," Irene said, locking gazes with Rex, "but I could have sworn our military adhered to a certain policy when it came to the men and women who voluntarily serve in its ranks. *I will never leave a fallen comrade to fall into the hands of the enemy*—isn't that how the Ranger Creed goes?"

That was precisely how the Ranger Creed went.

Irene's photographic memory made recall of the phrase a simple measure, but the optics of her question were not lost on Rex. Prior to his current role, the general had helmed Joint Special Operations Command, or JSOC. The aviator's appointment as the JSOC commander had not been without controversy. Unlike the snake eaters who usually occupied this role, Rex was an AC-130 pilot.

Even worse, he was an aviator with very little combat experience.

While Rex had checked the required boxes by first serving as the commander of 1st Special Operations Wing located at Hurlburt Field in Florida, he'd spent the majority of his time as a company and field-grade officer in staff billets rather than the cockpit of an AC-130J Ghostrider putting steel on target. As a nonshooter, there was a better-than-even chance that the general had never heard of the Ranger Creed, to say nothing of his ability to recite it from memory.

For a moment, Irene saw what lurked behind the general's congenial act. His warm blue eyes turned to shards of ice as the wattage on his bright smile dimmed. The index finger on his right hand was the real tell. The offending digit didn't so much move as vibrate, like a violin's plucked string.

Then his grin widened, and the squall passed as quickly as it had arrived.

"I'd never bet against a spy's memory," Rex said, "but in my business, we can't always bring everyone home. The mission comes first. Sometimes this means America's sons and daughters bear the cost of our poor choices. I advised against the raid on the HIG compound in the first place. I thought it was too provocative and had the potential to hang our service members out to dry. Now that the operation has gone off the rails, I don't think we should be throwing good money after bad. No one wants to rescue Sergeant Saxton more than me, but we run the risk of further antagonizing our Pakistani allies with a second covert operation conducted on their doorstep. I think this is a bridge too far."

Irene felt her blood pressure skyrocket even as her cold intellect prepared to rebut Rex's outrageous statements claim by claim. If the general was willing to sacrifice the lives of his troops on the altar of international diplomacy, so be it.

She was not.

Irene was opening her mouth to begin Rex's verbal dismemberment when President Alexander's voice cut through the air.

"Your concerns are duly noted, General Rex," Alexander said. "Again. I approved Irene's operation and she's going to run it. Questions?"

"No, sir," Rex said, his smile somehow even brighter. "I wish the best of luck to Director Kennedy's agent."

Kennedy had purposefully refused to reveal anything substantial about the operation, citing the old *sources and methods* standby even though Rex had pressed. She had no reason to suspect that the pompous aviator would actively sabotage her operation, but she wasn't taking any chances. When Rapp had called her from Jalalabad to brief his concept of the operation, the details had given her pause. What he was proposing was extreme even by his standards.

Then again, extreme times sometimes called for extreme measures.

Rapp's success depended on absolute operational secrecy. Under no circumstances would she divulge the details of Rapp's plan to this crowd. For reasons she still didn't quite understand, Rex seemed to take her refusal to elaborate as a personal affront. While Rex hadn't asked her outright for the identity of her agent or the insertion plan's particulars, the Air Force general had certainly nibbled around the edges. Government service types commonly desired access to classified material beyond their need to know for a variety of reasons, but this behavior was usually driven by a single cause.

Pride.

People wanted to be able to say that they were *in the know* when it came to clandestine or covert operations, even if they personally had nothing to do with the mission. Every training session on the handling of sensitive or classified material always began by stressing that a person's level of clearance had nothing to do with their importance.

While this was true in theory, the principle wasn't so clean in practice.

In a town in which status was derived from a person's proximity to power, everyone wanted to be in the room where it happened. For the president's staff and the sycophants who surrounded him, not possessing a security clearance was a barrier to entry. In order to truly be in the inner circle, an aide needed to have the requisite color badge and the appropriate initials after their name.

For Rex, this didn't apply quite so neatly.

The general might have the clearance to take part in a classified discussion, but when it came to the nuts and bolts of an ongoing CIA operation, Rex didn't have a need to know. That he pried for the information anyway suggested a vanity that fit with what Irene already knew about the man. Irene's distrust for the blowhard went beyond their professional disagreements. The same instinct that made her an excellent agent runner warned her that he couldn't be trusted.

Until Rex proved otherwise, Irene was going with her gut.

"Good," the president said. "Irene—anything more?"

"Not to do with this situation," Irene said, edging forward to lock gazes with the president. "But I would like to do a quick check-in on an administrative matter."

"Of course," the president said with a smile.

A smile that didn't quite reach his eyes.

CHAPTER 26

T HE president eyed Irene for a beat, his upraised eyebrows registering the significance of her statement.

Though the words were innocuous-sounding enough, the meaning behind them was not. Irene had learned long ago that even if people were not privy to the details discussed during her private conversations with the president, the fact that she was having a private conversation at all still drove speculation. Speculation that in turn drove wagging tongues. To avoid kick-starting the rumor mill every time she needed to see her boss alone, Irene had suggested a series of code words that would both alert the president to the true nature of her request and communicate its level of urgency. *Administrative matter* signified that her need was urgent and that it corresponded to one of her most important special access programs.

CRANKSHAFT.

"Sure," the president said, glancing at his watch, "but I've got a policy meeting with Ted and a couple senators in fifteen minutes. Is that enough time?"

"Plenty," Irene said.

Irene was seated next to the exit, which meant the departing principals filed past her to get to the door.

Most of the departures didn't register with her.

One did.

Rex placed a hand lightly on her shoulder as he walked past.

Anyone viewing the gesture would have discounted it as harmless. A moment of innocent contact between two coworkers as one edged past the other in a confined space. Maybe this was even how Rex had intended the touch.

This was not how Irene received it.

Her distaste for the general magnified the moment that his fingers were resting on her shoulder, stretching the touch's duration from a fraction of a second to something longer.

Intolerably longer.

Which took her somewhere else.

Irene felt her chest tighten as she struggled to breathe. She debated reaching for the mug resting on the table next to her elbow in order to fake choking on a swallow but didn't.

What if the president saw her shaking hand?

Irene fought to keep her expression blank even as touches from phantom fingers crawled across her skin like invisible spiders.

Not now.

Please, God, not now.

The Situation Room's heavy door swung shut with a resounding *thud*.

"Irene—are you okay?"

"Fine, sir," Irene said, forcing a smile.

The sound of the closing security door had somehow broken the spell.

She really was fine.

For now.

Alexander held her gaze for another moment and then slowly nodded. "Okay, then. I'm glad you grabbed me. I have some thoughts about your intention to send a CIA officer to the compound."

"Yes, sir," Irene said, her stomach sinking. "I wanted to update you on that. Nash is in Pakistan, as is our NOC. She'll be ready to make the approach by tomorrow."

She knew Alexander well enough to recognize when the president was getting cold feet. She was hoping that once he learned that the operation was already in motion, Alexander would stop second-guessing his decision.

"I'm not saying no," Alexander said. "I'm just saying that I want to call an audible."

For most people, this phrase was just a figure of speech. Not Joshua Alexander. The president had played football at Alabama until an injury his junior year had ended his hopes for what might have been a very promising postcollegiate NFL career.

President Alexander knew all about audibles.

"What do you mean, sir?" Irene said.

"The Ranger raid into Pakistan has caused us some headaches, but those are nothing compared to the shit storm that sending SEAL Team 6 to Abbottabad might unleash. We're not talking about a minor incursion into Pakistan. Our helicopters would have to cross almost the entire country to fly from J-Bad to the targeted compound. This isn't a simple raid. It's an invasion."

"I understand, sir," Irene said. "That's why it's vital that our officer confirms who's in the compound."

"You misunderstand me, Irene," Alexander said. "When it comes to getting proof, I'm in violent agreement with you. You can send your officer, but I want to add someone to the mission."

At first Irene didn't understand.

Then, she did.

"Mitch."

Alexander nodded. "This isn't a slight against you or your NOC.

You know how much faith I put in your word. But if I get this wrong, I could be taking us to the brink of war. I want Rapp in Abbottabad. That's nonnegotiable."

Irene sighed. "Then we have a bit of a problem, sir."

Alexander frowned. "What do you mean?"

Irene pointed to the TV. Alexander's features narrowed in confusion as he glanced at the video streaming from the still-loitering Reaper.

Then his eyes widened.

"That?" Alexander said, stabbing an index finger toward the display. "That's Rapp?"

"Who else?" Irene said.

"Anyone else," Alexander said, his voice thundering. "I thought you were inserting an agent. Some jihadi you'd flipped."

"Which is exactly what I wanted you and everyone else at the table to think," Irene said, holding firm against the president's anger. "No one but Rapp could pull this off. No one."

"I thought Rapp was chasing down the Iranian link to those killer missiles?"

"He is," Irene said. "The HIG warlord from the compound the Rangers hit was the second man in the Reaper video. The one Rapp was carrying over his shoulder."

"Holy hell," Alexander said. "You want to run that by me again?"

"The raid the Rangers executed against the HIG commander's compound was ambushed," Irene said, "and Colonel Dariush Ruyintan, an Iranian Quds Force operative, somehow knew the ambush was going to happen. The HIG warlord, CYCLONE, is the only link between Ruyintan, the missiles used to shoot down our Chinook, and maybe our missing Ranger. Rapp is going to pull on that thread."

"You said he was going to meet with Ashani in Kabul."

"He is," Irene said. "As soon as he finds Sergeant Saxton."

The words sounded ridiculous as she said them, but Irene was hoping that she was just overreacting.

Judging by the president's gobsmacked expression, she was not.

"Are you serious?"

"Absolutely," Irene said. "Rapp isn't scheduled to meet with Ashani for another six or seven hours. That should be plenty of time."

Only her years of running agents allowed Irene to make that statement with a straight face. She put all the conviction she could muster into her voice and hoped it would be enough to convince the leader of the free world that neither she nor her top counterterrorism agent was crazy. If the president believed her assurances, maybe she would too.

"I think you're both out of your minds, but I'm not questioning your judgment," Alexander said, lifting his hands in surrender. "By the same token, I don't expect you to question mine. I'm not sending our SEALs into Pakistan without ironclad proof of who is living in that compound, and I'm not sending a CIA NOC to knock on the compound's front door unless Rapp is there too. Understood?"

"Yes, sir," Irene said.

With a final nod, Alexander got to his feet.

As the president left the room, Irene found herself wondering how it was that the most powerful nation in the world was yet again placing its fate on the shoulders of just one man.

CHAPTER 27

"WHO are you truly, Abu al-Iraqi?"

Rapp had been anticipating some version of this question, but hearing it voiced so bluntly was still unsettling. Or maybe the source of his discomfort could be traced to the pair of bodyguards flanking CYCLONE. The gunmen were not the type of high-priced talent a minor Saudi prince would hire or the former Spetsnaz thugs that a Russian oligarch would employ. Their weather-beaten faces could have been crafted from leather, their beards were long and unkempt, and their clothes were worn and bleached by the sun. These were not the sort of men who watched over tech billionaires or babysat heirs to family fortunes.

The gunmen were killers, plain and simple.

And Rapp did not care for the way they were staring at him. The bodyguards looked less like a protective detail evaluating a potential threat and more like feral dogs assessing their chances against a cornered sheep.

Rapp finished chewing his mouthful of Afghan flatbread and sighed. "Who I am is none of your concern. You promised to help me if I freed you. I did. Now I'm beginning to think that you aren't going to honor your side of the bargain. This makes me upset, which should make you terrified."

Though he was speaking Arabic, Rapp's words appeared to register with the mangy dogs.

Or maybe it was his tone.

Either way, both men took a step nearer to CYCLONE.

Rapp found this amusing.

He and CYCLONE were sitting cross-legged on small cushions, eating food scooped from their individual bowls with chunks of bread. As was typical with Afghani meals, no utensils were offered, and Rapp found himself fervently hoping that the round of vaccines he'd received before heading to Pakistan were up to defeating whatever might be lurking beneath the dirty fingernails of the man who'd prepared the meal. But while a bout of dysentery might be funny in a gallows-humor sort of way, this was not why Rapp was amused.

Rapp was currently in the inner room of a compound that had been sunk into the side of a mountain. He was surrounded by armed men, himself weaponless, and seated on the floor. His only salvation lay with an unseen drone that was hopefully orbiting somewhere overhead. CYCLONE should have more to worry about from his undercooked food than Rapp, but somehow his guards knew differently.

The good ones always did.

As if sensing his thoughts, the fighter closest to Rapp fingered the scarred wooden stock of his AK-47. The man's pinched features reminded Rapp of a weasel, but his dark eyes radiated intelligence. His companion wasn't so much thin as emaciated. He looked like a fence post, but the gunman held his rifle with a shooter's familiar, easy manner.

Rapp had a rule about guns—he didn't let people point them in his direction. Neither guard had violated this ironclad tenet yet, but Ferret Face was getting close.

If things went sideways, he would die first.

In contrast to the guards, Rapp's implied threat seemed to wash over CYCLONE like rain running off a boulder. "Please don't take this the wrong way," CYCLONE said with a smile, "but your identity is very much my business. These are my mountains and I've lived among them for decades without once fearing the Americans. Now, in the space of twenty-four hours, I've been captured by commandos, interrogated, and then freed by a mysterious fighting force. A force I knew nothing about. These mountains and everything in them belong to me. Nothing exists in my territory without my knowledge. Nothing except you."

Rapp tore off another piece of flatbread, stuck it in his mouth, and chewed. The dry texture sucked away his saliva like a sponge. Rapp gazed longingly at the cup of tea situated within easy reach of his left hand, but he refrained. For the time being, he needed to manage his fluid intake carefully.

Very carefully.

"Have you no answer?" CYCLONE said.

There were two ways to play this.

One, Rapp could attempt to stroke the HIG warlord's ego.

Two, he could go for the jugular.

Rapp wasn't much for stroking egos.

"Listen to me, you backwoods fuck," Rapp said, dusting bread crumbs from his hands. "I am in this godforsaken land for one reason— to meet with an Iranian intelligence officer. You are not him. Since your memory apparently needs refreshing, the men who died attacking that convoy were from my organization, not yours. They were rescuing me, not you. Outside of this miserable valley and the inbred goat herders who call it home, nobody gives a rat's ass about you. Nobody. You begged for my help, not the other way around. You promised to settle your debt to me with interest if I saved you from the Americans. Payment is now due."

Rapp had tailored his speech to provoke a reaction.

He got one.

CYCLONE's smile grew even wider.

The warlord's guards didn't seem to share their employer's amusement.

Fence Post leaned over to whisper into CYCLONE's ear, while Ferret Face's index finger slid ever closer to his rifle's trigger guard. Rapp had never attended a Taliban weapons safety course, but he did know that the jihadis were notorious for suffering accidental weapons discharges. The odds were better than even that Ferret Face's rifle had a round in the chamber and that the weapon's selector switch was set to fire. Rapp was willing to give the scruffy fighter one inch. If the man's index finger moved even a centimeter farther, Rapp would consider the man a threat.

Ferret Face would not enjoy what happened next.

"Peace," CYCLONE said, holding up his hands. "My countrymen have been at war our entire lives—first with the Russians, then with each other, and now with the Americans. I've seen many people I thought friends become enemies and I've fought alongside men I'd once sworn to kill. In Afghanistan, you either become a crafty fox or die a trusting hare. There is no middle ground."

Rapp believed the HIG warlord, but he didn't give two shits about his martial philosophy. Perhaps when this dumpster fire of a war was finally over there'd be a market for a mujahideen version of Sun Tzu's *Art of War*. Until then, CYCLONE could save his philosophical musings for his henchman.

But Rapp didn't say that.

Contrary to what Irene might believe, he actually was capable of practicing restraint when the situation merited. And while CYCLONE hadn't explicitly said the words *I'm sorry*, Rapp could recognize an apology when he heard one. But apology or not, Rapp was of half a mind to just slay this douchebag and move on.

The clock was ticking.

After carrying the HIG warlord into the forest, Rapp had followed the gravel path CYCLONE had indicated for about three kilometers. Just when he was beginning to wonder if the jihadi had chosen the wrong goat trail, the foliage opened to reveal a village nestled in a small valley.

True to his word, CYCLONE did have people loyal to him in the village.

People in the form of armed men who were only too willing to pile Rapp and the HIG commander into the bed of a Hilux truck and cover them with sacks of corn, barley, and rice. Rapp glimpsed the sun long enough to confirm that the truck was heading generally south before the coarse fabric blotted out the sky.

With nothing else to do, Rapp settled in for the ride and tried to mark the time.

About an hour or so later, the truck came to a stop.

Unseen hands removed the burlap sacks and Rapp found himself eyeball to eyeball with Ferret Face and Fence Post. The two gunmen seemed indifferent to his presence, but the sight of CYCLONE provoked a much different reaction. They didn't salute, but the deference the pair showed the HIG warlord was obvious.

While the men were conversing in Pashtu, Rapp hopped out of the truck and stretched his kinked muscles. The Hilux was parked in front of yet another compound, but this one was different from the typical mud-brick construction in several important ways. One, the walls were made of much stronger concrete and the gate was constructed of interlocking steel slats. Two, the structure was embedded in the surrounding rocky cliff face, and its concrete exterior perfectly matched the dirty white shale sprouting from the ground.

Rather than a traditional gravel driveway, access to the compound required an off-road vehicle capable of navigating the scree-covered slope leading to the structure. Bits of stone were haphazardly stacked in front of the outer walls, obscuring their straight lines while strategically placed vegetation did the rest. Taken in sum, the natural camouflage rendered the structure difficult to detect from the ground and probably impossible to see from the air.

Rapp's gaze traveled from the compound to the jagged cliff faces on either side of the structure. Unless he missed his guess, he was looking at the foothills leading to the Spin Ghar mountains.

Success.

At least this is what Rapp had thought about an hour ago when he'd first arrived.

Now he wasn't so sure.

He'd hoped that the compound might hold the missing Ranger, but this did not seem to be the case. To make matters worse, CYCLONE was entirely too smart for his own good, and Rapp still did not like the vibe he was getting from the warlord's bodyguards.

Rapp could have just interrogated CYCLONE in J-Bad, but since the warlord had been captured at the same time the Ranger went missing, Rapp had been worried that the HIG commander would not know Saxton's location. Instead, Rapp had gambled that once CYCLONE was reunited with his men, they would either take their commander to where the Ranger was being held or tell him Saxton's location.

So far, this gamble had not paid off. If something didn't break loose in the next couple of minutes, Rapp intended to separate the warlord from his bodyguards and question him about the missing Ranger.

Forcefully.

Then Rapp would commandeer one of the Hilux trucks he'd seen parked beneath camouflage netting outside the compound and conduct his own search for Saxton using CYCLONE's best guess as his starting point. As long as the drone continued to float through the sky above him, Rapp had a way to signal Coleman and his hitters.

A way that could only be used once during a window that was rapidly closing thanks to the drone's prodigious fuel consumption.

And if this wasn't enough pressure, by now Ashani would have landed in Kabul. Rapp had to get this show on the road. In a world populated by dirtbags who needed killing, Rapp often felt busier than a one-legged man in an ass-kicking contest.

"If you have something to discuss, let's hear it," Rapp said. "Otherwise, I'm leaving."

"Arabs," CYCLONE said with another smile, "always so anxious. In some ways, you remind me of the Americans. They might have the watches, but we have all the time."

The word *Americans* sent a tendril of worry snaking through Rapp's gut.

Was CYCLONE trying to elicit some sort of reaction?

Rapp didn't know, nor did he intend to play mind games with the warlord. Rather than take the bait, he got to his feet. "Thank you for your hospitality. I need a phone. Now."

Hospitality wasn't just a quaint notion in this part of the world.

According to tribal tradition, CYCLONE had extended hospitality to Rapp by providing him with shelter and food. This meant that the HIG warlord was honor-bound to protect and aid Rapp. Still, the notion that there was no honor among thieves was doubly true for Afghan warlords who'd fought for the Northern Alliance, the Taliban, the HIG, and now perhaps the Iranians.

"Of course," CYCLONE said, standing as well. "Of course."

The warlord directed a stream of Pashtu at Ferret Face.

The man's disposition didn't grow any sunnier, but the fighter nodded and moved his finger away from the AK's trigger guard.

Progress.

Digging into his pocket, Fence Post produced a simple flip phone, which he handed to CYCLONE, who then passed it to Rapp.

Rapp was preparing to activate the device when the warlord spoke. "Just one more thing."

Rapp paused with his thumb hovering over the dial button. "What?"

"Before you leave, I thought we might discuss a business proposition."

Rapp sighed.

The HIG, like the Taliban, wasn't exactly an industrial powerhouse. Rapp assumed this conversation would center around the organization's one reliable export—opium. While it would be interesting to hear what the little toad was willing to offer, neither Rapp's timeline nor his legend permitted such a discussion. Farid Saeed wouldn't be interested in a deal to export poppy.

Rapp wasn't either.

"I don't traffic opium," Rapp said.

"Maybe that's true and maybe it isn't," CYCLONE said with a laugh, "but I have something even more valuable than heroin."

"What?" Rapp said.

"An American."

CHAPTER 28

RAPP stared at the Taliban commander, waiting for the punch line. CYCLONE grinned.

Had he not been in the troop transport truck with the jihadi, Rapp would have never guessed that just hours ago CYCLONE had been on his way to one of Afghanistan's most notorious prisons. Now the little shit looked positively serene. Like some version of an Afghan Buddha. When it became obvious that CYCLONE was content to wait all day if that's what it took, Rapp bit the bullet. "What American?"

"Ahh," CYCLONE said. "I thought that might interest you."

"Maybe," Rapp said. "Captured Americans bring with them a unique set of problems."

"What sort of problems?"

"Men with guns who drop on your head from helicopters in the dead of the night."

The wattage on CYCLONE's grin dimmed. "This American is worth the risk."

CYCLONE's reply sounded defensive.

Petulant even.

Rapp took the warlord's reaction as a sign that he wasn't the only one who had offered such advice. This was not a welcome development. If whoever else was whispering in the HIG commander's ear managed to sway the man, it would not be to the captured Ranger's benefit.

In this part of the world, liabilities were dealt with decisively.

Still, Rapp ran the risk of tipping his hand if he acted too interested in the captive. He was a financier from an Iraqi terrorist organization who was in Afghanistan to meet an Iranian intelligence officer. A man of Rapp's stature didn't concern himself with trivial matters like captured Americans.

Usually.

"Why?" Rapp said.

"Because," CYCLONE said, a portion of his Cheshire cat grin reappearing, "the captive isn't just any American. We have one of their Special Forces soldiers."

"You're a fool," Rapp said with a shake of his head. "You might be able to ransom a civilian, but the American military will not pay a dime for a captured soldier. And you've further compounded your mistake by your choice in captives. Do you know the lengths the Americans will go to recover one of their special operations warriors? If I were you, I'd kill him and be done with it."

"That would be extremely shortsighted," CYCLONE said. "But if that is how you truly feel, farewell. I remain in your debt. Go in peace."

Rapp made a show of considering the cell phone CYCLONE had loaned him as he furiously thought. It was clear the warlord knew that taking the Ranger hostage was the equivalent of poking a hornet's nest, but for some reason CYCLONE believed the risk was worth the reward.

As much as Rapp hated to admit it, the warrior hadn't lived this long by being stupid. CYCLONE had excused himself to make a series of calls after he and Rapp had arrived at the compound. At the time, Rapp had assumed that the wily old fighter was calling subordinates to head off the inevitable battle for succession that would have been waged by those postured to take his place had CYCLONE remained captured.

But perhaps Rapp had misjudged the calls' purpose.

Maybe CYCLONE had been working the phone to determine the market value of his new captive. Rapp thought the warlord likely shared the religious zeal common to his comrades in arms, but a fighter who'd switched allegiances as many times as CYCLONE also had a practical bent. According to the pre-mission brief Rapp had received from the J-Bad chief of base, the series of compounds CYCLONE was known to frequent were well constructed and somewhat luxurious by the region's standards. Rapp was willing to bet the generators, the fleet of Hilux trucks, and the contingent of guards to protect them hadn't been purchased on a HIG commander's salary. Perhaps Rapp had a chance to resolve this entire situation with something the Central Intelligence Agency had in an almost unlimited supply—cold, hard American cash.

Rapp activated the phone and was preparing to dial when CYCLONE spoke. "You're free to call whoever you will, but if you dial, my offer to show you the American expires."

"Why?" Rapp said, his finger frozen above the cell's number pad.

"Operational security," CYCLONE said. "I'm sure you understand."

Rapp did understand, but he'd been hoping the HIG warlord would not. Those hopes appeared to be in vain. CYCLONE apparently knew enough about the National Security Agency's digital exploitation capabilities to keep anyone interested in the captured American isolated from their cell phone. As Stan Hurley loved to say, in a war that had stretched for almost a decade, the dumb jihadis had died a long time ago. Rapp had certainly found occasion to dispute his mentor's assessment, but as was often the case, Stan was right more often than wrong.

Today was no exception.

Rapp gazed at the phone in silence for a beat.

Then he grunted his frustration and handed the device back to CYCLONE.

"Take me to the American."

• • •

An hour later, Rapp found himself in the bowels of the earth, fighting the urge to lay waste to everyone surrounding him.

Well, almost everyone.

In the hurricane of violence that was brewing in Rapp's soul, the American wearing a bloodied MultiCam uniform would form the eye of the storm.

Everyone else was fair game.

Especially the two shitheads of dubious origin attempting to out-bid him.

"Come, now," CYCLONE said, "that's a very reasonable offer from our Saudi friends. Surely you can do better."

Rapp could do better, but when it came to bidding against someone with the backing of the House of Saud, even the CIA's supply of cash started to look stingy. But it wasn't the Saudis who had Rapp most concerned. That honor went to the quiet man standing in the rear of the cave wearing a nondescript desert camouflage uniform.

The man who spoke Arabic with a Persian accent.

Rapp turned his attention from the mystery Iranian to CYCLONE. If the HIG commander felt any lingering sense of gratitude toward Rapp, he was hiding it well.

After voicing his intent to see the American, Rapp had been ushered out of the compound and into yet another Hilux truck. Though this time Rapp rode in the pickup's cab alongside CYCLONE rather than beneath burlap sacks in the truck bed, he still couldn't tell where they were taking him. This was because the HIG warlord had handed Rapp a blindfold as soon as he'd settled into his seat. Rather than protest, Rapp had dutifully tied the fabric across his eyes and focused on his other senses. Judging by the sound of the pickup's straining engine and the road's steep upward gradient, Rapp guessed that they were leaving the foothills for the Spin Ghar mountains proper.

After a jostling forty-five minutes, the truck came to a stop and Rapp's blindfold was removed, but it was sound rather than sight that first captured his attention. The sound of rushing water. A lot of it. Blinking against the sudden brightness, Rapp saw a waterfall several stories tall thundering down a rock face into a rushing river. To the right of the waterfall loomed the mouth of a cave complex reminiscent of the ones in which Al Qaeda elements had made their last stand during the initial invasion of Afghanistan.

That complex had been dubbed *Tora Bora*, Pashtu for *Black Cave*.

For all he knew, Rapp might have been looking at those exact same tunnels.

Resisting the urge to glance up at the hopefully still-loitering UAV, Rapp had followed Fence Post, Ferret Face, and CYCLONE into the subterranean lair. To his surprise, the accommodations were on par with the compound he'd just left. Lightbulbs ran the length of the ceiling in bundled strands to ward off the perpetual gloom, and thick rugs softened the rock floor. Strategically placed fans did an adequate job of circulating the air, and the smell of roasting meat and baking bread teased Rapp's nose. The tunnel complex had the vibe of a 1950s survivalist's bunker, which in Afghanistan was the equivalent of the Ritz-Carlton.

This luxury did not extend to the battered Ranger's accommodations.

The American was chained to the floor of a dank-looking depression about six feet below the ledge on which Rapp and the others were gathered. Rapp assumed that the cavern had been eroded by a now-dried-up underground stream, but regardless of how the depression had been formed, its purpose before it had been converted to a cell was easy to deduce.

An eye-watering stench wafted up from its dark confines.

A rock chimney climbing up the depression's far wall was probably intended to vent some of the noxious fumes aboveground, but the natural ventilation wasn't working nearly well enough for Rapp's taste. He knew that outfitting the cave with indoor plumbing was probably a bridge too far, but Rapp would have hoped the Afghans had the sense not to shit were they lived.

"I hate this country," Rapp said.

"Afghanistan isn't for everyone," CYCLONE said with a shrug.

"You misunderstand me," Rapp said. "It's not your country I hate. It's you."

"What?" CYLONE said. "You said you weren't interested in the American."

"I said you were a fool for capturing him," Rapp said. "You're not equipped to hide him. I am. My organization has trafficked several captured Westerners."

"Aid workers, journalists, and the occasional foolhardy tourist, yes. But not a Special Forces soldier."

"Correct," Rapp said, "which is why I was interested in this one. Now you want me to bid for the American? I saved your life."

"For which I am grateful," CYCLONE said, "but this is business."

"I thought you knew who I represented?" Rapp said.

"He doesn't, but I do."

The comment came from the quiet man in the desert camouflage uniform. The one who spoke Arabic with a Persian accent. The man smiled as he spoke, but the gesture didn't reach his cold eyes. The camouflage pattern, Persian accent, and confidence bordering on arrogance all pointed toward one conclusion—the man was Iranian.

Probably Quds Force.

To make things even more interesting, the Iranian looked familiar.

"I wasn't talking to you," Rapp said before turning back to CYCLONE.

"But I am talking to you."

While not particularly witty, the Iranian's comeback demanded Rapp's attention. Mainly because it was punctuated by the metal-on-leather whisper of a pistol sliding clear of its holster. With a sigh, Rapp turned to find himself staring down the barrel of a ZOAF PC-9 pistol. The Quds Force sidearm of choice.

Though Irene never seemed to believe him, this situation proved Rapp's point.

Sometimes violence really did choose him.

CHAPTER 29

RAPP turned from the pistol-wielding Iranian to CYCLONE. "What is this?"

To his credit, the HIG warlord looked surprised at the turn of events.

"Not sure," CYCLONE said, "but my Iranian friend has exactly three seconds to explain himself."

The HIG commander hadn't added the expected *or else*, but Ferret Face and Fence Post still got the message. Both men orientated their AK-47s toward the Iranian in the calm, easy manner displayed by men who were intimately familiar with violence.

The Iranian didn't waver, but the tip of his pistol trembled.

Slightly.

"I know this man," the Iranian said.

"My name is Farid Saeed," Rapp said, addressing the Iranian, "and I am in this country at the behest of Minister Ashani of the MOIS and Colonel Ruyintan of the Quds Force. I am quite certain that both of these men outrank you. Whatever bad blood you believe exists between us is trumped by their invitation. Lower your pistol and stand down. Now."

"Your sectarian quarrels are not my concern," CYCLONE said to the Iranian. "Mr. Saeed is my guest. He will be treated as such."

American intelligence analysts too often painted the various armed factions in Afghanistan with an overly broad brush. While the groups were mostly united in their hatred for the West, their motivation differed. Case in point, while the Taliban and the remnants of Al Qaeda might be true believers in the cause of radical Islam, other jihadis adhered to Islam in a manner similar to the way members of New York's Five Families professed their Catholicism. The mobsters might attend Mass, but they were not what anyone would call practicing Catholics. CYCLONE was a HIG warlord, but he also led a criminal enterprise. Judging by his efforts to auction the captured American, money, not Islam, was his primary motivation.

Rapp could work with that.

"Your guest is not Iraqi," the Iranian said. "He's American. An American known as *Malikul Mawt*."

Rapp had earned the *Angel of Death* moniker while slaying terrorists in Iraq. Most days he was rather proud that the jihadis had christened him with the nickname.

Today was not one of those days.

"If this man and I have a history, it's because I led my organization's efforts to destroy his Shia militias," Rapp said to CYCLONE. "One call to either of the Iranians I mentioned will put his suspicions to rest. Now, for the last time, tell him to lower his pistol."

Since Rapp's Saeed legend meant that he was Sunni, it made sense that members of his fictional organization would have crossed swords with the Iraqi Shia tribes backed by the Iranians. While much had been made of the struggle between militant Islam and the West, talking heads tended to forget that, prior to 9/11, Muslims had been killing each other with reckless abandon for decades. In fact, the longest and bloodiest war in modern Middle East history hadn't involved either the US or Israel.

That honor belonged to Iran and Iraq and their eight-year war.

Rapp was unarmed and secluded in a hidden cavern, but the Iranian was outnumbered four to one. Six to one, counting the Saudis. Rapp also had the advantage of an airtight legend, a recent history in which he'd saved CYCLONE from captivity, and a sizable bank account. Bottom line, CYCLONE was a thug. The thing about criminals is they're criminals.

At the end of the day, money talks and everything else walks.

"I do not know what Ashani or Ruyintan would say about this man," the Iranian said, "but I do know what my own eyes tell me. The last time I saw him, he was as close to me as he is now. Except that, instead of talking, he was slaughtering my Hezbollah and Quds Force companions while attempting to save Irene Kennedy."

"Who?" CYCLONE said.

"The director of the American Central Intelligence Agency," the Iranian said. "Your companion is a CIA officer who is undoubtedly here to rescue your prisoner. He is the most dangerous man I have ever met. Letting him live is the equivalent of grabbing a cobra by the tail."

While he was a little irritated that he'd missed one of men who'd perpetrated the vicious assault against Irene, Rapp was pleased with the Iranian's comparison. Over his long and storied career, Rapp had been called many things, but this was the first time he'd been likened to a viper.

On the negative side of the equation, the Iranian sounded convincing.

Very convincing.

Ignoring the Iranian, Rapp walked to the edge of the depression. Then he pulled down his trousers and began to piss. Hours of accumulated urine sprayed into the depression. Rapp hadn't had to pee this bad in . . . well . . . ever. He aimed most of his stream toward the rock chimney.

Most, but not all.

Offering a silent prayer for forgiveness, Rapp pissed across the soldier's shackled form.

The Ranger reacted predictably.

"Come down here and try that," Saxton bellowed. "I'll rip your pecker off and shove it down your throat."

Rapp had always liked Army Rangers.

While the soldiers didn't have the suave, surfer-boy reputation of their naval commando brethren, Rangers were the brawlers of the special operations community. If you needed a bunch of human wrecking balls to breach an enemy compound and punch the ticket of every Taliban shitbag inside, Army Rangers were the men for the job.

Rapp gave his pecker a final shake and then turned back to his astonished audience. "I'm here to rescue him?" Rapp said with a laugh. "I don't think so." Rapp locked gazes with CYCLONE. "You brought me here, not the other way around. I am interested in this American. Several of the jihadi groups we service would pay handsomely for the opportunity to execute him, but smuggling the soldier to Iraq won't be easy. I'm willing to pay two million. Not a penny more. Doesn't matter to me if you take it or leave it, but if that *kalb* doesn't lower his pistol by the time I count to five, I'm going to feed it to him."

Rapp stepped closer to the Iranian, positioning himself just behind and to the right of Fence Post. The bodyguard registered Rapp's presence with a slight shift of his head, but the rifleman's attention remained focused on the room's primary threat.

As did his AK-47.

"My Iraqi friend is correct," CYCLONE said to the Iranian. "Lower your pistol and—"

"One hundred million," the Iranian said. "I will pay you one hundred million US dollars."

"For the American?" CYCLONE said.

"For both Americans," the Iranian said. "Fifty million for the one in the pit and fifty more for the one standing behind you."

CYCLONE didn't answer.

He didn't have to.

Rapp felt the room's energy shift.

The thing about criminals is they're criminals.

CHAPTER 30

"**H**ow did you say you knew this asset again?"

"I didn't," Scott Coleman said, staring at the UAV feed.

"Come on, Scott. Frogman to frogman—what are we looking at here?"

Coleman sighed, trying to settle on an answer. Fortunately, this was an area in which he had considerable expertise. Hang around with Mitch Rapp long enough and you were sure to find yourself in an uncomfortable situation.

Or two.

This part of the conversation was nothing new, but Coleman's tap dancing act usually didn't involve misleading a fellow SEAL.

Especially one of Justin Garza's caliber.

Beneath his laid-back Texas vibe, Justin was a SEAL's SEAL. Though he and Coleman had served together early in Justin's career, the assaulter had spent the last decade as a SEAL Team 6 operator. While this achievement was more than enough to set Justin apart from the herd, the unassuming man with the soft Texas accent was also the Naval Special Warfare Command's subject matter expert on combatives. In nonmilitaryspeak, Justin was responsible for developing the hand-to-hand combat curriculum taught to every Navy SEAL. In furtherance of this goal, Justin had traveled the world to immerse himself in martial arts styles as varied as Israeli Krav Maga, Okinawan Kenpo, and Filipino Kali.

Justin was the real deal.

He was also the SEAL Team 6 liaison officer to the CIA in Afghanistan. Since there were currently no SEAL Team 6 operators in-country, Justin's current role centered more on providing a commando's viewpoint on all Agency and JSOC operations.

Technically, Justin was not read into Mitch's operation.

Technically.

But in Scott's experience, it was always better to have another frogman at your back.

Coleman took a quick look around the room before responding. The Agency's B-hut had become much busier since he'd first arrived in country. The chief of base, Steve, was sequestered in his office, probably updating the chief of station in Kabul on the operation's progress for the fiftieth time. The Ranger company commander, Mark Garner, was standing in front of a flat-screen TV with one of his lieutenants. The pair were studying a computer-rendered topographical map of the Spin Ghar mountains, no doubt plotting likely enemy locations. The sound of radios breaking squelch competed with murmured conversations from the bullpen as the agency analysts and case officers coordinated in real time with the pilot, sensor operator, and mission intelligence coordinator who were directing the orbiting UAV from half a world away.

The B-hut was a controlled-access building on a controlled-access compound. Coleman couldn't think of too many areas more secure than this one. Even so, he was reluctant to reveal too much about the operation. When he'd been in Justin's shoes, he'd hated the need-to-know bullshit. Now that he was on the other side of the table, the security didn't seem quite so unreasonable.

Especially considering what Rapp was attempting. Mitch was known for pushing the envelope, but this was some crazy shit even by his standards.

"Here's the deal," Coleman said, catching his voice low enough that the other SEAL had to lean closer. "That's not an Afghan asset. He's American."

Justin's bushy eyebrows shot up. "A case officer?"

Coleman shook his head. "Something like that. When did you come over to DEVGRU?"

Justin frowned. "Just prior to 9/11. Why?"

"Remember that Task Force 11 raid into Pakistan back in 2004?"

"The one with both SEALs and Delta boys?"

"That's it," Coleman said.

"Hell yeah," Justin said. "That was legendary."

"He's the one who developed the original intelligence to get the raid authorized and then conducted the sensitive site exploitation in Pakistan during the firefight."

Justin responded with a low whistle. "Holy shit. I heard that guy also had something to do with stopping a nuke from turning DC into a parking lot."

"Whatever you heard isn't half of what actually happened," Coleman said. "This dude has been in more slippery shit than most of the team guys combined. I've worked with him for the last ten years. He might not have a Trident, but if I was in a bad way, he'd be my first call, and that's no bullshit."

Justin digested this statement in silence.

Coleman understood.

There was a reason why SEALs signed every missive with LLTB. The letters stood for *Long Live the Brotherhood*. To a fellow frogman, what Coleman had just said was the equivalent of blasphemy.

But that didn't make his observation any less true.

"How much longer are we giving your guy?"

The question came from Mark Garner, who'd wandered over to join the conversation. Coleman didn't know when the Ranger company commander had started his vigil in the B-hut, but he'd been there when Scott showed up hours ago and hadn't left yet. Coleman's days of providing advice to young lieutenants and ensigns were long past, but he was tempted to make an exception with Mark. The junior officer looked like shit, and while Coleman understood all too well the anguish that came with knowing that one of your brothers-in-arms was at the mercy of jihadi barbarians, Garner had to be approaching a state of combat ineffectiveness.

"As long as he needs," Coleman said. "He is your Ranger's best chance for rescue. I know you want to go in there and start knocking heads, but putting a bunch of grunts on the ground is the quickest way to ensure your missing man gets a bullet in his skull."

"Saxton," Garner said. "His name is Sergeant Fred Saxton."

Coleman shared a look with Justin and the frogman nodded.

"Look, sir," Justin said, putting a hand on Garner's shoulder, "I know you're worried about your guy, but keeping a solo watch on this TV screen isn't doing him any good. When's the last time you've slept?"

The dark rings around Garner's eyes seemed answer enough, but the Ranger still looked like he wanted to dodge the question. "A while," Garner said finally.

Justin nodded. "Go grab some rack time. I promise nobody will leave without you."

"Okay, okay," Garner said, "but before I leave, at least tell me what we're looking for. All this Secret Squirrel shit just makes things worse."

Justin turned to Coleman and arched an eyebrow. "Our Ranger friend makes an excellent point."

Coleman sighed. "Mitch figured he'd be searched, so he's not carrying a beacon or radio."

"So, what," Justin said, "he's gonna send up smoke signals?"

Coleman felt vaguely irritated at the question but realized that he was probably more aggravated with himself. OPSEC was all well and good, but not at the expense of keeping the very people he was depending on to rescue Rapp in the dark.

Time to come clean.

"Not exactly," Coleman said. "He ingested a couple of special tablets. Something the agency's S-and-T folks dreamed up. Like Rapp's uniform, the pills are designed to allow us to passively track him. They slowly release a special compound into his bloodstream that makes his urine fluoresce in the spectrum monitored by the UAV's sensor."

"You've got to be kidding me," Justin said. "I've heard of pissing hot, but this takes the cake."

"Yeah," Coleman said, "pretty ingenious. He just needs to take a piss where our ISR asset can see him. Supposedly even the fumes from his urine will register."

"What will it look like?" Garner said. "Just another hot spot?"

"No," Coleman said. "The picture the agency guy sent me looked like a bed of sparkling diamonds."

"Kind of like that?" Garner said.

Coleman looked from the Ranger to the TV and swore.

"Exactly like that."

CHAPTER 31

RAPP could see the wheels turning in CYCLONE's head.

One hundred million dollars was a lot of money. With that kind of cash, the warlord could buy himself legitimacy. Maybe trade in the mountain compounds for a plush house in Islamabad. Or if living rough was more his style, CYCLONE could at least outfit his subterranean lair with indoor plumbing. Either way, one hundred million dollars was not something a criminal like CYCLONE would be willing to let slip by, Pashtu hospitality honor code or not.

Criminals were criminals.

Turning, Rapp stomped the inside of Fence Post's knee. He pictured his foot shattering bone and rupturing ligaments like a sledgehammer busting through drywall.

The guard's knee collapsed with a satisfying *pop*.

The man shrieked and stumbled, grabbing at Ferret Face's arm for support.

Which meant that his fingers were no longer on his rifle.

Snatching the man's AK, Rapp levered the stock around the guard's midsection. He sank to one knee as he moved, presenting a smaller target. Rapp fired a burst into Ferret Face and then tracked the muzzle toward the Iranian. Rapp was taking the slack out of the trigger when the now-one-legged Fence Post entered the fight. The jihadi raked his fingernails across Rapp's face just as the shot broke.

Both men missed their targets.

Rapp turned his head at the last moment, sacrificing his cheek to save his eyes even as the rounds he'd intended for the Iranian tore stone chunks from the cave's roof. Cursing, Rapp hammered an elbow into Fence Post's wrecked knee.

The man screamed.

Exploding to his feet, Rapp sank a shoulder into the bodyguard and sent him tumbling into the outhouse-turned-jail-cell. Turning, Rapp tracked the AK's iron sights toward the Iranian only to see the man vanish down one of the two corridors leading from the room.

Rapp caught motion to his right.

CYCLONE was sprinting for the second exit.

The AK's front sight post settled on the fleeing man's back seemingly of its own accord. Rapp slightly adjusted the aimpoint and pressed the trigger.

The rifle barked and puffs of red mist erupted from the warlord's leg.

CYCLONE crumpled.

The HIG commander grabbed his thigh and rolled onto his back, screaming. Crimson spilled from the wound, but there was no spurt of arterial blood. Gritting his teeth, CYCLONE pushed off with his good leg, crawling across the floor.

Rapp was impressed.

CYCLONE was as hard as woodpecker lips.

Crossing the room in two quick strides, Rapp stomped on CYCLONE's leg. He went rigid as if electricity rather than pain arced through his body. Gasping, the warlord opened his mouth to scream.

He didn't get the chance.

Snapping the wood stock down in a vicious arc, Rapp drove the rifle into the bridge of the man's nose. The thin bone ruptured, and blood sprayed from his face. CYCLONE went limp.

"Hey, Ranger," Rapp said, turning toward the depression. "You still down there?"

For a long moment no one answered.

Then a deep baritone replied.

"Who's asking?"

"Your ticket out of here," Rapp said. "Did you get the present I dropped you?"

"If by *present* you mean one of the nasty-assed jihadi guards, yes, yes, I did."

"Good," Rapp said. "Did he have the keys to your restraints?"

Another long pause. Then, "Maybe."

A pair of jihadis edged around the stone doorway of exit number one—the corridor through which the Iranian had run. Rapp dropped one of the shooters with a well-placed head shot, but the second slipped away. Knowing what was coming next, Rapp flattened himself behind CYCLONE's limp body.

The second shooter's AK-47 peeked around the corner and a tongue of fire erupted from the muzzle. Rapp cursed as stinging shards of rock peppered his neck and face. Professionals often derided the "spray and pray" method of engaging combatants, but the cave was a stone coffin. A ricochet from the walls, floor, or ceiling would kill just as easily as a direct hit. Rapp switched the rifle's selector switch to single and began squeezing off a series of slow, aimed pairs at the protruding barrel.

The rifle vanished.

"Listen up," Rapp yelled over the ringing in his ears, "the cavalry's coming, but they're not here yet. I've got two hallways to cover and one gun. How about lending a hand?"

"You pissed on me."

"I saved your life," Rapp said. "Suck it up, buttercup."

The rifle peeked back around the corner.

Rapp fired twice, but the first round did the trick. The AK clattered to the ground, and a scream echoed down the corridor. Rapp considered shooting again but didn't. As much as he wanted to flood the corridor with lead, he couldn't afford to waste ammunition.

"I thought Rangers liked to fight," Rapp said.

"We do."

The response came from just off Rapp's right shoulder. He turned to find the former captive crouched on the stone floor next to him. As if seeing the man triggered the rest of Rapp's senses, he could suddenly smell the gag-inducing stench from the Ranger's uniform.

"You need a shower," Rapp said.

"No shit."

Scooping up the AK-47 lying next to Rapp, the man ensured a round was chambered, checked that the magazine was seated, and then adjusted the selector switch. Setting the rifle to the side, the Ranger performed a quick but thorough search of the dead guard. His efforts yielded an additional pair of magazines. He tossed one to Rapp and shoved the second into his pocket.

"We taking this douchebag with us?" the Ranger said, pointing at CYCLONE.

"Yep," Rapp said.

The Ranger grunted but didn't argue. Instead he placed his rifle on the stone floor, undid his belt, and worked the thick webbing around the unconscious warlord's thigh. The Ranger was none too gentle as he cinched the ad hoc tourniquet, but the steady blood flow leaking from the fighter's leg dwindled to a trickle.

"What now?" the Ranger said as he scooped up his rifle.

"Your name's Fred, right?" Rapp said.

"To my friends."

"Well, Fred," Rapp said, "it's like this. My job was to find you and mark our position."

"Who's extracting us?" Saxton said.

"Your Rangers are providing the outer cordon," Rapp said, "but a SEAL friend of mine is doing the up-close work."

"You've got to be shitting me," Saxton said. "Bad enough I get pissed on, but a SEAL? Rangers don't get rescued by frogmen."

"They do today," Rapp said.

Saxton began to answer with what Rapp assumed would be another smart-assed comment when an ominous rumble drowned out the Ranger's words. The rock beneath Rapp's feet started to tremble and he stumbled forward, reaching for the wall.

The lights went out.

CHAPTER 32

"**W**HAT the hell?" Saxton said as the corridor plunged into darkness.

"That's the cavalry," Rapp said. "Hopefully."

"'Hopefully'?"

"This operation was heavy on execution," Rapp said, feeling for the cave's wall with his right hand while holding the AK with his left.

"And light on planning," Saxton said. "I've worked with SEALs before."

"You might want to cut my frogman friend a little slack," Rapp said. "He volunteered to come after your ass."

"So he could star in the movie somebody's gonna make."

"Quit bellyaching and grab that douchebag's cell," Rapp said.

"Why?" Saxton said.

"So I can call my friends," Rapp said.

"Won't do any good," Saxton said. "Never met a SEAL who could read a map."

"Give it a rest already."

"You been pissed on today? Thought not. Here's the phone. I used numbnuts' finger to unlock it."

Rapp accepted the device.

As expected, there was no cell coverage inside the cave, but the Wi-Fi icon signified a connection. The routers must be slaved to an emergency power source. In an odd turn of events, Rapp felt grateful for the thoroughness of whatever group of jihadi engineers had set up the cave's IT network. Shrugging off the strange thought, Rapp punched in a number, glad to have an excuse to end his argument with the cranky Ranger. While Saxton was wrong about SEALs, the man did have a point.

Rapp had not been pissed on today.

The call went through.

"Yes?"

"This is Ironman," Rapp said. "I authenticate Charlie One Seven Alpha."

"Authentication accepted, Ironman. This is Home Plate actual. Response is Whiskey Two Fiver Zulu."

The call sign Home Plate Actual meant that Rapp was speaking directly to the J-Bad chief of base, Steve. Hopefully that meant that Coleman and the Rangers were already on the way.

"Accepted," Rapp said, peering down the darkened corridor. "SITREP to follow." He felt more than heard Saxton slide into place next to him. Even carrying CYCLONE's deadweight, the Ranger moved like a panther.

"Send it, Ironman."

"Ironman has the precious cargo plus one. I am mobile but need immediate evac. Can you localize my position?"

SIGINT, or signals intelligence, had matured by leaps and bounds over the course of the near decade America had been fighting the Global War on Terror. Many of the commonplace digital intelligence-gathering methods employed by the NSA and other less well-known three-letter agencies would have been regarded as science fiction and not science fact only a handful of years ago.

Cell phone exploitation techniques were a perfect example.

Primarily driven by the need to feed actionable intelligence to the special mission units tasked with hunting down high-value targets in Iraq, the NSA's ability to glean information from a mobile device was astounding. But even the cyber ninjas who called Fort Meade home weren't omniscient.

"Okay, Ironman, I have you locked down to a five-kilometer radius. Your signal appears to be routing through several repeaters to mask the origin. Can you confirm your location?"

NSA analysts hadn't been the only ones learning about digital warfare.

The longer he waged war against terrorists, the less Rapp was surprised at the growing technological proficiency of his enemies. During the initial invasion of Afghanistan, Americans thought of the Taliban as barely literate cavemen. This had never really been true, and it was certainly not the case today. While the jihadi foot soldiers still counted a number of poorly educated fighters within their ranks, the upper echelons had begun to attract talent from across the Islamic Crescent. Since most jihadi communication was routed through encrypted message sites on the dark web, terrorist organizations heavily recruited computer scientists and IT specialists. The type of people able to employ a multitude of digital tricks.

Like masking a cell phone's location.

"I'm in a cave complex in the Spin Ghar mountains," Rapp said. "I entered through a southward opening elevation. I'm working my way back there now."

"Roger that, Ironman. QRF is en route. Are you still wearing your threads, over?"

As with the tablets he'd swallowed to taint his urine, Rapp had been skeptical about the purported effectiveness of his new wardrobe. While the eggheads who staffed the agency's Science and Technology, or S&T,

department meant well, the contraptions they tested in a laboratory's sterile confines often proved less than ideal in the real world.

"Affirmative," Rapp said.

"Good—the shirt showed up great on thermal. We were able to track you most of the way to the cave complex. The assault team will be on station in approximately five mikes, but we still have persistent ISR assets overhead. If you can self-rescue, do so. We'll vector you to safety once you're out of the cave."

That was good news, because even if he still had radioactive isotopes bouncing around in his bloodstream, Rapp's bladder was empty and not likely to be refilled anytime soon. While he wasn't normally part of full-up military operations, Rapp understood the fog of war especially as it pertained to a rescue operation with multiple moving pieces. His shirt would go a long way toward ensuring that he and Saxton weren't victims of friendly fire.

Which brought to mind a question he should have asked earlier.

"Is there a time limit on the effectiveness of my shirt?" Rapp said.

"Negative, Ironman. The treatment is woven into the fabric. As long as the cloth stays dry, it will work."

Even more good news. As part of his pre-mission planning, Rapp had received a brief from one of the Air Force weather specialists on loan to the agency. As per the norm in Jalalabad, the chance of rain over the next twenty-four hours was less than 5 percent.

He and Saxton had it made in the shade.

"Got it," Rapp said. "We are moving time now."

Saxton yelled something, but Rapp couldn't make out the Ranger's words over the sudden ringing in his ears.

Flashbangs were kind of loud.

CHAPTER 33

WHEN it came to displays of firepower, Scott Coleman was not easily impressed.

First as a SEAL, and then as the owner of a salvage/demolition company, he was well versed in the effects of high explosives. More than once, he'd had occasion to marvel at the way in which a well-placed breaching charge could turn even the most sturdy barrier into a gaping hole. In the same manner, Coleman had watched a twenty-thousand-ton steel monstrosity slide into the ocean's depths after he'd detonated the charges he and his team had carefully emplaced on the oil platform's undersea girders.

When it came to pyrotechnics, Coleman had seen it all.

Or so he'd thought.

But after watching the ridgeline a kilometer distant erupt under the combined effects of 155mm high-explosive artillery shells, he wasn't so sure. While he'd participated in more than his fair share of joking at his Army brethren's expense, one thing was for certain. When it came to putting indirect fire on target, Army Rangers had no equal.

Or at least their fire support officers didn't.

"Thirty seconds."

The shout came from the crew chief standing to Coleman's right. The update came verbally rather than through the Chinook's intercom because Scott had abandoned his headset and the snaking cable that went with it at the one-minute mark. The MH-47's internal communication system belonged with the helicopter.

Coleman did not.

After acknowledging the crew chief with an upraised thumb, Coleman keyed the transmit button on his radio and repeated the update for the benefit of his team. Will, seated in the driver's seat to Coleman's left, nodded his head to signify that he was tracking rather than respond via the radio like Charlie and Mas, who were in the passenger seats behind him. With less than thirty seconds until things went loud, there was no way Will was taking his hands off the steering wheel.

Coleman appreciated his teammate's singularity of focus. Working as a paramilitary officer required an attention to detail that rivaled a brain surgeon's, but the plan Scott had cooked up with Rapp was truly pushing things to the limit. Rather than dwell on the difficulty of the looming operation or the team's slim-to-nonexistent margin for error, Coleman dedicated his brainpower to something he could control.

Himself.

Coleman double-checked his restraint harness and cinched the belt as tight as it would go across his chest. Then he completed a final visual inspection of the M249 Squad Automatic Weapon machine gun mounted to his right. As the TC, or truck commander, Coleman was responsible for navigation as well as maintaining radio communication with the rest of the assault element. But when the shooting inevitably started, everyone had an offensive role to play. Mas had the M240 machine gun that fired the heavier 7.62mm round while Charlie was manning the top-mounted .50-caliber machine gun. Coleman's machine gun wasn't as sexy or hard-hitting as either of the other weapons systems, but his SAW could still put plenty of steel on target in a short amount of time.

Sometimes that could be the difference between life and death.

"Five seconds."

Coleman appreciated the warning, but he didn't need it. He could feel the Chinook flaring as it came to a hover, but more than that, he could see the mountaintop landing zone he'd selected materialize just beyond the helicopter's open ramp. With a dexterity Coleman would be hard-pressed to believe were he not witnessing it, the Chinook's pilots balanced the aircraft's extended ramp on the mountaintop even though the helicopter itself was still hovering in open air.

"Go! Go! Go!"

Coleman gave a thumbs-up to the crew chief with one hand and he reached for Will's arm with the other. Wrapping his fingers around the Marine's meaty biceps, Coleman squeezed. The all-terrain vehicle's turbo-diesel engine roared, launching it out of the Chinook's cabin and down the ramp. For a stomach-churning second, Coleman found himself wondering if the Night Stalker pilots had mistakenly allowed the dump truck of a helicopter to drift off the mountain.

Then the ATV's knobby front tires found purchase on the rocky soil.

The Chinook accelerated away from the ridgeline with a roar. The downdraft from the massive rotors rocked the ATV with hurricane-force winds, but Coleman scarcely noticed. His attention was focused on the moving map depicted on the tablet strapped to his thigh.

The tablet, as with the ATV, came courtesy of Justin Garza.

Though SEAL Team 6 was not currently in theater, several metal storage Conexes full of DEVGRU's equipment were already forward-deployed to J-Bad. Justin had allowed Coleman and his team to pick through the offerings, which included a prototype off-road tactical vehicle known as the MRZR, manufactured by Polaris. Small enough to fit in a Chinook but large enough to carry four armed assaulters with room for two or three more on a bench seat located at the vehicle's rear, the MRZR was fast, agile, and rugged. Most importantly, its powerful engine and reinforced suspension made the ATV ideal for navigating Afghanistan's treacherous mountainous terrain.

Coleman was in love.

"Turbine 33, this is Ghost 7," Coleman said after adjusting his boom mike. "We are clear of the LZ and proceeding to objective WILLIS, over."

"Roger that, Ghost. Turbine 33 is breaking station. Good hunting, over."

Coleman clicked the transmit button twice in response to the Chinook pilot's transmission before changing channels on his secondary radio from the air-to-ground frequency to the one monitored by the CIA personnel located at J-Bad airfield, thirty miles to the north. The distance was much too great for the Persistent Systems Wave Relay radio strapped to his tactical vest, but Coleman's transmission didn't have to reach anywhere near that far.

In addition to providing ISR coverage with its onboard suite of sensors, the Reaper UAV overhead served as a communications relay between Coleman and the operation's participants. As one of only four Americans on the ground, Coleman was glad to know that he and his men weren't alone, even though the departing MH-47's fleeing shadow suggested otherwise.

"Chaos Main, this is Ghost 7," Coleman said after toggling the transmit button. "We are one zero mikes from objective WILLIS. Request SITREP, over."

Coleman reflexively grabbed the MRZR's rollbar as Will spun the wheel to the left, nosing the vehicle down a boulder-strewn draw. The Marine was an excellent wheelman, but Coleman was still anxious about the route they'd chosen. Will had pronounced the path passable after hurriedly studying the satellite imagery of the terrain surrounding the landing zone, but Coleman wasn't quite as confident.

There was a reason why the locals still traveled these mountain passes on foot even in the era of modern transportation, but Scott had okayed the plan despite his misgivings. Special operators dealt with the world as it was, not as they wished it could be. Sometimes the plan had to work because there was no good alternative.

This was shaping up to be one of those times.

"Ghost 7, this is Chaos Main, read you loud and clear. We show ingress route BEARCAT clear of thermal signatures all the way to objective WILLIS. Fire mission will shift to smoke in five mikes. Assault force is orbiting vicinity GIBSON waiting for your go, over."

Coleman paused in order to visualize the tactical picture before replying.

Rapp's irradiated urine signaled that he'd located Sergeant Saxton, but the rescuers still knew nothing about the potential surface-to-air missile threat. Fortunately, Rapp's presence on the ground had been the catalyst needed to move the JSOC chain of command over their self-imposed speed bump. Or, knowing Rapp, this change of heart might have originated with their commander in chief.

Either way, just like Coleman had settled on a less-than-ideal route to objective WILLIS, the JSOC planners had figured out how to make lemonade out of lemons. Judging by the amount of artillery raining down from on high, the Ranger battalion staff had more than earned their keep. When confronted by the challenge represented by potential missileers guarding the cave complex, Captain Chris Jancosko, the battalion fires planner, had come up with an elegant solution worthy of the Ranger Regiment—give the bad guys something else to look at.

With this in mind, 155mm shells were currently pulverizing an unpopulated ridgeline just east of objective WILLIS. The same objective that Coleman was hurtling toward from the north and Garner's helicopter-borne Rangers would approach from the west. When Coleman reached the release point approximately one kilometer from the objective, the artillery barrage would transition from high-explosive shells to white phosphorus smoke.

In theory, the fireworks would allow Coleman to approach the cave complex unseen and unheard. If possible, they would spirit Rapp and the newly freed Ranger away to a clearing located due south of the cave complex where the 160th pilots would be waiting to evac them. If that didn't work, Coleman and his crew would become the reconnaissance element for the Rangers by providing real-time updates and suppressive fire as the helicopters disgorged the assaulters.

In theory.

In practice, operations seldom went exactly according to plan.

Judging by the collection of armed men just ahead, this operation was no different.

CHAPTER 34

RAPP was facing away from the pyrotechnic device when it detonated.

This bit of luck saved his life and a portion of his eyesight.

It did nothing to protect his hearing.

One moment Rapp was standing with the phone to his ear, deep in conversation. The next, unseen bells gonged and splashes of light danced across his vision. Dropping the phone, Rapp gripped his AK with both hands and crouched. Thumbing the selector switch to fully automatic, Rapp fired a long burst into the darkness, panning the rifle from right to left as he burned through a magazine. The muzzle flash illuminated stretches of the cavern, but between the all-encompassing darkness and his flash-blind eyes, Rapp couldn't see much.

What he did see wasn't encouraging.

A collection of bodies was entering from the far passageway. The figures were only visible for a millisecond, but the strobelike image lasted long enough for Rapp to form an impression—a tactical stack of at least six men.

Not good.

Rapp swapped magazines as a muzzle flash to his left announced that Saxton was still in the fight. Like Rapp, the Ranger hammered through his magazine in one continuous burst. This was not because the men lacked trigger discipline. This was their only chance to thwart the assault force. The stone walls meant that the entire cave was one big shooting gallery, and in tight quarters where every surface presented an opportunity for a ricochet, sometimes quantity really was a quality all its own. Like a pool player sinking balls during the break, Rapp was hoping that filling the air with a large volume of lead would knock down a few shooters and halt the assault's momentum.

If not, he was done for.

Rapp chambered a round as Saxton ran dry but didn't fire. He was down to his final thirty rounds and still shooting blind. The longer he lingered, the greater the odds that one of the attackers would score a lucky hit.

"We're leaving," Rapp said, grabbing Saxton by the ankle.

To his credit, the Ranger didn't argue. Saxton grunted as he hefted CYCLONE, then the soldier grabbed a fistful of Rapp's shirt.

"Go!"

Trailing his right hand on the cave's wall, Rapp moved forward as he clung to his AK-47 with his left. A series of *pops* provided mood music for their retreat as the assaulters filled the sudden silence with shots of their own. Shards of stone stung Rapp's face from a near miss, but a quick turn to the right cleared him from the line of fire. As the ringing in his ears slowly began to fade, Rapp almost began to smile. They might just make it out alive after all.

Then, Rapp realized he was missing something.

The phone.

CHAPTER 35

I N Afghanistan, telling friend from foe was never easy. Fortunately, one of the armed men possessed something that unequivocally moved him into the foe category—an RPG.

Unfortunately, the tube-launched munition was pointed at Scott.

"Contact front!" Coleman yelled as he depressed the M249's trigger.

The machine gun roared to life as the RPG tube belched flame.

Scott was no stranger to enemy fire. Though this unpleasantness normally came in the form of bullets, he had been on the wrong side of an RPG a time or two. Still, nothing in his previous experience had prepared him for this. Though the munition typically traveled faster than the human eye could track, today Coleman was head-to-head with the gunner. For an instant, the projectile seemed to hover just in front of Coleman, reminding him of the time he'd taken a fastball to the nose.

That collision had ended his baseball season.

This one had the potential to end quite a bit more.

The grenade screamed by, close enough that Coleman could feel the breeze generated by the projectile's stubby stabilizing fins. Panning the M249 left, Coleman walked the stream of crimson tracers through the jihadis while trying to remember how to breathe. The scarlet fire-flies sent at least two fighters tumbling to the ground while Will steered the MRZR into a third, crumpling the man with the ATV's left front bumper.

Then they were past the patrol.

Or what was left of it anyway.

Coleman was about to order Charlie to engage when the .50-caliber clamored to life. The Ma Deuce had first made its debut in the 1930s, but the weapon was still a fearsome sight to behold. Though he couldn't see the fireball emanating from the machine gun's gaping maw, the concussive muzzle blast hammered Coleman's shoulders and neck. The .50-cal sounded like a runaway jackhammer.

An *angry* runaway jackhammer.

Will wheeled the MRZR right, choosing to ramp over a shallow ravine rather than follow the gravel switchbacks. The ATV went air-borne before landing on the far side with a lurch that slammed Cole-man against his restraint harness.

The .50-cal fell silent.

"Don't know if I got the last one," Charlie said. "Our driver handles this beast like he's steering a shopping cart."

"If you wanna switch places let me know," Will said. "I actually hit where I aim."

"Quit your bitching," Mas said. "We're still alive. Though, I might have to clean out my britches."

A series of dry chuckles echoed over the intercom as the men tried to dissipate the tension. But even the best one-liner wouldn't have al-lowed Coleman to laugh away what had just happened. Gathering his thoughts, he keyed the transmit button.

"Chaos Main, this is Ghost 7," Coleman said. "We ran into a patrol just short of the release point. We suppressed and bypassed. Still en route to WILLIS, over."

"Ghost 7, Chaos Main copies all. Are you compromised, over?"

That was the million-dollar question. Coleman sighed as he tried to decide how to answer. Technically, they were compromised. He and Charlie had both opened up and neither of their machine guns was what anyone would term quiet.

That said, the man-made thunder was growing louder the closer the MRZR got to the cave complex. With the detonating artillery for cover, the jihadis might not have had heard the violent but brief fire-fight. The real question was whether a member of the patrol had a cell phone or walkie-talkie that they could use to alert the defenders.

Assuming that any members of the patrol were still capable of using either device.

Coleman knew he'd dropped at least two of the jihadis and that the man Will had run down was either dead or on his way to being so, which left the final shooter. Charlie might not have scored a direct hit, but the former SEAL Team 6 operator was no slouch with his weapon. The M2's half-inch-diameter armor-piercing rounds would have rico-cheted off the stone like shotgun pellets fired into a concrete floor. The patrol had probably been silenced before they could get off a warning.

Unless they hadn't been.

"Chaos Main, Ghost 7," Coleman said. "Our current heat state is unknown. We are still proceeding to WILLIS, over."

"Roger all, Ghost 7. Recommend you expedite. We see thermal sig-natures on the north side of WILLIS."

Of course they did.

CHAPTER 36

RAPP mentally reviewed his hike into the cave complex as he kept his right hand on the stone wall. He'd kept track of his pace count during the walk in and pegged the distance he'd traveled at just under four hundred meters.

No sweat.

Even a nonsprinter could cover a quarter of a mile in about two minutes. The darkness and the need to slow down for Saxton and the still-unconscious CYCLONE certainly put a cramp on Rapp's pace, but he'd be out of the complex in five or six minutes. Eight minutes tops.

That was the good news.

The bad was that if the HIG thugs had invested in backup generators, they ought to get their money back. While Rapp wholly approved of the distraction offered by the rolling artillery barrage, navigating the cave system in the dark was a bitch. To make matters worse, the last pair of shots from his pursuers had nearly taken his head off. While it was always better to be lucky than good, the shot placement seemed too accurate to attribute solely to luck. At least one of the jihadis probably had a night-vision device of some sort. Classic light-intensifying goggles wouldn't do much good this far underground, but if one of the mountain men had a thermal device, Rapp was a sitting duck.

Like the Russian thermal devices favored by the Iranians, for instance.

"How we doing up there?" Saxton said.

Excellent question.

"Need a rest?" Rapp said.

"I need to get the hell out of here."

If the Ranger was at all winded from carrying CYCLONE, he didn't show it. Saxton had been captured, beaten, and tossed in a makeshift outhouse, but he was still keeping up with Rapp while carrying one hundred and sixty pounds of deadweight over his shoulder. A long friendship with Coleman meant that Rapp was partial to SEALs, but Saxton was doing a great job representing his branch of service.

"You're in luck," Rapp said as his right hand found the gap he'd been expecting. "This is our stop."

Rapp was about to turn the corner when something made him freeze.

The whisper of sandals scraping against stone.

"What—"

Rapp blindly reached behind him, grabbed a handful of Saxton's shirt, and squeezed.

Hard.

The Ranger fell silent.

When it came to killing, few people had Rapp's experience, but Saxton was probably no slouch. One did not rise to the rank of sergeant in the Ranger Regiment without mixing it up on the battlefield a time or two. Rapp stopped breathing and closed his eyes, straining to pierce the all-encompassing darkness. After almost thirty seconds of silence, he'd been on the brink of believing that he'd imagined the sound when he heard the dry rasp of leather on stone again. Rapp considered easing his AK-47 around the corner and spraying but didn't. He had one magazine remaining and was probably facing multiple opponents.

Opponents who might also be equipped with thermal night-vision devices.

The correct play was to remain silent and let the approaching men grow closer. Hopefully he'd gain a better sense of how many militants he was facing. Engaging in a gunfight under these conditions was suicide. Rapp had just settled in to wait when Saxton grabbed his shoulder and squeezed.

Hard.

"Footsteps," Saxton whispered. "Behind us."

He didn't bother asking if the Ranger was sure. Instead, Rapp pictured the cave complex and the death that was approaching from two directions. He remembered being surprised as he'd followed CYCLONE into the cave proper. Surprised at the scale of the passageways as well their number. In fact, if Rapp was where he thought he was, there was a second passage on the opposite side of the hallway. He knew this because he'd expected for some reason to take the branch to the right and had been surprised when the group had turned left.

"Stay with me," Rapp said, his voice barely audible.

Saxton squeezed his shoulder and then grabbed the back of Rapp's shirt.

Rapp ghosted across the passageway and away from the safety offered by the wall. He kept his right arm out in front of him, fingers questing through the darkness like a blind man. The exercise brought to mind a spacewalker who had come untethered from his safety line. The wall he'd just left was his touchstone.

Without it, Rapp was adrift in a sea of black.

After several steps in which his outstretched fingertips touched nothing but air, Rapp began to worry. Like a pilot who inadvertently punches into a cloud bank and becomes disorientated, Rapp was concerned that he might be traveling parallel to the far wall instead of perpendicular. Resisting the urge to plunge blindly into the abyss, Rapp put one foot in front of the other while attempting to strike a balance between quick movement and running headlong into the unknown.

As if things weren't interesting enough, the now-unmistakable sound of footfalls echoed from just up ahead. If Rapp didn't find the passageway soon, he and Saxton would likely have what military tacticians charitably termed a meeting engagement with the approaching fighters. With no desire to repeat the battles of Gettysburg or Little Bighorn, Rapp lengthened his stride and stretched his right arm to its full extension.

His fingertips brushed stone.

A murmur of hushed voices now accompanied the footfalls to his right. The approaching guards were almost on top of him.

Saxton poked him in the kidney.

The men approaching from the opposite corridor had to be drawing nearer too.

For a heartbeat Rapp stood still, trying again to picture the intersection he'd briefly seen. His recollection was that the adjacent passageway was to his right, but with no way to chart his progress, he wasn't sure. If Rapp was wrong, he and Saxton would be pinned between the wall and one or both approaching groups of gunmen. Rapp had the urge to move left, but he was also left-handed. During moments of stress, people instinctively defaulted to their dominant side, which was why lost hikers often wandered in circles.

Now was the time to trust his memory, not his instincts.

Shifting the rifle from one hand to the other, Rapp touched the wall with his left hand and began to walk right. Five strides later, he felt a breeze emanating from the second passageway an instant before his fingers located a gap in the stone. Rapp took a giant stride into the new corridor and pulled the Ranger behind him.

"Stay here," Rapp hissed.

"Where the hell else you think I'm gonna go?" Saxton said.

Ignoring the panting Ranger, Rapp squatted. Leaning his rifle against the wall, Rapp felt across the floor with both hands until he found what he was seeking.

A rock.

Hiding in the corridor wasn't going to be enough. With two groups of armed men prowling the darkness, and at least one of them probably equipped with night observation devices, Rapp needed to even the odds.

Edging closer to the corner, Rapp pressed himself flat against the rough stone wall.

The footfalls grew louder, but Rapp waited. He had to time this perfectly. Too soon and he'd miss his mark. Too late and he'd be discovered. Rapp counted to ten, and then threw the rock down the hall to this right. He'd slung the stone sidearm like he was skipping a rock across a pond in the hopes of getting as many collisions from the throw as possible.

It worked.

The murmurs Rapp had heard earlier crescendoed into whispers.

Then gunshots.

Rapp scampered back down the passageway, chased into the darkness by the reports of multiple AK-47s firing on fully automatic. Either his adrenaline-fueled movement had caused Rapp to misjudge the distance he covered or Saxton had disobeyed his earlier admonishment to remain still.

Rapp crashed headlong into the Ranger.

To the stout soldier's credit, Saxton didn't fall, but he did stagger.

"What the hell?" Saxton said.

"My diversion worked," Rapp said as the firing continued. "Maybe a little too well."

"What do you mean?"

"I was hoping to send the group nearest us down the tunnel so that we could slide by them and make for the cave's entrance," Rapp said.

"Instead, you tricked them into shooting up their friends," Saxton said.

"Sounds that way," Rapp said.

"Which means if we try to sneak by, we're liable to catch a bullet," Saxton said. "What's the play?"

Rapp shrugged and then realized Saxton couldn't see the gesture.

"Hide here until the shooting stops. Sooner or later, they'll realize they have a blue-on-blue incident."

"Or run out of ammo."

"That works too," Rapp said. "Once the jihadis quit filling the air with lead, we can reassess. If they've done enough damage, maybe we can finish the job with the ammo we have on hand. If not, we sneak past and make for the entrance. The darkness is still our friend."

Then the overhead lights flickered.

CHAPTER 37

THE presence of thermals at the northern end of the cave complex wasn't surprising.

According to the digital timer at the top right corner of Coleman's tablet, the artillery bombardment had been going on for two minutes. By now the shock had worn off and the battle-hardened instincts of the cave's occupants would have taken over. While he vehemently disagreed with everything his Taliban adversaries stood for, Coleman had been in enough scuffles with the jihadis to respect the courage and tenacity of these mountain fighters. Staying huddled in their cave fortress might keep them safe from the artillery barrage, but it also meant they'd be sitting ducks for an advancing force. The mountain men were not stupid. It made sense that a few of the fighters would venture onto the ridgeline to scout out what the Americans were planning.

The question was what to do about the jihadis.

"Ghost 7, Chaos Main, stand by for SITREP, over."

The radio transmission gave Coleman an excuse to pause his deliberations.

"Go for Ghost 7," Coleman said.

"Roger that, 7. Be advised that Ironman has made contact. He has the precious cargo in hand and is egressing WILLIS time now, over."

Will bottomed the ATV into a dry ravine before turning the vehicle north. While the Recon Marine could sneak and peek with the best of them, Coleman thought Will might have missed his calling. He was the Mario Andretti of off-road driving. Which was actually a bit of a problem. Will was a minute ahead of schedule, which meant that Coleman needed to start the smoke barrage ahead of schedule too.

Unless Rapp's update meant that the diversion was no longer needed.

"Understood, Chaos Main," Coleman said. "Are you in contact with Ironman, over?"

"Stand by, Ghost 7."

The answer struck Coleman as odd.

Though the person manning the radio probably wasn't an operator, Coleman would have expected the man to anticipate his question. If Rapp was still on the line, of course Coleman would want to know. The rescue mission had gone well so far, but the hard part was still ahead. The greatest opportunity for fratricide always occurred when friendly elements had to link up on the battlefield.

Throw an artillery barrage and some pissed-off cavemen into the mix, and Coleman knew there was a very real chance the wrong person might catch a bullet even with the help of Rapp's special shirt. If he could talk directly to Rapp, Coleman could get a better sense of where his friend expected to emerge from the cave complex and learn what was potentially waiting for his team at the evac point.

Will eased off the gas after turning the MRZR's nose north. The entrance to the complex was only a hundred meters or so on the other side of the small foothill to their front. Once Will summited the rising terrain, Coleman and his crew would be visible to any defenders and therefore committed.

Decision time.

"Ghost 7, this is Chaos Main Actual. We are no longer in contact with Ironman. I say again, we are no longer in contact with Ironman, over."

For the first time Will turned his attention from the road to meet Coleman's gaze. The Marine didn't speak. He didn't have to. Coleman didn't know the J-Bad chief of base well, but the Chaos Main Actual call sign meant that Steve had chosen to relay the update himself rather than rely on his radio operator.

This was telling.

As was the tremor in the CIA officer's voice.

"Understood, Chaos Main Actual," Coleman said. "What was the last thing you heard before you lost contact with Ironman, over?"

"Gunshots."

CHAPTER 38

COLEMAN could forgive Steve for his less-than-steady radio voice, but he couldn't condone it. The J-Bad chief of base might be accustomed to high-pressure situations, but projecting calm in the middle of a kinetic operation that was going to shit was an acquired skill. Even so, the team leader's job was to be the eye of the storm. The center of tranquility for the rest of the operatives.

As Coleman had learned early in his career as a SEAL, maintaining control of your emotions wasn't just some macho bullshit. Fear was contagious.

But so was courage.

"Roger all, Chaos Main Actual," Coleman said, transmitting into the void before the bad news the CIA officer had just relayed could take root. "That isn't unusual when Ironman is in the mix. What's the status on Havok 6, over?"

"Break, break, Chaos 7, this is Havok 6," Mark Garner said. "We are two minutes from WILLIS. Are we a go, over?"

That was a very good question.

Conflict-avoidant people did not become soldiers. This sentiment went doubly so for those tough enough to make it through the grueling selection process required to earn the Ranger Regiment's coveted tan beret. That said, the Charge of the Light Brigade played great on the movie screen but was considerably less palatable in real life. Coleman knew that Mark and his band of marauders would fight their way into the caves to find Rapp without a second thought, but he was no longer sure this was the right course of action.

As much as Coleman didn't want to admit it, the gunshots Steve had reported changed the equation. Rapp was industrious and he could improvise, adapt, and overcome with the best of them, but he was not invincible. If faced with armed resistance, Rapp would either overwhelm the aggressors immediately or try to find an alternate egress route. Coleman could imagine a scenario in which Rapp had managed to arm himself, but even if he had a weapon, Rapp would still be a singleton with a possibly injured Army Ranger in tow.

One of the reasons why Rapp was so effective was that he precisely chose the time and place for most of his kills. He wouldn't shirk from a fight, but neither would Rapp allow the enemy to dictate the terms of the engagement. If the main egress route was clear, Rapp would be out of the caves momentarily. If not, it made no sense to send the Rangers in after him. Rapp was probably already searching for a secondary exit.

"Havok 6, this is Chaos 7," Coleman said. "Do not proceed to WILLIS. I say again, do not proceed to WILLIS. I think Ironman will seek an alternate egress point. I want to get a closer look at the objective."

"Chaos 7, this is Havok 6. Understand all. What element will be conducting the recon, over?"

"This one."

CHAPTER 39

THE strand of lights flickered to life like a scene from a B-grade horror movie.

Though the filaments barely illuminated, the change from cavernous darkness to hazy light was still shocking. One moment Rapp couldn't see his hand in front of his face. The next a string of hanging bulbs revealed the passage in a wavering kaleidoscope of shadows. The overhead lighting buzzed as the load posed by the countless bulbs warred against unseen generators laboring to provide power. A sickly orange flooded the passage.

Then the filaments burst into full brilliance.

"Shit," Saxton said.

The Ranger's whisper conveyed a scream's worth of emotion. The gunshots in the hallway gave way to shouts in at least two different languages.

The gig was up.

"Down the corridor," Rapp said. "Go."

Shouldering the still-limp CYCLONE, the Ranger moved at a respectable trot. While no longer a competitive endurance athlete, Rapp could still match the pace of men half his age. But loaded down with the deadweight of someone CYCLONE's size, Rapp doubted he'd have been able keep up with Saxton.

They must build them strong in the Ranger Regiment.

Rapp gave the Ranger a bit of a head start and then followed. He ran for half a dozen steps before pausing to clear the passageway behind them. The presence of two patrols meant that he and Saxton were being hunted. It wouldn't take the jihadis long to sort out their confusion. The narrow passageways weren't big enough for more than two men to pass abreast, but this advantage evaporated if the jihadis were fine with killing rather than capturing their prey. In that scenario, the engagement would be like shooting fish in a barrel.

As if to add emphasis to his thoughts, the *clank* of metal striking stone sounded from the passageway's mouth. Rapp tried to yell a warning, but his words were drowned out by an ear-shattering detonation. The concussion slapped against Rapp and Saxton staggered.

The passageway formed a Y just ahead of the Ranger.

"Right!" Rapp yelled. "Go right!"

Saxton groaned, but he staggered toward the branch Rapp had indicated. Turning to face their pursuers, Rapp dropped to one knee, sighted toward the mouth of the passageway, and squeezed off a controlled burst. Rapp waited for the report's echo to fade and then fired again. The passageway's mouth remained empty, and he risked a glance over his shoulder in time to see Saxton limping down the intersection.

Perfect.

Rapp turned back to the entrance in time to see three tennis-ball-size objects tumble into view. Rapp dove toward the Y-intersection, stretching to full extension. He didn't so much hear the exploding grenades as feel them deep in his core. The concussion prompted an instant bout of nausea as shock waves buffeted his internal organs. His right foot jerked as if someone had smacked the sole of his foot with a rubber mallet. Pins and needles shot the length of his leg, but Rapp ignored the pain in favor of a more pressing priority.

Staying alive.

Squirming onto his back, Rapp aimed at the entrance. Though his ears were still ringing, his eyes worked just fine. Two men raced into the area cleared by the explosion, their AKs belching fire. Rapp centered his rifle's front sight post on the lead assaulter's center mass, aligned the rear sights, and pressed the trigger.

The man dropped.

Rapp transferred his aim to the second man and fired again. He was expecting a three- or four-round burst. The AK sounded just once.

His magazine was empty.

The assaulter stumbled but didn't crumple like his partner. Dropping the rifle, Rapp pushed himself backward. If his ears were ringing, the shooters pursuing him had to be half-deaf. Hopefully it would take them a moment to realize that Rapp was no longer shooting back.

A scrum of bodies poured into the hallway.

Rapp swore.

If he got to his feet, he'd be cut down in a volley of rifle fire. If he stayed on his back, he'd never make the intersection before the jihadis gathered their wits and aimed at the figure squirming across the ground.

He was in trouble.

A hand grabbed him by the shoulder and jerked him up. Saxton churned forward in a low crouch, dragging Rapp across the intersection like he was an offensive lineman exploding out of a three-point stance. Rapp's foot caught on the uneven stone, and he stumbled, fouling Saxton's legs in the process. He slapped his forearms onto the ground to keep from face-planting onto the rock.

Saxton wasn't so fortunate.

The Ranger's face bounced off the stone and his lip split in a burst of red.

"This is the worst rescue I've ever seen," Saxton hissed. "We're gonna die."

"Nope," Rapp said, "we're out of here."

"How?" Saxton said.

"That's how," Rapp said.

Rapp pointed to a bubbling stream that disappeared under a rock face to their right. The instant he saw the underground tributary, Rapp understood what had subconsciously prompted him to take the intersection to the right.

The smell of water.

Rapp remembered the waterfall at the front of the cave complex's entrance. The rock tunnels must serve as a natural aqueduct for the spring water the farmers in the surrounding village used to irrigate their crops. The underground river moved at a quick but navigable pace. Rapp took this to mean that the tunnels were wide enough not to constrict the river's flow. In other words, the rock channels were probably large enough to contain air pockets.

Probably.

"Not gonna happen," Saxton said.

"Look," Rapp said, not trying to hide his exasperation. "I get that it isn't an ideal solution, but I saw the pool this stream empties into. The current is manageable, and the tunnel is taller than the water by at least a foot or so. We'll be able to breathe. Besides, the alternative isn't exactly promising."

As if to underscore Rapp's point, another volley of shots echoed from the passageway they'd just vacated. With the air saturated with dust, their pursuers might not have seen which corridor Rapp and Saxton had chosen in the confusion surrounding their escape, but with only two branches to choose from, the jihadis had a fifty-fifty chance. Based on the way Rapp's luck had been breaking lately, he didn't love those odds.

"I can't swim," Saxton said.

Rapp stared at the Ranger, his mind refusing to make sense of the man's words.

"What?"

"I. Can't. Swim."

"How the hell does a Ranger not know how to swim?" Rapp said.

"I joined the Army, not the Navy," Saxton said. "Swimming wasn't in the job description."

This time splintering rocks and the buzzing of bullets snapping through the sound barrier accompanied the bark of AK-47s firing. The assaulters had either chosen correctly or split their numbers to cover both branches.

Rapp was out of time.

"No problem," Rapp said, taking a step closer to Saxton. "I know exactly what you need to do."

"What?" Saxton said, looking over his shoulder at the corridor.

"Learn."

Rapp smashed both hands into the Ranger's back, torquing his hips into the thrust. With a cry, Saxton tumbled into the river still clutching CYCLONE. Rapp gave the men a body-length lead and then dove after them.

A moment later, the gaping tunnel swallowed them.

CHAPTER 40

T HE foaming water closed around Rapp with an icy embrace.

He knew the river was sourced from both ice melt and a natural spring and he'd expected the water to be cold.

But it wasn't cold.

It was frigid.

After finding his footing on the rocky floor, Rapp pushed up with both feet, gasping for air the moment his head broke the surface. The cold was significant, and if he spent too long bobbing in the Taliban's version of the Lazy River, he would have to start watching for the telltale mental sluggishness and deadened limbs that announced the onset of hypothermia.

But that was a problem for later.

First, he needed to locate his nonswimming companion.

Fortunately, the sputtering and cursing gave Rapp a pretty good idea where to look. The tunnel wasn't lit, and the illumination provided by the lightbulb strands behind them was fading fast. Rapp stroked toward the commotion with distance-eating kicks, desperate to link up with Saxton before the encroaching darkness made the task exponentially more difficult.

On the fifth stroke, his questing fingers touched fabric.

"I've got you," Rapp said, looping an arm around Saxton's neck. "Just relax."

The Ranger instinctively fought, but Rapp was ready for the man's drowning response. Sliding beneath the soldier's flailing arms, Rapp transferred his hold to something like a rear naked choke and flipped Saxton onto his back.

"Relax," Rapp hissed. "If you keep fighting, you'll drown us both. Just breathe and let me do the rest."

Rapp's words must have penetrated Saxton's fear-saturated brain because the Ranger stopped struggling and began hacking.

"Lesson number one," Rapp said, "hold your breath underwater."

"Fuck you," Saxton said between coughs. "I told you I couldn't swim."

"And I told you I didn't care," Rapp said, beginning a sidestroke. "It was the river or die. Easy choice."

"Funny," Saxton said, "'cause that sounds like the same choice to me."

"They don't teach water survival training in Ranger School?" Rapp said.

"They do, but I. Can't. Swim. What happened to the shithead I was carrying?"

"He swims like you," Rapp said.

Fingers of darkness were stretching across the turbulent water. Rapp scanned the foaming surface for a glimpse of CYCLONE but didn't see the warlord. While he was disappointed that he wouldn't be able to question the jihadi later, Rapp was also thankful he didn't have to try to keep two men afloat.

"What's that roaring?" Saxton said, still sputtering.

"I've got good news and bad news," Rapp said, adjusting his hold on Saxton's neck.

"What?"

"The rushing sound means we're almost out of this cavern."

"Fantastic."

"The bad news is that I sugarcoated our exit."

"What do you mean?" Saxton said.

"There's a waterfall." Rapp said.

"A what?"

"Don't get all weak-kneed on me. It's a short drop."

"I hate you," Saxton said.

"Get ready," Rapp said as the roar grew louder. "We're about to get flushed down the toilet."

Saxton might have tried to say something, but Rapp couldn't hear the Ranger over the thundering rapids.

That was probably for the best.

CHAPTER 41

As someone who hunted his nation's enemies on their turf, Rapp had been in some tight spots. In Paris, he'd once entered a hotel room through the window to find a team of killers with automatic weapons waiting in ambush. On another continent in another operation gone sideways, Rapp had allowed himself to be captured by Hezbollah thugs in hopes of locating and saving Stan Hurley before the jihadis executed his curmudgeon of a mentor.

Those encounters had nothing on rocketing down a pitch-black rock tunnel with a nonswimming Ranger in his arms and the sound of a churning waterfall in his ears. On the positive side of the ledger, the growling rapids made conversation with Saxton almost impossible.

Almost.

When it came to communicating his feelings, the Ranger was extremely persistent.

"I swear to God I'm going to kill you!" Saxton screamed.

Rapp didn't bother pointing out the hilarity of the Ranger's statement. By simply releasing the man's shirt and scissor-kicking with the current, Rapp could rid himself of any threat the soldier posed. But he didn't do so, mainly because he thought Saxton had a point. If they survived the journey through the aqueduct, the waterfall, and the unpredictable currents sure to be roiling the water below, Rapp was of a mind to kick his own ass. But first he had to live through the next two minutes.

This was no sure proposition.

"When we get to the waterfall, I'm gonna let go and swim ahead of you," Rapp yelled.

"The hell you say?"

"I need to put space between us," Rapp said. "Otherwise we might knock heads during the fall."

"I thought it was a short drop," Saxton sputtered.

"Short might be in the eye of the beholder," Rapp said. "You're going to fall for what will seem like forever. Once you hit the water, the current's gonna grab you. Don't fight it. Not at first. Go limp for a five-count. Then breathe out and watch for bubbles. If you're near the bottom, push off the riverbed. If not, just kick your legs and follow the bubbles. Your body is buoyant. It wants to float."

"Mine doesn't," Saxton said.

"Five seconds," Rapp said, "and don't cheat. Give me the full one-Mississippi, two-Mississippi. Once you break the surface, I'll be there. We'll get to shore together. Okay?"

"Let me go," Saxton said. "I'm gonna try something."

Though the Ranger was doing an admirable job of not panicking, Rapp was worried that Saxton would devolve back to thrashing his limbs if Rapp released his hold. Still, Saxton had put his life in Rapp's hands. The least Rapp could do was show the Ranger a little trust of his own.

"Okay," Rapp said, uncurling his arm from around Saxton's neck. "You're free."

Rapp felt Saxton grip his shirt with a strength only available to Rangers and drowning men. Then he heard the sound of Saxton submerging. Rapp was in the process of reaching for the Ranger when he heard the soldier coughing up water.

"Grab me," Saxton said. "Hurry."

Once again Rapp snaked his right arm around Saxton's neck, but this time the Ranger didn't resist. Something felt different. Rapp did a test sidestroke to confirm his suspicion. The Ranger was more buoyant.

"What did you do?" Rapp said.

"Inflated my shirt," Saxton said. "Can't swim, but I've done my share of drownproofing. Maybe it will help once I hit the pool."

Rapp was familiar with the technique and thought Saxton's hopes were wishful thinking. The air pocket the Ranger had created inside his shirt would not survive the fall, let alone the harsh landing that followed. But in survival situations, attitude was everything. If Saxton felt more confident, Rapp wasn't going to argue.

A blast of air smacked Rapp in the face and the darkness began to lift. The waterfall.

"This is it!" Rapp screamed. "See you at the bottom."

Rapp squeezed Saxton's shoulder and then released the Ranger.

Saxton didn't reflexively grab for him, but Rapp wasn't going to press his luck. Turning onto his stomach, Rapp stroked toward the tunnel's mouth, desperate to put space between himself and his companion. Rapp intended to exit the aqueduct feetfirst. A leg fractured by a boulder was survivable.

The same couldn't be said for a broken neck or skull.

Rapp churned through the water, counting each stroke. He'd allotted himself ten kicks. Then he'd rotate in the water, pull his legs to his chest, and cannonball out the rock tunnel. Once airborne, he'd straighten his legs, cross his feet at the ankles, guard his face and nose with his hands, and hope for the best.

Ten kicks sounded reasonable.

He made it to eight.

On the ninth stroke, Rapp lunged forward with his powerful left arm, expecting to still feel water.

He didn't.

CHAPTER 42

RAPP had imagined many potential operational pitfalls while he'd been riding in a truck jammed shoulder to shoulder with a crew of smelly jihadis.

Plunging headfirst down a waterfall hadn't made the list.

The instant Rapp felt open space instead of water, he cupped his hands over his nose. This was the prescribed method for entering an unfamiliar body of water of unknown depth and assuming a feetfirst fall.

Rapp was not falling feetfirst.

He tried to orient himself into a more suitable entry position in midair, but he was no more a competitive diver than ballerina. After several excruciating seconds of useless flailing, Rapp belly-flopped into the water with the grace of a sack of mulch falling off a tailgate. The impact drove the air from his lungs. He'd estimated the waterfall to be about twenty feet high, but that had been optimistic. The water felt like concrete.

Then the current dragged him under.

Rapp fought the urge to reflexively take a breath even as the turbulence sent him tumbling head over heels. Heeding his advice to Saxton, Rapp didn't fight the current at first, but after a five-count of getting banged against the riverbed, he flutter-kicked his legs in long, powerful strokes. Though he would have given his left arm for a pair of fins, Rapp's hours of open-water swimming paid dividends. After several more seconds of getting tossed about, he swam clear of the roiling maelstrom, angled for the surface, and ascended.

Three kicks later, his head burst from the water.

Judging by how the rescue had gone so far, Rapp was going to owe his Ranger friend a beer when this was over. Maybe a case of them. Rapp would put his swimming skills up against anyone not wearing a Trident, but the trip down the waterfall had still been a doozy.

Saxton was going to have trouble.

Unfortunately, drowning was now the least of Rapp's worries. The anemic moon revealed several black forms standing on the cliff overlooking the pool.

Black forms with AK-47s.

The human eye was attuned to motion, especially at night, but fortunately, Rapp had help. In the same way in which background noise like static or falling rain dampens a person's sense of hearing, the constant motion generated by the waterfall would help to camouflage Rapp's movement.

To a point.

The deluge of water thundering into the basin did create a blind spot of sorts, but once he swam clear of the visual disturbance, Rapp's motion would set him apart from the relatively placid river chortling downstream of the waterfall. But that was a problem for later. Since Saxton had yet to surface, Rapp assumed that the Ranger was caught somewhere in the vortex of converging currents he'd just escaped.

Taking a deep breath, Rapp marked where he would begin his search grid and prepared to swim back into the cyclone. The sound of splashing water stopped him.

Turning, Rapp saw Saxton flailing on the water's surface.

So did the jihadis.

CHAPTER 43

THE first burst of rifle fire missed.

The rounds cratered the water, raising divots that geysered skyward before splashing back to the churning surface. Perhaps mercifully, Saxton seemed unaware that he was now a target. If the Ranger's water survival training had helped him navigate the deadly currents earlier, it was failing him now.

Saxton's hands slapped the water even as his head barely crested the surface.

Then he was gone.

Like he was coming off the starting platform, Rapp freestyled toward the stricken Ranger for all he was worth. The good news about having his face buried in the water was that Rapp could no longer hear or see the gunmen.

The bad news was pretty much everything else.

There was no way Rapp was going to let Saxton drown. Besides, in theory this wasn't a solo op. While there were days when Rapp found himself wishing that he was still a solo operator hunting his prey across Europe, these thoughts mostly came after spending too much time on Langley's seventh floor.

Yes, he missed the carefree days of his youth when he'd lived the cover of a traveling computer software salesman, but if Rapp were being honest, there was something to be said for a team of shooters ready to wreak havoc on his behalf. As the bullet-shaped mass of puckered flesh in Rapp's shoulder could attest, sometimes shit just went sideways. Now when the bad days happened, Coleman and his hitters had Rapp's back. Hopefully Scott and the crew were positioned in overwatch, ready to intervene.

If not, this was going to be a very short swim.

CHAPTER 44

"**G**HOST 7 is in position," Coleman whispered.

"Ghost 9 copies all," Will said. "Good hunting, 7."

Coleman wasn't normally a big believer in luck.

Normally.

But tonight, Coleman would take all the luck he could get.

"I've got eyes on the entrance to WILLIS. How do you want to play this?"

The whispered question came from Charlie, who was nestled in a shallow depression about two feet to Coleman's left. While Coleman considered himself more than adequate with a long gun, there was no question that Charlie was the better long-distance shooter. Accepting that not all operators were created equal was one of the keys to success in the special operations community. Besides, on this operation Coleman was not just another shooter. He was the team leader, which meant he had more important considerations than just putting steel on target.

Like trying to figure out what Rapp was up to.

"You've got the thermal sight," Coleman said, "so keep your attention on the exits. I'll take the jihadis meandering around the entrance."

"You're the boss, boss."

Even Charlie's whisper seemed at ease. As if the sniper were lying in the sun on a beach somewhere rather than huddled beneath a length of camouflage netting hoping not to be discovered by a roving jihadi patrol. To be fair, Will and Mas were waiting in the MRZR on the other side of the sloping terrain about fifty meters back. The two men functioned as rear security as well as a makeshift QRF, but there was no getting around the fact that he and Charlie were hanging in the breeze.

"Ghost 7, this is Chaos Main. The fire mission is rounds complete. Do you want to transition to smoke, over?"

Coleman thought about how to answer as he surveyed the outcropping. His night-vision goggles "saw" in a different spectrum than Charlie's thermal sight. This meant that the image intensifiers needed ambient light in order to work their magic. On low illumination nights, or in caves, thermal sights were much more valuable, but tonight's quarter moon was custom-made for Coleman's goggles.

The downside to this equation was that Coleman couldn't see Rapp's specially treated shirt. This was why he had Charlie scanning for additional egress points to the cave complex while he kept an eye on the jihadis lining the cliffs. And like ants emerging from a disturbed nest, more bad guys were crawling out of the caves every minute. The original plan had called for transitioning from high-explosive to smoke shells in order to obscure the objective as Garner's Rangers made their approach.

While that plan had now been overcome by events, Coleman was still considering employing the white phosphorus artillery rounds. The thick white smoke the shells produced would obscure his visibility, and hopefully that of the jihadis, but would not hamper Charlie's thermal sight. In essence, Coleman might be able to provide Rapp with a cloak of invisibility, assuming that the shells didn't land in the vicinity of where he was exiting. White phosphorus burned at more than fifteen hundred degrees Fahrenheit and was almost impossible to extinguish. The best invisibility cloak in the world wouldn't do a bit of good if Coleman accidentally turned Rapp's egress route into the gates of hell.

Maybe smoke wasn't such a good idea after all.

"Chaos Main, this is Ghost 7," Coleman said. "What's the time of flight on those shells, over?"

"Ghost 7, this is Chaos Main Actual. Wait one."

Coleman breathed a sigh of relief that Steve didn't attempt to field the question. The time of flight for artillery shells was a technical question that could only be answered after factoring a wide range of variables. The chief of base was a spy, not an artilleryman.

"Ghost 6, this is Havok 13. The guns are already loaded with Willie Pete shells. I'll have steel on target ninety seconds after you tell me to execute, over."

Once again Coleman found himself grudgingly admitting that he was thankful that the Ranger fire support officer was on the job. Though to be fair, Captain Jancosko was actually a Marine, which meant that he was technically part of the Department of the Navy.

Maybe Coleman didn't owe the Army thanks after all.

"Roger that, Chaos Main," Coleman said. "Stand by to *shit*—"

Like all serious operatives, Coleman prided himself on his radio etiquette. In a career spanning several decades, he'd never lost his cool on the radio and certainly never cursed.

Apparently, there was a first time for everything.

Like watching three bodies tumble down a waterfall. The action happened so quickly, Coleman wasn't sure that he'd seen what he'd thought he'd seen.

Then a head popped out of the water.

A single head.

"Shit," Coleman said again, this time to himself.

"What do you have?" Charlie said.

"Ghost 7, this is Chaos Main. Say again, over?"

Ignoring the understandably confused fire support officer, Coleman turned to Charlie.

"Three bodies just fell down the waterfall," Coleman said. "Can you see them?"

Charlie shifted his rifle and then said, "Negative. But that water's freaking cold. It's probably masking their signatures."

A second head bobbed to the surface closer to Coleman but quickly went under. The first person must have seen or heard the disturbance in the water because they started stroking for where the second person had disappeared. Coleman had spent his life in and around water. He knew how this would end.

No way would the first swimmer reach the drowning man in time.

"That's gotta be Rapp," Coleman said, "which means the non-swimmer is our precious cargo. Cover me."

"On it," Charlie said.

Dropping his rifle, Coleman sprinted for the pool of water. The second head popped above the surface again, but the man slipped below much sooner than the first time. The swimmer, Rapp, redoubled his efforts, but it wasn't going to be enough.

The drowning man was fading.

"Chaos Main, this is Ghost 7," Coleman said after triggering the transmit button. "Fire for effect on target reference point Alpha 7. I say again, fire for effect on Alpha 7, over."

"Ghost 7, this is—"

Coleman dove into the pool while Captain Jancosko was still mid-sentence. Call-for-fire protocol dictated that the fire support officer receive a final confirmation before he sent artillery rounds streaking toward their target, but Coleman was hoping the Marine was intuitive enough to know when to break the rules.

If not, this might be Coleman's final swim.

While the jihadis guarding the exit to the cave complex might not have seen three bodies tumble from the aqueduct, there was no way they could miss Coleman's mad sprint from the underbrush. Either Jancosko obscured Coleman's rescue with some well-placed Willie Pete, or the tranquil pool was about to become a shooting gallery.

Either way, this was no longer Coleman's concern.

The entirety of his being was now focused on the patch of water he'd mentally marked as his target. The patch where he'd seen the struggling man slide beneath the surface.

Coleman was no stranger to rescuing unresponsive swimmers.

During BUD/S, or Basic Underwater Demolition/SEAL training, Coleman had been a victim of a shallow-water blackout. One minute he'd been wrestling with his dive gear, trying to unknot the rat's nest the instructor had made of his regulator hose, and the next he'd found himself on the concrete pool deck as a medic berated him for forgetting to breathe. Just because a struggling swimmer was underwater did not mean he was unsavable.

But that equation changed rapidly the longer his brain went without oxygen.

Filling his air with lungs, Coleman dove beneath the water to the sound of AK-47s firing. As the water closed in around him, Coleman came face-to-face with the enormity of his task. SEALs were trained to conduct underwater grid searches, but without air to breathe, a light source, or even a dive mask, Coleman was at a huge disadvantage. He wasn't exactly swimming in the crystal waters of the Bahamas, and the faint moonlight wasn't penetrating the river's murky depths.

Coleman swam deeper, scissoring his legs while spreading his arms wide in the hopes of enlarging his search. For the first time, Coleman was forced to consider that he might not find the Ranger. That after all the effort Rapp and the entire CIA/JSOC team had expended on this rescue, they could still come out short. The anger that accompanied the disheartening thought gave renewed effort to Coleman's strokes. He kicked like a sprinter, determined to cover as much ground as possible before his dwindling air supply forced him to the surface. His outstretched fingers bumped the rocky bottom and Coleman adjusted his dive angle, skimming along the riverbed in an attempt to locate a prone form.

Nothing.

With his chest on fire, Coleman stroked upward. Ignoring the urge to rocket toward the surface to fill his quivering lungs with oxygen, Coleman slowed his ascent to minimize the ripples when he surfaced.

He needn't have bothered.

One moment, Coleman was stroking through darkness.

The next, it was as if the Almighty had said, *Let there be light.*

The ridgeline overlooking the pool erupted in flame as a sheath of white phosphorus shells detonated. Sheets of fire spilled down the rock, accompanied by dense, choking white smoke. If the jihadis had still been firing their rifles at Coleman, they weren't any longer. But safety from the gunmen was only half of the reason why Coleman found himself smiling.

The other half was flailing his arms just a body length away.

"Easy, now," Coleman said, reaching for the floundering man. "I've got you."

Coleman slid his arm around the man's neck in a modified rescue hold and was pleasantly surprised to feel the swimmer relax rather than fight his efforts.

"Who are you?" the man sputtered.

"The guy that's gonna get you out of here," Coleman said.

"That's what the first guy said right after he pissed on me."

Definitely Rapp.

"I told you that wasn't personal."

Coleman suppressed a chuckle as Rapp swam over, seemingly no worse for the wear. "Glad to see you," Coleman said. "The natives were getting restless."

"You don't say," Rapp said. "Need a hand?"

"Nah, I've got him. Head to shore and link up with Charlie. Tell him to call Will forward so we can get the hell out of here."

"Sounds like a plan," Rapp said.

Rapp scythed through the water with an efficiency of motion that made Coleman jealous. Even years after giving up competitive racing,

Rapp could still move out. Coleman gave his friend a several-second head start and then began sidestroking for shore with the Ranger in tow.

"Just tell me one thing," Saxton said. "Are you a SEAL?"

"Yep," Coleman said.

"Then let me drown."

In spite of everything, Coleman found himself chuckling.

"Don't sweat it, kid," Coleman said. "Even Rangers need heroes."

CHAPTER 45

A ZAD Ashani held two tickets in his hand.
Though the printouts weighed just ounces, the paper stock felt unnaturally heavy in his fingers. Perhaps it was because the weight of his life and that of his family rested on which ticket Ashani decided to use.

"Excuse me, is this seat taken?"

For a facility located in the capital city of a nation that had been in a near-constant state of war for decades, the airport was a busy place. The complex now boasted a recently opened international terminal, and upward of three hundred passengers a day made use of the multiple airlines that frequented Kabul International Airport. This meant that the seating areas were surprisingly full.

This morning was no exception.

Though he'd been to Kabul many times, Ashani was always struck by the diversity of passengers. Yes, many of the men wore the white Islamic *Taqiyah* skullcaps or the Afghan *pakol* hat, but many more were bareheaded. In the same manner, Western-style shirts, jeans, and sneakers rivaled for primacy with the flowing tunic-style *Perahan* shirts and the

loose *tunban* pants. The woman by and large dressed more conserva-
tively, but a fair amount of leggings, jeans, and modest blouses competed
with the more traditional long dresses and hijab head covering.

The person addressing Ashani was male, clean-shaven, and decidedly Western in his sport coat, button-down shirt, jeans, and brown
loafers. He could have been a businessman, journalist, or an employee
for one of the legions of nongovernmental organizations that plied their
trade in Afghanistan.

Or something else entirely.

"No," Ashani said, "feel free."

He replied in English since that was the language the questioner
had used, but judging by the man's accent, Ashani didn't think that was
his native tongue. The questioner was Caucasian, but his diction and
pronunciation suggested a hint of a French accent. Ashani's heart rate
began to accelerate as the man settled into the seat next to him. Looking
over the man's shoulder, Ashani consulted the large analog clock
mounted to the wall.

Nine a.m.

Fourteen hours past the time when he and Mitch Rapp were to have
met.

While the profession of espionage was not by any means an exact
science, there were certain aspects of the trade that were absolutes.
One of these was the window of time in which a handler was scheduled to meet with his asset. These windows were structured around
gaps—gaps in surveillance, gaps in schedule, and in its most literal
sense, gaps between buildings. Moments in which two people could
talk privately and exchange vital information.

Ashani had purposefully chosen his meet time with Rapp to occur
after he'd finished his summit with Iran's new operational partners
and before his trip to the airport. A period in which a normal person
would be expected to fall off the radar as they took in the city, slept,
packed bags, checked for flight delays, caught up on last-minute
emails, or made a few before-travel calls.

In other words, the perfect explainable gap.

A gap that Rapp had not filled.

The businessman seated next to Ashani shifted in his seat and withdrew a newspaper from his leather satchel. The movement was slight and perfectly explainable.

Ashani prepared himself for what was coming next.

As an intelligence officer who'd plied his trade for three decades, Ashani knew that clandestine contact could occur in any number of ways. Old-school tradecraft would have dictated a few surreptitiously whispered words, a note dropped in Ashani's pocket, or perhaps instructions scribbled in the margins of a newspaper left on the man's seat after he departed.

Then again, since this was the twenty-first century, contact could have just as easily been made digitally via an air-dropped text, image, or website link. In either case, Ashani's role remained the same.

Wait for contact.

But Ashani's window was closing.

The clock on the wall clicked as the minute hand lunged forward.

Five minutes.

Ashani had five minutes to decide which ticket to use. One routed through several countries before eventually terminating in Paris, where his wife and daughters waited. The other, the one his government was expecting him to use, was a flight to Islamabad.

Ashani felt his lungs quiver, but for the first time, the spasm didn't prompt a hacking cough. His ever-present scarlet handkerchief still rested in his right front pocket, but the material was dry. Ashani wanted to believe that this was because his immune system was rallying and had fought the cancer devouring his lungs to a standstill.

In his heart, he knew this wasn't true.

A far more likely explanation was that the tumors had destroyed enough of the healthy tissue that Ashani had nothing left to hack up. The act of walking now winded him, to say nothing of climbing stairs. He didn't know how much lung capacity he had remaining or when his blood oxygen would plummet to levels too low to sustain consciousness, but Ashani understood that he was on borrowed time. The question was whether he should rendezvous with his family and enact his fallback plan or continue to push his operational luck and travel to Islamabad.

The answer all came down to Rapp.

Without help from the American, Ashani knew that the odds of successfully evacuating his family from France were slim. The information he possessed about the looming Iranian operation in Afghanistan was Ashani's currency. While there was a possibility that Ashani could exchange this currency at the American embassy in Paris, this would be a final act of desperation. The Iranian MOIS was a competent intelligence service. He would be burned the moment he entered the embassy, which meant the elegant solution he'd imagined for his disappearance would no longer be possible. To place his family forever beyond the clutches of his former comrades or, worse, the Quds Force lunatics, he needed Rapp.

But Rapp was nowhere to be found.

A gate agent's voice echoed through the terminal, announcing that the flight terminating in Paris was now boarding. A couple seated to Ashani's right struggled to their feet. The father was loaded down with his family's carry-on luggage as well as a diaper bag. The mother had a baby in a carrier strapped to her chest and two toddlers gripping each hand. A final little girl, perhaps six, rounded out the crew. She was old enough to pull her own tiny carry-on and she fearlessly led the family toward the gate.

Ashani teared up as the procession marched past him. His emotions had been a roller coaster since he'd received his terminal diagnosis. Some days he raged against the injustice of dying before he could experience the joy of holding grandchildren on his lap. Other days he found himself overwhelmed with gratitude for the life he'd been so fortunate to live.

Ashani fought the urge to call out to the parents as they trudged past. He hadn't been as present as he could have been when his girls had been that little, but he'd told more than his fair share of bedtime stories and relished in lively dinner chatter. He wanted to place a hand on the father's shoulder and entreat him to savor the moments when his little girls wanted to dance around the living room with Daddy. He wanted to hug the mother and tell her that the dark days of nighttime feedings and cranky toddlers would soon end.

More than anything, Ashani wanted to wrap his arms around his lovely Samira and listen as his girls talked and laughed together. His raven-haired beauties were now twenty-three, twenty, and eighteen. Many years had passed since he had carried diaper bags while Samira herded the girls, but in that instant, those years seemed just a whisper away.

The businessman seated next to Ashani joined the exodus.

He did not leave his paper.

Ashani checked his pockets and glanced at his phone even though he knew what he'd find.

Nothing.

Absolutely nothing.

Ashani had been monitoring Rapp's Farid Saeed legend and knew that the CIA officer had traveled to Kabul the previous day. What had transpired in the ensuing twenty-four hours was still a mystery. Shortly after landing, CCTV cameras showed Rapp departing the international terminal and disappearing into the hustle and bustle of Kabul.

Ashani had been unable to piece together what had happened next. While this wasn't exactly surprising, it was disheartening. Mitch Rapp was a clandestine operative of considerable skill, with the physical and verbal aptitude to pass for many nationalities. Of course he could vanish should the need arise. The question was *why*. Why had the American been sufficiently intrigued to come to Kabul but not interested enough to actually meet with the Iranian who'd requested his presence?

The family showed their tickets to the gate agent and then passed down the jet bridge out of sight. Of the businessman, Ashani saw no sign. With a harried look, the gate agent unclipped the microphone attached to her podium and made the announcement Ashani had been expecting in three languages.

Final boarding call.

Ashani struggled to his feet. Specks of darkness flitted across his vision, and he almost lost his balance. Thankfully, his groping hand found the chair's metal armrest. He took comfort in the feel of the cool metal as he waited for the vertigo to pass. He did not have long, and he would spend what time he had remaining with those he loved.

His decision made, Ashani pressed through the crowd toward the gate agent. The young woman smiled encouragingly at his unsteady progress as if she were cheering on a child's first steps rather than the doddering strides of a dying, middle-aged man.

His pocket pulsed.

Ashani withdrew his phone with trembling fingers. It was a text message, but not from Rapp.

The sender was Ruyintan.

We need to talk.

Yes, they did.

With the foresight of one who had waged war from the shadows his entire career, Ashani knew how this would end. Traveling to Paris might buy him time with his family, but without the deal he intended to exact from Rapp, they would never be safe.

And Rapp wasn't here.

Sighing, Ashani dropped his ticket to Paris into the trash receptacle and joined the queue for the flight to Islamabad. With shaking fingers, he texted a reply.

Coming.

CHAPTER 46

MIKE Nash shifted in his leather reclining seat as the Gulfstream's engines spooled down. Fifteen hours after Irene had tasked him with conducting his first international trip in his new capacity as a CIA executive, Nash sat on the tarmac of Islamabad International Airport. For fifteen hours, Nash had war-gamed how to achieve the diplomatic and operational goals Irene had outlined ahead of his unscheduled visit.

Now, the time for planning was over.

"Ready, sir?"

Nash looked from the jet's open doorway to his aide. Bill Thompson was both impossibly young and unabashedly eager. For some reason, these two qualities had the combined effect of making Nash feel impossibly ancient and deeply cynical. Maybe part of Nash's poor attitude could be attributed to the fact that he wasn't used to being called *sir*.

At least not anymore.

Sure, as a captain in the Marine Corps, Nash had been accustomed to the honorifics paid to his rank. Still, as more than one noncommissioned officer had helpfully pointed out when Nash had still been a wet-behind-the-ears second lieutenant, calling Nash *sir* and rendering him a hand salute were a tribute to the fact that he was an officer, not to him personally. Hopefully that situation would change as Nash grew into his role, but to gain the respect of the Marines he led, he'd first have to earn it. Nash had relished the challenge and thought he could hear a difference in the single-syllable word's inflection after he'd served as a platoon commander in combat with his Marines.

That was the opposite of this.

Now Nash was a *sir* because he was a GS-15.

His ascent into the government's Senior Executive Service was the equivalent of achieving flag rank in the military. Except Nash was no longer a rifle-toting Marine, a knuckle-dragging paramilitary officer, or even a cubicle-dwelling bureaucrat. No, his new incarnation had transformed Nash into something much more despised.

Senior management.

And he had his old pal Rapp to thank.

Or blame.

"Just a sec," Nash said, powering down his laptop.

To be fair, the gig did have its share of perks. While Nash had certainly traveled on an Agency Gulfstream before, this was the first time that his rank merited a jet just for him. If a person had to fly the seven thousand or so miles from Andrews Air Force Base in Maryland to Islamabad, Pakistan, a Gulfstream V was the way to make the trip. The jet was fast and its cruising altitude of fifty-plus thousand feet put the aircraft and its passengers in the smooth air above most of the turbulence.

The jet belonged to the CIA, so its interior didn't match the opulence of the Gulfstreams favored by rock stars or tech overlords, but the supple seats, plush couch, and narrow but serviceable bed beat the hell out of flying commercial. Though he still felt grimy from wearing the same clothes for the last thirteen hours, Nash was rested and ready to begin his day of meetings. The United States might have been left off the invitation list for the Regional Stability Conference that Pakistan was host-

ing, but Nash's Pakistani counterparts had assured him that the slight
had been unintentional. Nash thought that was about as likely as Stan
Hurley opening a florist shop once he retired.

No matter.

The ISI leadership had made up for their supposed oversight by
scheduling Nash for a meeting with the president of Pakistan just hours
after his arrival. Nash had shadowed Irene in enough head-of-state
summits to know that this conversation was a formality and that the
real talks would occur between his counterpart and him in a much
smaller venue.

Even so, Nash was prepared for fireworks.

Pakistan was notionally an ally in the Global War on Terror, but it
was becoming harder and harder for the US administration to ignore
the nation's double dealing. On one hand, Pakistan had legitimately
aided the US after 9/11. On the other, the Pakistani army had mostly
abandoned their much-hyped campaign to root terrorists out of the
Federally Administered Trible Areas, or FATA, a no-man's-land that
made up much of the border between Afghanistan and Pakistan.

The divide within Pakistan's intelligence service, the ISI, or Inter-
Services Intelligence, was even more stark. It was no secret that the Taliban came to power in large part through financial aid from the ISI and
Pakistan's Interior Ministry. Supposedly this had been part of a national
strategy to use Afghanistan as a buffer against foreign incursion into
Pakistan's sphere of influence. A strategy that was officially renounced
after receiving some very direct communication from Washington. Before the dust on Ground Zero had fully settled, the American president
had provided his Pakistani counterpart with the lay of the world in
commendably unambiguous terms—you're either with us or against us.
After seeing the rapidity and brutality with which the Americans had
dealt with Al Qaeda, the choice had been easy to make.

Then.

Now, ten years later, the ground was much less firm. Though he
wouldn't confess his feelings even to Maggie, Nash knew in his heart

that the effort in Afghanistan was mired in a swamp. While his CIA brothers and sisters were still ruthlessly dispatching terrorists, the American military was on a far less certain footing.

With the exception of the Special Mission Units and some members of the special operations community, the generals guiding the efforts of US boots on the ground increasingly seemed to be in search of a job. Were they nation-building? Trying to win hearts and minds? Building a stable democracy? Or killing bad guys in Afghanistan so that the jihadis didn't have the chance to kill Americans on US soil?

Nash was no longer sure.

Neither were America's allies.

If nature abhors a vacuum, regional stability does doubly so. Nash was angry that Pakistan wasn't taking a more active role in stabilizing the conflict raging on their doorstep, but the Marine in him understood. You had to fight the war you found yourself in, not the one you hoped for.

Pakistan's leaders guided their country with a pragmaticism born from years of navigating the region's turbulent waters. They were nothing if not experts at judging the way the wind blew and tacking their nation's course accordingly. If the United States was no longer certain how to solve the problem of Afghanistan, Pakistan was not going to do the work for them. Nash was in Islamabad to show the flag, as the old saying went. To remind his Pakistani counterparts that the US was still in the business of exterminating terrorists and America expected some sort of measurable return on investment for the more than ten billion dollars in "aid" that had flowed into Pakistani coffers since 9/11.

At least that was Nash's official story.

The truth was that Nash's visit was meant to be provocative if not outright confrontational. Thanks to Rapp, Nash was a war-on-terrorism hero, the public face for the countless men and women who operated behind the veil of operational secrecy. Nash's trip to Pakistan was as overt as the message he was conveying from the occupant of 1600 Pennsylvania Avenue—*you're either with us or against us*. Nash didn't know President

Saad Chutani, but he had enough familiarity with the quasi-dictator to understand that this message wasn't going to be received well, especially in light of the botched Ranger raid against the HIG compound.

A compound notionally located on Pakistani soil.

But a diplomatic fireworks display was exactly what Irene had in mind.

The more the Pakistani political class and their enablers in the ISI were focused on Nash's visit, the less they might be paying attention to Rapp's shenanigans as he cowboyed along across Afghanistan and Pakistan.

Not to mention the NOC, Noreen Ahmed, who'd also slipped into country.

It was Noreen's presence more than the need to bring the Pakistanis back to the straight and narrow that had prompted Nash's trip. That said, as much as he detested the fact that he was wearing a suit instead of the outdoor wear that normally served as the uniform of the day for a Rapp operation, Nash was committed to accomplishing his goal. Once a covert officer's cover was rolled back, he could never be reinserted into the clandestine world. And nothing said rolling back your cover like the president of the United States pinning a medal on your chest in front of a roomful of reporters. Like it or not, this was Nash's new job and he'd be damned if he'd end his first official trip with nothing more to show for his efforts than a few diplomatic niceties and a couple of handshakes. Once a Marine, always a Marine, and Marines didn't phone it in.

Ever.

"All right," Nash said after locking his laptop in the Gulfstream's safe, "let's go give 'em hell."

Judging by the stricken expression on poor Bill's face, this was not the expression Nash's predecessor employed while preparing his team for a round of diplomatic sparring.

Maybe that was part of the problem.

CHAPTER 47

"I'M telling you, he was Iranian."

Mitch Rapp made the statement in a tone that brooked no argument. The tone of a person who spoke Farsi and knew a Persian accent when he heard one. From an evidentiary perspective, this should have been one of Rapp's less controversial statements.

It was not.

"I'm not saying he wasn't," Colonel Nick Petrie said, his patronizing tone suggesting that he was doing exactly that. "We've certainly had our share of dustups with Iranian special operations types and intelligence officers smuggling weapons and fighters, but that was in the Western theater. We're in RC East."

While Rapp did not concern himself with the overall strategy of the war in Afghanistan, he could certainly see that things weren't progressing according to plan. He hadn't devoted much brainpower to reasoning out the cause of the current morass. Rapp was an intelligence officer, not a military strategist. But with men like this in charge, it wasn't hard to understand why America was doing little better than treading water as the Taliban and other unsavory elements solidified their hold on the populace.

"This is not a debate," Rapp said, his expression challenging the colonel to say otherwise. "Besides the HIG shitbird, there were three other men in that cavern bidding for Ranger Saxton. Two spoke Arabic with Saudi accents, and the other one was Iranian. An Iranian who said he knew me from a prior dustup I had with some Quds Force and Hezbollah douchebags. If I were in your shoes, I might devote more energy to finding out why that collection of talent was huddled together in a cave thirty minutes south of here and less to trying to explain away a problem by pretending it doesn't exist."

As much as he'd hoped for a different response, Rapp had expected this reaction from Petrie. September 11, 2001, was a tragedy of unspeakable magnitude, and it had galvanized the military and intelligence services in a manner not seen in Rapp's lifetime. For the first time since December 8, 1941, America's populace, politicians, and the men and women who carried out kinetic diplomacy on their behalf had been fused with a unity of purpose. The initial invasion into Afghanistan had been facilitated and controlled by CIA Jawbreaker teams with Army Special Forces A-teams providing the muscle. Those days had been the Wild, Wild West, but shit had gotten done. Within two months of the American invasion, the Taliban had been on the run, Al Qaeda was all but destroyed, and US-backed forces had taken control of the majority of Afghanistan.

That had been a decade ago.

Many of the brave men and women who'd thrown caution to the wind while executing some of the most audacious operations since the Normandy landing were long gone, replaced by careerists who often seemed more concerned with gaining their next star or setting up a lucrative postmilitary career than with winning the war.

Petrie was Exhibit A.

"We won't be conducting operations in the vicinity of the Spin Ghar mountains. Period."

The rejoinder came from a lean man dressed in civilian clothes who was seated to the colonel's right. This back-and-forth bullshit was the exact scenario Rapp had been trying to avoid when he'd marched into the brigade tactical operations center, or TOC, and asked to see Colonel Petrie along with his S2, or intelligence officer, in a closed-door meeting. The brigade commander had intimated that his schedule was extremely busy, but he would try to work Rapp in sometime in the next several hours.

Rapp had intimated that Colonel Petrie could walk into the conference room or be dragged.

The conversation had gone downhill from there.

Colonel Petrie was now seated in his secure conference room, but the meeting was not the cozy conversation Rapp had envisioned. In addition to Petrie's S2—his aide-de-camp whose purpose seemed to be to satisfy the colonel's never-ending craving for Diet Cokes—the S3, or operations officer, and a trio of nervous-looking captains, the colonel was flanked by the man in civvies.

The man now inserting himself where he most assuredly didn't belong.

"What's your name?" Rapp said.

"Tim," the man said. "Tim Sellers. I'm with the Department of Agriculture."

"Why are you here?" Rapp said.

Tim's cheeks colored. "The Department of Agriculture has been designated by the Department of State as the lead agency to oversee reconstruction efforts in this area of RC East. Our charter is to work with both governmental and nongovernmental organizations to bring stability to Afghanistan via three pillars: education—"

"Stop," Rapp said.

"Stop what?" Tim said, the flush on his cheeks deepening.

"The words coming out of your mouth," Rapp said. "I'm sure you're doing your best to bring unicorns and rainbows to the children of Afghanistan, but I don't give a shit. I'm here to fight a war, not nation-build. I need you to un-ass this conference room so the grown-ups can talk."

"No," Tim said.

This was not a word Rapp often encountered.

Between the early part of his career in which he'd answered only to Kennedy and the later portion in which he was afforded great latitude by the president of the United States, Rapp was used to getting his way. On the rare occasion when he encountered someone naïve enough to erect a roadblock in his operational path, Rapp either bulldozed his way through or went around the person. Having the White House on speed dial was a kind of institutional laxative all its own. Even the most self-important bureaucrat quickly found religion after a call from 1600 Pennsylvania Avenue.

Usually.

But today might just be the exception that proved the rule.

After returning to J-Bad from the rescue operation, Rapp had found himself at a crossroads. His efforts to save Saxton had proven successful, but not much else had gone right. The HIG commander, CYCLONE, had drowned during the chaos surrounding the rescue, and the data from his waterlogged phone had proven to be unrecoverable.

The Chinook shootdown had confirmed Ruyintan's tip, but Rapp was still no closer to understanding what the Iranian Quds Force colonel was planning. At present, Rapp knew only that CYCLONE had been equipped with missiles capable of targeting American helicopters at night. It stood to reason that Ruyintan had probably provided those missiles, but Rapp didn't know this for certain.

To be fair, Rapp knew very little for certain.

He had no idea how the missiles' targeting system worked, whether more missiles existed, and if so, what Ruyintan intended to do with them. Presumably, Ashani would have been able to answer at least some of these questions, but Rapp had also missed his window to meet with the MOIS officer.

After landing back at Jalalabad with a wet but otherwise no worse-for-wear Ranger Fred Saxton, Rapp had been the recipient of more bad news, this time from the CIA's Kabul chief of station. A name trace had yielded a hit on one of Ashani's known aliases. The MOIS officer had been listed on the manifest for a passenger flight that had recently departed Kabul International Airport for Islamabad. A review of hacked CCTV feed from inside the airport confirmed the worst—Ashani had boarded the flight.

With Ashani gone and CYCLONE dead, Rapp had intended to concentrate his efforts on finding and interrogating the Iranian he'd encountered in the cave complex. The man was more than likely one of Ruyintan's minions, and even if he wasn't directly linked to Ruyintan, the Iranian certainly wasn't in Afghanistan to sightsee. At a minimum, he would be able to provide Rapp with another piece of the Ruyintan operational puzzle. But to locate the missing Iranian, Rapp would need to cast a wide net. This could only be accomplished with boots on the ground.

Lots of them.

While the JSOC folks were hell on wheels when it came to capturing high-value targets, they were not equipped for house-to-house and village-to-village searches. This would be the law enforcement equivalent of sending a SWAT team rather than patrol officers to conduct a neighborhood canvass. The rugged section of Afghanistan that Rapp needed to search offered ample places for the Iranian to hide or, worse still, disappear across the porous border with Pakistan. To lock down the likely avenues of escape while conducting an organized manhunt, Rapp would need help from an organization he didn't often work with—conventional military forces.

With this in mind, Rapp had left the JSOC compound after finishing the mission debrief and crossed the street to make the acquaintance of Colonel Petrie. Special operations and the CIA worked together on a regular basis, but this was not the case with conventional units. Their chain of command was much broader and more unwieldy and often institutionally averse to working with three-letter agencies.

That said, Rapp knew that regular infantry units enjoyed getting after the enemy just as much as their special operations brothers in arms. He might have spent the majority of his career with spooks, spies, and snake eaters, but Rapp deeply respected the conventional military. The special operations community was sexy, but winning a war required gaining and holding terrain, and that could only be done by massing soldiers on the battlefield. Colonel Petrie commanded an infantry brigade, and the operation Rapp was proposing should have been right up the warfighter's alley.

Should have been.

Unfortunately, Colonel Petrie didn't seem to be much on warfighting at the moment.

Ignoring the troublesome USDA civilian, Rapp instead focused on Colonel Petrie. In addition to the requisite eagle denoting his rank of colonel, Rapp noticed two things that did not bode well. One, the section of uniform above the colonel's right shoulder that should have been occupied by a combat patch was empty. Two, the unit patch on his left shoulder indicated that his brigade was part of the National Guard. Petrie was on his first combat tour, and he was not an active-duty officer. While neither of these indications was a disqualifier per se, it could go a long way toward explaining the deference the military officer was showing to his Department of Agriculture contemporary. Someone who had risen to the rank of colonel without ever going into harm's way was bound to be cautious on his first combat deployment.

By the same token, while the majority of Reserve and Guard units had served with distinction in both Iraq and Afghanistan, sometimes the familiarity of fighting alongside people who were your civilian neighbors and coworkers could manifest in unhealthy ways. A commander should never commit the lives of his or her troops needlessly, but death was often the unfortunate outcome of combat. A leader who focused on their subordinates to the exclusion of the mission did a disservice to both. An infantryman's job was to close with and kill the enemy.

Leaders who forgot this did so at their own peril.

"Colonel Petrie, what is your mission in Afghanistan?" Rapp said.

The colonel's thin brown eyebrows bunched together in confusion as if Rapp had asked a trick question.

Not a good sign.

"What do you mean?"

"Your mission," Rapp said, spacing out the words as if speaking to a toddler. "What are your standing orders?"

"I don't see what that has to do with—" Tim interrupted.

"If you speak again without permission," Rapp said, turning to the Department of Agriculture bureaucrat, "I will physically remove you from this room. Got it?"

The flush that had begun in the man's cheeks had now enveloped his face and was creeping down his neck. Tim opened his mouth but then slowly closed it. Rapp had changed out of his local garb and into a flight suit. The tan one-piece overalls were devoid of insignia or organizational markings and featured no name tag. No rank bestowed instant authority and no skill badges afforded immediate respect. Even so, there must have been something about Rapp's presence. The bureaucrat might have murder in his eyes, but Tim's mouth remained closed.

Progress.

"My mission is to secure and hold the area of operations assigned to my brigade," Petrie said.

"Good," Rapp said with a helpful nod. "I'm offering you a chance to do just that. The Iranian I have to find is a foreign intelligence officer bent on destabilizing not just your area of operations but all of Afghanistan. I need your subordinate battalions to conduct a search for this man, going house-to-house if necessary. Once you find him, I will assume custody of the Iranian, and you will never hear from me again. Okay?"

"No," Tim said, slapping his palm against the table. "It's not okay, and I don't give a shit who you are. The bullshit raids your JSOC friends conducted over the last twenty-four hours have already done enough damage. In one fell swoop, you have undone weeks of bilateral talks between the HIG, the village elders, and other local leaders. I will not sit here and allow this farce of a conversation to continue."

Rapp sighed before turning to the bureaucrat.

On this point, he agreed.

The time for talking was over.

CHAPTER 48

"Did you have to hit him?" Coleman said.

"Absolutely," Rapp said.

Coleman paused to consider his friend. The conviction in Rapp's voice gave even him pause. Maybe there was a rational explanation for the storm of violence that had just engulfed an otherwise placid brigade headquarters.

"Why?" Coleman said.

"Do you know what the Department of Agriculture does?"

Coleman shook his head. "Not really."

"Exactly. So why in the hell should some bean counter from a nonsense government agency be directing our Afghanistan wartime strategy?"

Coleman didn't have an answer. Rather than try to come up with one, he looked from his friend to the wooden B-hut that served as the combination TOC and conference room for the infantry brigade's leadership team.

The structure was still standing.

This was not always a given after Rapp lost his cool. On the other hand, the two guards posted on either side of the entrance were giving Rapp serious side-eye. The soldiers weren't reaching for their sidearms, but their fingers were fluttering close to the black matte pistol grips.

This could be because moments earlier Rapp had exploded out of the B-hut's front door while dragging a sputtering man by the nape of his neck. To his credit, Rapp hadn't hit the man, but he did deposit the civilian on the dusty ground in a tangled heap of arms, legs, and freshly pressed khakis. The pair of guards had seemed unsure how to read the situation, especially after he got to his feet and took a swing at Rapp.

That had been a mistake.

Now the man was recovering at the J-Bad aid station and Rapp and Coleman were persona non grata inside the brigade headquarters. The head of the guard detail had delivered this news with the calm, soothing voice a circus trainer might use with a lion that had escaped his cage. Rapp had taken the pronouncement in stride, but judging by their rigid body language, the soldiers were still uneasy.

Coleman could sympathize.

If he had a dollar for every panic attack Rapp had induced in a protective detail, he'd be a rich man.

A very rich man.

"I take it the ground pounders aren't going to help us find the missing Iranian?" Coleman said.

The look of disgust on Rapp's face was answer enough.

"I really think we might lose this thing," Rapp said, turning to Coleman.

"What?" Coleman said. "Our chance to find the Quds Force officer?"

Rapp shook his head. "The war, Scott. The whole goddamn war. The special operations boys and girls across the street are still getting after it, but the jihadis aren't going to be crushed by spies and snake eaters alone. Look, I'm all for giving the local populace a reason to support us, but we've got leaders who think that it's a better use of our soldiers' time to build schools instead of kill shitbags."

Coleman was nowhere near old enough to have experienced Vietnam, but as a young frogman he'd known several senior chiefs who had. While he hadn't doubted their observations on what it was like to serve in the long, unpopular, and ultimately unsuccessful war, Coleman had never been able to come to terms with the conflict's outcome. How could America piss away the lives of fifty-five thousand of her sons and daughters over seven bloody years and still settle for defeat?

It had never made sense to him then.

It was starting to now.

"My team is reloaded and ready to go, but I'm not sure where to point them," Coleman said.

In a situation that was as unique as it was unsettling, Coleman was unsure about a number of things. While working with Rapp gave new meaning to the phrase *ready, fire, aim*, the SEAL always took it on faith that Rapp had a plan even if what he was thinking wasn't abundantly clear.

To anyone.

But this felt different.

Rapp felt different.

Coleman eyed his friend, trying to find the source for the verdict his subconscious had just rendered. Rapp was still Rapp, but he seemed . . . distracted. One of the things Coleman admired most about Rapp was his ability to compartmentalize.

No, that wasn't quite right.

Compartmentalize suggested that Rapp locked away pieces of himself while operating. That wasn't accurate. Rapp brought all of himself to every operation. All of his anger, all of his intuition, and all of his experience. It wasn't that he turned into an emotionless killing machine as much as he became hyperfocused in a manner that superseded distraction. But if Coleman were pressed to describe his friend right now, that would be the word he'd choose.

Distracted.

"This whole thing has me second-guessing myself," Rapp said.

Coleman stared at Rapp, unsure if he'd heard correctly.

Rapp second-guessing himself?

They were in uncharted territory.

"About rescuing Saxton?" Coleman said.

Rapp shook his head. "That was the right play, even if it meant missing Ashani. We don't leave our people behind. No, I'm second-guessing a decision I made a couple of years ago. Some shitheads I didn't kill but maybe should have."

Coleman nodded as if he understood.

He didn't.

When it came to killing bad guys, Rapp was both decisive and effective. His moral compass, while calibrated differently than the average person's, never pointed anywhere but Rapp's version of true north. Rapp was one of the most vicious operatives Coleman had ever worked with. Rapp had no issue climbing into the gutter with his nation's enemies if that's what it took to end a threat to his countrymen.

What made Rapp unique wasn't just his skill at waging death. It was that it didn't morally or psychologically stain him. Rapp slept soundly at night, not because he was a psychopath, but because he believed in the absolute righteousness of his cause and the undeniable depravity of those he hunted. Rapp never killed a man who didn't deserve to die any more than he allowed a threat to his nation to continue to draw breath.

Until now.

"Someone I know?" Coleman said.

"Remember the thugs who grabbed Irene?" Rapp said.

"Of course."

"I'd thought that getting rid of the Hezbollah ringleader, Mukhtar, would be enough."

"Now you don't?"

Rapp didn't answer right away, which only increased Coleman's anxiety.

Rapp was as methodical in his speech as he was in his killing. He wasn't prone to overlong deliberations or navel-gazing. Rapp intuitively understood a tactical situation the way Mozart knew music. Rapp decided on a course of action at a speed that almost seemed instanta-neous. He didn't second-guess himself or suffer a loss for words.

Ever.

"Has Irene seemed . . . different?" Rapp said.

Coleman hadn't seen this coming.

"How?"

Rapp shrugged. "Like maybe the Iranians got inside her head."

Rapp was undoubtedly referring to Irene's capture and interrogation at the hands of Iranian Quds Forces operatives and Hezbollah terrorists. Coleman's relationship with Kennedy wasn't on the same level as Rapp's, but anyone who'd been subjected to what she'd endured would certainly view life differently. She'd been beaten and humiliated by murderous an-imals who'd been a hair trigger away from raping and executing her.

Coleman could only imagine the resulting psychological scars.

"Sorry," Coleman said, shaking his head, "I'm not following."

"I smoked a bunch of Quds Force officers during Irene's capture and later killed Mukhtar. I assumed the rest of the Iranians got the mes-sage. Maybe I should have made sure."

Coming from anyone else, the observation would have sounded like a schoolyard boast. Iran's Quds Force officers were capable and experi-enced killers, and unlike the terrorists Rapp normally hunted, they had the resources of a nation-state at their disposal.

A nation-state with aspirations of joining the nuclear weapons club.

Stan Hurley had done more than his fair share of wet work while running assets in East Germany and other nations on the wrong side of the Iron Curtain, but what Rapp was musing about was more akin to decapitating the KGB than an operative-on-operative skirmish.

"Where's that leave us?" Coleman said.

The question wasn't just a prompt.

Coleman still didn't understand everything that went on in his friend's brain, but he usually had a fairly good idea of where they were headed.

Not today.

"The conventional forces aren't going to help us find the missing Iranian Quds Force officer without some major prodding," Rapp said. "I could ask Irene to go to work on the president, but by the time the order trickles down to here, the Iranian will be across the border into Pakistan. I need to get at this a different way."

"What can I do?" Coleman said.

"Act as my point man here and be ready to execute at a moment's notice."

"What about you?"

"It's time for the mountain to go to Muhammad."

CHAPTER 49

FOUR hours later, Nash was ready to reassess his previously optimistic attitude.

No, that wasn't quite right.

Nash was ready to flip the bird to the men seated on the long, cream-colored couch across from him, get back on his shiny Gulfstream, and fly home. But one did not flip the bird to the chief of the Army staff for the Pakistani Army, especially when the president of Pakistan was watching.

"The operation you conducted on our border was needlessly destabilizing."

General Davi's comment had been the culmination of an overly long soliloquy in which Pakistan's most senior member of the armed forces ran through a list of grievances both real and imagined against his American counterparts. Some of the general's complaints had merit, but many were meant to obscure his own failures.

Nash bit back the first response that leaped to mind.

The one that had *Rapp* written all over it.

Nash wasn't Rapp.

While Rapp would have undoubtedly pointed out how Pakistan's practice of allowing Taliban and HIG thugs to cross the porous Afghan border with impunity was destabilizing to the entire region, Nash did not want to the blow the summit out of the water.

Yet.

"Just so I understand," Nash said, "are you objecting to our raid's target or the manner in which it was carried out?"

Nash wore his best earnest expression as he spoke. The one he'd perfected during spats with Maggie. He loved his wife deeply, but when it came to arguing with her, Nash was at a severe disadvantage. First off, Maggie was hot, and her attractiveness increased in direct proportion to her anger. Second, she was a lawyer.

A damned good lawyer.

Which meant that when it came to verbal jousting, Nash did not often win the day. Accordingly, he'd adopted the strategy he was now employing—look earnest and try for the sympathy win.

"Both. You targeted a Pakistani citizen in Pakistani-controlled territory without our knowledge or permission. This is not how allies behave."

So apparently Nash's earnest expression worked best on Maggie.

Or maybe *only* on Maggie.

The rejoinder had come from a gentleman seated on the couch to General Davi's right. Unlike the general's tan dress uniform adorned with flashy medals and colorful ribbons, the man who had spoken wore a Western-style suit, white shirt, and conservative blue tie.

"Sorry," Nash said with a smile. "Who are you exactly?"

The room in which the meeting was taking place had a décor reminiscent of a 1970s-era funeral home. Dark wood paneling covered the walls, and the only window was obscured by beige floor-to-ceiling curtains. The room's occupants were relegated to a pair of couches facing each other across a no-man's-land dominated by an ornate rug.

Nash, his assistant Bill Thompson, and Justin Freeman, the State Department representative, sat on the American couch with the head of Nash's protective detail, Emily Welch, standing just off his right shoulder.

The Pakistani couch boasted five occupants, including General Davi.

President Saad Chutani was the exception to this arrangement. The former general and current quasi-elected leader of Pakistan occupied a plush white chair at the room's head, as if he were mediating the squabbles of unruly children.

This characterization wasn't far from the truth.

The meeting had begun amicably enough, if a bit frosty.

While the official purpose of Nash's visit was billed as American participation in the Regional Stability Conference that Pakistan was hosting, he and his Pakistani counterparts knew this was not the case. America had just executed a cross-border raid into Pakistan. A raid that had resulted in the deaths of several Americans and the destruction of a special operations Chinook helicopter. Pakistan's leadership could be persuaded to look the other way on covert American activity when the operations were successful and discreet.

The raid on the HIG compound had been neither.

Accordingly, the Pakistanis believed Nash was coming hat in hand to apologize for egregious behavior. Given the history between the two nations, this was a reasonable assumption.

It was also completely wrong.

Nash's marching orders from Irene had been twofold—deliver a message to the Pakistanis while stirring up trouble in the process. Irene theorized that the more visible Nash made his presence while in Islamabad, the more ISI resources and assets would be focused on the troublesome CIA executive, leaving fewer to hunt for the solitary NOC, or non-official cover, CIA officer clandestinely making her way to Abbottabad.

The NOC in question, Noreen Ahmed, was tasked with determining whether or not CRANKSHAFT truly resided in the Abbottabad compound, while it was Nash's job to provide her with cover in the form of diplomatic distractions coupled with an active itinerary that commanded the attention of as many ISI surveillance teams as possible. Put simply, Nash was charged with making a nuisance of himself.

He was only too happy to oblige.

Unfortunately, President Chutani hadn't assumed the role of quasi-dictator by being naïve. Nash had expected to join the already under-way conference, but he'd received an invitation to meet with the Pakistani president first. Nash had of course accepted, assuming that the face-to-face would be a chance for Chutani to quietly express his frustrations with his ally while reaffirming his commitment to America's Global War on Terror and the billions of US dollars that came along with it.

Nash had been wrong.

After agreeing to the State Department rep's belated request to ac-company him to the meeting, Nash had arrived at the Presidential Palace with his small retinue only to be shown into a receiving area.

Things were not as he'd expected.

Instead of an intimate meeting with President Chutani, Nash found himself in a room crowded with military, ISI, and political representa-tives. Without the niceties or introductions typical at the beginning of such a gathering, Nash and his comrades had been pointed toward their couch.

Then the lambasting had commenced.

Now, almost twenty minutes after the fun had begun, Nash was ready to go on the offensive, starting with the suited man who'd fol-lowed General Davi's tirade. Contrary to what he'd said, Nash was inti-mately familiar with the slight, bespectacled man who looked ready to fight. Maahir Alavi was the Pakistani equivalent of a political lobbyist except that instead of representing companies looking for congressional handouts like his US counterparts, Alavi advocated on behalf of a more select constituency.

Terrorist groups.

Terrorist groups like the HIG.

Alavi glared back at Nash. His dark eyes burned even though the lobbyist's lips were compressed into a thin, hard line. The man seemed to be vibrating with tension. Perfect. Nash decided it was high time to channel his inner Rapp.

"Oh," Nash said, slapping his knee, "my apologies. I do know you. You're the mouthpiece for that jihadi piece of trash we rolled up during our raid on the HIG compound."

The simmering pot that was the room boiled over in a chorus of angry voices. To put it mildly, Nash had struck a nerve. Now he had the opportunity to sit back and watch the fault lines as alliances frayed. Who was really running point when it came to the government's relationship with the jihadis? ISI? The military? Or did the tendrils of corruption reach all the way to the nation's highest elected office? What happened next would be a gold mine of intelligence.

"I believe this would be an opportune time for a short break," Justin said.

Or perhaps not.

Not for the first time, Nash found himself wishing he could strangle a member of the State Department.

"Yes," President Chutani said, "that would be helpful. Mr. Nash must be exhausted from his travels, and I have other things that require my attention. Let's convene again this evening prior to the state dinner."

"Thank you very much, sir," Justin said. "We look forward to continuing our conversation tonight."

Nash stood along with the rest of the room as the president rose and made for the door. The couch opposite Nash emptied as the Pakistani movers and shakers trooped out behind Chutani, leaving the Americans in the hands of a trio of aides.

Nash seethed.

"All right, then," Justin said to the remaining Pakistanis, "should we go over the itinerary for the rest of Mr. Nash's visit?"

Mike wanted nothing to do with revisiting the daily schedule that had already been the topic of three separate conversations. What he wanted to do was to pull the State Department rep into a huddle room for a little wall-to-wall counseling. The twit had sacrificed an opportunity to witness the inner workings of the Pakistani government in the name of avoiding conflict.

This was American diplomacy at its worst.

"Excuse me, Mr. Nash. Do you have a minute?"

Nash had been so busy staring daggers at his fellow American that he'd missed the approach of the diminutive Pakistani man currently standing respectfully in front of him. Though he hadn't traded his paramilitary garb for a suit that long ago, Nash was already losing his tactical edge.

Nash glanced at Emily and saw that while he might have been wool-gathering, the leader of his protective detail was still on the job. Like a sheepdog, she'd separated the man from the rest of the crowd, and while her posture was respectful, Emily was on point. Her green eyes locked on Nash as she waited for an indication of how he wanted to play this. Nash acknowledged her unasked question with a short nod and then turned to the aide.

"Forgive my ignorance," Nash said. "I don't know your name."

This time, Nash wasn't faking.

He didn't know the man's identity or his position within the government, and the Pakistani's appearance didn't provide any obvious clues. Unlike the military generals who had flanked the president, he wasn't wearing a uniform, nor did his physique or posture suggest a martial influence. His Western-style suit was appropriate for the occasion but neither the cut nor material suggested that it had been hand-made on Savile Row like those of his contemporaries. Nash had about six inches and fifty pounds on him, but the Pakistani's trim build suggested an active lifestyle. He had a clean-shaven, earnest face that was pleasant but forgettable.

"That is not surprising," the man said with a smile. "I make it a practice not to be known. My name is Bilal Dogar and I work for the ISI."

This time Nash kept his expression blank for a different reason.

Agency analysts prided themselves on their knowledge of the Pakistani intelligence service, especially its personnel. If the man standing in front of him was telling the truth, Nash had just made the acquaintance of someone important enough to attend a meeting between his president and a CIA deputy director, but with a profile that had afforded him the ability to escape the CIA's notice.

Interesting.

"Pleased to meet you," Nash said. "How can I help?"

"Perhaps we could talk somewhere a bit more private?" Dogar said, lowering his voice.

"Can you tell me the topic of our conversation?" Nash said.

"The Iranians."

CHAPTER 50

N ASH stared at Dogar, waiting for the punch line.

It didn't come.

Instead, the intelligence officer stared back at him expectantly.

Admittedly, this was Nash's first overseas trip in which he was openly representing the CIA's interests instead of clandestinely working to further them, so he was a bit green when it came to diplomatic engagements.

Even so, Nash didn't think this was a common occurrence.

"Okay," Nash said, "where do you want to talk?"

"If you'll come with me," Dogar said, this time loud enough for his voice to carry, "I'd be happy to show you the exhibit."

Nash got it.

"Emily, I'm gonna take a walk with Mr. Dogar," Nash said. "We'll be back in ten."

"I'll go with you, sir," Emily said. "Jason can keep an eye on things here."

Nash suppressed a smile.

While his announcement to Emily was more to set the stage for the rest of the room's occupants, the head of his protective detail had done a little communicating of her own. Secret Squirrel stuff was all well and good, but she wasn't letting Nash out of her sight.

Fair enough.

"This way, sir," Dogar said.

If the ISI operative was upset about Emily tagging along, he didn't show it. Then again, if the man was truly an intelligence professional, he understood how the game was played.

"President Chutani is an unabashed patron of the arts," Dogar said, playing the role of tour guide as they walked. "One of his first acts after assuming office was to turn one of the palace front rooms into a rotating exhibition of Pakistani artisans. The current display features a collection of contemporary artists."

"Like Ahmed Parvez?" Nash said.

Dogar gave Nash an appraising look. "Yes. Mr. Parvez is one of the artists featured in the exhibit. You know of him?"

"A little. My wife loves him. She purchased one of his paintings for our home."

"Then she has excellent taste. Did you know he lived in America for a time?"

Nash did not.

What he did know was that they had left the receiving room and were now proceeding deeper into the palace. Unlike its equivalent in the White House, space here was not at a premium.

"Several Iranian officials are in Islamabad," Dogar said, catching his voice lower.

"Why?" Nash said.

Though there was a significant Shia population in Pakistan, the nation was a Sunni-majority state. As to the religious fault lines that divided the Middle East, Pakistan more often leaned toward the Sunni leadership of Saudi Arabia than the Shia theocracy of Iran. But with everything involving Pakistan, alliances were both complicated and often in flux. In truth, Pakistan played competing interests against each other, happy to take funds and money from both sides while refusing to commit wholeheartedly to anyone. In this regard, Pakistan's treatment of their Middle East allies wasn't all that different than the game it played with the United States.

Nash supposed he should give the Pakistanis credit for consistency.

"That is not important," Dogar said. "What *is* important is that I've been asked to serve as their intermediary. One of them would like to meet with you."

"When?" Nash said.

Dogar turned a corner into a room lit with soft, natural lighting. The walls were lined with paintings. While the subtlety of art was lost on Nash, even he found the exhibit impressive.

"This is one of Mr. Parvez's most important works," Dogar said, again speaking loud enough to ensure his voice carried. "If you look closely, you can see his masterful use of color."

Nash bent to examine the painting.

As he did so, Dogar's hand touched his pocket.

The brush pass was expertly done.

Had Nash's peripheral vision not caught the blur of motion from the Pakistani's hand, he didn't think he would have sensed it. Even now, he couldn't feel anything in his front pocket, but he had no doubt that something was there.

"We consider this piece to be one of our national treasures," Dogar said. "I hope you found this detour of sorts worthwhile."

Nash straightened from his examination and shoved both hands deep into his front pockets. His left hand encountered nothing but a stray ball of lint. His right touched something else.

A piece of paper.

"Spending time with fellow art enthusiasts is always worthwhile," Nash said with a smile. "Thank you for sharing your knowledge."

"Of course," Dogar said. "Now, if you'll follow me, I'll reunite you with your delegation.

The small man continued his tutorial on Pakistani artists as they retraced their steps, but Nash's thoughts were focused on something else.

Iranians.

CHAPTER 51

DARIAN Moradi took a deep breath of mountain air.

Though the Islamabad skyline jutting through the fog was only a few kilometers away, the reaching green canopies of countless oak trees surrounding the Daman-e-Koh viewing area made the urban sprawl seem impossibly distant. Here, amid the beauty of Allah's creation, Moradi could for a moment pretend his problems were as distant as the partially obscured skyscrapers.

"You are a hard man to find."

Moradi stifled a gasp, but only just barely. He might be the deputy minister of the MOIS, but he wasn't a spy.

Not really.

Moradi had been awarded the post because he was a protégé of one of the Guardian Council's influential mullahs and a fellow cleric. While he knew little of running agents or scratching chalk marks on abandoned buildings in the middle of the night, he understood political intrigue and had been navigating its treacherous currents since he'd first come to the notice of his mentor years ago.

Those same dangers were what had driven him to seek solace in this picturesque hilltop garden. He'd had decisions to make and wanted to think through them away from the prying eyes of his fellow countrymen who were also guests at the Regional Stability Conference.

Evidently, he hadn't succeeded.

"I didn't realize you were looking," Moradi said, turning away from the beautiful vista to the man standing next to him.

Daman-e-Koh was a corruption of two Persian words that roughly translated to *foothills*. The magical slice of greenery more than lived up to its name. Part of a series of hilltop gardens, the Daman-e-Koh overlook consisted of a pair of tiered semicircular concrete and stone viewing platforms separated by two sets of stairs. Since the upper platform was connected to the rest of the park's trails and therefore much more heavily trafficked, Moradi had chosen the more isolated lower tier for his moment of personal reflection.

Unfortunately, it hadn't been isolated enough.

Moradi now shared the iron railing that protected the unwary from a tumble down a five-hundred-foot cliff face with Dariush Ruyintan. As always, Ruyintan was impeccably dressed. Rather than the crisply starched, deep green military uniform he favored while in Tehran, Ruyintan wore an expensive yet conservative Western-style suit with a dress shirt open at the collar. Moradi was again struck by the Quds Force officer's charisma. Ruyintan had the looks and force of personality to be a politician with the exception of his unblinking eyes.

They were the eyes of a killer.

"That is the nature of our business, is it not?" Ruyintan said. "To always look even though we rarely find?"

Moradi understood the subtext at play but chose to ignore it. Verbal jousting with Ruyintan made Moradi feel like a fish out of water.

No, that wasn't quite right.

More like a bait fish dangled in front of a barracuda.

"I wanted to be alone with my thoughts," Moradi said. "What about you?"

Moradi knew he was not physically imposing. Nor did he possess martial skills that made up for his slight stature. Unlike the wolf clothed in sheepskin standing next to him, Moradi had not achieved his station because of battlefield prowess. Even so, he possessed two attributes that made him a formidable adversary—brains and proximity to power.

Surviving this encounter would require both.

"We are ambitious men," Ruyintan said. "Sometimes ambitious men make mistakes."

A movement to Moradi's left punctuated Ruyintan's statement.

Turning, Moradi saw Ruyintan's ever-present security detail. Two members of the protective detail had taken positions on the upper dais, while the remaining pair were posted behind their principal at the foot of each stairwell. Unless he decided to take his chances with the oak trees, Moradi wasn't going anywhere.

"Speak plainly," Moradi said. "It's late, and I'm jet-lagged."

Ruyintan chuckled, a dry rasping sound entirely free of mirth. "For a cleric, you are refreshingly straightforward. I will endeavor to be the same. Earlier today, I received a call from one of my operatives in Afghanistan. He was attending an auction."

"An auction for what?"

"A captured American soldier."

Moradi studied the operative's face, looking for a sign that Ruyintan was joking.

He found none.

"Are you mad?" Moradi said.

"The American wasn't just any soldier. The man was a Ranger— a member of their special operations contingent."

"And you thought this was a good idea?"

Ruyintan scowled. "My men are taught to exercise initiative, as are yours. In any case, the wisdom of his decision is not important."

Moradi would have begged to differ, but he held his tongue.

Ruyintan was still talking.

"What is important is the man my operative found with the captive in the cave. A man the Iraqis call *Malikul Mawt*. Do you know of him?"

Moradi did know of him, but not for the reason Ruyintan might suppose. The *Angel of Death* was the nom de guerre given to the CIA operative Mitch Rapp. The same operative who Ashani had convinced Moradi was their sole chance of avoiding war with the Americans. Moradi had bet his life on the intelligence officer's plan.

Now the stakes were coming into focus.

"Of course I know of him," Moradi said.

"Have you ever met Rapp?"

On its surface, the question sounded innocent enough, but Moradi thought he detected an undertone in Ruyintan's voice. A dangerous one.

"Until two months ago, I was an aide to a member of the Guardian Council. I've been a cleric my entire adult life. On what occasion would I have met this Mitch Rapp?"

"*Yes* or *no* will suffice."

This time, the danger was front and center in Ruyintan's icy reply.

Moradi's stomach knotted, and he could feel sweat beginning to gather at the nape of his neck. It occurred to him that while his position in the MOIS and his friendliness with his old boss were protection of sorts, that protection only extended so far. While he'd seen several fellow hikers during his trek to the lookout, Moradi couldn't help but notice that the two tiers were now conspicuously absent of bystanders.

Islamabad was a major city with major city problems. Crime was low, but not nonexistent. Tourists who were foolish enough to wander the sprawling nature preserve alone were responsible for what befell them. The park was full of wild animals like the leopards that lived in the surrounding hills.

There were also dangerous beasts that walked about on two legs rather than four.

"No," Moradi said, infusing his reply with outrage. "Why do you ask?"

"Because you steered me toward him."

Moradi furrowed his brow as he furiously thought. He was prepared for Ruyintan to make this connection eventually, but his realization was supposed to have occurred *after* the Americans had disrupted the Quds Force plot in Afghanistan. But Rapp had missed his rendezvous with Ashani. Moradi had attempted to smooth out this wrinkle by sending word to Mike Nash that he wanted to talk. Ironically, Moradi had come to this secluded space to collect his thoughts ahead of his scheduled meeting with the CIA officer.

Now Ruyintan would be part of those deliberations.

"I have no idea what you're talking about," Moradi said.

"Farid Saeed. Why did you suggest that I meet with him?"

"For the exact reasons I told you. His organization is a gateway to the Sunni militias in Iraq. Getting him on board with our operation would allow us to duplicate your Afghanistan success in Iraq."

"But why Saeed specifically?"

Ruyintan's question was no louder than a whisper, but Moradi nearly flinched at the vehemence behind the words.

This was it.

The moment of truth.

"As you say, I'm a cleric," Moradi said with a shrug. "I'm still learning the operational details of my job. Like you, I'm second-in-command of a substantial organization. Also like you, I have aspirations beyond my current role. Ashani mentioned Saeed's potential utility in passing. I decided to act on his idea."

"So you gave me the dossier without Ashani's knowledge?"

Moradi nodded.

Ruyintan laughed again. The merriment did not reach his eyes.

"You might be a fine cleric, but you have much to learn about the profession of espionage."

"What do you mean?" Moradi said. Moradi raised his voice as he spoke, hoping to use anger to disguise his fear.

"Ashani played you. The man you sent me to meet is no Sunni financier. In fact, he's not even Arab."

"Then who is he?"

"An American. An American by the name of Mitch Rapp."

CHAPTER 52

MORADI stared at Ruyintan with an expression of shock. He allowed his mouth to slowly open even as he silently counted the passing seconds. When his internal clock reached five, he closed his lips, swallowed twice, and cleared his throat. It was a performance he'd rehearsed numerous times in front of his hotel mirror.

Hopefully, his practice had just paid off.

"What?" Moradi croaked.

"Either you have the worst luck of any intelligence officer who's ever lived, or your superior used you as a cutout to funnel information to me. Information that might have gotten me killed."

"I . . . I didn't know."

Moradi endured the Quds Force officer's stare for what seemed like an eternity.

Then, Ruyintan slowly nodded.

"You weren't the only one taken in by Ashani's duplicity. I accepted the Saeed dossier and his whereabouts on face value and saw what I expected to see. Had I run the information past my own intelligence analysts, they would have no doubt made the connection to Rapp."

Moradi did not need to be convinced that this was true. Ashani had voiced this exact pitfall. While still a clandestine operative of sorts, Mitch Rapp was well-known to his enemies. Any competent intelligence organization would possess the counterterrorism operative's likeness on file.

But they still had to look for the information.

Despite the risks, Moradi had agreed to implement Ashani's plan. Using Ruyintan to unwittingly convey a message to Rapp from Ashani was an elegant solution to their current problem and would protect Moradi with two layers of deniability. One, it had been Ashani, not Moradi, who had come up with the idea of using Farid Saeed to gain access to the Iraqi militias. Two, it had been Ruyintan, not Moradi, who had been face-to-face with America's most deadly assassin and not known it.

"Where is Rapp now?" Moradi said.

"That is an excellent question. We know he landed in Kabul under the same French legend he was using when I met with him in Islamabad, but his trail goes cold once he leaves the airport."

"Did Rapp meet with Ashani?"

"That is an even better question. One I would like your help answering."

Tendrils of dread snaked through Moradi's gut.

A hawk screeched as it wheeled overhead. The raptor's wingtips made minute adjustments in response to the rising thermals as the bird's head jerked from side to side, scanning for prey. The hawk's appearance felt like an omen, but Moradi wasn't sure if he was the predator or the prey.

Time to find out.

"How can I assisst you?" Moradi said.

"As we speak, Ashani is on his way to Islamabad at my request. If for some reason he develops second thoughts about meeting with me, I would like you to let me know."

"Of course," Moradi said. "He is a traitor to the revolution."

"Just so, and he will die for his betrayal. Now, I'll leave you to your thoughts."

Ruyintan turned and walked away without waiting for a reply.

That was just as well.

Moradi was too terrified to speak.

CHAPTER 53

MORADI waited until the last footfall from Ruyintan and his entourage faded.

Then he waited some more.

This time, Moradi's delay wasn't because he needed additional time to think. To the contrary, he'd had more than enough time to dwell upon what had just transpired. Moradi remained at the railing because he wanted to ensure he didn't run into the Quds Force thugs on the trek down to his car. As he'd truthfully told Ruyintan, Moradi was no intelligence officer. His acting had taxed his meager abilities to their limits. Moradi needed time to regroup before braving another interaction with Ruyintan.

Or Ashani.

With a shudder Moradi considered how quickly their scheme was unraveling. Even now, Afghan Shia militiamen armed with the Iranian-modified shoulder-fired missiles and their Quds Force handlers were moving into preplanned staging areas. Far from using Mitch Rapp to interdict Ruyintan's operation before the attacks could be launched, Ashani had only muddied the water. Thanks to him, the Americans knew that the Iranians were at least aware of the Afghan operation while Ruyintan had deduced that there was a traitor in the Iranian ranks.

Moradi wasn't sure how things could get any worse.

Then he heard footfalls.

The gait and cadence of the footsteps suggested that they belonged to a single person. Moradi took this as a hopeful sign even as he reached into the folds of his clerical robes. Had Ruyintan meant him harm, the Quds Force officer would have acted while in the company of his protective detail. The bodyguards were fellow Quds Force operatives and therefore no stranger to murder.

This was something different.

Moradi's fingers closed around the grip of a pistol holstered against his chest.

Billed by the manufacturer as a "Baby Glock," the miniature pistol was easy to conceal and required very little skill to employ at close distances. In other words, the Glock 26 was the perfect weapon for a man like Moradi. With a deep breath to fortify himself, Moradi turned to confront the newcomer.

Death stared back at him.

Moradi's stomach fluttered, and his heart accelerated as cold sweat popped out of his pores. This was not unlike the time he'd stumbled across a spider-tailed viper while hiking as a youth. The shocking realization that what he'd thought was a benign spider was actually a lethal serpent. On that day, the venomous reptile had been sluggish due to the cold and its strike had been halfhearted and ineffective.

There was nothing sluggish about the man standing next to him.

Moradi tried to speak, but his suddenly dry mouth meant that he had to swallow first. That might have been just as well. His obvious startlement was embarrassing, but it gave Moradi a moment to survey his adversary.

"Surprised to see me?" Rapp said.

Meeting the American in person was jarring. Perhaps the equivalent of coming face-to-face with a tiger after only seeing one in pictures. Rapp's presence provoked a visceral fight-or-flight response, and Moradi struggled to keep his hands from shaking.

"Why are you here?" Moradi said.

"As opposed to chasing your countrymen across Afghanistan?" Rapp said.

Moradi stiffened as he realized that where they were having the conversation was just as dangerous as the topic the two men were discussing. Rapp wasn't Moradi's only source of peril. If the wrong person saw him talking with an American intelligence officer, Moradi's interrogation would likely begin with torture and end with a bullet to the back of his skull.

"What do you want?" Moradi said.

"Details," Rapp said. "What are your Quds Force friends planning and where are they now?"

Moradi was at the edge of a precipice.

He was not a traitor, but neither was he suicidal.

Contrary to what Ruyintan might believe, Moradi agreed with Ashani's assessment that the American president did have red lines. Red lines that he would enforce. If the Quds Force officer succeeded, Alexander would respond to Iran's provocation with overwhelming military force. Using airpower alone, the Americans had the ability to send the Iranian navy to the bottom of the Persian Gulf, destroy what remained of the Iranian air force, and turn Iran's oil refineries into smoking piles of charred metal. To be sure there was no misunderstanding, the same fleet of attack aircraft and strategic bombers could also declare open season on Quds Force or MOIS officers operating in Syria and Iraq via pinpoint strikes on known Iranian compounds.

Then it would be a simple matter to let nature run its course.

Between Saudi Arabia, Yemen, and the United Arab Emirates, there was no shortage of Sunni powers tired of being antagonized by proxies funded by their troublesome Shia neighbor. Without its military might or the ability to generate cash through the sale of oil, Iran would be nothing more than a nation surrounded by enemies, with a stagnant economy and a civilian population roiled by unrest.

The Islamic Republic would not survive such a scenario.

But what choice did Moradi have?

The answer came in a flash.

He could delay.

Delay by giving Rapp enough to get the American out of his hair while buying himself time to consult with Ashani. Perhaps the MOIS operative had already developed a fallback plan to address his failure to meet with Rapp in Kabul. Or perhaps Ruyintan would get to the MOIS officer first. If that happened, Moradi had no doubt that Ashani would eventually confess.

To everything.

Quds Force interrogators were nothing if not persuasive. Either way, Ruyintan would realize that, thanks to Ashani's leak to the Americans, his plan would no longer be tenable. The Quds Force officer would then be forced to call off the Afghanistan operation. While there was a chance Ashani would implicate him as well, Moradi was willing to run that risk. He'd already planted the seeds of Ashani's duplicity with Ruyintan by fingering the MOIS officer as the source of the Saeed dossier. Now he just needed time for those seeds to bear fruit.

Delaying was Moradi's only hope.

"I can't tell you that," Moradi said, shaking his head, "because I don't know myself. It's a Quds Force, not MOIS, operation. But I'll keep digging. This is the best I can do."

Rapp stared back at him.

The American's black orbs seemed to be looking past Moradi's flesh into the darkest parts of his soul. Moradi tightened his grip on the Glock. He was no marksman, but it would be a simple matter to rotate the pistol and fire through his robes into Rapp's chest.

Moradi's finger tightened on the trigger.

The American slowly nodded.

"Okay," Rapp said. "I know you're in a tough spot. Even though we're never going to see eye to eye, I respect you as a fellow professional."

In a turn of events Moradi would have never seen coming, Rapp offered a handshake.

Moradi reflexively accepted.

Like the viper of Moradi's youth, Rapp struck. But unlike that hapless snake, Rapp didn't miss. The American snared Moradi's wrist while body-checking him into the railing. The steel bit into Moradi's rib cage, driving the air from his lungs while pinning his other arm against his chest.

That was the least of his worries.

Rapp used his newfound leverage to torque Moradi's wrist. He couldn't quite see what the American had done, but he could feel it.

Oh, how he could feel it.

"Release the pistol or I will snap your fucking wrist like kindling," Rapp said.

Moradi complied.

"Now grab the railing with your free hand."

The pressure grinding him into the railing eased slightly, but the agony from his snared wrist doubled as bones shifted and tendons strained.

"Okay," Moradi hissed. "Okay."

He worked his hand free from the folds of his robes and dutifully grabbed the cool steel. With movements too quick to follow, Rapp relieved him of the concealed Glock. Then, as if he were caught in a python's tightening coils, Moradi felt the crushing pressure against his midsection return as the American smashed him into the railing.

"Listen to me, you ungrateful little pissant," Rapp said, his voice barely louder than a whisper. "I already don't think much of Iranians. Your Quds Force thugs snatched one of my closest friends and beat the shit out of her."

Rapp's words seemed to be coming from far away. As if the pain radiating up Moradi's arm had fogged his brain. The American's voice was the faintest of lights flashing a warning atop dark waves of agony.

What friend of Rapp's had been snatched by the Quds Force?

Then Moradi knew.

"I had nothing to do with Director Kennedy's kidnapping," Moradi said, fighting to keep the terror from his voice. "Nothing!"

"Which is why you're still breathing," Rapp said, "but lately I've been second-guessing that decision. Know what a doctor does when he finds cancer? He cuts out the tumor *and* some of the surrounding tissue, just to be safe. You might not be the cancer, but you're damn sure surrounding tissue."

Somehow Rapp's whisper was more terrifying than a scream.

"I want to help," Moradi said, hissing the words through clenched teeth.

"You bet your ass you do," Rapp said. "When I punch someone's ticket, it's clean and professional. Just like the way I did that Hezbollah shitbag who kidnapped Director Kennedy. But if your MOIS or Quds Force comrades think you're a traitor, your death won't be nearly so clean. How long do you think someone like you would last in Evin Prison?"

Rapp cranked Moradi's wrist, and a white-hot poker stabbed him in the forearm.

He thought he'd known pain before.

He hadn't.

Moradi stifled the urge to vomit as he stumbled out a question. "What do you want to know? What? WHAT?"

"Everything," Rapp said. "Start talking."

Moradi did.

CHAPTER 54

"Yes?"

"Irene, it's me."

Rapp did the time conversion in his head as he waited for his boss to respond. He and Irene complemented each other well. While not prone to going off half-cocked, Rapp also wasn't one to dither. In his experience, the simplest solution was almost always the correct one. Operatives who spent too long analyzing the third- and fourth-order effects of their actions tended to fall into one of two camps.

Ineffective or dead.

"Where are you calling from?"

On the other hand, there were times when deep thinking was necessary. When strategy rather than just tactics should be consulted. If this were a football team, Rapp would consider himself the quarterback and Kennedy the coach. While he was perfectly comfortable calling the plays 99 percent of the time, sometimes it made sense to talk with someone who had a bird's-eye view of the field.

This was one of those times.

"That's complicated," Rapp said. "I need to run some things by you, but I'm not in a position to place the call from the office."

In this context, the words *the office* referred to the US embassy in Islamabad. Deep within the bowels of this building lay a space guarded by multiple cypher locks and insulated from prying eyes and ears both human and otherwise. The CIA annex held the secure voice and video communications that would have allowed Rapp to connect with Kennedy in a much more mundane manner.

Rapp was not in the embassy.

After leaving Moradi, he had made his way back to his car as quickly as possible without running and thereby attracting attention. He'd thought about calling Irene from the garden's parking lot but hadn't. His time-sensitive information would be useless if he was sitting in a jail cell and thereby unable to relay it. While he didn't think Moradi would go to the Pakistani authorities, it was better to be safe than sorry, which meant he needed to put distance between himself and the scene of their rather forceful conversation.

With this in mind, Rapp had driven along the road that wound through the park at precisely the posted speed limit. After reaching the entrance, he had motored southeast down Seventh Avenue past leafy jogging trails and two colleges before reaching the intersection of busy Jinnah Avenue. From here Rapp had proceeded west for several blocks before pulling into the parking lot of a combination Kentucky Fried Chicken and gas station. Nosing the car into a slot that offered excellent sight lines in all directions, Rapp shut off the engine and paused to think.

As anyone with passing familiarity with the world of espionage knew, embassies came with embassy watchers—employees of foreign intelligence services who documented the comings and goings of everyone who entered the island of US soil. Like every case officer worth his or her salt, Rapp had snuck into an embassy before. These entrances ran the gamut from high-tech solutions like disguises meant to defeat the biometric devices employed by watchers to the decidedly low-tech stow-away-in-a-car-trunk solution.

Neither option was appropriate today.

Rapp had come into Pakistan dark. With Mike Nash already serving as the diplomatic pincushion designed to draw attention away from the NOC, Rapp hadn't wanted to upset the applecart. Though Nash now stood higher than Rapp in the government service rank system, this would mean little to the Pakistanis. If Rapp dropped into the country under his true name, he would immediately upstage Nash's efforts. This would be counterproductive to Irene's strategy and hamstring Rapp's ability to clandestinely meet Ashani.

True-name travel was out.

Plan B would have normally been to slide into Pakistan using one of his many carefully cultivated legends, but this wouldn't work either. Though he still didn't understand exactly what the Iranians were up to, Rapp knew enough to intuit that his need to speak with Ashani was time-sensitive. This precluded the normal method of changing legends, which would have involved a flight from Afghanistan to a neutral country, a liaison with local CIA officers to facilitate a document and possible appearance change, followed by another series of flights that bounced around the region before terminating in Islamabad.

This left plan C.

Plan C was what Irene would have probably termed *risky*, while Rapp's mentor and former Cold War legend Stan Hurley would have labeled it *getting shit done*. Even though Pakistan was a country that enforced its borders, there were ways to get into town unnoticed.

Or at least overlooked.

Ever since a 2005 earthquake had rocked the Pakistani territory of Kashmir, relief efforts had flowed by air from Bagram to the stricken towns. This arrangement originally came into being because the former Soviet Air Force base was already the American logistical hub for Afghanistan. It had proven to be a simple matter to load Chinooks with much-needed food, water, and medical supplies and fly the aircraft into the devastated areas. Now, six years later, the flights continued, though responsibility had shifted from the military to various nongovernmental organizations, or NGOs.

Whether or not the aid was still needed was a logical question, but in Afghanistan, logical questions often went unanswered. Like the war effort itself, the earthquake relief effort was functioning on autopilot. As a taxpayer, Rapp was as disgusted by this waste as he was with the rudderless wartime strategy. A strategy that burned through funds at a frightening rate with little to show for the investment. But as a clandestine operative, Rapp was only too happy to hop on a relief flight and head east.

As was usually the case in austere parts of the world where money flowed and bad actors flourished, the CIA had brokered an "agreement" with one of the NGOs chartered with moving the unending supply of American largesse into Pakistan. This agreement was as simple as it was profitable. Occasionally, an extra worker would be added to the flight manifest. Once the helicopter landed, said worker exited the aircraft and melted into the countryside with no one the wiser. After boarding the Chinook, Rapp had recognized one of the pilots and negotiated a slight detour in the helicopter's return flight.

A detour to Islamabad.

The helicopter had set down in an abandoned field, and Rapp clandestinely entered Pakistan. Existing as a ghost had its own operational difficulties, chief among them communication. Fortunately, after hiking to a small village, Rapp was able hail a cab that deposited him in the city proper. From there it had been a simple matter to procure a burner phone and one of the CIA's prestaged vehicles.

Unlike many of his Agency counterparts, Rapp did not believe in secure communications. Though he didn't pretend to understand how modern cryptology worked well enough to critique its performance from a scientific aspect, Rapp knew history was littered with battles lost and wars forfeited because one side or the other found out the hard way that their "secure" codes weren't so unbreakable. As such, Rapp treated every electronic communication as if it were already compromised.

"Okay," Kennedy said, drawing out the word. "How do you want to do this?"

Though he was calling on an unsecure line, Rapp had taken several precautions, the first being the phone itself. Unless the ISI had seeded every disposable phone in Islamabad with malware, it was reasonable to assume that Rapp's handset wasn't compromised.

The second precaution came via the telephone line Rapp had dialed, or rather the one he hadn't. Though the connection had ultimately been routed to Kennedy's desk, Rapp had dialed a throwaway number. In a nod to the old "one-time pads" that had been used during the Cold War to encrypt written messages with a single-use and therefore theoretically unbreakable code, the Agency's Science and Technology Department had implemented a number of phone numbers that were tied to single-use VPNs.

These VPNs fed into secure VoIP channels, which in turn were routed to the red phone at Irene's desk. Rapp felt confident communicating to Kennedy in broad terms, but the information he had to deliver required more detail than he felt comfortable trusting to the wizardry of ones and zeroes.

"I've got some grunt work to do," Rapp said. "Send me one of the interns from accounting."

Rapp's response was code for a crash meeting request. While Rapp had no intentions of going to the embassy, the embassy could come to him in the form of one of the in-country case officers. The man or woman wouldn't have time to run a full SDR, or surveillance detection route, but the risk was worth the reward. The information he'd extracted from Moradi was time-sensitive, meaning that Rapp couldn't afford to entrust it to a dead drop.

He needed to talk to a human being.

Now.

"I'll send an intern," Kennedy said, "but I'm going to need you to work something else after you debrief them."

Rapp suppressed a flash of irritation. Kennedy knew better than to superced his on-the-ground decisions. "Look, I'm kind of busy and—"

"It's about CRANKSHAFT," Kennedy said.

CHAPTER 55

"CAPTAIN Garner, do you have a minute?" Scott Coleman said.

The Ranger Company commander looked up from where he'd been stenciling red grease pencil marks on the clear acetate overlaying a set of military maps covering the far wall of the TOC. Much to Scott Coleman's satisfaction, someone still preferred good old-fashioned paper and pens to computer wizardry. This was not to imply that Coleman didn't appreciate technology.

He did.

He also had seen it fail firsthand, usually in a spectacular fashion at the exact moment it was most needed. Handheld digital tablets that showcased a networked common operating picture might be all the rage, but a paper map never ran out of battery power or glitched in the middle of a firefight.

"For you? Of course. I heard you were the one who pulled Sergeant Saxton out of the water."

"Guilty," Coleman said with a smile. "How'd you know?"

"Saxton tried to turn in his Ranger tab. Said he couldn't handle the shame of being saved by a SEAL."

Coleman laughed as Garner held out his hand. "All bullshit aside, thank you for saving my Ranger. I owe you one."

"I don't know about the saving part," Coleman said, accepting Garner's handshake. "Your boy was doing pretty good on his own. I just pointed him in the right direction."

"Bullshit," Garner said after pausing to spit a stream of brown liquid into a paper coffee cup. "Sergeant Saxton is the kind of Ranger you want at your back when bullets are flying, but I've seen rocks that could swim better. When we get back to the States, I'm sending his ass to SCUBA school."

Coleman chuckled.

The interservice rivalry between SEALs and Rangers was more hype than reality, but working with someone from another service was always dicey. As a SEAL, Coleman instinctively knew what he was getting when someone with a Trident walked into the room. It wasn't that he thought SEALs were superhuman as much as he understood a frogman's strengths and weaknesses because he was one. Working with Rangers could be the equivalent of suiting up with a new football team for the first time. They might be capable athletes, but Coleman needed to ensure that he and his unfamiliar teammates were all operating from the same playbook, preferably before they took the field. That said, Garner had a sense of humor and none of the bravado that sometimes infected members of this unique community, especially when they had to swallow their pride and acknowledge the contributions of operators outside their chosen branch. Coleman thought he could work with Garner.

Hopefully, the feeling was mutual.

"Dive school requires equal parts ability and grit," Coleman said. "One of those characteristics can be taught. The other can't. You're either born with grit or you aren't. Based on what I saw, Saxton has no issues in that department."

"That's a fact," Garner said. "Now I've just got to get my Ranger to the YMCA for swimming lessons. Okay, Mr. Coleman, I don't think you're here to shoot the shit. What can I do you for?"

"It's Scott," Coleman said with a smile. "How serious were you about owing me one?"

"Should have seen that coming," Garner said. "What can I do for the fine men and women of the Central Intelligence Agency?"

Coleman paused to gather his thoughts.

Though he'd been expecting to hear from Rapp, the call had come from Irene instead. With the no-nonsense manner for which she was known, Kennedy had relayed what Rapp had learned from Moradi. Unfortunately, it wasn't much. Moradi knew where the Iranians were crossing with their HIG militia members into Afghanistan, but he didn't know the group's targets.

Hopefully, that would be enough.

"I need some muscle," Coleman said. "Bad guys are coming across the Pakistani border with bad attitudes and bad intentions. I need help showing them the error of their ways."

Garner frowned before answering. "I'm all about bringing the wrath of God down on deserving souls, but why don't you just put warheads on their foreheads and call it a day?"

"Excellent question," Coleman said. "This is a mixed group of shitbags. Most of them are your garden-variety HIG operatives trained in Iran, but a couple are Quds Force officers. I need at least one of the Iranians alive."

"For questioning?"

"*Questioning* is too gentle a term for what I have in mind," Coleman said, his smile evaporating. "I plan to interrogate the shit out of them. They're carrying time-sensitive information about an imminent attack against American interests using Iranian modified surface-to-air missiles, and they may not be the only group of fighters entering Afghanistan. If I don't get answers, people will die."

Garner spat another brown stream into his cup before speaking. "Don't take this the wrong way, Scott, but are you sure my men are the ones for this job? If you need a compound leveled, we're your guys, but Rangers are more baseball bat than scalpel. Maybe you want to talk to the special mission folks?"

If Coleman had had any remaining doubts about Garner, they vanished. Possessing the mental and physical toughness needed to survive the legendary special operations pipeline was rare.

Knowing when your particular set of skills wasn't up for the task was rarer still.

"I appreciate the honesty," Coleman said, "but a baseball bat is exactly what I'm looking for. I've got a crew of hitters who can take care of securing the high-value targets. I need a blocking force to keep them in place and a QRF standing by in case things go sideways."

"Blocking force," Garner said. "I don't know that I've ever heard a SEAL use a doctrinally correct term. Maybe the End Days really are upon us. Give me the details on your target convoy."

"We're looking for three vehicles coming through the Torkham border crossing," Coleman said, ignoring the Ranger's dig. Sometimes, the truth hurt.

"Shit," Garner said, frowning as he traced the route from Pakistan on the map. "You know that's the most highly trafficked border checkpoint in the country, right? Most of what comes into Afghanistan by ground uses that crossing. Do you know where they're headed? It would be easier to interdict them farther west once the traffic thins."

"No," Coleman said, "and there's more bad news. We also need to find the convoy."

"Seriously?" Garner said. "Usually, hits come to us with the full package—Preds overhead and signals intelligence-driven geolocation from phones or radios courtesy of the NSA. All we worry about is kicking ass and taking names."

"Not today," Coleman said. "No SIGINT and no Preds on station. The ISR bird had a malfunction and returned to base. The replacement is en route, but it's still an hour or more out. Our intel says the convoy's already moving. We can't wait for ISR coverage."

"You're supposed to hit a time-sensitive target that you can't find, and you have zero ISR assets to help with the search," Garner said. "Did I miss anything?"

"That's about the size of it," Coleman said, his heart sinking.

"Then you need more than a blocking force. Someone's got to do a zone reconnaissance to find your convoy."

"Your boys?" Coleman said.

Garner shook his head as he studied the map. "I can't cover an area that large. To be safe, the recon would need to begin ten or fifteen kilometers on the western side of the border and work east toward Pakistan. That's a mission for the cavalry."

"Cavalry?" Coleman said. "Like cowboys and Indians?"

"Forget what I said about you being an enlightened SEAL," Garner said. "Yes, like cowboys and Indians, except the cavalry I'm thinking about uses helicopters instead of horses."

"Helicopters?" Coleman said.

"Apache gunships to be exact," Garner said.

"And you can task them?" Coleman said.

Garner laughed. "Not a chance. The flyboys don't work for me, but I know the troop commander. I can put in a good word, but the mission request has to come from you."

"Do I need to fill out paperwork?" Coleman said.

"Nah," Garner said. "Gunship pilots love to do two things and one of them is flying. Unfortunately, they're in the middle of doing the other thing right now."

"I'm afraid to ask," Coleman said.

Garner laughed again. "It's better if you take a gander yourself. Two-Six Cavalry is set up on the non-SOF side of the compound. Turn right once you leave my TOC and follow the smell."

"The smell of what?"

"Steak."

CHAPTER 56

As a SEAL, Coleman was certainly familiar with Army flyboys, but his experience had been almost exclusively with the 160th Night Stalkers, not general aviation. As such, he wasn't sure what he would find as he followed the mouthwatering scent of grilling meat out the gates that delineated SOF country toward the section of airfield that housed the general aviation units.

Like all kids of the eighties, he'd grown up watching the movies his parents would have never approved of on cable long after they'd gone to bed. One of these cinematic masterpieces had kept him from swimming in the ocean for far too many years, while another had given him a healthy fear of both evil spirits and the priests who exorcised them. Still others had simply been too much for his young mind to comprehend. This category included a flick about Vietnam that touched his warrior soul even though he had little understanding of the film's dark theme. The one thing he did remember were the cowboy hats.

Black Stetsons to be exact.

Coleman found himself awash in a sea of black Stetsons as he slipped onto the aviation compound.

Stetsons and flight suits.

"Here for the BBQ?"

Coleman turned from the sight of three charcoal grills belching clouds of smoke to the Stetson-wearing soldier who'd asked the question. The gold chevrons flashing from his hat marked him as a staff sergeant, which probably explained why he was wearing a desert camouflage uniform rather than a flight suit. Apache gunships were two-seaters, meaning that, unlike Chinooks or Black Hawks, the enlisted men and women who served as crew chiefs didn't fly with their birds. But this restriction apparently didn't apply to cowboy hats or the silver spurs that glittered from the staff sergeant's brown suede desert boots.

"No," Coleman said. "I need to talk with someone about flying a mission."

"Nothing's flying," the sergeant said. "It's a safety stand-down day."

Coleman waited for the punch line, but the NCO stared back at him with a straight face, apparently not seeing the irony in stopping operations to talk about safety in the middle of a war. Then again, this was an aviation unit. Aviators might be in the military, but their reality was worlds away from the lives of normal grunts.

"How about taking me to your CO?" Coleman said.

"No problem," the sergeant said. "Want to stop by the mess tent first? Another batch of steaks just came off the grill. And there's ice cream. Chocolate's gone, but there's still a carton of strawberry."

Once again, Coleman waited for the punch line.

Once again, the sergeant stared back with a blank expression.

Aviators.

"I hear you've got a mission for us."

The comment came from a fit-looking man wearing the twin silver bars of an Army captain on his Stetson. With his sunglasses, Bristol Aviator watch, tan flight suit, and fat cigar, the cavalry trooper more than matched the stereotype Coleman had first encountered in *Apoca-*

lypse Now years ago. Contrary to Robert Duvall's iconic character, this aviator didn't seem interested in surfing. But he did appear eager to work.

"I do," Coleman said, "but your NCO said you weren't flying today."

"Headquarters isn't flying today," the captain corrected. "But headquarters is all the way up in Bagram. We're down here where the rubber meets the road. My boss told me we had to comply with the brigade's safety stand-down day, no excuses. However, he also said that we have to remain responsive to the operational needs of the units we support."

"What does that mean?" Coleman said.

"This is the cavalry," the captain said. "When confronted with orders that are vague, cavalry troopers err on the side of initiative. Which brings me to an important question—who the hell are you?"

Coleman hesitated, thinking about the best way to answer. While the CIA's presence in Afghanistan wasn't exactly a secret, there was a reason why intelligence personnel were sequestered from the general population of soldiers and civilians who fought the war. Case in point, Coleman was addressing the aviation captain in the midst of a table full of pilots piled with plates of surf and turf and empty bottles of nonalcoholic beer.

At least Scott hoped the beverages were nonalcoholic.

Either way, for CIA officers, anonymity was a way of life, especially in a small outpost like FOB Fenty. While the smaller FOB had nowhere near the number of Afghans present at the sprawling city of Bagram, there were still more ears than Coleman would have liked. And the local nationals weren't the only people who talked. Soldiers were as notorious for their propensity to gossip as aviators were for telling flying stories.

But Coleman had to say something.

Even if the aviators weren't on a safety stand-down day, they didn't just fly on behalf of whoever walked in the door. The captain's cavalier attitude aside, Apache gunships were a finite resource, and Coleman was willing to bet that the number of mission requests the cavalry troop received far outnumbered their capacity to support them. Coleman needed to give the man something, but "Mitch Rapp's Lonely Hearts Club" didn't seem like the way to go either.

"My name is Scott Coleman. I'm OGA."

Coleman's pronouncement brought a round of snickers from the aviators.

Not the reaction he'd anticipated.

"Of course you are," the captain said. "My name is Kelsey Smith and let me guess—you need gunship support and the 160th boys are all in Iraq?"

This was a common refrain in Afghanistan, especially the more mountainous areas whose steep elevation precluded the use of AH-6 Little Birds, or Killer Eggs, as the ground pounders called the aircraft. Though the single-engine helicopters had been heavily modified in the almost four decades since they'd originally entered service, the birds still lacked the power to fly at the elevations needed to service mountaintop landing zones.

The Direct Action Penetrators, or DAPs—Black Hawks the 160th SOAR had transformed into gunships by adding rocket pods, miniguns, and a fixed chain gun—had no problem filling this role, but the airframes had by and large been moved to the conflict in Iraq. More often than not, rotary-wing close air support in Afghanistan was provided by conventional units. In Coleman's experience, no gunship pilot worth his or her salt shied away from missions supporting SOF, but this support didn't come without a little good-natured ribbing.

"Here's the deal," Coleman said. "I need to interdict a set of high-value targets. Are you in or not? Because I can always go down the road and see what the Hog pilots are doing."

Coleman's threat to use A-10s was mostly bluster. Though the Warthog was undoubtedly the best close air support aircraft ever fielded, winding mountain roads combined with an unknown target location equaled helicopters as far as he was concerned.

"Please," Smith said. "Everyone knows the Air Force doesn't fly when the chow hall's serving surf and turf. Save the BS and fill me in on the mission specifics."

"Convoy of three vehicles entering Afghanistan via the Torkham border crossing," Coleman said. "I need you to smoke the lead and trail cars. My team will take the remaining one."

"Why not just let us hit all three?" Smith said.

"Because I need to talk to the HVTs in the middle vehicle," Coleman said.

"Okay," Smith said. "Do you have eyes on the convoy?"

"No," Coleman said with a sigh. "They're currently on the move, and I don't have a location. I was hoping you could find them."

"Hope is not a method nor a combat multiplier," Smith said, "but you've come to the right place. This is a cavalry troop, which means we know a thing or two about conducting a reconnaissance."

"Great," Coleman said. "One more thing—the vehicle we're after is carrying shoulder-fired missiles."

"Like the one that brought down the 160th Chinook?"

"Exactly like that one."

Captain Smith frowned and turned to one of the pilots seated next to him. "Darrin—what do you think?"

Like Smith, the pilot was wearing a flight suit, Stetson, and a flight suit patch bearing a rendition of his aviator wings and a name—Darrin Swan. But unlike the captain, Darrin's rank consisted of the three dots meaning that he was a CW3, or Chief Warrant Officer Three.

"MANPADS are no joke," Darrin said, "but shoulder-fired missiles work best in an ambush scenario. For this, I don't think we have anything to worry about. It's not like the jihadis are going to shoot a missile out the window as they're driving down the highway."

"Agreed," Smith said before turning back to Coleman. "We're in."

"Fantastic," Coleman said. "When can you be ready?"

"Imminently," Smith said, climbing to his feet. "I'll get the QRF birds spun up and launched while I muster the rest of the troop for a quick air mission brief. I intend to be airborne within thirty minutes. Does your team have a ride?"

Coleman shook his head. "The 160th was going to be my next stop."

"Don't bother," Smith said. "Getting permission from those guys for a daylight infil requires an act of God. I command a cavalry troop–plus. That means, in addition to my Apaches, I've got four Black Hawks and two Chinooks. You and your men can ride in the command-and-control bird with me. Sound good?"

It did sound good to Coleman.

Very good.

CHAPTER 57

N OREEN Ahmed trudged up the stairs to her third-floor apartment.

Though the atmosphere in the little complex seemed almost festive, she felt none of her fellow residents' glee. Like her, they were only here temporarily. The entire complex was built with short-term rentals in mind. Families or even single visitors coming to make use of the resort town's amenities. But unlike her neighbors, Noreen wasn't here to visit a son or daughter at the nearby Pakistan Military Academy, hike the Miranjani mountains, or swim in the pool beneath the breathtaking Sajikot waterfall. Noreen might be dressed as a tourist in hiking pants, a sweat-wicking shirt, and sturdy boots, but she was not in Abbottabad for pleasure.

A chorus of squeals drifted from the courtyard as Noreen made the final turn up the concrete stairwell. It wasn't lost on her that children were part of the reason she was leaving the CIA and, in her final assignment for the Agency, she was surrounded by them. The screams, shrieks, and laughs emanating from the cluster of brown bodies swarming a soccer ball sounded like heaven. Noreen enjoyed the sound of the children at play and would have loved to open the windows to her apartment to let the joy serenade her while she prepared dinner.

She couldn't.

As much as her idyllic surroundings suggested otherwise, Noreen wasn't on vacation. She was in the nation of her birth for one reason— to obtain definitive proof that the man who'd engineered the slaughter of almost three thousand innocents on a crisp morning in September had finally been found.

Noreen understood the criticality of her task just as she knew that if bin Laden was really here, heads would roll. Agency analysts had been working overtime to reconstruct the origin of the compound that served as his potential residence and put a timeline around when he'd arrived. Current estimates had bin Laden moving in seven years ago, and if the world's most wanted terrorist really had lived in a resort town known for its population of retired military officers and the nation's version of West Point without detection, only two conclusions could be drawn: elements within the Pakistan security services were helping the mass murderer, or they were incompetent.

Or both.

Noreen was operating under the assumption that unfriendly eyes were watching her every move. Eyes that wanted to both protect Abbottabad's most famous resident and save the nation the embarrassment the military and intelligence services would suffer if bin Laden was discovered right under their nose. Unlike her sibling in-country CIA case officers, Noreen was operating as a NOC. Coming in dark allowed her the latitude to go places her declared coworkers could not, but it also meant she had no diplomatic backstop. If things went sideways for declared Agency personnel, the Pakistani government might deem them persona non grata and expel them from Pakistan. In contrast, Noreen would be looking at jail in a best-case scenario.

She tried not to think about the worst case.

Arriving at her door, Noreen dropped her pack and took a moment to stretch the kinks out of her back. In staying true with her legend as a travel blogger, Noreen was a bit sore from the series of hikes she'd undertaken.

But this was not why she was stretching.

Technology had inarguably advanced the profession of espionage in ways unimaginable to the Cold War spies who'd helped solidify the CIA's reputation, but there was a reason why chalk marks, dead drops, and brush passes were still taught at the Farm. These analog methods were often overlooked by twenty-first-century counterintelligence officers more accustomed to digital surveillance than pounding the pavement. While earning her stripes as a case officer, Noreen had learned how to use *tells* to safeguard important items. Like the strand of black hair fastened to the corner of her apartment door with a droplet of clear superglue, for instance.

Noreen eyed the unbroken strand as she fished her keys from her pocket.

In an odd way, she'd almost been hoping to find the tell disturbed. While conducting her SDR this morning, she'd felt the tingling at the back of her neck that she normally associated with a surveillance team. Though her multi-hour trek of seemingly random stops, double backs, and turns had yielded nothing, Noreen hadn't been able to shake the feeling. Trusting her gut, she'd engaged in a more aggressive maneuver that, while indiscreet, had cleaned her of any watchers.

But this decision came with trade-offs.

Yes, she'd known she was clean while she'd conducted her reconnaissance of the dirt road leading to bin Laden's compound, but her obvious attempt to shake a tail would be a pretty good indication to a surveillance team that they were onto something. If she had been in the phantom team's position, Noreen would have gone to her apartment and searched it. The strand, if broken, would have at least confirmed that Noreen's hypothesis was correct, but the length of hair was intact.

Was she too focused on her post-CIA life?

These were questions that Noreen did not want to consider, but consider them she must. With a sigh that was not staged, Noreen inserted her key and unlocked the dead bolt. Then she shouldered her pack, opened the door, and slipped into the apartment's dark confines. The dim lighting was a balm to her tired eyes after hours spent beneath the blazing sun, but there was just one problem.

She'd left the kitchen light on.

CHAPTER 58

T HOUGH it had been billed as a small two-bedroom, Noreen considered the apartment spacious, especially by DC standards. The front door opened into a sitting room with hardwood floors and vaulted ceilings. The couch, two love seats, and matching end tables were worn but comfortable. Built-in shelves lined with hardback books covered the wall to Noreen's left. A long dining table fashioned from a single length of oak divided the front room from the expansive and well-equipped kitchen.

A man was seated at the table.

Despite her training, Noreen froze.

She'd taken two steps into the apartment before her eyes had adjusted well enough to make out the form at the table. In another sign that perhaps her head wasn't completely in the game, both of her hands were occupied. Her right held the door handle of the still partially open door while her left was wedged into the strap of her backpack.

She was better than this.

"Shut the door, Noreen," the man said. "You're letting in mosquitoes."

The man's American-accented English was sharply at odds with his appearance. Though he wasn't Pakistani, he could have passed for half a dozen nationalities, none of which would garner attention in Abbottabad. His olive skin, dark hair, and full beard screamed Arab, but Noreen wasn't sure.

For one, his English was too good.

As someone who spoke three languages, Noreen knew how hard it was to master a particular region's syntax and accent. Then there was his appearance. The attributes that would pass over the head of a casual observer stood out like red flags to Noreen. His shirt disguised his build, but judging by the man's rippling forearms, the fabric probably covered a chiseled physique. His sun-darkened face spoke of a life spent outdoors, but his skin didn't have the premature aging of someone who had regularly weathered the elements.

His eyes were the deciding factor.

Hard pieces of obsidian that reflected the single light illuminated above the stove.

With exaggeration motions, Noreen took another step into the apartment and closed the door behind her. If the man was part of a team, she had just limited their ability to influence what happened next. If he was a lone operative, she would rather have him in front of her than at her back.

"Don't hurt me," Noreen said, stammering over her words. "I'm just a—"

Noreen tossed her backpack at the man.

Most people believed they could multitask. This wasn't true. A human was capable of switching their attention from one subject to another at impressively quick rates, but the mind could only concentrate on one thing at a time. Between her words and the visual and audio stimulation provided by the backpack as it crashed to the wooden floor, she was hoping that her visitor would focus on something besides her. The distraction need only be good for an instant.

With silky motions sharply at odds with her earlier performance, she palmed the space beneath the coffee table and ripped away the baby Glock secured beneath. The sound of Velcro tearing filled the air, but Noreen didn't care. She had a pistol in her hands and its stubby front sight post was bisecting the man's forehead.

Things were looking up.

"Not bad," the man said. "Now put the pistol down so we can talk."

"Who are you?" Noreen said.

Her heart was hammering, but her voice was level. Better still, the front sight post never wavered. Maybe she'd been too hard on herself earlier.

"It's not loaded."

Noreen knew she'd chambered a round in the Glock before securing the pistol to the Velcro. She also knew that the tell outside her apartment's only entrance was still intact. The dwelling should be empty.

It was not.

Without taking her eyes from the man, she racked the Glock's slide with the smooth, economical movements her Ground Branch instructor had drilled into her head on the Farm's pistol range. The muzzle was back on target in a microsecond. If the man had been lying and there had been a round in the chamber, it would have sailed across the room, but there were still plenty more in the magazine. If he wasn't lying, Noreen had just remedied her problem.

Simple.

Or not.

Instead of shuttling a fresh 9mm round into the Glock's chamber, the slide locked to the rear. Not only was the bullet she'd loaded no longer present, the magazine was empty. Without breaking eye contact, the seated man opened his left hand. A deluge of bullets cascaded onto the table in a silver waterfall.

Shit.

"Put the pistol down," the man said. "We've got work to do."

Noreen slowly lowered the pistol.

"Who are you?"

"Mitch Rapp."

Shit.

CHAPTER 59

"You did well by the way."

Noreen eyed Rapp as she chewed, trying to decide if he was patronizing her.

"I'm serious," Rapp said, taking an orange from the bowl on the table and peeling it. "Operatives way more senior than you would have lost their head. You kept your cool."

"Do you get off on scaring the shit out of people?" Noreen said.

Rapp stopped with an orange slice midway to his mouth. "Do you know who I am?"

Noreen nodded.

She did know who Rapp was.

Everyone at the Agency knew who Rapp was.

Perhaps not by sight, but anyone who worked as a case officer had heard rumors about the Agency's top counterterrorism operative even if they took the form of whispers exchanged at the water cooler. While Mitch Rapp certainly wasn't a feature at Langley like many of the other career-focused bureaucrats, he'd pulled off some of the most storied operations in the CIA's recent history. She knew who Rapp was and now

Noreen was pissed that her introduction to the living legend had begun with her pointing a gun at him.

An unloaded gun.

"Then you should know better than to ask such a stupid question," Rapp said. "Why do you think I did what I did?"

"I don't know," Noreen said, her answer sounding defensive even to her.

"Of course you do," Rapp said. "You've got a grand total of one operational tour of duty under your belt and you're on your way out the door. You're Farm-trained, but you've never worked as a NOC and you sure as shit haven't done anything like this. You're here because you have the right profile to work this op, but I don't entrust my life to performance evaluations."

"So you decided to test me?"

"Damn right I did. The SDR you ran this morning was adequate and the tell on your front door was well done. Real old-school stuff. But tradecraft is only part of what makes a good case officer. Ops never go according to plan. I needed to know how you'd react to the unexpected."

Noreen unscrewed the plastic water bottle opposite her plate and took a drink. The gesture had less to do with thirst and more that she needed time to think. Was she pissed-off that Rapp had purposefully scared the shit out of her?

Yes.

Had she come dangerously close to losing it after realizing the Glock was empty?

Also yes.

But she hadn't lost it. This certainly hadn't been how she'd imagined her day would end when she'd laced up her hiking boots this morning, but she was glad for Rapp's presence. Working as a lone wolf was cool in the movies, but after experiencing it in real life, Noreen would use a different descriptor.

Terrifying.

For the first time since arriving in Pakistan, Noreen felt like she could breathe. The scope of her mission was enormous and the consequences for failure were still unthinkable, but she was no longer alone.

"Was the plan for me to link up with you all along?" Noreen said. "I thought this was a solo op."

Rapp shook his head. "You're not on this alone. There's an Agency safehouse located within line of sight of the compound. It's chock-full of antennas, cameras, and mikes along with half a dozen stir-crazy CIA officers. You know what they've got?"

Noreen shook her head.

"Jack shit," Rapp said. "Whoever's living in that compound is a careful son of a bitch. Eighteen-foot walls topped with razor wire ring the place, while the inner building is protected by a second seven-foot wall that cordons it off from the courtyard. They have electricity and gas, but no telephone or internet service. The inner courtyard has a bunch of vegetable gardens and a small farm—chickens, goats, rabbits, the works. The only people who go in and out of the compound are the two couriers and occasionally their kids. The families even burn their trash. Our safehouse has been operational for close to a month. Other than confirming that there are a shitload of people living inside the compound based on the amount of laundry drying on the clotheslines, the CIA officers have come up with nothing."

Noreen knew some of this.

After she'd agreed to Nash's pitch, there hadn't been much time to bring her up to speed. She'd squeezed in a single classified briefing at headquarters that had covered the basics before catching a flight out of Dulles. A little less than eight hours had elapsed from the time she'd answered Nash's call to the moment she fastened her seat belt on a plane heading east.

To say her husband, Brian, hadn't been pleased was an understatement. But at the end of the day, he'd done what he'd always done— kissed her forehead and told her that she'd be in his prayers. Though she'd been raised Muslim, Noreen wasn't practicing. Usually she considered Brian's devout Christian faith an endearing, if confusing, facet of the man she loved.

Not this time.

Until she completed this operation, Noreen would welcome all the divine help she could get.

"If you weren't part of the initial plan, why are you here now?" Noreen said.

"Things have changed," Rapp said, "and not for the better. What was your mission?"

Noreen paused before replying. Surely Rapp knew what she'd been instructed to do, so why was he asking? The answer followed on the heels of her question. For the same reason he'd slipped inside her apartment and waited for her in the darkness. He was testing her. Not her recall, but her understanding of what was at stake.

"Mike Nash was my briefing officer," Noreen said, "and his instructions were a bit vague. He told me to come to Abbottabad, rent an apartment, and establish my legend as a travel writer. He wanted me out and about, but away from the city proper. Further instructions would be issued via my COVCOM device."

"Sure," Rapp said, waving away her explanation. "That's what he said. What did Nash mean?"

Noreen took a deep breath.

She'd been thinking on this subject seemingly nonstop since she'd received her orders. Her operational experience, while admittedly limited, didn't jibe with such an open-ended tasking. Case officers were not exactly a dime a dozen and bringing one of them into country dark took some doing. After flying out of Dulles, Noreen had spent the next twenty-four hours hopping planes, trains, and automobiles to clear her tail.

A considerable amount of time and resources had been expended getting her in-country clean, including Mike Nash's presence in Islamabad. To do this without giving her a clear purpose didn't make sense.

After reflecting on this contradiction, Noreen could think of just one explanation.

"I'm a pinch hitter," Noreen said. "I speak the language, look like I belong, and spent part of my life in Pakistan. My guess is that plan A didn't work and neither did versions B, C, D, and E. I'm the Hail Mary. The high-risk, high-reward operation that only gets approved when the ops folks have nothing left."

Rapp stared at her in silence for an uncomfortably long period of time.

Then, he spoke.

"Your chief of station was an idiot," Rapp said.

"Why?"

"You're smart and can think on your feet. That can't be taught. Recruiting assets takes time to master. Some people pick it up right away. Other go through a bit of a learning curve. But your operational sense is far more mature than what someone with your limited experience should possess. Your chief of station should have recognized that and structured your evaluation accordingly. Once we're done, I'll set things right."

Noreen swallowed, unprepared for the level of emotion Rapp's statement engendered. Yes, she'd certainly thought herself better than her abysmal performance evaluation depicted, but she really didn't know. The Congo had been her first tour. Competition between fellow case officers was fierce and promotions through the government service, or GS, scale was directly linked to the number of successful asset recruitments.

In her darkest moments, of which there had been more than a few, Noreen found herself wondering if perhaps her boss had been correct. Maybe this wasn't the life for her. While she couldn't say for sure whether her decision to exit the Agency might have gone differently if she'd departed Africa as a success rather than a failure, a positive evaluation certainly would have helped.

But that was neither here nor there.

She and Brian had agreed that leaving the CIA was the best thing for their family. She was in Pakistan because she was a patriotic American willing to answer her nation's call a final time. Nothing more. Rapp's assessment and his offer to right what he perceived as a wrong were a balm to Noreen's injured pride, but that was it.

At least that's what she told herself.

"Thank you," Noreen said. "So what's the plan?"

Mercifully, her voice didn't break and the hot pinpricks at the corners of her eyes didn't materialize into tears. She might not have recruiting assets completely licked as of yet, but she had mastered the science of masking her emotions.

"I'm still working on that part," Rapp said. "Here's what I know. Our friends in the safehouse had a final play and it didn't pan out. The other adults living in the compound don't leave, but their kids sometimes do. While observing the compound kids playing with the nearby farm children, one of the analysts came up with a pretty inspired plan—get a DNA sample from the kids and bounce it up against bin Laden's."

"That is a good idea," Noreen said. "How were they going to obtain it?"

"Vaccinations," Rapp said. "Polio is still rampant in Pakistan and Afghanistan. We vaccinate the kids, and if possible, their mothers."

"And grab the DNA from the used syringes," Noreen said. "That sounds like a great plan."

"It didn't work."

"Why?"

"Because the doctor they sent was a man."

Noreen understood immediately even as she wondered how the Agency planners who'd advocated for the scenario hadn't anticipated this obstacle. While not exactly a bastion of liberal democracy, Pakistan was a progressive country by the standards of Fertile Crescent. In the Islamic Republic of Iran, home to Ayatollah Ali Hoseini-Nassiri, who was considered the preeminent Shia theologian, women were required to wear the hijab and cover their legs, arms, and torsos. Saudi Arabia, home to Islam's holiest city of Mecca and the Islamic pilgrimage known as the hajj, forbade women to drive and prohibited travel abroad without a male guardian. Bin Laden's radical form of Sunni Islam more mirrored the beliefs of Afghanistan's Taliban. Women were considered fit for little beyond bearing children and domestic duties. As part of this belief structure, segregation between men and women was strictly enforced. It was no wonder that the compound residents had refused to allow a male doctor access to the facility.

"Did the doctor vaccinate anyone?" Noreen said.

Rapp shook his head. "They didn't even open the door."

"So we're going to give it a go with a female doctor?" Noreen said.

"No time to find one," Rapp said. "Besides, I have something better than a doctor."

"What?"

"You."

Noreen thought she knew where the conversation had been headed, but Rapp's words still came with a finality. An ominous sense of finality. Two days ago, she'd been napping beside her husband as she burned away the final bit of leave accumulated by her six years as an employee of the Central Intelligence Agency. Now she was half a world away, about to walk into the compound housing the most wanted man on earth with nothing more than a syringe full of saline and her wits.

"What if they won't open the door?" Noreen said.

"They will," Rapp said.

Rapp hadn't asked if she was willing to do her part, at least not directly, but Noreen understood what he was waiting for all the same. She was not a Ground Branch shooter or a veteran of the special operations community. Up until this moment, she'd been a failed case officer about to trade in her blue badge for FBI creds. No doubt there were trainees at the Farm who would kill for an opportunity like this one.

Not Noreen.

But that didn't matter.

Sometimes the moment really did choose you. Noreen was the only person who could do this. The only person who had a prayer of deter-mining whether the compound's mysterious resident really was the most evil man of the twenty-first century.

"Okay," Noreen said. "What's next?"

"Grab your bag. We'll talk in the car."

CHAPTER 60

Sixty minutes later, Coleman was reconsidering his earlier optimism. While Captain Smith had proven true to his word, the operation had not gone according to plan.

Anyone's plan.

In the first reality check of the day, the original Black Hawk slotted for the flight had developed a maintenance issue. One the positive side, Captain Smith seemed to know his business. A spare Black Hawk had already been idling and Coleman and his crew had been quickly bumped to the replacement aircraft.

This was where things got tricky.

The second aircraft lacked the command-and-control console present in its predecessor. This meant that, rather than a flat-screen display the size of a small television populated by a moving map, the operational graphics, and the blue and red icons representing friendly or enemy units, Smith had to run the operation via a small tablet and his paper map. Also missing from the new aircraft was the communications panel that had linked Smith to five different radios. The new configuration limited Smith to two frequencies via the standard intercom, and he needed the help of one of the pilots to switch from channel to channel.

Not ideal, but certainly doable.

The second limitation had to do with the space inside the Black Hawk.

Or lack of it.

In the first iteration of the plan, Coleman's assault element had been divided between two aircraft. The support element, consisting of Charlie, would be located in the second aircraft while Coleman, Will, and Mas would ride in the first. Scott had broken down the manifest this way so that his sniper could infil separately, but this was no longer possible. Now a single Black Hawk held all of the CIA shooters along with Smith. Not ideal, but Scott would make it work.

Assuming, of course, they ever found the convoy.

"Shock 6, this is Shock 16. We are phase line JAMESON with negative contact, over."

"One Six, this is Shock 6," Smith said. "Roger that. Shock 26, this is Shock 6. Status, over?"

"Shock 6, this is Shock 26. We are two klicks west of JAMESON, over."

"Roger that, 26," Smith said. "Call phase line JAMESON, over."

"Shock 26 copies all, over."

Coleman peered over Smith's shoulder, orienting himself to the cavalry officer's map. In the way of military operations, Smith was using phase lines to control the progress of his Apaches as they conducted a reconnaissance that moved from west to east. After hearing Coleman's estimates for the convoy's start time and rate of travel, Smith had done some quick calculations to project where the jihadis might currently be. The information Rapp had passed to Coleman via Kennedy suggested that the convoy would enter Afghanistan at the popular Torkham border crossing, approximately seventy-five kilometers southeast of Jalalabad.

With this in mind, Smith had task organized his troop into two

teams of four Apaches each, with an additional two in reserve. The gunships were stacked north to south, with Smith's two platoon leaders,
radio call signs Shock 16 and Shock 26, controlling their own platoons.
Shock 16 commanded the northernmost team while Shock 26 was in
charge of the southern aircraft. The north–south running phase lines,
named after whiskey brands, were placed over easily identifiable terrain
features like roads, valleys, or rivers and were arrayed from west to east.
The phase lines controlled the aircraft's eastern progress in the same
way that yard lines on a football field delineated the ball's position with
respect to either end zone.

Even though Coleman believed the convoy was much closer to the
border, Smith had begun his reconnaissance twenty kilometers west of
Torkham. The cavalry officer's reasoning was sound—he could only
conduct the reconnaissance in one direction. If the Apaches began at
the border and then followed the road northwest, the slow, deliberate
pace of the reconnaissance gave the potentially faster-moving convoy
the opportunity to lose themselves in any of the secondary roads and
villages that branched from Highway 7 into Afghanistan's interior. By
beginning closer to Jalalabad and following the highway toward the Pakistani border, the gunships stood a better chance of intercepting the
convoy away from prying eyes—another necessity, from Coleman's perspective.

But so far, the cavalry troop had come up empty.

Coleman leaned over Smith's shoulder, examining the tactical map.
The reconnaissance's limit of advance was FOUR BRANCHES. To Coleman's eye, only six or so kilometers stretched from the dirt road that was
JAMESON to the dry riverbed that served both as FOUR BRANCHES
and the unofficial border between Afghanistan and Pakistan.

"We'll find them," Smith said, this time over the helicopter's intercom system rather than the radio. "Recons are almost always this way—
long periods of boredom followed by brief moments of excitement."

Coleman nodded, but he wasn't convinced. The cavalry officer
knew his craft, but Coleman was no stranger to the no-man's-land that

formed the border area. In some ways, this search was easier than others Coleman had been a party to because the convoy had to stay on paved roads rather than make use of the network of goat paths that spider-webbed through the mountain crossings. But vehicular traffic still came with its own challenges.

Even at this time of the day, traffic along the route wasn't exactly sparse. Much of America's supplies for the war effort came through Pakistan, and while Rapp had provided Coleman with a description of the target vehicles, the constant flow of cars and trucks meant that the heli-copter aircrews stayed busy. Each time a potential vehicle was discov-ered, it had to be cleared, and this further halted the recon's progress.

Then there was the elephant in the room.

While Rapp, and by extension Coleman, was confident that the fight-ers and their deadly cargo were progressing northwest to Jalalabad, numerous more sparsely used roads branched off from the main thorough-fare. If Rapp was wrong about the Iranians' destination or perhaps, more unsettling, wrong about their route of travel, there was every like-lihood that the convoy would disappear along a gravel path or a hard-packed dirt road.

If this happened, Coleman would be back to square one.

"Shock 6, this is 16. I've got a three-vehicle convoy headed north-west approximately two klicks west of phase line FOUR BRANCHES. Grid coordinates as follows, over."

Coleman listened as the platoon leader relayed the series of letters and numbers that converted the convoy's position into a grid reference system employed by military maps. Captain Smith annotated the con-voy on the clear acetate covering his map with his ever-present grease pencil. The coordinates corresponded to a stretch of road just north of the small town of Sadat.

"Shock 6 copies all," Smith said. "Can you send me a TADS shot, over."

"Roger that, 6. Stand by."

"My birds have an upgraded sensor package," Smith said to Coleman as he fiddled with the tablet strapped to his kneeboard. "In addition to new optics, the system can data-burst still images across the HF radio. Not near the fidelity of a Reaper or Predator, but we should at least be able to take a look-see."

Coleman nodded, only partially paying attention. Locating the convoy was the easy part.

Interdicting it was something else entirely.

Next to hostage rescue, vehicle interdiction was the most difficult mission set in a SEAL team's mission portfolio. Decimating a moving convoy was easy. Drop a couple of Hellfires on the vehicles and call it a day. But stopping moving vehicles in a way that negated the occupants' ability to kill you while keeping them alive for questioning was especially difficult.

And that was just the tactical portion of the operation.

Coleman wanted to spring his trap away from prying eyes or potential collateral damage. The road snaked north through the mountains before branching northeast through a valley containing a settlement and at least one mosque. The populated area was a nonstarter. Coleman needed to hit the vehicles before the convoy broke out into the open.

"Shock 6, this is 16. Images sent, over."

Smith's tablet pulsed.

The cavalryman tapped the screen and a picture of three vehicles moving single file up an incline replaced the digital map.

"That's them," Coleman said.

"You sure?" Smith said.

"Positive. We're looking for a Suzuki van and a pair of Toyota Corollas. That's our convoy."

Coleman had to hand it to the Iranians. The Quds Force operatives knew their business. Suzuki vans were extremely common in Pakistan, while the Corolla seemed to be the Afghan car of choice. The trio of vehicles would blend in nicely with the traffic crossing the border. Even more importantly, the Suzuki had more than enough cargo space to transport the Iranian-modified shoulder-fired missiles.

"Okay," Smith said. "Where do you want to take them?"

"Here."

Coleman indicated a section of road that offered several tactical advantages. One, it changed direction by more than ninety degrees from northeast to northwest. Two, the pass was sandwiched between a pair of mountains, which would block the view of what happened from the populous valley to the northwest or the city of Sadat to the south. Most importantly, the stretch was located just before the summit. This meant that the convoy would be traveling at its slowest as the drivers navigated both the steep incline and the twisty road that would eventually lead to the valley below.

It was about as perfect as Coleman would find.

"Where do you want to set up?" Smith said.

"My support by fire team here," Coleman said, pointing to another section of map. The ridgeline he indicated would offer a commanding view of the road and unobstructed access to the kill zone.

"What about your main effort?" Smith said.

That was a very good question.

"This will be a precision engagement," Coleman said. "I'll need your birds to trigger the ambush by knocking out the rear and trail vehicles. How will you do that?"

Smith frowned as he looked from his map to the image on the tablet.

"In a perfect world, I'd hit the lead and trail vehicles with Hellfires, but that's not gonna work. The spacing is too close. I'm afraid your HVT would catch shrapnel from one or both missiles. I have the same concern for a rocket engagement, so that leaves thirty-millimeter."

"Won't that cause collateral damage?" Coleman said.

"Might," Smith said, "but it's less risky. The thirty-millimeter rounds have shaped charges, but their burst radius is only four meters. I can fire a burst just ahead of the lead Corolla. The shrapnel will tear the shit out of the car and probably kill the driver and front passenger, but you won't get secondaries or the shock wave a Hellfire would generate."

"What about the rear Toyota?" Coleman said.

"Two options," Smith said. "We can try the thirty-millimeter trick in reverse by walking the rounds toward him from the rear. If he slows down in response to the lead vehicle biting it, there should be no problem."

"If he doesn't?"

Smith shrugged. "You tell me. If he pulls a one-eighty to head back down the mountain toward Pakistan, I can put a Hellfire through his roof. Same if he drives around the lead Corolla. But if he gets too close to the van, we could be in trouble."

Coleman nodded.

It was impossible to completely de-risk any kinetic operation and this was doubly true for engagements planned on the fly. That said, there was a difference between acceptable risk and idiocy. Coleman had shed blood with every member of his team. He was confident in their abilities. He couldn't say the same for his new aviator friends.

"No bullshit," Coleman said. "What's danger close for a thirty-millimeter engagement on the lead vehicle."

The question the SEAL was asking sounded simple.

It was not.

The definition of *danger close* was different for each ordnance, but the concept was easy to understand—the minimum safe distance between friendly forces and an exploding munition. But what Coleman was proposing threw some very large wrinkles into that equation. The Apache gunships would actually be aiming at an offset impact point from their targets.

From their *moving* targets.

"The textbook answer is seventy meters for thirty-millimeter rounds," Smith said, "but nothing about this is textbook. My troopers are good, but the cannon is an area weapons system. Diving fire helps tighten the shot group and we can run our engagement parallel to the target to cut down the risk of short rounds, but I'd say you probably want to be eighty meters away to be safe."

Eighty meters.

Almost the length of a football field. A combat-loaded man would require twenty seconds or more to sprint eighty meters. Too long. Coleman needed to surprise the occupants of the second vehicle.

He had to be closer.

"What about here?" Coleman said, indicating a dip in the terrain about twenty yards off the road. "This depression could be our foxhole. If we're hugging the dirt, we should be okay even if a burst of thirty-millimeter falls short."

Smith studied the map and slowly nodded. "It's gonna be loud, but you'll be out of our line of fire. If you're good with it, I am."

Coleman wasn't sure that *good with it* was an accurate characterization of how he felt. He'd seen enough clips of Apache gun tape to know what the 30mm munitions did to a human body. The munitions were point-detonating, meaning that they exploded when the bullets made contact with the ground. It would be noisy as hell, but the razor-sharp shards of metal that were so effective at slicing apart a target should pass harmlessly overhead. Unless a pilot fired a burst directly into Coleman's foxhole.

If that happened, there wouldn't be enough left of Scott to fill a trash bag.

But at least his ending would be quick.

"Okay," Coleman said. "Here's how we'll run it."

CHAPTER 61

" **H**ERE we go."

Mitch Rapp looked from the computer screen to the anxious CIA analyst sitting behind the keyboard. His name was Taylor Moore and he spoke with the slow diction and smooth vowels of someone who'd grown up south of the Mason-Dixon Line. Though Rapp hadn't spent a ton of time with the kid, Moore seemed to know his stuff. That said, Rapp might still have to kill him if the twenty-something kept with the running commentary.

Rapp was standing in the living area of a CIA safehouse located in the Bilal Town suburb of Abbottabad. As safehouses went, the accommodations weren't bad. The place had the vibe of a vacation home in the country. The house was nestled at the base of the foothills leading to the lesser Himalayas. The property was surrounded by trees and boasted its own modest privacy wall.

The rural locale meant that the dwelling was bordered by wheat fields, and a solitary dirt road provided the only vehicular access. A mangy dog prowled the property grounds at will and provided an alarm of sorts, while a rooster of uncertain origin strutted along the tops of the privacy wall and crowed at random intervals. Rapp would charitably describe the house's furnishings as rustic, but he'd certainly seen worse.

Dusty couches and odd décor aside, Rapp was most interested in the high-tech equipment that had turned the safehouse's large living room into an intelligence fusion cell. No fewer than six laptops sat open on a series of folding tables that had been converted to desks, while a bevy of secure communications equipment graced the kitchen counter. The dining room was devoted to a pair of monitors that displayed the results from the impressive amount of signals data being collected, correlated, and deciphered by several surreptitiously installed antennas.

The safehouse was manned with a mixture of case officers and analysts with a lone paramilitary officer named Jason Beighley thrown in for good measure. Until Rapp's appearance, the crew had been passively monitoring the bin Laden compound, which was within line of sight of the safehouse's large bay windows. Now that the passivity had been replaced with the hustle and bustle that accompanied an ongoing operation, the air seemed saturated with equal parts adrenaline and fear. Even so, there was a way to deal with mission jitters without aggravating fellow teammates.

Moore had yet to learn this lesson.

"You sure your girl knows what she's doing?"

Rapp's eyes narrowed as he looked from the computer monitor to the man standing next to him. "What kind of dumbass question is that?"

His response carried through the house. To his credit, the man who'd spoken, a case officer named Connor Sullivan, had the grace to look embarrassed, but Rapp wasn't ready to let bygones be bygones just yet. Moore could be forgiven his nerves. The kid was manning the laptop attached to a low-profile high-definition camera mounted to the safehouse's roof.

This was Moore's first operational tour, and it was a doozy. He was charged with monitoring a compound that might just hold the terrorist mastermind of the century in a country full of people who bordered between indifference and outright contempt for Americans. Many of these same people considered the man in the compound a hero. The men who staffed Pakistan's government weren't much different. If the safehouse became compromised, Moore would get a firsthand look at a Pakistani jail.

But Connor Sullivan was a different matter.

"Sorry, Mitch," Connor said. "That was out of line."

Rapp could have just accepted the apology and moved on.

He did not.

As the senior-ranking person, Sullivan set the culture for the men and women he led. Rapp was no stranger to long surveillance operations and the friction they generated between teammates. Take five high-performing individuals, stuff them into a house meant to hold two people, and give them a job that incorporates hours of boredom interspersed with infrequent and brief moments of terror. Viewed from that perspective, it was a wonder any long-duration surveillance team came through the operation without killing each other.

But that was the job.

More importantly, it was the job of team leaders like Sullivan to show his subordinates the correct way to manage the stress and defuse petty squabbles. Rapp knew that the three men and two women who staffed the safehouse and had manned its surveillance tools for the last three weeks were frustrated.

That was understandable.

But allowing their frustration to boil over into disparaging comments about adjacent teammates had the potential to put the mission at risk.

"That woman is a Farm-trained case officer," Rapp said. "She grew up in Pakistan, speaks the language, and looks like she belongs here, which is something no one else in this house can claim. She was recruited for this operation by Mike Nash and vetted by me. She's good to go because I say she's good to go. Anyone have a problem with that?"

Judging by the answering silence, no one did.

The gang was on edge. Not only were they at risk of constant detection, but the pressure from headquarters to figure out who was in the compound kept increasing. SEAL Team 6 assaulters had been practicing on a compound identical to the one he was viewing on the combination day TV/infrared sensor for three weeks. At some point, the national command authority had to authorize the mission or the decision would be made for them. While the Agency people surveilling the compound were good, they were not perfect. Sooner or later, a mistake or even just bad luck would tip the balance. A local would get suspicious of the strangers and whisper something into the wrong ear. Or maybe one of the couriers would get tipped off to the Agency presence courtesy of a countersurveillance team of their own. There was also the possibility that the compound's mysterious resident might get antsy and decide to change locations.

If the man who paced the compound's grounds in loose-fitting clothing and a broad-brimmed hat really was bin Laden, he'd managed to remain undetected for almost ten years. A person couldn't stay free for that long without developing some sort of sixth sense about his enemies. Bottom line, the Agency surveillance team was on borrowed time and needed to produce results.

Which was exactly what Rapp intended to do.

"No questions about her performance," Sullivan said, answering for the team, "but this is the first USPER to approach the compound. If things go bad, what are we prepared to do?"

This time Sullivan was asking a good question.

USPER stood for United States Person. It was a generic term used to delineate assets from people with US citizenship and/or a legitimate reason to consider America their home.

People like Noreen.

The doctor who'd been turned away during his attempt to vaccinate the compound's occupants was Pakistani and therefore an asset. While his safety and well-being were important to his handler and the CIA writ large, he was not in the same category as Noreen. The cold, hard truth was that assets were often deemed expendable.

Case officers were not.

But Sullivan's question got at something even deeper. Sullivan might be asking about Noreen, but Rapp thought the question also applied to bin Laden. If Noreen somehow spooked the terrorist, would Rapp stand by while the Al Qaeda leader slipped through their fingers?

No.

But Rapp didn't say this to Sullivan.

The CIA officer was already under enough stress. No sense adding Rapp's potential one-man assassination operation to his worry list. Instead, Rapp decided to go with something reassuring.

"If Noreen gets into trouble, we will do whatever is necessary to extract her. Questions?"

"Right on," Taylor said.

Rapp eyed the analyst, considering.

His remark to Sullivan wasn't pure bluster. Rapp had no intention of letting anything happen to Noreen. He'd gone into hell multiple times before to save comrades, and he wasn't planning on changing strategies now. That said, there was something to having a fellow operative watching your back.

As legendary Marine Jim Mattis had once said, when going to a gunfight it was wise to bring all your friends with guns. But that was a thought for later. At the moment, Rapp had more pressing concerns.

Noreen was knocking on the compound's gate.

CHAPTER 62

FOR once, Noreen was grateful for the unseasonably warm and humid weather.

The thick humidity wrapped her in a stifling blanket, but the 85-degree temperatures also provided cover for the rivulets of sweat dripping down her face. She'd once heard a Farm instructor describe a spy's glamorous life as standing outside an apartment building in the pouring rain, aiming a bit of electronics at one particular door and praying that this wasn't the night you went to jail.

Noreen had laughed at the anecdote along with the rest of her class. She wasn't laughing now.

The compound had seemed big in the surveillance pictures Rapp had provided. Standing next to the green metal gate, it looked positively massive. Though the structure was imposing, it also had a slightly decrepit air. The gray cinder-block walls towered above her, but the sides were pitted and damp with condensation. Lime-colored mildew covered the sections not exposed to direct sunlight, giving off a moldy smell. Razor wire glittered from the top of the wall, reflecting the sunlight like an alligator's gleaming teeth. Her head knew that the one-man wrecking ball that was Rapp was watching her every move from the safehouse.

Her heart wasn't so sure.

She'd experienced the Rapp effect firsthand and now understood why he was able to so easily bend politicians, Agency bureaucrats, and captured terrorists to his will. Rapp's presence was tangible. He exuded raw intensity. After hearing his plan and her part in it, Noreen had been ready to run through a brick wall. Now that she was faced with one made from cinder blocks, she wasn't as confident.

Much to her surprise, the steel gate had begun to swing open at her first knock, but Noreen didn't stop pounding on the metal. For one thing, her legend said she was a nurse delivering a vaccine to the rural parts of Abbottabad. The compound, while impressive, was just one of many houses she needed to visit today.

But that was only part of the reason.

Pounding on the rusted gate gave Noreen's hands something to do besides quiver.

Even though it had to weigh twice as much as she did, the gate opened smoothly. One moment Noreen had been confronting a pitted, rust-flecked surface. The next she was face-to-face with a dark-complected man.

A frowning dark-complected man.

According to safehouse analysts, two Al Qaeda couriers lived in the compound and served as the conduit between the structure's unseen residents and the outside world. The men posed as brothers claiming to be Pakistanis who had been born in Kuwait. Whether this was true or not, Noreen didn't know or particularly care. The men's origins were no more important to her than their true names.

To cut through the multiple aliases associated with each man, Agency analysts had come up with an easy solution. The skinny courier was given the code name FLACO, while his portly companion had been christened GORDO.

Noreen had just met FLACO.

"What?" FLACO said with all the welcome of a junkyard dog.

"Hello," Noreen said, undeterred. "I'm here to vaccinate this household."

"Go away."

The steel gate began to swing shut.

Noreen wasn't having it.

Throwing her shoulder into the mass of metal, Noreen set her feet and locked her legs. "I have been instructed to vaccinate everyone in this compound. Let me do my job or I'll have to report your non-compliance to my superiors."

Noreen stretched the lanyard hanging around her neck that identified her as a government health worker. For an instant she thought the man was going to slam his weight into the gate and knock her on her ass.

Then the resistance stopped.

"Why?" FLACO said, not bothering to hide his suspicion.

"Polio," Noreen said, still holding the badge in front of her as if it were a shield. "Infections have doubled in Abbottabad. Everyone gets vaccinated. You can call this number if you have questions."

FLACO's gaze drifted from her face to her badge. His fingers moved toward his pocket and then froze, confirming a hunch Rapp had voiced. Even though the analysts manning the safehouse's SIGINT tools hadn't detected so much as a whiff of cellular energy since they'd set up shop, the courier might be carrying a mobile.

FLACO's dark eyes narrowed. "Why did they send a . . ."

"Woman?" Noreen said, finishing the sentence. "Because there are more women and children in this part of town than men. Now, are you going to let me vaccinate your family or not?"

FLACO scowled for a long moment.

Then, he spoke.

"Be quick."

She intended to.

CHAPTER 63

NOREEN had thought that getting into the compound would be the tough part.

She wasn't a doctor and hadn't taken any medical training beyond the Agency's version of the tactical combat casualty care course, but what she needed to do wasn't rocket science. In her backpack Noreen had a box full of syringes, alcohol swabs, a sharps container for used needles, and a dozen ten-dose vials of single-antigen inactivated polio vaccine. Her job was to jab everyone in the compound, place the syringes in a specifically marked bag, and walk to the next house on the dirt road and repeat the process.

Simple.

There was nothing simple about what was happening now.

Noreen had just taken a step into the compound's courtyard when the steel gate slammed closed behind her. She turned to FLACO with a puzzled look.

"We have animals," FLACO said.

There were in fact animals inside.

The compound formed an upside-down triangle with the base to the north and the point oriented due south. North–south running walls further segmented the structure into three main areas: western, center, and eastern. Noreen had entered via the western side, which had been turned into a makeshift barnyard for the cows, chickens, and other animals meandering across the hardpacked dirt. Several gardens were laid out in neat rows. Though she couldn't see it over the twelve-foot-high wall to the east, Noreen knew from satellite imagery that the compound's main living areas resided in the structure's center segment. The eastern segment was bounded by walls like the other sections and was used primarily for agricultural purposes.

As Noreen watched, a pair of young children attacked weeds sprouting between the vegetables under the supervision of what appeared to be an older sibling. More children were doing chores in the stables while a trio of toddlers chased each other in the dirt. Two boys entered from a door leading to the structure's center segment. The pair headed for the gate Noreen had just used at a dead sprint. FLACO yelled a string of orders that arrested their break for freedom. With slumped shoulders, the would-be escapees trudged back to the woman who had come through the door behind them. Grabbing each by their ear, she gave the pair a tongue-lashing that would have made Noreen's own mother proud before directing them toward their laboring siblings.

Setting her knapsack on the ground, Noreen undid the top flap.

"How many people are here?" Noreen said.

"Why?"

FLACO's suspicious tone might have warranted an angry response, but Noreen opted for a tired sigh. "So I know how many needles to prepare."

Noreen began unpacking. Though her heart was thundering, her hands moved with quick efficiency. This, more than anything else, seemed to break through the courier's suspicions.

"Okay," FLACO said. "Let me get the others."

He hadn't answered her question, but Noreen was still encouraged.

This was actually going to work.

Then the eastern door banged open.

CHAPTER 64

"SHE'S in. Holy crap, she's in."

In a turn of events that surprised even him, Rapp found himself smiling along with Taylor Moore's enthusiasm. Rapp had instructed Noreen not to wear a wire or carry a weapon. While both clandestine tools were useful in the right scenario, today they would be more hindrance than help. A person wearing a wire or carrying a knife or pistol acted differently.

Thought differently.

Noreen had enough on her mind. She didn't need to add to the list her fear that her microphone and transmitter would be discovered or she'd be forced to use her weapon. Her best defense was to believe with every fiber of her being that she was nothing more than a simple nurse tasked with inoculating the compound's occupants.

Well, that and the knowledge that if things went wrong, Mitch Rapp was waiting.

"Of course she's in," Rapp said. "Switch to sat feed."

While he was just as excited that Noreen had made it inside the compound, Rapp wanted to make sure the safehouse's residents understood that they were still on war footing. Much could go wrong, and Rapp needed everyone anticipating the bad things that could happen to Noreen in order to stay one step ahead of them. Celebrations were for after the operation.

"Sat feed online . . . now."

If Moore was conscious of Rapp's rebuke, the kid didn't show it. His fingers flew across his laptop's keyboard with the unerring certainty of a concert pianist. A moment later, the high-definition video was replaced with an overhead thermal view courtesy of a low-earth-orbit satellite.

This was the other reason that time was of the essence.

Satellites had been retasked to provide imagery of the compound, but they were not in a geosynchronous orbit for fear of drawing attention and unwanted questions from the Pakistanis or other sharp-eyed adversaries. This meant that a live feed was only available for the short window in which the satellite was overhead.

While he would have preferred a Predator's persistent stare, Rapp had nixed this idea for operational security reasons. One, if the compound contained who they thought it did, Rapp didn't want to run the risk of accidentally alerting him. Engineers had been making great strides at reducing the UAV's acoustic signature, but the ambient conditions were hard to account for. The lawn mower–like sound of the aircraft's Honeywell turboprop engine often carried to the ground at inopportune times.

And then there were the Pakistanis.

While the country's political leadership was willing to look the other way, or in some cases privately aid, CIA drone strikes on its territory, these kinetic operations had been reserved almost exclusively for the hinterlands. The Wild West area in Pakistan's western border with Afghanistan, a construct that existed more on maps than in the reality of the people who called the region home.

But there was a limit to Pakistani forbearance.

The government might privately tolerate targeted assassinations along the western border even as they publicly raged against the drone strikes, but Abbottabad didn't fall into that category. The city had a population of several hundred thousand and was located on the eastern side of Pakistan, only fourteen or so miles from the border with India. Operating a drone above the compound would require the aircraft to transit the length of Pakistan undetected.

That was a bridge too far, so satellite feed was the only answer.

The imagery was good, considering it was coming from a camera hundreds of miles away. Even so, Rapp found himself frowning. The high-definition television feed he'd been watching earlier provided the illusion that Rapp was just over Noreen's shoulder, able to reach out and touch a bad guy if things went south.

The satellite imagery put that fantasy to rest.

Watching the meet unfold made Rapp feel like a staff weenie back on Langley's seventh floor rather than an operative. Not to mention that if things did go sideways, Noreen would be on her own until Rapp covered the kilometer separating the safehouse from the compound. Not for the first time, Rapp wished that Charlie Wicker were up on the safehouse roof with his eye behind an optic and the buttstock of his rifle snugged into his shoulder.

But that was a nonstarter. Coleman and his crew were still in Afghanistan doing God's work. Besides, Noreen seemed to be just fine.

So far.

Rapp snugged the Bluetooth-equipped earbud deeper into his right ear. The device was linked to a trio of low-profile microphones trained on the compound from various vantage points within the safehouse. An analyst seated next to Taylor was in charge of the audio. Like Taylor, her fingers flitted across the keyboard as she tried for the optimum mix. Rapp knew she was doing her best, but the feed sounded like garbage.

He was missing about every third word as the analyst cycled between the mikes. An Urdu speaker seated next to the analyst was attempting to translate the conversation to English in real time, but FLACO's thick Waziri accent only exacerbated the delay.

"...*go*..."

While the words were somewhat garbled, the courier's tone came through loud and clear. The Al Qaeda operative's Spidey senses were definitely tingling.

"...*how many people*..."

Noreen was striking the right balance between annoyance at the delay posed by the man's obstinance and unease at the man's increasingly belligerent attitude. Unlike day TV, the satellite's infrared imagery carried with it none of the visual cues Rapp was used to deciphering. He couldn't see the courier's facial expressions or determine whether his shoulders were hunched or fingers balled into fists.

"...*why*..."

This wasn't working.

Rapp snatched a burner phone from the table. "Can you patch the audio into this?"

The blond analyst nodded.

"Good," Rapp said, sliding the phone into his back pocket. "I need Noreen's audio in my right ear and an open line to the safehouse in my left."

"Want company?"

The question came from Jason Beighley, the paramilitary officer.

Rapp paused to take stock of the man. He liked what he saw—a wiry build and a calm demeanor that suggested Jason had been some places and seen some things. "What'd you do before the Agency?"

"I was a sniper in the Unit."

Excellent.

"That compound's a klick away—can you handle it?"

"Easy day."

Rapp nodded. "Then grab your rifle and get set up. I might need you."

"On it."

Rapp headed for the safehouse door.

"Where are you going?" Connor Sullivan asked.

"To pay CRANKSHAFT a visit."

CHAPTER 65

I n an enormous display of willpower, Noreen didn't look toward the heavy footfalls echoing from the eastern door. Instead, she reached into her knapsack for the cooler containing the vaccine vials.

That was a mistake.

One moment she was head down, rummaging in her backpack.

The next, she was on her back, looking at the sky.

The newcomer, GORDO, had bowled her over with the casual disregard one might show a bug. Noreen had reflexively cradled the serum container to her chest, which meant she had no way to shield herself from the man's sandaled foot. Turning, she curled into a fetal position, hoping to absorb the blow with her back muscles.

It never came.

Instead, she was treated to the sound of the two men screaming in Arabic. FLACO had interposed himself between her and GORDO, but the second courier had his hands balled into fists.

Fists he looked ready to use on Noreen.

"Are you crazy?" Noreen said.

The emotion in her voice was genuine, as were her tears.

GORDO stopped his Arabic tirade and turned to consider her with hate-filled eyes.

Then, he lunged past FLACO.

CHAPTER 66

R APP ducked out of the safehouse and ran for the collection of dusty vehicles parked in the walled courtyard. Ignoring the sedan, SUV, and single truck, Rapp approached a dirty van. The words *Hazara Electric Supply Company* were stenciled on the side panel in bright red Urdu script. Rapp felt beneath the rear bumper and retrieved a key secured in a magnetic holder. He unlocked and opened the driver's-side door and slid into the worn seat.

After inserting the key, Rapp turned the ignition.

CIA officers were great at collecting intelligence but sometimes faltered at the less glamorous chores associated with their chosen profession. Chores like ensuring that the fleet of vehicles assigned to the safehouse remained in good working order.

The engine coughed and sputtered.

Rapp snarled as he envisioned murdering a fellow Agency employee.

Then the motor caught.

Slamming the transmission into drive, Rapp spun the wheel and stomped on the gas. The V-8 responded as if seeking to atone for its earlier reluctance. Rapp angled the van toward the vehicular gate, paused as the pressure sensor actioned the opening mechanism, and then floored the accelerator before the gate was all the way open. For a moment, he thought his impatience might have gotten the best of him as he jiggered the wheel to avoid dinging the concrete barrier.

Then he was through.

Rapp drove with one hand and snagged the shirt resting in the passenger seat with the other. While he'd intended to monitor the operation from the safehouse, Rapp had also anticipated the need to get a bit closer to the action. Hence the shirt. Switching his grip, he slipped his arms through the sleeves and began buttoning up the front. After fastening the top three buttons, Rapp unmuted his phone.

"This is Ironman," Rapp said. "Give me a SITREP."

"Roger that, Ironman," Sullivan said. "Beighley is in place on the roof, but he has no line of sight into the compound. Our audio tech is working the three mikes, but as best as we can figure someone is dragging Noreen toward the segment of the compound that houses the living quarters. Do you want us to launch a mini-drone?"

"No," Rapp said, spinning the wheel with his right hand as he finished buttoning the shirt with his left. "We can't risk spooking the bad guys. Stick with the satellite feed."

"Okay, but we're gonna lose it in just under two minutes."

Rapp resisted the urge to point out that if the situation continued to deteriorate, Noreen would probably be dead much sooner than that. Sullivan was just doing his job.

Now Rapp intended to do his.

"Is Noreen still in the courtyard," Rapp said.

"Affirmative," Sullivan said. "They're dragging her toward the eastern door, but she's struggling."

Good girl.

"Okay," Rapp said, a plan coming together in his mind. "Can Beighley hear me on this channel?"

"That's a negative, but we can relay."

"Won't work," Rapp said. "This needs to be synchronized. Either find a way to get him on this frequency or head upstairs and sit with him. I'm talking close enough to squeeze his shoulder. Beighley needs to send a round downrange the instant I give the word."

"Stand by."

Sullivan was redeeming himself.

"Okay, I'm with Beighley on the roof."

Rapp braked as he came to the turnoff for the dirt road leading to the compound.

While he wanted to continue rocketing down the hardpacked mud, he couldn't. The van's suspension and oversize engine were probably up to the challenge, but he was more worried about observers unseen and otherwise. The CIA safehouse team had identified several surveillance cameras on the compound's exterior, at least two of which had commanding views of the road. Racing hell-bent for leather down a mostly private street was a great way to get attention.

The wrong kind of attention.

"Tell Beighley there are a series of four electric meters mounted on the northeast corner of the compound," Rapp said. "Let me know when he has them."

"Stand by."

Rapp bumped down the road, trying to stay clear of the biggest potholes. He maintained an even twenty kilometers per hour. Slow enough to keep from knocking his head against the ceiling as the van's tires traveled from one rut to another, but fast enough to project a sense of urgency. A gaggle of kids playing soccer grudgingly made way. Rapp waved as he drove past.

"Beighley has them," Sullivan said.

Rapp exhaled. This gambit had come together on the fly, and he hadn't been sure the roof even offered Beighley a line of sight to the electric meters.

Maybe this was going to work after all.

"Ironman, we're out of time. They're at the eastern door."

"Tell Beighley to shoot exactly when I say," Rapp said, depressing the accelerator. "Exactly. I'm going to give him a three-count and then the execute command. He's to fire on the word *execute*. Got it?"

For the first time, Rapp saw the compound in person. The structure gave off a prison vibe. The razor wire glinted in the sun and fissures had already begun to form in the concrete. While it was certainly better living conditions than the caves of Tora Bora, Rapp had expected something different. Something more akin to the opulence of a European castle or the decadence of a Saudi hotel suite.

"Tracking," Sullivan said, "they're opening the eastern door."

Steering the van to the right, Rapp pulled the vehicle up to the compound's gate and braked. "Three," Rapp said, slamming the transmission into park, "two, one. Execute, execute, execute."

Rapp laid on the van's horn an instant before giving the execute command. The ground branch sniper undoubtedly had a suppressor attached to his rifle's muzzle, and while this would muffle the report, it would not completely eliminate it. Worse still, the can would do nothing for the distinctive crack a rifle bullet made as it transited the sound barrier. With this in mind, Rapp decided to use an old-school sound-suppression system.

The horn.

"Round complete," Sullivan said.

Rapp gave the horn one last blast for good measure before hopping out of the van and slamming the door closed behind him. Now it was time to see if the Ground Branch sniper had earned his money. Striding up to the compound's iron gate, Rapp banged on the metal with a closed fist.

For a long moment, nothing happened.

Then it opened.

CHAPTER 67

RAPP felt an immediate distaste for the man staring back at him. This could be because he'd just been dragging a fellow CIA officer across his yard by her hair, or it could have been the less-than-friendly expression on his face. It might also have been because, if the Agency eggheads were correct, this shitbag had helped bin Laden evade justice. Regardless of the reason, the result was the same.

Rapp wanted to kill him.

Unfortunately, that wasn't going to happen just yet, so Rapp suppressed his anger and channeled his annoyance into a suitable facial expression.

"Your meter," Rapp said, before FLACO could even get a word in. "Something's wrong with it."

Whatever the courier had been expecting, this clearly wasn't it. FLACO's eyes went from Rapp's shirt, which had the word *HAZECO* prominently emblazoned above his left breast, to the van behind him. The van that was stenciled with the words *Hazara Electric Supply Company*—Abbottabad's electricity provider.

FLACO replied in heavily accented Urdu.

"I don't understand you," Rapp said, speaking in Arabic, "but I need to check the electric line inside. Something's wrong with your meter."

Rapp moved to push past FLACO, but the gangly courier stood in his way. Rapp collided with the man and stumbled. He reached for the gate to steady himself and gave it a hearty push as he regained his balance. The barrier swung open, offering Rapp a view of the compound's interior.

And Noreen.

The case officer was still on her feet. Barely. Her bag full of medical equipment had fallen, spilling syringes and serum vials across the dirty ground. Her hair was askew and GORDO had his hand drawn back, clearly about to administer a slap.

"What is going on?" Rapp said, allowing anger but not rage to color his voice.

With Rapp, there was a difference.

Anger was an inconvenience.

Rage was lethal.

Pakistan was not a Western country, but neither was it Saudi Arabia. If Rapp had a daughter, he wouldn't want her to grow up here, but Pakistani women weren't considered subhuman by their male counterparts. The Pakistani military had women members, as did parliament. Unlike Afghanistan during the Taliban's rule, in present-day Pakistan a woman couldn't be beaten and dragged about by her hair for no reason. This realization seemed to dawn on FLACO and his fake brother at same time. GORDO released his hold on Noreen, and FLACO began jawing in Arabic about a misunderstanding.

Ignoring them both, Rapp called across the courtyard to Noreen. "Are you okay?"

To her credit, Noreen kept her cool. Perhaps not trusting her voice, the case officer gave a short nod. Then she bent and began scooping up the spilled medical supplies and shoving them back into her bag.

"You sure?" Rapp said, shouldering past FLACO.

"Yes," Noreen said as she slung the bag across her shoulder. "These men can die of polio for all I care."

With a final glare at the couriers, Noreen walked past Rapp and out the gate.

"What were you doing with that woman?" Rapp said.

"I told you, it was a misunderstanding," FLACO said. The courier's eyes narrowed. "Why are you here?"

"And I told you," Rapp said, "I'm from HAZECO. There is a problem with your meter, and I need to check the electric hookup."

"How do I know that is true?"

Rapp looked down at his shirt and then back at the man. "I don't have time for this nonsense," Rapp said. "Call my office if you'd like or don't, I don't care. Let me do my job and I'll be out of your hair."

The couriers hadn't made any calls since the safehouse had begun surveillance, and the compound had no visible landline. Per the operational security one would expect if bin Laden really was present, the jihadis utilized a rotating series of public call booths at least an hour's drive from Abbottabad when they needed to talk. As such, Rapp thought the likelihood of them calling his bluff low. If they did, Sullivan was prepared. The safehouse had a device designed to swallow all nearby wireless signals by mimicking a cell phone tower. If a cell inside the compound activated, the call would ring through to an Agency-employed Urdu speaker who would pose as a bored receptionist for the electric company.

Simple.

Unless of course the men decided to use a sat phone.

As if hearing Rapp's thought, FLACO pulled a sat phone from his pocket.

The analytical part of Rapp's mind absorbed as much information about the device as possible with the intention of relaying the data to Sullivan later. The part of Rapp's brain responsible for keeping him alive went about planning how he was going to kill both men to ensure that there *was* a later.

FLACO flipped open the device and was preparing to dial when his fellow courier covered the keypad with his hand.

"Wait," GORDO said. "You said there was a problem with our meter, right?"

"Yes," Rapp said.

"Then let's go see it. Together."

GORDO's fingers floated toward the back of his pants.

Rapp knew what the motion heralded, but a meter reader from HAZECO would not. So rather than react to this provocation, Rapp ignored it.

"Procedure says that I need to check the lines first," Rapp said, making as if to move past the men. "In case there's a break. Live electrical lines can kill someone who touches them."

"Meter first."

GORDO slid over so that he was shoulder-to-shoulder with FLACO. This time the meaning would be clear even to an employee of HAZECO. Rapp wasn't going a step farther into the compound.

Unless he went through the men.

For a long moment, Rapp considered doing just that.

He still didn't know if bin Laden was present, but he had zero qualms with dropping these two douchebags. The way they'd treated Noreen aside, both men were known Al Qaeda members and active couriers for the terrorist organization. As far as Rapp was concerned, both had been added to his list by way of their association to other shitbags he'd either killed or planned on killing. Sooner or later, their number would come up, and there was no time like the present. Rapp did the kill math with about as much effort as it took a normal person to decide whether they wanted a donut to go with their coffee. The men believed that proximity to their pistols, coupled with the fact that they were on home turf, meant safety.

They couldn't have been more wrong.

Though Rapp was also armed, if things went kinetic, he wouldn't be reaching for his pistol. The closest shitbag, FLACO, would get a punch to the throat that would put him out of the game.

Permanently.

GORDO would live about a half second longer only because it would take Rapp that long to close distance while flicking open his matte-black ZT knife. An eye gouge would cause GORDO to hunch forward, exposing his brainpan, which Rapp would obligingly turn into scrambled eggs with one quick thrust followed by an equally quick turn of the blade. Then it would be back to shitbag one. Rapp intended to help FLACO forget about his crushed windpipe by ventilating the courier's jugular.

Two dead men.

Five seconds.

Call it seven seconds tops.

Rapp's assessment was not a brag. He was simply providing an estimate in the same manner a good home contractor could eyeball a kitchen and ballpark the remodeling cost. Rapp was a craftsman and killing was his craft.

The eastern door banged open, and children flooded onto the hard-packed soil. A trio of boys chased two squealing girls. The five of them moved across the courtyard in a squirming jumble of laughs and shrieks. The leader of the pack, a brunette who looked about six, caught sight of the three men and screamed a single word.

"Baba!"

Father.

GORDO, who moments before had been dragging Noreen by her hair, turned and let loose a stream of Arabic admonishing the child. The little girl's face transformed from a look of pure adulation into a thundercloud. Fat tears leaked from her eyes as she turned away, tiny shoulders shuddering.

Rapp kept his expression neutral even as he considered his options. While he did not kill women or children, this stipulation did not exempt dirtbags who chose to use them as human shields. On the other

hand, Rapp also did not make messes, and this had the makings of a co-
lossal one. The couriers needed to be removed from circulation, but this
was not the time or place. Agency estimates had at least five adult males
living in the compound. As much as he wanted to put the pair of jokers
flanking him in the dirt, Rapp knew the difference between audacity
and stupidity.

"You want to start with the meter?" Rapp said. "Fine. Let's go."

Rapp moved toward the gate. His skin crawled as he turned his
back on the two Al Qaeda couriers, but it couldn't be helped. He was
still in character, and this is what a meter man would do.

But that didn't mean he had to like it.

Rapp's shoulders loosened as he crossed the compound's threshold
and then tightened again when he heard the crunch of footfalls. In all
the excitement, he'd neglected to confirm that Beighley had hit his target. If the paramilitary officer had missed, or if his hit hadn't done a
convincing job, this cold war would turn hot in a hurry. Rapp quickened his step, hoping to get to the meters before the couriers so that he
could assess the situation and spin an alternative plan if necessary.

His hopes were in vain.

Like the sense of potential energy that saturated the air the instant
before lightning struck, Rapp could feel the couriers closing on him.
Whatever awaited around the side of the compound, they'd see it together. He rounded the corner of the pockmarked wall and gestured to
the section of wall on which the meters were affixed. "See?" he said.
"Problem with the meter."

Problem was a bit of an understatement.

While most dwellings had a single meter, the compound had four,
but the meter closest to Rapp had been reduced to splinters.

"What happened?" FLACO said.

The courier went to touch the still-intact housing, but Rapp stayed
his hand. "Careful. Those plastic shards can be sharp, and the electronics might still be live. I'd hate for you to get shocked."

FLACO jerked his hand back from the cratered housing, but his partner wasn't so easily swayed. "What caused this?" GORDO said, using his front knuckle to sift through the shattered pieces.

Rapp thought it would be too suspicious if he tried to stop the second man's efforts, but he was still worried. The 7.62mm round Beighley had fired would have hit the meter like a runaway freight train. In all likelihood, the bullet had ricocheted off the concrete, but on the off chance he was wrong, Rapp didn't want the courier discovering a flattened projectile in the back of the meter.

"Probably kids playing football or cricket nearby," Rapp said, pulling a cell phone from his pocket. "We get this all the time. Let me take a picture for the office."

At the word *picture* GORDO jerked back his hand like a scalded cat.

"Wait," GORDO said, backing up a step.

Rapp nodded distractedly as he fiddled with his phone. The fact that GORDO didn't want to be in the picture was another data point, but like the rest of the intelligence he'd collected thus far, it was inconclusive. The answers Rapp needed were inside the compound, not out here.

"All right," Rapp said, "let's take a look at the junction boxes inside."

"Why?" GORDO said.

Rapp gestured toward the shattered meter. "I think this was probably the work of children, but I'm not sure. There's always a chance the meter could have shattered due to an electricity surge. This can happen when the line's damaged. Kind of like a kink in a garden hose."

Rapp had no idea if any of this was true, but since it sounded plausible to him, he was hoping it sounded plausible to the couriers.

"How does the line become kinked?" GORDO said.

Another excellent question.

"Sometimes herd animals step on the lines," Rap said. "A kinked line can short. Depending on the voltage load, the short can cause a fire or even catastrophically fail."

GORDO paled and Rapp thought he was in. Then FLACO's satellite phone vibrated. The courier examined the device and then turned to Rapp.

"We'll call you if there's a problem with the line," FLACO said. "There's no need to go back inside."

Though everything in his being desperately wanted to get back in the compound, Rapp shrugged and said, "Suit yourself. Here's my card." He fished in his shirt pocket, withdrew a business card, and handed it to FLACO. "Call the number on the bottom if you lose service. I'll get someone out here to fix the meter in a couple of days."

"Why can't you fix it now?"

GORDO again.

"I only triage," Rapp said. "A repair crew follows behind me. If you give me your number, I'll have them call before they show."

"That will not be necessary," GORDO said, his eyes hardening. "We will be here."

Of that Rapp had no doubt.

CHAPTER 68

"How are we doing this?"

The question came from Mas. Coleman suppressed a sigh. Most days, the team of operatives Rapp had assembled over the years functioned like a well-oiled machine.

Today was not one of those days.

"Hearing him explain it again won't make the answer any better."

This comment came from Will. That the men on Coleman's team hailed from different services usually wasn't an issue.

Usually.

"Here's the deal," Coleman said, hissing his answer. "The gunships are gonna take out the lead vehicle with their cannon while Charlie hits the driver of the second vehicle and covers our assault across the objective. The second pair of gunships will have the rear vehicle. We grab the Iranians out of car two, bag-and-tag 'em, and secure the missiles. Then the Black Hawks pick us up. Simple."

"You're right," Mas said. "The plan really isn't any better when you hear it the second time."

Will chuckled, but the laugh sounded forced. It probably was. Will had been fine with the *make shit happen* vibe of this mission, but Mas was less enthused, probably because he understood how difficult it would be to get men out of the vehicle alive without dying in the process.

Coleman sympathized with the former Delta operator's concern because he shared it.

His team was risking their lives because Rapp needed information. Were it not for the requirement to interrogate the Iranians, Coleman could have let Captain Smith drop Hellfires on the convoy and called it a day.

But this was the nature of the intelligence business.

Unlike conventional forces whose charter centered on closing with and destroying the enemy, paramilitary operatives operated in the gray area in which the intelligence gleaned from high-value targets was often more important than taking them off the battlefield. This was why the army's Delta Force now worked almost exclusively in Iraq. Winning the fight against the insurgency raging across the Arab nation required the ability to both decapitate the heads of terrorist militias and understand their chain of command, funding mechanisms, training regimes, and so much more.

Coleman believed in his team, but he would love to turn over the kinetic portion of this mission to a troop of Delta assaulters right about now. But neither SEAL Team 6 nor Delta Force was here to save the day. If Scott and his band of ruffians didn't make shit happen, the intelligence held in the minds of his targets would go up in smoke.

"Chaos 7, this is Shock 6. Lead vehicle is ten seconds out, over."

Captain Smith's radio call put an end to Coleman's internal deliberations.

For better or worse, the operation was now in motion.

"Shock 6, this is Chaos 7," Coleman said. "Roger all. You are cleared hot, over."

"Shock 6 confirming cleared hot. Stand by."

Stand by was such an aviator thing to say. Coleman was huddled body-to-body with his team in a rain-filled depression half a length away from a road that was about to become a scene of unmitigated violence. Captain Smith might have been working at an insurance call center for all the tension in the cavalryman's voice.

But that characterization wasn't entirely fair.

Smith was also helpless in the sense that he wasn't taking the shot. Instead, an aviator under his command was about to fire at a target with Americans hunkered well inside the danger-close guidelines. Smith's life might not be in danger, but Coleman knew that behind the calm radio demeanor the cavalryman must also be feeling pretty helpless. Except Smith's version of helpless didn't have him squatting in a hole while praying that a man he'd never met hadn't skimped on gunnery practice.

Maybe this whole paramilitary gig was overrated.

Putting aside his increasingly pessimistic thoughts, Coleman pressed the transmit button on his second radio. "Zeus, this is Chaos 7. You are weapons-free."

"Roger that, 7. Zeus is weapons-free."

Charlie's voice also seemed absurdly relaxed, but for a different reason. The former SEAL was in the zone, embracing the battlefield Zen practiced by all snipers. Though the distance to target was only two hundred meters, Charlie would still retard his heart rate and respiration. The key to being a great long-distance shooter was to treat each engagement as if it were a kilometer-plus shot. Besides, this wouldn't exactly be a walk in the park even though the distance was minimal. Charlie was charged with shooting accurately through the windshield of a moving car in order to kill the driver.

Not exactly a cakewalk.

Though his teammates could monitor his conversation with the sniper element, Coleman still reached over with his left hand to squeeze Will's shoulder. Was the gesture unnecessary? Probably. But there were already too many variables in the tactical equation Coleman couldn't control. He wasn't going to add his team accidentally missing the execute signal to the mix.

A moment later Coleman felt two squeezes on his left biceps courtesy of Mas.

The assault team was ready to execute.

Now it was up to the aviators.

Even though he was a veteran of countless kinetic operations, Scott wasn't any less susceptible to the mind tricks that accompanied combat. Tricks like a warped perception of time. As seconds seemed to become minutes, Coleman had to fight the urge to press his radio's transmit button to ask for an update. The gunship pilots had enough on their plates. The last thing Captain Smith needed was an anxious SEAL crawling into the cockpit with him.

At least that's what the logical part of Scott's mind told him.

The lizard portion of his brain wasn't so sure.

Maybe Smith was trying to call him and couldn't get through. Coleman was debating whether to conduct a radio check when thunder rent his world. The noise was difficult to describe—a string of detonations that sounded a bit like firecrackers exploding but with much more menace. A mechanical clacking vaguely reminiscent of a jackhammer on speed accompanied by a *pop, pop, pop* of detonating 30mm rounds. Coleman kept his chest pressed against the muddy ground as a second round of detonations sounded.

Then he peered over the ledge.

The good news was that the Apaches had hit their mark. The lead Corolla was resting on the rims of two blown front tires. The engine was leaking fluid and spewing steam, and the windshield was shattered. Coleman couldn't speak to the status of the vehicle's occupants, but that Toyota wasn't going anywhere.

The bad news was that the same couldn't be said of the target vehicle. Rather than screeching to a halt behind the stricken lead Corolla, the driver of the Suzuki van decided that it was time to get the hell out of Dodge. The lead vehicle was sprawled across both lanes, blocking traffic. Instead of trying to weave around the totaled sedan, the van had elected to make an off-road escape.

An escape headed straight toward Coleman.

CHAPTER 69

USUALLY, the phrase *coming straight at you* was something of an exaggeration.

Not today.

The Suzuki hurtled toward Coleman with an unerring accuracy as if it were a heat-seeking missile locked on to a dumpster fire. The front tire snagged a piece of rock as the van tore up the slight incline, sending the hood wobbling to the left.

For an instant.

Then the wheels angled right, and the bumper was once again centered on Coleman's belly button. Without thought, Coleman brought his rifle to his shoulder, laid his optic's crimson dot on the driver's midsection, moved the selector switch to fire, and pressed the trigger. A distant part of his brain registered the rifle's report as the buttstock slapped his shoulder, but the majority of Coleman's intellect was focused on just one task.

Hammering through his magazine.

Feeling like a matador staring down a charging bull, Coleman bent his knees and leaned into engagement even as he continued to fire.

Running never entered his mind. He simply worked the trigger, bring-ing the red dot back onto target each time the muzzle climb lifted it toward the van's roof.

The Suzuki kept coming.

Coleman kept shooting.

Now he was in a macabre race to see if he could reach the end of his thirty-round magazine before the van's mud-crusted black bumper crushed his pelvis. Coleman didn't know why emptying his magazine before dying seemed so important, only that he had the fleeting thought that a gunfighter shouldn't die with rounds still left in his weapon. He wondered if it would hurt when the vehicle broke his body in two or whether his brain would just short-circuit on his way to oblivion.

One moment he was nose-to-nose with the radiator.

The next he was flat on his back, staring at the sky.

For an instant, he felt nothing but rage as he realized that his bolt had not locked to the rear. There were still rounds left in his magazine. Then he had another realization.

He was still alive.

"You crazy fucker," Will said.

Coleman wasn't sure how to respond. Fortunately, he didn't have to. Given that the Suzuki that had been trying to turn him into a hood or-nament was nose-down in the depression he'd been occupying seconds ago, friendly banter wasn't high on his to-do list.

As if hearing his thoughts, the van's front passenger door squeaked open.

"On the ground," Coleman said as he clambered to his feet. "Now."

Just to ensure that the passenger got the message, Coleman re-peated his instructions in two more languages. Whether it was his way with words, the crash, or seeing the man seated next to him impaled by high-velocity rifle rounds, the passenger sank to his knees, hands in the air.

"Clear the rest of the vehicle," Coleman said.

"On it," Mas said.

The Delta assaulter glided forward like a panther, his rifle's muzzle locked on the Suzuki's rear passenger window like it was a bird dog's nose. At just short of the window, Mas edged around and did a quick peek into the interior.

"Clear," Mas said. "The driver and rear passenger are both KIA. No one else inside."

"Chaos 7, this is Shock 6. Trail and rear vehicles have both been neutralized. What's your status, over?"

Without being told, Will had slapped flex-cuffs on the survivor's wrists and ankles before sliding a black bag over the man's head. Mas was searching the van, rummaging through the interior.

What was his status?

The interdiction hadn't gone as Coleman had envisioned, but his teammates were safe, they had a prisoner to interrogate, and the danger posed by the Iranian-modified shoulder-fired missiles had just been mitigated.

All things considered, Coleman's status was pretty damn good.

"Chaos 7, this is Zeus, all threats neutralized. I'm ready for exfil, over."

"Roger that, Zeus," Coleman said, feeling his lips twist into a smile. "I'm on the horn with Shock 6 now. Exfil birds should be en route momentarily."

Charlie responded with two clicks of the radio transmit button. Coleman reached for the push-to-talk on the radio that was tuned to Shock's air-to-ground frequency.

They'd actually done it.

"I think we've got a problem!" Mas yelled.

Coleman turned toward the voice, his index finger hovering over the transmit button. Mas's headed poked from the Suzuki's open door.

He didn't look happy.

"What kind of problem?" Coleman said.

"The kind that's gonna ruin your day."

CHAPTER 70

ISLAMABAD, PAKISTAN

Though it was difficult for his Persian pride to stomach, Azad Ashani believed the Islamabad Serena Hotel was perhaps the most magnificent resort in the Middle East and easily among the top five in the world. Located in the northeastern corner of Islamabad within hiking distance of Shakarparian National Park and Rawal Lake, the resort was more a destination than a simple place to spend the night. With fourteen acres of gardens, six restaurants, a full spa and heated outdoor pool, and a stunning façade influenced by Islamic architecture, it was easy to understand why the Serena was Pakistan's only five-star hotel.

But Ashani was not here for the amenities.

The hotel's outdoor gardens featured dozens of paths that meandered past ponds, courtyards, benches, gazebos, and countless other secluded nooks and crannies. Though the architects who designed the facility had surely not had this in mind, the pedestrian area offered multiple opportunities for a spy with much on his mind to ensure that he wasn't being followed. But even this wasn't the reason why Ashani found himself seated on a bench in a quiet corner of the garden with a wall of nicotine-colored stone to his back and a leafy privacy hedge to his front. He was here because the hotel was famous for housing another contingency besides vacationers.

Foreign delegations.

Ashani fished a cell phone from his pocket with trembling fingers.

The tremors had begun during his flight from Kabul and had continued intermittently for the next several hours. Though he wished otherwise, Ashani could not attribute the shaking to fear. While in a particularly morbid mood, Ashani had once forced his doctor to detail how his final days on earth would be spent. The physician had explained that Ashani would experience neurological symptoms during what the doctor had euphemistically termed the "final stage."

Uncontrollable trembling was one of those symptoms.

After a few embarrassing mishaps, Ashani managed to extract the phone and place the device on the bench next to him.

As he stretched an index finger toward the phone icon, the tremors ceased.

The flight from Kabul to Islamabad, while short, had provided Ashani with much-needed time to think. With no faces of passersby to keep track of, no text messages to answer, and no emails to read, Ashani was able to devote the sum of his intellect to his current situation. While his body was in a state of terminal decay, Ashani's mind was as sharp as ever and the period of intense introspection had yielded several valuable conclusions. One, until he secured a deal with the Americans, his family would remain vulnerable. Two, Rapp's failure to meet must be an indication that the terms Ashani had previously offered were no longer lucrative enough to garner the American's attention. To address conclusion one, Ashani was left with a singular course of action.

Propose a bigger deal.

Ashani had arrived at this conclusion fairly quickly and had spent the remainder of the flight strategizing over how to structure this new deal. After the Kennedy kidnapping debacle, he'd done his best to demonstrate to both the CIA director and her top assassin that the horrors perpetrated against her were the work of a few rogue operatives rather than a reflection of official Iranian policy. Ashani had established a back-channel relationship with Kennedy prior to her kidnapping, and he'd redoubled his efforts after the incident.

In addition to the intelligence on Hezbollah and other regional bad actors, Ashani had tried to shape the American assessment of the Iranian leadership through a series of carefully curated leaks. Leaks detailing deliberations between the Guardian Council and Iranian elected officials. While his superiors would certainly not have approved of his actions, Ashani did not consider his leaks traitorous but rather an influence campaign. He loved his country and believed that its best chance of survival lay with convincing the Americans that the Persian people were not a threat.

Ashani was no traitor.

And this was the source of his difficulties.

As head of the MOIS, Ashani possessed many secrets the Americans would love to have. Secrets that would expose his country and make it vulnerable on the world stage. Ashani might detest Quds Force operatives like Ruyintan and the officer's enablers in the Iranian ruling class, but he loved his fellow countrymen. Ashani needed to offer something that would tantalize the CIA without harming his nation in the process. Ashani had but one piece of information that would satisfy these diametrically opposite criteria.

One secret to trade in exchange for his family's safety.

Hopefully, it would be enough.

Where are you?

The text from Ruyintan only underscored Ashani's urgency.

Ashani was at the Serena Hotel and not the Iranian embassy in Islamabad with Ruyintan for one reason—Mike Nash. The CIA assistant director and his retinue were guests at the Serena, but Ashani was not about to place the entirety of his hopes in Nash's hands. The assistant director was no doubt a capable clandestine officer, but he did not have the authority to broker the deal Ashani was seeking. Ashani would spill his secret to Nash, but only if his terms were first met.

On my way, Ashani texted to Ruyintan.

Then he dialed a new number.

CHAPTER 71

"WHAT'S your assessment?"

Rapp eyed the card table on the other side of the safe-house's living room as he considered his answer. He had long ago come to terms with the notion that he did not have a normal job. In fact, what he did for a living wasn't even in the same universe with the nine-to-fivers who made up the majority of his countrymen. Still, there was something unnerving about trying to answer a question of this magnitude while eyeball to eyeball with a greasy carton of takeout, a day-old newspaper, and a Mark Greaney paperback.

Even CIA officers loved *The Gray Man*.

"He's in there, Irene," Rapp said. "I could feel him."

Rapp answered without filtering his thoughts, as was his custom when speaking with his longtime boss and friend. Nor did he pause to consider how odd his response would sound. Taylor Moore stopped pecking on his laptop long enough to give Rapp a strange look, but that was fine. From anyone else on the planet the notion of being able to sense the location of Al Qaeda's leader would sound ridiculous.

Not from Rapp.

"Other than your intuition, is there anything I can take to the president?" Irene said.

Rapp turned to face the window.

Though he couldn't see the compound from where he was standing, Rapp could have pointed to it through the wall. It was as if the structure were a magnetic pole and his finger a compass needle. His pause wasn't driven by offense at Irene's question. At times she lent greater credence to his instincts than he did. Irene had authorized operations solely on his gut before and if she had been the deciding authority on this one, Rapp knew she would again.

But Irene wasn't the deciding voice.

That honor resided with President Alexander.

"No," Rapp said, replaying the events at the compound in his mind. "I pressed as far as I could, but I couldn't make it happen. Not in a way that would have allowed me to walk out afterward. For a moment, I thought I had a window to prosecute the target. It didn't pan out."

If Irene was surprised to hear that Rapp had been considering punching bin Laden's ticket, she didn't say. Irene knew Rapp as well as his own mother did. Maybe better. You don't turn a wolf loose in a henhouse and then act surprised when he comes out with feathers in his mouth.

"What about STORMRIDER?" Irene said.

Even though the phone connection was routed through three encryption devices and therefore considered secure, Kennedy was still using the randomly generated cypher referring to Noreen. Irene shared Rapp's paranoia when it came to secure communications not because she was ill-informed but because she was a former agent runner. There was something to be said for staffing the leadership of the world's premier intelligence organization with case officers who knew what it was like to operate in the field one step ahead of people who wanted to kill you.

As if she knew she was the topic of conversation, Noreen looked up from where she'd been composing her after-action review on another of the safehouse's secure laptops. After leaving the compound, Rapp had made the decision to rendezvous with Noreen and bring her in from the cold. Her performance in the compound had impressed him, and Rapp judged her to be more valuable as a potential team member than as a solo operative still maintaining her NOC cover.

"It was a bust," Rapp said. "STORMRIDER played it perfectly, but FLACO and GORDO are pretty wily customers. "If I'm wrong and CRANKSHAFT isn't in that compound, we should kill whoever they're protecting. How are things on your end?"

"Alexander isn't budging. No proof of life, no mission."

This pronouncement irritated Rapp for all the usual reasons, but there was something in Kennedy's tone he didn't like. "What aren't you telling me, boss?"

A sigh echoed through the phone.

"We're on borrowed time with CRANKSHAFT. Illumination conditions are only conducive for a mission for the next couple of nights. After that, we'll need to push the operation a minimum of thirty days. I don't think we can wait that long."

"Why?" Rapp said. He understood the concerns about illumination. The helicopters carrying the bin Laden assault team would be flying blacked out. Between the phases of the moon and the overhead cloud coverage, environmental conditions dictated a very narrow window in which the ambient light would be strong enough for the pilot's night-vision goggles, but not so bright as to spotlight the helicopters. But he thought Irene had concerns beyond just the weather.

"I have a feeling of my own. I think CRANKSHAFT is about to slip through our fingers."

"Agreed," Rapp said. "And not just because I want to shoot the shit-bag in the face. The couriers were on edge. Beyond just operational paranoia. Either the strain of living in close quarters while confined to that compound is wearing on them, or they have operational intelligence that we're getting close, or maybe both. STORMRIDER did a great job, but these guys learned a long time ago that safe is better than sorry."

His answer was met by a long, unbroken silence.

Rapp didn't mind.

He had a unique vantage point into Kennedy's mind. Her silence did not equate to doubt. In fact, the opposite was true. Irene was probably framing the argument she intended to make to President Alexander on Rapp's behalf. Like a lawyer deposing a witness, she was identifying vulnerabilities in Rapp's testimony and considering ways to shore them up.

"Your gut won't be enough," Irene said finally. "Not this time."

"Politics?"

"Partly, but more than that. You know what it will mean if it turns out that one of our allies was harboring the world's most wanted man. This has implications beyond just the presidency. If Alexander approves the operation and things go wrong, the fallout could undo our progress in Afghanistan."

Rapp thought about his rather unfruitful meeting with the National Guard brigade commander. If that was progress, he'd hate to see the alternative.

"We need honest-to-God proof," Irene continued. "The kind the president can slap down on the table in front of the American people."

Rapp sighed.

"Have preparations for this thing started?" Rapp said.

"Yes."

"Are the shooters in position?"

"Not yet," Irene said. "They're in-country, but still at Bagram."

"Because the president's waiting for his proof?"

"Yes."

Irene didn't elaborate.

She didn't have to.

Rapp understood the significance. When fifty of the most highly trained men on the planet showed up at a small outpost like Fenty in Jalalabad, people noticed. Countless foreign nationals worked on each FOB and even if the arrival of the strike package went unnoticed, the men's presence wouldn't be. The longer the assaulters sat waiting for strike authorization, the greater the likelihood they would be noticed. If the president forward-deployed the Tier 1 operators, he needed to use them.

Quickly.

"Tell your boss to send the welcoming committee," Rapp said. "I will identify our mystery guest in time for them to launch. He has my word."

Another stretch of silence.

This time Rapp thought the quiet was for him. Irene never second-guessed him, but she did occasionally give Rapp room to reexamine his assessments. Rapp had a deserved reputation for being headstrong, but he also possessed the rare quality of knowing his blind spot. Dr. Lewis, the only Agency shrink completely read into Rapp's operational portfolio, termed the attribute emotional intelligence.

Rapp liked to think of it as common sense.

"Tell him, Irene."

"Would you like to share with me how you intend to get that proof?"

"I don't know yet, but as soon as I get off the phone with you, I'll get on the horn with Coleman and tell him to get his ass here. Between his team and our assets in-country, I will come up with something. Tell the president to send them, Irene. My gut says that they need to go tonight or we risk losing CRANKSHAFT."

This time, the silence stretched even longer.

"I thought you might say something like that," Irene finally said, "and I've got one more avenue to pursue."

"What?"

"Ashani."

"What the hell has he got to do with this?"

"I just received a message from him," Irene said. "He called one of the encrypted digital dead-drop voicemails he's been using to pass me back-channel information."

"I know he's probably pissed that I blew off my meeting with him, but the missing Ranger was more important. By now Coleman should have interdicted the Iranian convoy from Pakistan. With any luck he's got a prisoner or two we can interrogate to understand whatever in the hell the Quds Force was planning to do with those missiles. Ashani's important, but he doesn't trump CRANKSHAFT."

"Agreed. Which is why I thought you'd be interested to hear that he's offering intelligence on CRANKSHAFT."

Rapp frowned as he replayed Irene's words, trying to understand if he'd somehow misunderstood. "What do you mean?"

"Exactly what I said. Ashani is currently in Islamabad, and he claims to know CRANKSHAFT's whereabouts. He's willing to trade this information for his family. His wife and daughters are playing tourist in Paris, and he wants my assurance that we will exfil them to America. If I agree, he will relay what he knows to Nash."

Rapp surveyed the scrum of Agency workers spread out across the living room. His first thought was that their operational security had been breached and the CRANKSHAFT mission was now penetrated. How else could Ashani know exactly what they were seeking?

But that wasn't the only explanation.

Rapp could feel the compound's presence as he was caught in the structure's gravitational pull. Sometimes operations came together through a confluence of seemingly unrelated events. A series of random-appearing happenings that rippled through time and space after originating from a single inflection point.

"Mitch?"

"I'm thinking."

Rapp took stock of the team he had and the options they represented. Could he mount an operation to verify who was in the compound?

Yes.

Would it be successful with this team?

Probably not.

Rapp needed to approach the reconnaissance of the compound with the mindset that it was a no-fail mission. He had to be prepared to prosecute the target then and there if his effort failed to garner the proof the president required, or worse still, spooked the compound's inhabitants. This was the definition of a high-risk/high-reward operation. One did not attempt to win the Super Bowl with a roster consisting of the neighborhood pickup team. To do this right, Rapp needed his varsity players.

Coleman's crew.

"Confirm the deal with Ashani," Rapp said, looking at his watch and computing drive times. "I'll handle things on this end, but you've got to get those frogmen to J-Bad."

"Are you sure, Mitch?"

Rapp understood his boss's true question. To get Alexander to forward-deploy SEAL Team 6, Irene would have to be creative in her update. She would need to put her credibility as the director of the Central Intelligence Agency on the line based solely on Rapp's word.

This was not a small ask.

"It's an hour flight from Bagram to Fenty plus whatever time it takes the frogmen to pack up their shit and load it aboard the helicopters, but this mission isn't going off until nightfall at the earliest. I'm betting it will be closer to the middle of the night to ensure our targets are deep in their sleep cycle before our boys come knocking. By the time the sun sets, I'll have proof of life, Irene. I promise."

This time there was no hesitation in Irene's reply.

"Okay. I'll send the confirmation signal to Ashani and speak with President Alexander. The ball's in your court, Mitch. Good luck."

"Thanks, boss."

The call ended.

On the whole, he only disagreed with one thing Kennedy had said.

It wasn't a ball that had just dropped in his court.

It was a grenade.

CHAPTER 72

" **C** OLEMAN."

"Scott, it's me," Rapp said, turning the wheel with one hand as he held the burner phone to his ear with the other. "I need you and the boys to join me. What's the status on your op?"

"Sorry for not getting back to you sooner," Coleman said, "but things here have been a bit hairy."

Rapp gritted his teeth and hammered the accelerator. As per standard operating procedure, the safehouse's fleet of vehicles reflected the most commonly seen trucks and cars on Pakistan's street. This was a great strategy when a CIA officer needed to blend in while conducting surveillance or an asset meet. It wasn't such a great plan if said officer needed to cover the one hundred and forty kilometers between Abbottabad and Islamabad as quickly as possible. The gray Honda Civic that Rapp was piloting was a reliable car, but it was a bit lacking in the horsepower department.

"Give me the short version," Rapp said. "We're on the clock."

Noreen stirred in the seat next to him. She'd offered to drive while he made calls, but Rapp had declined and put the cell on speaker mode instead. His decision wasn't an indictment of the case officer's skills but an acknowledgment of his own shortcomings. Like a shark, Rapp needed to be in constant motion. The two-hour trip would be painful enough without him sitting in the passenger seat, twiddling his thumbs.

"We hit the convoy and captured a Quds Force officer and one of the HIG fighters," Coleman said.

"That's good."

"Not really. The Iranian made a grab for one of the Afghan's weapons. He was shot and killed in the struggle. We've still got the HIG jihadi, but he's only a foot soldier."

"Fuck," Rapp said.

"I'm afraid that's not the worst of it. We secured the missiles, but we're two short."

Noreen stifled a gasp as Rapp threaded the car between a pair of slower-moving vehicles. Had Rapp been able to make the trip from Abbottabad to Islamabad by air, he could have covered the fifty-kilometer straight-line distance in minutes. Instead he was forced to box around the mountain range separating the two cities by following the M-15 Motorway southwest for fifty kilometers, then picking up the M-1 Motorway heading southeast before hopping on the Srinagar Highway and driving northeast for the final portion of his journey.

While he could do nothing to shorten the distance, Rapp was determined to push the Honda to its limits, even if his driving elicited the occasional gulp from his passenger.

"Explain," Rapp said.

"You said we were looking for eight missiles. The convoy only had six."

"Shit," Rapp said. "Did you get any intel from your prisoner?"

"I turned him over to the Afghans," Coleman said. "They're working on him, but he hasn't given up much. Says that they were heading to Kabul but claims that only the Iranians knew the actual targets. He did confirm the existence of the two missing missiles. Said they're part of another convoy."

"What do you mean?"

"Two Quds Force officers and four HIG fighters split off from the main convoy before it left Pakistan. They took the missiles with them. He doesn't know where the second convoy is headed."

Or he's refusing to say.

Not for the first time, Rapp wished he could be in two places at once. Next to Irene, Coleman was the person he trusted most, but Rapp also knew the SEAL's limitations. Scott had the ruthlessness required to do the things that were sometimes necessary to get evil men to give up their secrets, but he didn't possess Rapp's intuition. Even if Coleman put the phone on speaker so that Rapp could listen as the Afghans did their work, it wouldn't be the same. Rapp needed to smell a prisoner's fear, see their expressions, and hear their voice. He needed to be present for the interrogation, not two hundred miles away.

"Here's the deal," Rapp said. "I need your help here, but those missing missiles have me worried. Very worried. Any ideas on this second convoy?"

Coleman sighed.

"I've been thinking about that nonstop. Iranians smuggling weapons into Afghanistan isn't new. The Brits have even interdicted MANPADS shipments out by Herat, near Afghanistan's western border with Iran, but this is the first time the Quds Force has tried to bring munitions in from the east."

"What are you driving at?" Rapp said.

"Smuggling Iranian weapons and fighters into Afghanistan from Pakistan is the equivalent of heading west from New York to get to Paris. The convoy we interdicted came in through Torkham. That means they would have had to cross over seven hundred miles of Pakistan-controlled territory just to reach the Pakistani-Afghanistan border checkpoint. Why in the hell would they do that?"

Rapp pictured the geography as he thought about Scott's question. While Afghanistan shared an almost four-hundred-mile western border with Iran, Pakistan encompassed its southern and western sides. The

Torkham border crossing was heavily trafficked, but why would the Iranian convoys risk discovery by skirting Afghanistan's entire southern border for hundreds and hundreds of miles?

Unless they hadn't.

"Pakistan's Regional Stability Conference," Rapp said. "What do you want to bet those motherfuckers flew the missiles into Islamabad with the Iranian delegation? From Islamabad to Torkham is only, what, one hundred miles? They knew we'd probably catch them if they tried smuggling the weapons in from the west—"

"So they did it from the east," Coleman said. "But the second convoy split before they crossed the border—"

"Which means the Iranians were smart enough to hedge their bets," Rapp said. "The missing missiles must be coming into Afghanistan via another border crossing. Maybe farther south toward Khost or north up in the Kunar. Shit, shit, shit."

"What do you want me to do?"

That was a great question.

What Rapp wanted was for Coleman and his crew to saddle up and head for Pakistan, but the situation with the missing missiles was sounding more and more dire by the moment.

"I don't have the situational awareness to make that call from here, Scott," Rapp said. "If you think you can get something more out of the HIG fighter, work that angle. Call in any assets you need, and if you run into a roadblock feel free to invoke my name. If you think it's a dry hole, get yourself and the team here."

"On it."

"Good hunting," Rapp said, and ended the call.

"Where's that leave us?" Noreen said.

"With too much road and not enough time."

CHAPTER 73

MIKE Nash was not having what anyone would consider a successful trip.

After verbally jousting with his Pakistani hosts and getting crossways with his own colleague at the Department of State, Nash had been looking forward to his off-the-books meeting with the number two at the MOIS, Darian Moradi. Nash didn't claim to be a diplomat and had no expertise resolving interservice rivalries between State and the CIA, but he did know a thing or two about being a spy.

While the meet was supposed to occur at a brightly lit Islamabad coffee shop rather than the back alleys or decrepit safehouses more familiar to Nash, he still felt on safe ground for the first time on this godforsaken trip.

Except that Moradi had never showed.

Now Nash was beginning to wonder if he was cut out for a desk job.

Strike that.

Nash *knew* he wasn't cut out for a desk job, which was why he had never put in for one in the first place. In the blissful days before Mitch Rapp had turned him into a national hero while simultaneously guaranteeing that Nash would never again work clandestinely, he'd occasionally pondered his exit strategy.

Okay, so perhaps more than occasionally.

Between the aches and pains that grew ever more persistent and Maggie's increasingly less-than-subtle hints that their relationship needed to undergo a strategic rebalancing, Nash had known that his days as a paramilitary officer were numbered. Unlike Rapp, who had nothing and no one to live for besides the job, Nash's children were hurtling toward adulthood and his wife was a hotshot attorney at one of the nation's most prestigious law firms.

Something had to give.

And it had.

But not in the way he'd imagined.

Nash's gaze slid across the room's sterile confines. Known as "the bubble" in Agency lexicon, the room was the most secure space in a CIA station. The bubble was surrounded by a Faraday cage to mitigate electronic eavesdropping and insulated from the floor and structure of the building to prevent the unintentional transference of sound waves. It was the Holy of Holies. The place where the most secure conversations were held and the most sensitive emails read. Nash had always associated the bubble with executives huddled around stacks of classified documents, and he'd done his best to avoid the space.

Now he was one of those executives.

His eyes drifted back to his secure laptop and the cable he was trying to compose to Irene. Sending a SITREP to his boss was nothing new, but Nash had been struggling with the verbiage for the last fifteen minutes.

Okay, so maybe that wasn't entirely true.

His issue was more with the tone and substance of his update. Even to Nash's eyes, the text read like a whiny missive written by someone who was angry they'd been sidelined. That all of that was true didn't make the transgression any less serious. Nash was not some prima donna Ivy Leaguer upset that his first Agency posting had been to Mozambique rather than Vienna. No one was holding a gun to Nash's head. He could leave the Agency tomorrow and his family would be fine until he found another job.

More than fine.

Maggie made a shit ton of money, and though their lifestyle was a bit ostentatious for Nash's liking, they lived well beneath their means. Nash needed to either get with the program or get out the door.

This business was too serious to be lukewarm.

With a sigh, Nash deleted much of what he'd written and prepared to start over. As his fingers flew over the keyboard, he had another moment of personal revelation—this one even less pleasant than his self-induced attitude correction. For the first time since he'd joined the Agency, Nash hadn't responded with revulsion when he'd considered what a post-CIA life might look like.

As usual, Maggie was right.

A come-to-Jesus was in order.

The reinforced steel door behind him banged open and Nash frowned.

It was customary to at least knock before barging into the Holy of Holies. The kind of conversations held in its sacred space were of the sort meant for station chiefs and presidents.

Someone needed to learn some manners.

As Nash turned, the frustration he'd been holding at bay boiled over. "Were you raised in a barn?" Nash said.

"Look who's taken to the executive persona like a duck to water. Just because you've adopted the seventh floor's dress code doesn't mean you have to copy their attitude too."

Other than Maggie, the number of people who could talk to Nash in this manner and still boast a picture-worthy smile was in the low single digits.

Digit number one was framed in the doorway.

"What if I'd been on the phone with someone important?" Nash sputtered, trying to cover for his irritation.

"More important than me?" Rapp said. "Impossible. Now, are you going to keep pissing and moaning or do you want to get back in the game?"

Nash wanted to be mad.

He really did.

Though he'd shucked his jacket and rolled up the sleeves on his dress shirt, he knew that Rapp was right. He looked like any of the other SES bureaucrats who lorded over their Washington fiefdoms.

Rapp, on the other hand, looked like . . . Rapp.

Where Nash's pants and shirt still displayed some of their dry-cleaner-induced stiffness, Rapp's wardrobe gave off a different vibe. His pants were wrinkle-free, but the cuffs had a slight coating of dust. Similarly, his shirt, while clean, was open at the neck and untucked. The sleeves were rolled and the fabric bunched as if perhaps its wearer had been in a recent wrestling match.

Knowing Rapp, this was entirely possible.

But it was the vibe that radiated from his former partner that most irritated Nash. Rapp brought to mind an athlete who'd just stepped off the field for halftime. He was in his element, warmed up, and ready to give the other team hell. Nash, on the other hand, wasn't even the former starter who was now offering encouragement from the sidelines. He was in the owner's box with the rest of the has-beens and never-was's. But as much as Nash wanted to direct his irritation at his former teammate, he couldn't. Not because he'd suddenly outgrown his admittedly childish behavior. No, his change of heart stemmed from something Rapp had just offered.

A chance to lace up his cleats and join the team.

"Tell me," Nash said.

He cringed at the needy tone that accompanied his answer and prepped himself for Rapp's ribbing. It didn't come.

"Shit's going sideways," Rapp said. "I need your help."

"In the field?" Nash said.

"Sort of," Rapp said. "I want to put your newly minted clout as a senior Agency executive to work."

"What are you talking about?" Nash said, a sinking feeling settling in his stomach.

This didn't sound like donning a chest plate or grabbing a rifle.

"Ashani's here. I need to meet with him."

"Not gonna happen," Nash said, shaking his head. "The Islamabad chief of station showed me a breakdown of the Iranian delegation. It's rife with Quds Force minders. Your picture is probably on every urinal in the Iranian embassy. No way can you get within a mile of Ashani."

"I know," Rapp said. "That's why you're going to set up the meeting. Invite Ashani to coffee. A mano a mano between the head of the MOIS and the CIA's deputy director for counterterrorism. Hold the meeting in your hotel suite. I'll join you."

Nash shook his head. "He won't accept. I was supposed to meet with Ashani's number two earlier, but he stood me up."

"Moradi?"

"Yep."

Rapp smiled. "Ashani will accept. He already reached out to Irene to set the conditions. He's going to provide us with information in exchange for his family's safety."

"On the missiles?"

"That and something more."

"What?"

"CRANKSHAFT."

Inwardly Nash sighed, but he kept his expression blank. While this wasn't an invitation to be Rapp's number two man in the tactical stack, it sure beat the hell out of hobnobbing with Pakistanis.

"Sure," Nash said. "When?"

"Now."

CHAPTER 74

I T had been a long time since Nash had sat at a table with candles and a linen tablecloth, anxiously awaiting the arrival of a pretty girl. The separate dining area in Nash's presidential suite wasn't a restaurant, but with a mahogany table that could seat eight and the fancy place settings and plates of steaming food, it could have been. By the same token, the person Nash was waiting for was neither female nor someone he was interested in dating, but the sensation felt similar.

With the exception of the panther pacing behind him.

"Where the fuck is this guy?"

Nash had tried ignoring Rapp.

It hadn't worked.

Though his friend was normally the cool head in almost any scenario, Rapp's legendary low tolerance for bullshit was getting the better of him.

To be fair, Nash was also a little uptight.

The plan to meet with the MOIS minister was a variation of hiding in plain sight. Contrary to their depictions in pop culture, these types of ministerial gatherings weren't all cocktail parties any more than they were adrenaline-charged meetings held around impossibly long diplomatic tables. In the real world of espionage and diplomacy, it was often the one-off liaisons that were more important than anything annotated on the official itinerary.

"Do you know what's driving Ashani's desire to defect?" Nash said.

Rapp shrugged. "Haven't really had time to think about it before now. Do you have a theory?"

"Yes. Cancer."

A stillness enveloped the room.

"Explain," Rapp said.

"Ashani's been good at hiding his movements, but we learned that he's been seeking treatment outside Iran for a respiratory illness. Specialists in Europe as you would expect from a member of the Iranian elite, but there's an interesting correlation between the doctors he's been seeing. All of them consulted with their US counterparts who were treating the emergence of post-9/11 cancers endemic to first responders and victims of the attacks in New York."

"The Isfahan nuclear facility," Rapp said. "The Mossad brought it down and Ashani was one of the few survivors. He must have breathed in a shit ton of concrete dust and now he has cancer. Is he looking for a treatment in the West?"

"The opposite," Nash said. "I think he's come to terms with a terminal diagnosis. He's not trying to save himself. He's trying to save his family."

"Because he has enemies in the Iranian government," Rapp said. "And he'll have even more once it comes out that he helped us thwart their Afghanistan operation. He's dying and won't be able to protect his wife and daughters."

"Exactly," Nash said.

Rapp squeezed his shoulder. "That's some good work, Mike. Really. But it only makes this meeting more urgent. CRANKSHAFT aside, I need to figure out what Ruyintan has planned for that missing convoy. I'm still not connecting the dots."

"What do you mean?" Nash said.

Rapp shrugged. "Sending a bunch of jihadis into Afghanistan with shoulder-fired missiles isn't big enough. Westerners see militant Islamic leaders foam at that mouth as they thunder their intentions to murder us and shrug. No matter how large the German shepherd, if all he ever does is bark, eventually you tune him out. Only people like us understand that these killers mean what they say. It isn't lack of intent that keeps them from biting us. It's a big chain-link fence. And if the dog thinks that someone left the gate open . . ."

"They bite," Nash said.

"Exactly," Rapp said. "This shit with the missiles—it's a nibble. Would it throw a wrench in our plans if our helicopters were vulnerable at night? Sure. But we'd adjust tactics to mitigate the threat just like we did once Iranian explosively formed penetrators started blowing up Humvees in Iraq. Besides, the missiles are finite. Yes, the Quds Force shitheads almost got one past us by sneaking six through Pakistan, but that's a one-trick pony. Ruyintan thinks bigger than that."

Nash stared at Rapp as he turned over what he'd just said.

Rapp was absolutely correct.

If the Iranians were willing to go through the operational hurdles of moving a team of Afghan HIG militants into Iran for training, equip them with a limited supply of modified surface-to-air missiles, coordinate for transportation through Pakistan, and assign Quds Force minders to ensure they successfully executed their mission, it wouldn't be for a series of piecemeal attacks against coalition aircraft. It was almost as if . . .

"Holy shit," Nash said, turning in his chair, "the missing missiles. Everything else was the distraction. Those MANPADS and the men carrying them are the main effort."

"That's what I'm afraid of," Rapp said, "but there's only one man that can tell of us if that's true."

As if on cue, someone knocked on the door. The pattern was unique—three long raps, two short ones, and then a final three long.

Ashani.

"Come in," Nash said, getting to his feet.

The door swung open, revealing the visitor.

It was not Ashani.

CHAPTER 75

"WHAT is he doing here?"

The man asking the question was none other than Darian Moradi.

While Nash was surprised to see the deputy minister attending in place of his boss, the expression on the cleric's face wasn't shock or even annoyance.

It was terror.

"Great to see you again," Rapp said.

"You," Moradi stammered. "You!"

The MOIS number two turned to grab the door, but his fingers never connected with the handle. With a speed that would have been difficult to believe had Nash not spent most of his professional career watching Rapp at work, his friend snagged the Iranian. In a measured display of aggression, Rapp spun the slight man and planted him into the open chair at the head of the table. Rapp completed the sequence by throwing the door's dead bolt and then positioning himself between Moradi and escape.

Game, set, and match.

"I take it you two know each other?" Nash said.

"Ashani said I could trust you," Moradi said, jabbing an index finger at Nash.

The movement caused the MOIS officer's sleeve to flutter, revealing what looked like a splint affixed to his forearm.

"Keep your pants on," Rapp said, stepping closer to Moradi. "We're here to talk. Unless your start with the shitty attitude again. Then I'm gonna finish what I started on your wrist. Why isn't your boss here?"

Of course the splint was Rapp's work.

Why would Nash ever assume differently?

"Ashani promised me we'd be alone," Moradi said, again to Nash.

The small man completely ignored Rapp in the same way that a child might close their eyes when presented with something scary. As if pretending that Rapp didn't exist would somehow mitigate the danger he represented. Or maybe the cleric was under the misguided assumption that the CIA organization chart indicating that Nash was Rapp's boss somehow gave him authority over the assassin.

Better to put that pipe dream to rest now.

"You can trust me," Nash said, "but the time for subterfuge is over. We have questions that require immediate answers. Help us, and we'll help you."

"Or what?" Moradi said. "You'll unchain your dog?"

Nash laughed. "I'm afraid you misunderstand the situation. I don't tell him what to do. No one tells him what to do."

For a split second, Moradi's indignant expression transformed into one of horror.

Then his head bounced off the table.

"Listen carefully," Rapp said, yanking the cleric's head backward by his hair. "I'm done fucking around. Tell me exactly what I need to know, or I will gut you like a fish."

"They will kill me," Moradi sputtered.

Rapp thumbed open his ZT blade. "Your countrymen are running around with two shoulder-fired missiles and a team of HIG fanatics.

Fanatics they trained. You are going to tell me why Ashani isn't at this meeting and where to find him or I am going to remove your eyeball. If those Quds Force shitheads employ their missiles against an American target, my president will hold your nation responsible. Our first strike will sink your navy and decapitate your government. It only gets worse from there. You can work with me and stop this madness or be the one-eyed guy who has to explain to the Guardian Council why they should expect random visits from Hellfire missiles. Choose."

The matte-black blade descended toward Moradi's left eyeball.

Nash swallowed.

Usually, he had a pretty good handle on what Rapp was thinking.

Not tonight.

Nash considered intervening. Taking the gloves off while interrogating terrorists was one thing, but killing the number two man at the MOIS was something else.

"You fucks are the world's largest state sponsors of terrorism," Rapp said, as if reading Nash's mind. "It's long past time we started treating you the same way we treat the mindless jihadis you pay to die on your behalf."

The ZT's tip dimpled Moradi's skin.

Nash clenched his fists.

He couldn't allow this to happen.

"I don't know anything else," Moradi said, screaming his answer. "Ruyintan never talked about a secondary target."

"Ashani," Rapp said, increasing pressure on the blade. "Where is he?"

A single drop of crimson welled up from the cleric's cheek.

"They took him," Moradi said.

"Who?" Rapp said.

"Ruyintan. That's what I came to tell you. Ruyintan and his thugs arrested Ashani."

"When?" Rapp said.

"About an hour ago," Moradi said. "They were going to question him in the embassy and then take him back to Tehran."

"How?"

"A chartered jet from Islamabad International Airport."

Rapp released Moradi's hair and closed the folding knife. Turning to Nash, he uttered just two words.

"Call Irene."

CHAPTER 76

RENE Kennedy had weathered many a tense moment in the White House.

In her more than two decades of service with the CIA, she had spent almost half as an executive. Her mentor, Thomas Stansfield, had been grooming her to replace him long before cancer claimed his life. As such, she'd accompanied her surrogate father to 1600 Pennsylvania Avenue countless times before assuming his role as the director of the world's premier intelligence organization. In this capacity, Irene had sat in war rooms with multiple presidential administrations.

She'd seen a thing or two.

None of that held a candle to this.

Irene often wondered what it might have been like in the Roosevelt White House as the president and his staff anxiously waited for word from the armada of ships carrying an army of nearly 130,000 troops poised to hit the beaches of Normandy as part of the D-Day invasion. The restless hours must have been absolutely agonizing, but Irene thought that her lot might be even worse. She was just as helpless, but today's technology allowed her to watch events unfolding half a world away in real time.

It was maddening.

"Final inspections complete. Strike package boarding their aircraft."

An Air Force general was translating what was happening on the television into words. Originally, the plan had been for the president to wait for news of the operation's success or failure from the Situation Room's much larger conference room, but the siren song of technology had proven too great. Someone had let slip that a single officer was monitoring a livestreaming satellite feed from a much smaller anteroom, and the president had promptly joined him. Now a space meant to hold three or four was packed with bodies all mesmerized by a flight of idling helicopters parked on the J-Bad tarmac.

Though she wanted to zone out with the other cabinet members, Irene couldn't. She had made a promise to the president. A promise still unfulfilled. True to his word, President Alexander was launching the mission based on her assurances that Rapp would come through with final validation of bin Laden's whereabouts before the SEAL Team 6 assaulters fast-roped onto the Abbottabad compound. But as the ghostly figures boarding the helicopters could attest, time was running out.

Irene felt the weight of the president's gaze.

Turning to make eye contact with her boss, she shook her head.

Alexander's features hardened and he gave a short nod in return. The aircraft would launch without Rapp's report, but the Pakistani border was the president's red line. Traversing the width of Pakistan uninvited could be classified as an act of war. An act of war against a notional ally, no less. In a counterbalance to the momentous failure that had led to the 9/11 attacks, this time the CIA had to get the intelligence right.

One hundred percent right.

Irene glanced at the clock.

Twenty minutes.

That was how long she had once the aircraft departed the airfield

before the helicopters would be in Pakistani airspace. Twenty minutes
to confirm that she was not sending twenty-six men on the most dangerous mission of their lives just to assault a compound full of children
and low-level Al Qaeda operatives. To his credit, Joshua Alexander was
risking it all—the presidency, his legacy, and maybe even war—solely
on her say-so.

Where was Mitch?

Her chest tightened.

The question brought to mind the other time she'd desperately
wondered where Rapp was and what he was doing. Back then, the
stakes had been much more personal. Instead of the lives of anonymous
commandos, Irene had spent her time in that dank cell worrying about
something much closer to home.

Her own life.

The lighting dimmed and her respiration quickened.

Not now.

This couldn't be happening now.

Her boss was on the brink of taking the nation to war and she was
having a panic attack. Irene closed her eyes and massaged her temples,
feigning a headache as she tried to block out the sensation of a rubber
hose stinging her bare back or the fists striking her face and body or the
indignity of being doused in her own urine or the—

"Director Kennedy?"

Irene snapped open her eyes.

She slowly turned toward the sound of the voice, resisting the urge
to leap from her chair and run toward the speaker like a drowning
swimmer lurching for a lifeline. She was the director of the Central Intelligence Agency. Men were about to live and die based on her word.
This was not the time to give the impression that she was losing her
grip.

Even if she was precariously close to doing just that.

"Yes?" Irene said.

The speaker was a young woman with short, dark hair and an earnest expression. To Irene's eye the woman looked about twelve, but maybe it was because she lacked the sense of chic jadedness that the more senior interns tried to project. Part of Irene wanted to thank the woman for her service while the other half wanted to scream at her to run while there was still time.

"There's a phone call, ma'am," the woman said. "The secure line."

"Coming," Irene said, getting to her feet.

She caught the president's eye as she headed for the door.

He didn't speak.

He didn't have to.

CHAPTER 77

"**D**IRECTOR Kennedy speaking," Irene said, clutching the phone to her ear.

"Irene, it's me."

Irene grabbed the desk for support as her knees suddenly went wobbly. The voice on the other end of the line did not belong to Rapp.

The caller was Mike Nash.

Maintaining her balance took more effort than Irene cared to admit. After checking over her shoulder to ensure that she was still alone in the little huddle room, Irene sank into a leather chair.

"What's happening, Mike?" Irene said.

She tried to keep her tone neutral, but it was hard not to let her disappointment seep through. Nash was in Pakistan to keep the Pakistanis occupied while Rapp and the NOC officer did the real work. Though it was perhaps unfair to Mike, Irene couldn't think of anyone she'd rather hear from less at this moment.

"I need to pass along an operational update," Nash said.

Irene straightened as the room swam back into focus.

"On CRANKSHAFT?" Irene said.

"In a manner of speaking. Ruyintan just arrested Ashani. He intends to rendition him to Iran."

"Okay," Irene said, drawing out the word. "Can you provide specifics?"

"Not really. Moradi was the source. That's all he knew."

"How confident are you in Moradi's reporting?"

"Very," Nash said. "Rapp was the one asking the questions."

Kennedy paused to consider the ramifications of that statement.

Was Rapp known for employing extreme measures when interrogating terrorists who might have knowledge of a pending attack against US interests?

Absolutely.

But Moradi wasn't a run-of-the-mill jihadi. He was an influential cleric and the second-in-command of the MOIS. The KGB was infamous for employing rough-and-tumble "Moscow Rules" tactics during the heyday of Cold War espionage, but this was not that. Assaulting the senior leadership of another intelligence service could be grounds for war.

Except the Iranians had allowed Hezbollah to do just that to her.

Perhaps a little turnabout was fair play.

"What is Mr. Moradi's current condition?" Kennedy said.

"Other than a small cut above his right eye and a couple of bruises, he's fine. Physically, anyway."

An enemy combatant who encountered Rapp and lived to tell about it undoubtedly came away with more than just a few bumps and bruises. As Irene knew firsthand, there was an emotional component to being manhandled. Chances were that Moradi would wake up in a cold sweat more than once with thoughts of Rapp hovering at the edge of his consciousness.

Good.

"Where is Mitch now?" Kennedy said. "And why isn't he the one on the phone?"

While she didn't know the answer to her first question, Irene thought she could guess at the second. Rapp wasn't on the phone because he was in the middle of making things happen. But she wanted to hear this from Nash. He needed to show the strength of character required to inform his boss that her top counterterrorism operative hadn't made it a priority to personally keep her abreast of what he was doing. Either Nash was going to grow into his new role, or she'd need to find him another.

His response would be a good indicator of which way the wind was blowing.

"Our surveillance team confirmed that the Iranian delegation left their embassy minutes ago," Nash said. "Based on Moradi's information, we believe they're en route to Islamabad International Airport with Ashani. Mitch is putting together a plan to interdict Ashani before Ruyintan renditions him from Pakistan. I'm currently idling on the tarmac in the Gulfstream. I'm the one calling because Rapp is busy and I'm not."

"Why aren't you in the air already?" Irene said.

As part of Nash's pre-trip briefing, Irene had discussed with him the possibility that the CRANKSHAFT operation might launch during his trip. If this happened, she wanted him out of Pakistan before the commandos hit bin Laden's compound. Tensions were bound to run high in the mission's aftermath no matter its outcome. The last thing Irene wanted to do was provide the Pakistanis with potential bargaining chips in the form of American CIA officers.

"Because Rapp needs my help."

"Help how?"

"It would probably be better if you didn't know."

Irene swallowed her instinctive reply, determined not take out her frustration with Mitch on Nash. Was she angry that her top operative was running an unapproved and ad hoc kinetic operation on Pakistani soil moments before the launch of the riskiest clandestine undertaking of the last decade?

Yes.

Was she surprised?

Not in the least.

"Did Mr. Rapp happen to relay any information that might be helpful?" Irene said.

She managed to keep the sarcasm from her voice, but not the disappointment. For this to work, Nash needed to come into his own as opposed to just being Rapp's errand boy. Then again, she'd run Rapp for years and knew firsthand the struggles Mike was facing. Managing Rapp wasn't so much riding a bridleless mustang as trying to surf a tsunami.

"Yes," Nash said. "He said to trust him."

Of course he did.

CHAPTER 78

BILAL Din was not a happy man.

To be fair, he knew he had only himself to blame. While the salary he earned as a corporal in Pakistan's Airport Security Forces, or ASF, was not extravagant, it did provide Bilal with enough to take care of his small family.

And therein lay the problem.

Bilal did not want a small family. He wanted a house full of children. Boys and girls who would grow up to a world outside of Pakistan and careers beyond government service. Bilal wanted his offspring to study at the best universities and earn diplomas with exotic names like *Oxford*, *Cambridge*, or *Harvard*.

Bilal was a practical man and knew that achieving these dreams required money. Money on a scale that his government career couldn't provide. With this in mind, Bilal had taken on a second, more lucrative job.

A job with the CIA.

But Bilal wasn't a spy.

He was a purveyor of information. He provided his handler with tidbits concerning the comings and goings of people and cargo through Islamabad International Airport's busy terminals.

In exchange for his service, his offshore bank accounts received regular deposits.

Though he knew that what he was doing was wrong, Bilal slept soundly at night. As part of his agreement with his Agency handler, he did not provide information on Pakistani officials or trade in national secrets. He bore his birth country no ill will and did not consider himself a traitor. Bilal was simply a pair of eyes and ears for the Americans, who no doubt had countless more officials like him on their payroll. In the five years since he'd first brokered the arrangement, Bilal had never had cause to second-guess his decision to work for the Agency.

Until now.

"Do you have the uniforms?"

The idyllic setting provided a strange backdrop for the question. A question loaded with intent. Bilal stood on the gravel-lined access road just south of the Rama Dam spillway. The site offered a picturesque view of the man-made lake to the east and was a prime spot for anglers during daylight hours. At this time of the night, however, no fishing poles jutted out from the concrete flood barriers lining the shore and no vehicles were parked among the green weeds spouting between the loose rock.

Well, almost no vehicles.

In addition to Bilal's patrol car, a battered blue Honda Civic occupied the sought-after fishing spot. A Honda Civic bearing two people.

The question had come from the slighter of the pair.

The woman.

Though the woman spoke flawless Urdu in a perfect accent, Bilal did not believe she was Pakistani. Everything about her appearance and speech might suggest otherwise, but Bilal sensed an arrogance found in only one place.

America.

Or maybe that was his anger speaking.

Without answering, Bilal opened the passenger door to his patrol car, withdrew a pair of Airport Security Forces uniforms, and handed them to the woman. He instinctively disliked her, but Bilal kept his eyes fixed on her face. She was attractive, but that wasn't why Bilal refused to look at her companion.

The man terrified him.

Dark-skinned, with a thick beard and wavy black hair, her companion could have hailed from a half a dozen countries. Bilal didn't think the man was Pakistani either, but he was making a concerted effort not to appear interested in the stranger. The man had done nothing that could be construed as aggressive, but Bilal instinctively placed him in a different threat category. He had never seen the pair before and, Allah willing, would never see them again. The less he knew about whatever they were planning, the better.

His task complete, Bilal was turning back to his vehicle when a voice stopped him.

A male voice.

"Wait."

Bilal froze, hating himself for responding. As a member of the ASF, he was charged with keeping airports and, more importantly, passengers safe. As such, he'd developed a law enforcement officer's instincts when it came to identifying dangerous men. While the man standing in front of him was not particularly physically imposing, nor was his stature provocative, Bilal's sixth sense still screamed a single word.

Beware.

"I provided the uniforms," Bilal said. "My part is done."

"Not quite," the man said. "We need your car."

Bilal rested his right hand on the butt of his service revolver.

To anyone who understood the language of violence, his message was clear.

This conversation was at an end.

"Uniforms sometimes go missing," he said. "The same can't be said of patrol cars. Besides, if I gave it to you, how I would get back to the airport?"

Bilal inwardly grimaced at his response. Besides providing the man with an opportunity to offer a rebuttal, his lapse had done something worse—display weakness. As he'd done during his initial meeting with his handler, Bilal knew that he had to establish and maintain the terms of this relationship. Dangerous people could sense weakness in the same manner in which a shark could smell blood.

Still, his question was valid.

For obvious reasons, the meeting was being held away from the airport, but the dam was only a kilometer or so straight-line distance from the airfield. The fishing area was open to the public, but Bilal had made the trip via the airport's perimeter roads, which could be traveled only by the ASF. The distance to the airport proper was short enough for Bilal to hike, but arriving back at his duty station without his patrol car would raise questions.

Questions that the man and woman would undoubtedly want to avoid.

Bilal caught himself before he smiled, but he still reveled in the sudden surge of joy. He'd discovered a way out of this situation that didn't involve betraying his country.

"We don't want you to abandon your car," the man said. "We want you to drive it."

Or perhaps not.

CHAPTER 79

D AMON Sanger ran his eyes across the Beechjet 400A's instrument
panel as he acknowledged the radio call from Islamabad International Airport's air traffic control.

"Roger, Islamabad Tower, JS Charter Kilo Juliet is holding short of
taxiway Romeo for runway One Zero right."

The three multipurpose displays that made up the bulk of the business jet's digital cockpit showed that both engines' temperatures were in
the green and the flight plan's navigational waypoints were loaded. The
taxiway off the Beechjet's nose was an expanse of empty blackness
bounded by strings of blue edge lights. Beyond the taxiway, the southern-
most runway was waiting with its two miles of concrete delineated by
white lighting. As Damon watched, the aircraft he was holding short
for, an Air Force C-37A Gulfstream business jet painted in an unmistakable blue and white livery with the words *United States of America*
stenciled above the seven cabin windows, taxied to the runway's
threshold.

In Damon's world everything was perfect.

Everything outside his jet, anyway.

"What do you think is going on back there?"

Like Damon, his copilot was also an expat. But while Damon's radio transmissions were flavored with an American accent, Nico Romano's English had a decidedly Italian flair. Nico, like Damon, had flown for his nation's military before transitioning to life as a commercial pilot. For Nico, it had been Eurofighter Typhoons, while Damon's aircraft of choice had been three variations of the venerable AH-64 Apache helicopter gunship.

Damon liked his job and coworkers. While not as prestigious as flying for a major airline, life as a charter pilot had its perks. Damon enjoyed the variety that came with piloting business jets for high-end customers. The exotic destinations, ever-changing schedule, and generous pay combined with Islamabad's relatively low cost of living meant that his Army pension went a lot further here than in the States. VIP passengers could be demanding but their demands were normally a problem for the flight attendants.

Normally.

Today there were no flight attendants, and the clients had requested zero contact with the flight crew. At first, Damon hadn't understood the strange request.

Now he did.

"Our job is to fly the plane, Nico," Damon said, "not supervise the passengers. How's the weather at our destination?"

"Tehran, you mean?" Nico said. "It is as perfect as it ever gets in that part of the world. Do you think our passengers will all be alive to experience it?"

Damon sighed as he willed the American government jet to expedite its power check so that he could take the runway. He and Nico had honored the customers' demands. Instead of welcoming the passengers as they'd boarded, the flight crew had remained in the cockpit with the door closed.

But he and Nico weren't blind.

Unlike regular passenger pickups, this one hadn't taken place on the large tarmac reserved for general aviation just to the west of the main terminal and due north of the active runways. Instead Damon had been instructed to taxi to the southwestern corner of the airfield and wait for the passengers on a stretch of asphalt that abutted four isolated hangars. Though the taxiway was present on Damon's airport diagram, it wasn't labeled and the hangars it serviced were conspicuously absent. This section of the airfield was obviously under the Pakistani military's jurisdiction. Accordingly, Damon had assumed that their passengers would be high-ranking officers or civilians in the armed forces.

This assumption had proven to be incorrect.

Though only the Beechjet's position lights had been illuminated, Damon had still seen five men exit the pair of Range Rovers that had pulled alongside his jet. The men were dark-complected, but not Pakistani or Indian. Based on the charter's destination, Damon guessed they were Iranian.

Damon didn't have a problem flying Iranians.

Passengers were passengers.

But the figure who'd been half-carried, half-dragged from the rear of the lead Range Rover didn't really qualify as a passenger. In Damon's experience, a person wearing handcuffs was best described using a different P-word.

Prisoner.

"It does not bother you that we are conducting a rendition?" Nico said. "Most likely an illegal one?"

Nico's English was always flawless, but his accent grew more pronounced under pressure. At this point his intonation was thick enough to slice with a knife. But accent or not, Nico had a point.

A point that Damon had been trying to ignore.

Was he willing to participate in a kidnapping?

Or worse?

Iranian government officials weren't known for their model human rights practices. And if this was some sort of rendition, what were the potential consequences for Nico and him? Would he be able to off-load the passengers in Tehran, refuel, and head back to Islamabad, or might a problem unexpectedly develop with his passport or flight plan?

"Islamabad Tower, Shogun One Five is aborting our takeoff and diverting to taxiway Romeo."

Damon sighed.

Rather than disappear into the night sky, the American Gulfstream had aborted its takeoff roll and was now taxiing onto an adjacent taxiway. Islamabad International was Pakistan's second-busiest airport and its two active runways were prime real estate. With that in mind, it made sense that the Americans had chosen to move from the active runway to where Damon was holding short, but the tower probably wasn't going to like their decision.

"Shogun One Five, this is Islamabad Tower. Taxiway Romeo is restricted. Please continue to taxiway Charlie."

"Too late," Nico said.

The Gulfstream had already taxied onto Taxiway Romeo, which meant the pilots were committed. No doubt reacting to the tower's command, the pilots braked, bringing the jet to a stop.

"Unable, Tower. We've already taken Romeo."

The Gulfstream was now impeding Damon's access to the runway.

"The Yanks are about to catch hell," Nico said.

"Islamabad Tower, this is Shogun One Five. I apologize. We have an issue with our nosewheel steering. Request permission to proceed south on taxiway Romeo so we can troubleshoot."

"When pigs fly," Damon muttered.

Damon's Beechjet was holding on a secondary taxiway that branched to the southwest from Romeo, the taxiway the Americans were currently occupying. As long as Damon maintained his position, the Americans could taxi south, turn around at the semicircular cul-de-sac-like area to Damon's right, and retake the active. But to do this, the American Gulfstream would need to further encroach into restricted territory.

"Shogun One Five, this is Islamabad Tower. Negative. Maintain current position."

Nico started the auxiliary power unit, or APU, and pulled the jet's engines back to idle. It was the correct decision from a fuel management perspective, as the smaller APU used far less jet fuel than the larger engines. Because of the Americans' poor etiquette, Damon was not going anywhere until the Gulfstream moved, which meant they needed to conserve fuel. But as the Italian aviator seemed to forget from time to time, Nico was no longer flying a single-pilot aircraft.

They had passengers to consider.

As if reading Damon's mind, the intercom linking the pilots to the cabin buzzed.

Normally, passenger communications were handled by the flight attendants.

Tonight, Damon had that duty.

"This is the pilot speaking," Damon said.

"Why did the engines go to idle?"

The specificity of the question gave Damon pause. While he was accustomed to fielding inquiries about schedule delays both real and imagined, most passengers neither knew nor cared about the status of the aircraft's engines. This was yet another indication that the men occupying the Beechjet's cabin were not run-of-the-mill passengers.

"The plane ahead of us aborted its takeoff and diverted to our taxiway," Damon said. "It's blocking access to the runway."

The detail was much greater than what Damon would have normally provided, but he thought that the level of specificity might head off further inquiries.

It did not.

"The jet can either taxi out of the way or the airport's crash rescue team can push it into the grass. I don't care which, but I expect to be airborne in five minutes."

Damon saw Nico's angry expression, but he raised his hand, forestalling the Italian's outburst.

He was the captain.

This was his problem.

"I'm sorry, but I don't think that's going to happen," Damon said.

"I assure you it will," the passenger said. "We have a priority clearance from the Pakistani government. If we aren't rolling in the next thirty seconds, I will place a call to the director general of the Inter-Services Intelligence of Pakistan. He will then contact the airport directly. Either you coordinate with air traffic control, or I will."

Nico reached for his seat belt's release, but Damon grabbed the Italian's hand.

"Look," Damon said, pointing out the windshield.

A single airport security vehicle raced onto the tarmac with its red and blue lights flashing. The four-door sedan came to a stop between the American Gulfstream and Damon's Beechjet. The car's doors opened, and three figures exited—two men and a woman. One of the men angled toward the idling American jet while the second man and his woman companion headed for Damon's aircraft. Stopping just off the Beechjet's nose, the man pointed at the cockpit and motioned for the staircase to be let down.

"What do they want?" Nico said.

"Don't know," Damon said, unbuckling. "You have the jet. I'll find out."

"Are you sure?" Nico said. "You are the captain."

"Precisely. The captain gets the hard jobs."

"Be careful."

Damon squeezed Nico's shoulder as he stood. "Look on the bright side—maybe our customers will fire us."

Damon didn't put much stock in this outcome.

Judging by Nico's look, his copilot didn't either.

CHAPTER 80

"**R**EADY?" Rapp said.

Noreen nodded. This was partly because she didn't think she'd be heard over the screaming of four jet engines.

But only partly.

Now that the moment of truth was upon her, Noreen wasn't sure she could trust her voice. The plan Rapp had briefed had sounded ambitious even in the sterile confines of the ASF sedan. Now that she was face-to-face with their target, she might choose a different word to describe his concept of the operation.

Insane.

"Remember—your job is to get their attention and stay out of the way. Okay?"

"Yes!" Noreen shouted, putting steel into her voice.

A steel she didn't feel.

Walking into the compound that had potentially held Osama bin Laden had been frightening, but not debilitatingly so. She'd known in an abstract manner that there had been a possibility of violence, but she'd put the odds at very low. That those low odds had still materialized had been disconcerting, but part of the job. Things might have turned out differently had Rapp not been there, but at the end of the day, the largest injury she'd suffered had been to her dignity.

This was the antithesis of that.

Noreen could sense violence fermenting on the business jet in the same manner that a black cloud brewed with electricity. She just hoped she wasn't at ground zero when lightning struck.

As Rapp had predicted, the jet's crew had let down the staircase. Though she was no tactical ninja, Noreen knew that storming an airplane with hostages was a dicey endeavor. Even the operations that are counted as a success generally came with collateral damage in the form of injured or killed hostages. Failures, on the other hand, occurred when the assaulters were detected during the boarding process and never gained entry to the plane. Fortunately, Rapp had a plan to get them aboard the jet. The CIA Gulfstream had fenced in the Iranian jet, and Bilal had set the stage.

Now it was up to Noreen to walk into the spotlight.

"Can I help you?"

The question was voiced by the pilot standing at the top of the retractable stairwell. He spoke with an American accent and Noreen thought she detected a hint of stress in his voice.

Welcome to the club.

As per Rapp's instructions, she pointed to her ears and then continued up the stairs while grasping the metal railing. The steel felt cool and slightly damp from condensation.

Or perhaps the dampness was due to her sweaty palms.

"Inside," Noreen said with a thick Urdu accent. "Too loud."

She could feel Rapp just behind her and she didn't slow her progress as she summited the steps. For a moment, her stomach clenched at the possibility that the pilot might refuse to move. Then she pushed away her fear. One way or another, she was entering the airplane. The man could either move or suffer the indignity of being shoved aside by a woman he outweighed by one hundred pounds.

The pilot seemed to sense her determination. He hesitated, then gave a short nod and edged into the cabin.

Noreen followed.

CHAPTER 81

MARTIAL arts aficionados love to talk about the proverbial "fight in an elevator."

A hand-to-hand combat scenario in an enclosed space or under circumstances in which the victim's mobility was severely limited. The old *would your fighting style still work if your back was against a brick wall* question. To Rapp's way of thinking, most of this was just wasteful bloviating. Though he was a devotee of several styles of unarmed combat, he had long ago come to terms with the truth that no one fighting style addressed all potential martial scenarios.

Better still, most of the armchair warriors who liked to participate in this fruitless debate had never actually fought an opponent in an elevator, let alone a narrow stairwell or a dingy hotel room. Compared to what he was facing now, those scenarios might as well have been arena bouts. There was fighting in an elevator and then there was engaging in mortal combat inside a narrow metal tube that barely afforded an attacker the ability to stand. Rapp was much too young to have hunted Viet Cong as a tunnel rat, but those tight confines couldn't have been much narrower than what he currently faced.

CHAPTER 82

D AMON might have hung up his flight helmet two years ago, but he still had an attack helicopter pilot's instincts. Right now his gut was screaming that an unseen threat was sliding into a shooting position at his six o'clock. A bandit approaching from out of the sun, intent on shredding his aircraft with high-explosive rounds.

The woman didn't look like much.

Pretty, with dark, expressive eyes and an athletic figure that even her unflattering ASF uniform couldn't quite mask. But other than the fact that the officer's raven hair cascaded to her shoulders absent the confines of the expected hijab, there wasn't anything about her that Damon could lay his finger on. Nothing that should have his fight-or-flight response sparking like a live wire.

Then death slid by.

After realizing that the woman was determined to board his airplane, Damon had reluctantly made room for her in the small space between the cockpit and the Beechjet's cabin. While the business jet's accommodations were nothing to sneeze at, the aircraft was not a Gulfstream GVI with a full galley, couches, and a bedroom or wet bar.

The interior could accommodate six passengers in its pairs of leather reclining seats, but the cabin space was relatively modest. Damon had edged to the starboard as the woman entered, clearing the narrow corridor leading from the cockpit to the passenger area. He'd assumed that she wanted to address his passengers.

She didn't.

Instead, the ASF officer had followed Damon, crowding him against the bulkhead.

At first Damon hadn't understood.

Now, he did.

Though she'd been the one doing the talking, the woman was not the main attraction. Her job had been to draw everyone's attention while making room for the star.

Her partner.

The woman had attempted to distract Damon with a loud burst of Urdu. Her expressive body language was coupled with indecipherable hand gestures and head motions that made the most of her unbound hair.

The woman's efforts had almost worked.

Almost.

Despite her captivating performance, Damon was a gunship pilot. A gunship pilot who'd once gone head-to-head with a ZSU-23-4 antiaircraft system while spearheading the American invasion into Iraq. The sensation he felt now was eerily similar to the moment when his Apache had been locked up by the ZSU's fire control radar and golf ball–size projectiles began hurtling past his cockpit.

The man who flowed into the cabin wasn't physically intimidating. As with the woman, he was dressed in the ASF uniform, which featured a woodland camouflage pattern. Also like the woman, the bulky uniform masked his physique. He was neither fat nor unduly muscled—an average build for an average man.

The way he moved was not average.

While stationed in Thailand, Damon had once witnessed a cage fight between a mongoose and a cobra. The cobra was death personified, but the mongoose had been created with a singular purpose—to kill cobras. As the man slid past with a gait reminiscent of a surging tide, Damon was struck by the image of a mongoose.

A mongoose entering a den of snakes.

CHAPTER 83

Ashani fought against a haze of pain and drug-induced paranoia.

He was determined to remain conscious. Or at least as conscious as
his wounds and the heavy dose of the barbiturate that Quds Force officers were partial to using during interrogations permitted. Asleep,
Ashani would be swept along to his eventual rendezvous with Evin
Prison and a custom-made gallows from which he would hang.

A gallows no doubt already under construction.

Awake, Ashani had a chance to alter his destiny. A chance that
might be so slight as to be almost nonexistent, but a chance all the same.
Despite his best efforts, it had become harder and harder for Ashani to
differentiate between his surroundings and the pain-free euphoria to
which his mind begged to retreat. Twice he'd seen his wife and daughters and tried to call out, only to be jerked awake as an unconscious
spasm inflamed his injuries. Riding the pain, Ashani had clawed his
way to lucidity long enough to mark his surroundings.

He was on a plane.

A small business jet.

A change in the sound made by the roaring engines prompted Ashani to turn toward the window next to his seat. The jolt of agony accompanying the small gesture took his breath away, but the new information the pain garnered was worth the price.

They were still on the ground.

So why was the engine noise quieting?

The lessening ambient noise allowed Ashani to make out a cluster of voices echoing from the front of the cabin. Gritting his teeth, he tried to sit up for a better view. The movement sent bolts of lightning arcing through his abdomen. Brilliant points of light flared across his vision, but the tears leaking from his eyes weren't just from the unspeakable pain.

Three figures were clustered around the cockpit door.

Two he didn't recognize.

One he did.

CHAPTER 84

For a long moment, Ashani just stared at Rapp.

Was the American really here?

Ashani knew the delusions that a tortured man's brain was capable of forming. Hallucinations constructed of equal parts pain and hopelessness. Like a person stranded in a desert who sees an oasis as they're dying of thirst, prisoners desperate for rescue often construed salvation from thin air.

Maybe Rapp was just a phantasm.

The phantasm began to move.

The woman standing beside the assassin edged the pilot out of the way, clearing a corridor from the cockpit to the cabin. A corridor Rapp employed like a bullet screaming down a rifle's barrel. One moment Rapp had been entering the cabin from the airstairs with his head down and his shaggy hair covering his face in wet strands.

His hands had been empty.

They weren't empty any longer.

A pistol's report battered Ashani's ears, drowning out the idling engines. The unexpectedness of a gunman firing an unsuppressed weapon in close quarters had the effect of a detonating flashbang.

For an instant, Ashani's tormentors were stunned.

And then Rapp wasn't the only person moving.

Ashani resisted the urge to cower until the storm of violence passed. If he'd learned anything in his dealings with Ruyintan, it was that the Quds Force operative had instilled an unmatched ferocity coupled with an unparalleled capacity for violence into his men. Rapp might have the upper hand now, but he wouldn't retain it.

There were five armed Iranians on the plane.

That was too many.

Ashani thrust to his left, turning himself into a human spear. The pull of restraints against his wounds tore a scream from his lips, but not before the crown of his head connected with his seatmate's shooting arm. A pistol discharged and the muzzle blast buffeted his face. Reeling, Ashani battled the urge to retch as men screamed and weapons fired. The pungent odor of gunpowder filled the air along with the rustlike smell of blood and the putrid stench of perforated bowels.

Ashani's seatmate plunged his pistol into Ashani's chest.

And pulled the trigger.

The explosion of agony made what Ashani had felt earlier seem like a love tap. A milky gauze enveloped him, blanketing the pain and softening the edges of his awareness.

Hadn't he done enough?

Couldn't he just let go?

He saw Samira's beautiful face.

Rapp was a man of his word, but he was also a cold-blooded killer. He did not trade in charity. Ashani trusted the assassin to save his family, but not if he died without telling the CIA officer what he knew.

He had to fight.

Ignoring the fire burning in his chest and the blood soaking his shirt, Ashani flung himself against his seatmate a second time. He fell onto the Quds Force officer like a pile of wet laundry, lacking the strength to cause harm.

But even wet laundry could spoil a man's aim.

The Quds Officer cursed and rocketed an elbow into Ashani's temple.

The blow accomplished what the gunshot wound had not.

Blackness claimed him.

CHAPTER 85

RAPP squeezed the trigger and sent a 9mm round into the brain-pan of the Iranian seated next to Ashani. The Quds Force officer's head snapped back as a splatter of bone and brain matter sprayed against the fuselage with a wet-sounding slap. Panning to his left and right, Rapp surveyed the cabin over his pistol's stubby front sight post, looking for additional threats.

He found none.

The gunfight had taken the term *close-quarters battle* to an entirely new level. He was no stranger to violence, but he'd never killed five men in such tight confines. The once-luxurious cabin was covered in gore. Blood and other bodily fluids dripped down the leather seats and gathered on the beige-carpeted floor in putrid puddles. The stench made Rapp want to vomit and the ringing in his ears and his proximity to multiple muzzle blasts made his balance a bit unsteady. Catching movement to his left, Rapp saw a Quds Force operative pawing at his chest.

Rapp shot him in the forehead.

The Iranian went limp.

Though he'd survived the carnage without serious injury, a burning across the top of Rapp's left shoulder suggested that this was a near thing. After completing a final sweep of the cabin, Rapp eyed his shoulder. The thin stream of blood combined with the painful but free movement of the joint confirmed his early diagnosis—a graze.

He was fine.

Ashani was not.

The Iranian's face had been beaten to a pulp. His eyes were almost swollen shut and ringed by discolored circles. His nose was cartoonishly flat—more caricature than something resembling a normal appendage. Ashani's lips were split and dripping blood and at least one of his teeth was cracked, but it was the wetness on his chest that most concerned Rapp.

Crossing the cabin, Rapp holstered his pistol and examined the wound. The hole was in the vicinity of the Iranian's heart. Even if the MOIS officer had been in an operating room under the care of a world-class surgeon, Rapp would have put slim odds on his survival. In a cabin full of death with medical help nowhere in sight, Ashani had minutes to live.

Maybe less.

Ashani's eyes opened, and he beckoned Rapp closer with a weak wave.

"You will save my family?" Ashani gurgled.

"Yes," Rapp said.

Ashani sighed but the sound was more a whistle of air leaking from a punctured tire than a proper exhale. "Ruyintan is with the missing missiles."

"Where is he going?" Rapp said.

"Abbottabad. The missiles were intended to be used here. Against planes carrying diplomatic envoys. Now Ruyintan is taking them to bin Laden's compound."

"Why?"

"You."

Ashani's breath rattled in his chest.

Then, he was still.

"Bloody hell."

Rapp turned from his latest failure only to confront another. The comment had come from the pilot. The man's once-white uniform was now splattered with blood, but he seemed unhurt.

The woman he was crouching over was not.

Rapp bounded up the corridor and dropped to his knees beside Noreen. A dime-size entrance wound dimpled her skull just above her right ear. Noreen's thick black hair almost obscured the small hole, but nothing could hide the hideous exit wound at the back of her head.

The CIA officer was gone.

CHAPTER 86

M IKE Nash stared out the Gulfstream's oval window.

He might be a suit-wearing bureaucrat, but his mind still functioned like an operator's.

Rapp was taking too long.

Much too long.

"Sir, ground control is asking for an update on our mechanical issue. We're not going to be able to keep up this charade much longer."

Nash turned from the Iranian plane to the pilot standing in the cockpit's open door. Because his ruse of a visit to Pakistan was not just another diplomatic mission, Nash had requested and received pilots from the Agency's Air Branch. These men and women generally had a background in military special operations aviation prior to joining the CIA and most if not at all had combat deployments under their belts.

Bottom line: the aviators were not easily excitable.

His current pilot was a perfect example.

While the man was dressed in the livery typical of an aviator, his eyes exhibited a hardness at odds with his plain black pants, white dress shirt, and captain's shoulder boards. The man's name was Derek Richardson. Nash had reviewed his personnel jacket and knew Derek was in his early forties, but the pilot's full head of hair was mostly gray with only a scattering of the original black. Nash had seen this premature aging before and knew its source.

Combat.

"It's Derek, right?" Nash said.

"Yes, sir," the pilot said, nodding.

"You fly for special operations before the Agency?" Nash said.

Another nod.

"Army 160th?"

"Army, but a different unit."

Nash understood the significance of Derek's answer. The Night Stalkers might be the best-known special operations aviation entity, but they weren't the only game in town.

Not by a long shot.

Derek had seen a thing or two before he'd joined the Agency.

"Thought so," Nash said. "Here's the deal—two Agency operatives just boarded that Beechjet. We need to give them time to do what they have to do without attracting the attention of prying eyes. Understand?"

"Yes, sir," Derek said. "We need a reason to be here that's serious enough to keep us from taking off but not so serious that ground control will spin up security, maintenance, or crash and rescue."

"Exactly," Nash said.

"Okay," Derek said. "I can manage that for a bit longer, but we won't be able to sit on this taxiway indefinitely. Ten minutes. Fifteen tops. After that, we'll need to either taxi back to the general aviation ramp or take the active and depart."

Nash didn't like the pilot's answer, but he accepted it. People with Derek's résumé made the impossible seem routine. If the aviator thought they were near the end of their rope, Nash had to believe him. Nash was preparing to acknowledge Derek's update when another voice carried through the cabin.

The copilot's.

"Derek—outside. Now!"

For a profession that prided itself on maintaining a calm radio demeanor even when their aircraft was disintegrating around them, the copilot seemed a bit excited. Nash glanced out the cabin window and understood why.

Rapp was crossing the tarmac separating the two airplanes.

A limp body was cradled in his arms.

CHAPTER 87

"KILL the outside lights," Nash said. "Now."

To avoid additional attention from ground control or the airfield security forces, as well as give the illusion that their maintenance issue was temporary, the Gulfstream's landing lights were illuminated. But now those same high-intensity beams were a liability. To his credit, the copilot didn't wait for confirmation from Derek. The lights extinguished, plunging the taxiway into darkness.

"Extend the airstairs," Nash said, getting to his feet.

Derek pressed the necessary buttons on a touchscreen located on the bulkhead nearest the Gulfstream's single entrance. A moment later, the airfield's ambient noise flooded the cabin as the jet's door opened and airstairs unfolded. Nash reached for the metal railing, but Derek grabbed his shoulder, halting him.

Rapp was already on the staircase.

Nash reached down to help his former boss into the jet, but Rapp shouldered away his hand. Nash had served with Rapp long enough to recognize the set of the man's jaw. No one was going to help him carry the dead CIA officer.

No one.

Rapp looked half-feral. His shirt was smeared with blood and his black eyes blazed fury. Nash had to fight the urge to step backward. Rage distorted the air around Rapp like heat shimmering above black-top on a hot summer day.

Rapp's wild eyes found Nash.

"I need you to fly her to Bagram. The airplane on the tarmac in front of you is going to follow. Once you both land, get a team of our guys to bag-and-tag the Iranians and sanitize the aircraft. Then send the jet back here. It's a charter and the pilots are expats and former military officers. They'll play ball."

Rapp reverently lowered Noreen's body onto the leather couch as he spoke. Grabbing a blanket, he shook it out and covered her face.

Then he turned back to Nash.

"Questions?"

"Is the other bird flight-worthy?"

Rapp shrugged. "I think the exact words the pilot used were 'big plane, little bullets.' They have a couple new holes in the upholstery, but nothing to keep them from making the hop to Bagram."

"What about Irene's question? Did you get the answer?"

Rapp looked over Nash's shoulder.

The ASF corporal who had accompanied Rapp and Noreen onto the tarmac had long since retreated to his car. This meant that the jet's occupants were all Agency personnel, but Nash understood Rapp's reti-cence. The old Ben Franklin quote about three people's ability to keep a secret depended on two of them being dead still applied even to CIA officers. The bin Laden raid was classified at the code word level and most of the people in the Gulfstream had neither the required clearance nor the all-important "need to know."

"Get in the air before you get caught in the shit storm that's brew-ing," Rapp said. "I'll go direct with Irene."

Nash flushed. While he'd worked with Rapp long enough to know the man was no one's idea of politically correct, his friend's response felt unnecessarily harsh. Then Nash's gaze settled on Noreen's shrouded form. "Okay. We'll be wheels-up as soon as you're off. Anything else?"

Nash had meant the question as a throwaway.

An olive branch.

Rapp would most certainly turn him down. Irene had raised him to be a lone wolf. Though the agency's premier counterterrorism operative had come a long way from stalking jihadis by himself, Rapp still believed in planning and sourcing his own operations.

He never asked for help.

Ever.

"I need one of your pilots," Rapp said, turning from Nash to the cockpit. "Can either of you fly a helicopter?"

Derek looked over Rapp's shoulder at Nash.

Nash nodded.

"I'm qualified in a bunch of types," Derek said. "Both military and civilian."

"You guys were parked over in general aviation, right?" Rapp said.

"Correct," Derek said, "and yes, I saw the Bell JetRanger for rent at the adjacent flight school. I can fly it."

"What if someone misplaced the keys?" Rapp said.

Derek smiled. "It just so happens that the CIA's version of pilot training has an extra class or two that military flight school omits. As long as the bird is topped off with fuel, we should be good to go."

"Great," Rapp said. "Grab your shit and follow me."

For a moment Nash thought that his friend was going to disappear back down the airstairs without a parting word. Then Rapp caught his eye.

"You did good, Mike," Rapp said. "If you hadn't engineered this distraction, the Iranians would have smuggled Ashani home with us none the wiser. You did good."

Rapp was not one to hand out empty compliments, but any sense of pride the words engendered vanished as Nash's gaze settled on Noreen.

"Later," Rapp said, squeezing Nash's shoulder. "First, we have to see this thing through. Get back to Bagram and clean up my mess. I'll sort things here."

Nash nodded, not because he didn't trust himself to speak but because he didn't know what to say. Things were a long way from being sorted. Navy SEALs were about to enter Pakistani airspace for a raid on a compound that might or might not hold bin Laden. An Iranian special operations team and their HIG goons were in the wind with a pair of shoulder-fired missiles.

Things were about as far from sorted as Nash could imagine.

"Ready," Derek said, returning from the cockpit.

Rapp studied the pilot with an intensity that Nash could feel from across the cabin.

Then Rapp nodded. "Let's get this done."

Rapp disappeared down the airstairs with Derek in tow.

Rapp's exit bothered Nash.

He wanted to believe that his irritation was grounded in his friend's brusque manner or because Rapp was leaving Nash behind to deal with a plane full of Iranian bodies.

It wasn't.

Rapp was just being Rapp. When things went sideways, he didn't wait to be tossed from the frying pan into the fire. He leaped for the flames headfirst.

For the first time, Nash wasn't leaping with him.

CHAPTER 88

RAPP hunched against the drizzle, trying to protect his phone. The agency's S&T folks swore the cell was secure. Rapp had his doubts about that, but he was quite certain that the device was not weatherproof. As his long association with the tech geeks who designed James Bond gear for the clandestine service spooks had proven more than once, never assume a scientist will solve the unstated problem. In this case, he was happy for the semi-secure mode of communication he'd pilfered from Nash's jet before leaving with Derek, but he couldn't help but notice the lack of an environmental cover for the phone.

One problem at a time.

"Almost there," Derek called.

Rapp waved an acknowledgment as he punched numbers into the cell's dial pad. The former Army aviator either knew how to steal the Bell JetRanger or he didn't. Rapp was of no help in that regard. Judging by the trouble Derek was having getting past the aircraft's door lock, Rapp thought they might be in for a rough ride, but that was neither here nor there.

He had bigger fish to fry.

After entering the final digit, Rapp thumbed the send button.

As operations went, this would not go down as his finest. Rapp was standing on the tarmac of the general aviation section of the airfield facing south toward Islamabad International's two runways. Nash's jet rolled down the active as Rapp watched, the blue and white paint scheme distinct even against the surrounding darkness. Almost as soon as the American jet was in the air, the charter full of dead Iranians taxied onto the runway behind it. With a shriek of engine noise, the nimble Beechjet screamed down the runway, rotated, and then rocketed into the sky, chasing the C-37's fading position lights.

"Got it," Derek whispered as he opened the helicopter's door. "Let me flip on the battery and check fuel levels."

Rapp nodded but didn't reply. His call had gone through and a familiar voice was speaking.

"Hello?"

"Irene, it's me," Rapp said. "CRANKSHAFT is in Abbottabad. I have confirmation from Ashani."

An exhaled breath echoed through the phone. "Thank God. The strike package is sixty minutes from the target. This is cutting it close, even for you."

Rapp knew Irene intended the comment as a joke.

It wasn't funny.

"We're not out of the woods yet," Rapp said as Derek slid into the JetRanger's right seat. "Ashani's dead. So is STORMRIDER. Ruyintan is missing. We think he has the remaining two missiles."

Over his two-decade-plus career as a covert operative, Rapp had provided Irene with some pretty damning updates. They hadn't held a candle to this one.

Ashani.

Noreen.

Ruyintan.

Each name felt like a body blow to his liver.

Huddled against the rain in clothes covered in blood with only his pistol and cell phone, Rapp wasn't sure things could get much worse.

"Quarter of a tank," Derek said. "We can get to Abbottabad. Barely. But it'll be a one-way trip."

"What was that?" Irene said.

"Nothing. Just an update from my pilot."

"Pilot?"

"Yeah—I've got to track down Ruyintan and those missiles."

"Why?"

"He's headed for Abbottabad."

After a moment of silence, Irene said, "I assume Ruyintan's choice of destination is not a coincidence?"

"Correct," Rapp said. "Ashani said Ruyintan is taking them to bin Laden's compound."

"Why?"

"Because of me."

What had been a slight drizzle was now becoming a respectable downpour. Rain bounced off the tarmac in fat drops. The airfield's rotating white beacon sliced through growing fog, but Rapp knew they needed to get this show on the road or risk being grounded by the weather.

"What does that mean?" Irene said.

"No idea. That's one of the many questions I plan on asking Ruyintan face-to-face."

"Well then how does he know we're coming for CRANKSHAFT?"

"How did Ashani even know CRANKSHAFT was in Abbottabad?" Rapp said.

Rapp made eye contact with Derek and made a circle in the air with his index finger. The former Army aviator nodded and started flipping switches.

God bless helicopter pilots.

"I might be able to answer that one," Irene said. "CRANKSHAFT's wives must be in the compound. We know they took refuge in Iran with his children shortly after 9/11. It didn't work out. The Iranians expelled them in 2010, and the family fell off our radar soon after. I assume the MOIS did a better job of keeping track of where the wives and children landed than we did."

A pair of headlights burned through the darkness, tracking toward the flight school from the service road to Rapp's right. In theory, that road was open to the general public so that members of the flying club could gain access to the facility, but Rapp didn't imagine that anyone was planning on grabbing some stick time in the middle of the night. Maybe Derek had triggered an alarm on the JetRanger or perhaps the airfield security officer, Bilal, had suddenly sprung a conscience.

The end result was the same—he and Derek were in trouble.

"I don't know how Ruyintan put the pieces together," Rapp said, "but Ashani was in bad shape. I think Ruyintan broke him and learned that Ashani intended to trade us information on CRANKSHAFT's where-abouts for his family's safety. Maybe Ruyintan figures we're coming for CRANKSHAFT tonight, or maybe he just wants to arrange a final *fuck you* before he ducks out of country. Hell, it could be that Ruyintan only intends to warn CRANKSHAFT that we're onto him. At this point, the *why* doesn't really matter. Bottom line—Ruyintan can't be allowed to get to Abbottabad, and I'm the only one who can stop him."

Rapp slid the phone between his cheek and shoulder so that he could use both hands to eject the pistol's magazine and verify the remaining rounds.

Eight.

David had once gone into battle against a giant with just five smooth stones and a sling. Then again, Israel's future king been the re-cipient of divine intervention. Rapp didn't make a practice of asking the Almighty for help, but he wouldn't turn down an extra magazine or two right about now.

The headlights slid right as the vehicle turned from the perimeter road to the gravel driveway leading to the flight school.

Go time.

"Fifty-nine minutes, Mitch. Men will be fast-roping onto that compound in fifty-nine minutes."

"If you tell the president about the missiles, his advisors will pressure him to abort," Rapp said as he slid into the copilot's seat. "We'll lose CRANKSHAFT. Maybe forever. I've got this, boss. Keep those helicopters on course."

Rapp plugged his right ear with his finger and squeezed the phone against his left, trying to hear Irene over the engine noise.

Headlights played across the JetRanger as the vehicle accelerated.

"I thought you might say that," Irene said, "so I sent you some help."

"What kind of help?"

"You should see a vehicle coming toward you. I think you'll like what's inside. Godspeed, Mitch."

Irene disconnected.

Rapp stared at the approaching headlights with equal parts irritation and curiosity. Was he bothered that Irene had inserted herself into his operational planning? A little. Rapp didn't appreciate back seat drivers whether the person offering suggestions was his longtime boss or the president of the United States.

And yet.

And yet he needed to find, fix, and finish an Iranian intelligence officer in the company of an unknown number of underlings and two shoulder-fired missiles. Missiles that had been modified specifically to acquire and destroy aerial targets at night.

Maybe he could use a bit of help.

"Hang tight," Rapp said as he unbuckled his seat belt.

"Where you going?" Derek said.

"To see what's in the car. I'm leaving the cockpit door open. If I start shooting, hover over and get me."

"No problem," Derek said, "but if you've gotta kill someone, do it quick. We're burning gas."

God bless helicopter pilots.

CHAPTER 89

R APP held his pistol with his left hand and shaded his eyes with his right.

The muzzle was pointed at the ground, but that could change in a heartbeat. If the person in the car had been sent by Irene, she or he would be expecting Rapp to be armed. If they weren't, Rapp was splitting the difference between the provocative vibes holding the weapon at low ready would send and the state of unpreparedness that holstering the pistol would engender.

Fortunately, whoever was driving the four-door sedan seemed to get the message. The headlights extinguished as the car rolled onto the tarmac, showing little regard for the aircraft tied down at regular intervals along the blacktop or the slew of airfield regulations that undoubtedly prohibited random cars from weaving across the apron.

If anything, killing the headlights seemed to imbue the driver with more confidence.

The sedan's engine roared as the vehicle put on a burst of speed.

Rapp was in the middle of rethinking his unprovocative stance when the sedan's hood nosed to Rapp's left, putting him abeam the driver. The car skidded to a halt as the vehicle drew even with Rapp, but not before plowing through a puddle.

Rapp could now add *drenched* to the list of adjectives describing his wardrobe.

In the time it took Rapp to wipe the moisture from his eyes, the motor died, and the driver's-side door swung open.

"You look like a drowned cat who tangled with the wrong dog."

There was precisely one human being on the entirety of planet Earth who could talk to Rapp this way. Stan Hurley appeared in a cloud of cigarette smoke as if he were the devil himself newly summoned from the gates of hell.

"What are you doing here?" Rapp said.

"What kind of dipshit question is that? Saving your ass, of course. Now, if you're done playing grab-ass, make yourself useful and help me with this kit. Irene said we're on the clock."

Fifteen precious minutes later, Rapp was in right rear passenger seat of the JetRanger, trying to connect the dongle he'd pulled from one of Stan's kit bags to his phone.

True to his word, Hurley had brought help—in a big way.

From two innocuous go-bags haphazardly resting on the back seat of Stan's vehicle, Rapp had unpacked a pair of HK416 carbines mounted with EOTECH holographic sights and integrated suppressors, plate-carrier body armor equipped with tactical chest rigs, and about a dozen magazines all loaded with 5.56mm hollow-points. A smaller, padded bag for electronics contained two sets of night-vision goggles, two tactical tablets, the low-profile Bluetooth communication system Nash had been pushing, and an assortment of batteries, dongles, cables, and chargers.

Rapp felt like he'd just scored a free shopping spree at Gunfighters "R" Us.

The uptick in his equipment situation almost made up for Stan's piss-poor attitude.

"You were planning on saving the day with only a half-empty pistol?

I swear to God, one day I'm gonna find whoever trained you and punch that son of a bitch in the mouth."

Stan Hurley's exact age was perhaps the most closely guarded secret in the free world. Like the archeological practice of estimating the antiquity of an object by correlating it with the items buried alongside it, Rapp tended to view Hurley through the lens of the historical events the operative had taken part in. Though Stan was not old enough to have caused havoc behind German lines during World War II with Wild Bill Donovan and Thomas Stansfield, he'd begun his clandestine career in the decade after the war's conclusion. Stan was a hard man who'd done hard things in conflict zones too numerous to count.

He was also the person who'd trained Rapp.

If there was one human being to whom Rapp should afford deference, it was Stan.

"Are you done?" Rapp said. "If so, I could use your help. If not, feel free to hop out."

Rapp was not big on deference.

"Don't get your panties in a bunch," Stan said. "I'm just blowing off steam."

Rapp thought this was only partly true. Since they were currently hurtling north as fast as Derek could push the little helicopter, Rapp didn't think Hurley was anxious to take him up on his offer to exit the aircraft. But he also thought that Stan might be a little sore that he hadn't been invited to the Islamabad party before now. Still, if anyone could drop into the mountain range north of Islamabad and walk out unharmed, it would be Stan Hurley. The old codger had certainly aged, but he was still as wiry as a steel trap.

A rusted, ornery steel trap.

"Besides, I'm not mad at you," Stan said after a pause. "Or at least not just at you. I was working a thing in Vienna when Irene called. I landed in Islamabad three hours ago, and I still had to kick an untold number of shitbirds out of bed just to score a vehicle and two assaulter packs. Irene needs to get her ass over here and clean house. Too many of our people have forgotten they're supposed to be fighting a war."

Rapp digested this in silence as he finally got the cell phone connected to his flight headset. He was preparing to dial when the Jet-Ranger bucked, throwing him against his harness.

The phone tumbled to the cabin floor.

Rapp cursed as he strained to reach the cell.

"Sorry," Derek said. "Turbulence is always bad this close to mountains. We're burning JP8 like it's going out of style. I'm gonna need to revise my fuel estimate."

This was another problem Rapp did not need.

Based on when the charter pilot, Damon, had told him that the Iranians and Ashani had boarded his jet, Rapp figured that Ruyintan had departed Islamabad for Abbottabad at least an hour and a half earlier. The head start would have been no factor had Derek been able to travel in a straight line between the two cities, but that was a nonstarter. The helicopter's engine wasn't powerful enough to achieve the minimum safe altitude required to fly over the craggy peaks.

Had the weather been more cooperative, Derek might have tried to poke his way through some of the lower passes, but the poor visibility prohibited this course of action too. Instead, the Army aviator had elected to swing west before turning back northeast in an effort to skirt the rolling foothills. This meant their flight time was about thirty minutes versus Ruyintan's drive time of almost two hours.

It was going to be close.

"Do you at least know what kind of car we're trying to find?" Stan said.

Rapp did not, but he was hoping that was about to change. "Here's the deal—we're looking for two shoulder-fired missiles, a Quds Forces colonel, his bodyguards, and maybe a HIG fighter or two. I don't know what they're driving, but I know where they're going—bin Laden's compound in Abbottabad."

"I'm sorry," Derek said. "Can you say that again?"

"It gets better," Rapp said. "Two Black Hawks full of SEAL Team 6 assaulters are en route to that same compound. We need to find the Iranians and remove them from the equation so that they're not a factor in the SEAL raid. Best case, Ruyintan wants to warn bin Laden that we're coming. Worse case, he knows about the raid and intends to shoot down the Black Hawks. Speaking of which, you might want to set your watch's countdown timer for thirty minutes. That's the strike package's time on target."

"Fuck me running," Stan said. "I should have stayed in Vienna."

"It's gonna be close," Derek said as the helicopter's nose dipped. "I'm redlining the engine, but higher airspeed means a higher rate of fuel consumption. I think I can get us to Abbottabad about fifteen minutes before the strike package, but we'll have less than ten minutes of gas."

"Get us there as fast as you can," Rapp said. "Stan and I will deal with the Iranians."

"Fan-fucking-tastic," Hurley said.

The old codger really had a way with words.

CHAPTER 90

"**M**ARCUS, it's me."

Rapp resisted the urge to shout into his headset's mic. The noise-canceling algorithms did a fair job of negating the worst of the howling engine, but a helicopter's cabin was no one's idea of a library.

"Hey, Mitch. What's up?"

Marcus Drummond had attended the Massachusetts Institute of Technology with Rapp's younger brother. But unlike Steven Rapp, who made his millions though legitimate investments in the stock market, Marcus had gone a different route—hacking. His criminal career, while illustrious from the standpoint of his successful hacks, had not been lengthy. After a string of successes, Marcus had soon found himself a target of the FBI and, shortly thereafter, in a jail cell.

After learning of his friend's incarceration, Steven had suggested that Rapp might find a use for a cyber warrior of Marcus's abilities. Rapp had given Marcus a trial run, and the hacker had proven his worth countless times since.

Rapp was hoping this would be another one of those times.

"I know you're on vacation," Rapp said, "but I need your help. Now."

"Thank God. I can't take much more of this family reunion. What's up?"

"Do you have your laptop?" Rapp said.

"I'm going to pretend you didn't just ask that. Tell me what you need."

Rapp pictured the business card Ruyintan had given him what felt like a lifetime ago. The business card with a number scribbled across the front in the Iranian's precise handwriting. "I need to lock down a phone that's somewhere between Islamabad and Abbottabad. Ready to copy?"

"Shoot."

Rapp relayed the string of digits.

"Got it," Marcus said after reading them back. "Give me ten minutes."

"You have five. No bullshit. This is a ticking-time-bomb sort of tasking. Invoke whatever protocols you need to bump this to the top of the list."

"Up to and including the president?"

"Up to and including the Holy Trinity. I mean it, Marcus. We have to find this phone. Now."

"All right, stand by."

Rapp's seat dropped out from beneath him like he was strapped into a runaway elevator. After a second of heart-stopping descent, the rotor noise increased and the helicopter clawed its way into a steep climb, pressing him into the upholstery.

"What the fuck?" Stan said.

"Sorry," Derek answered. "Wasn't expecting the downdraft. There's a thunderstorm brewing over Islamabad. The air should be cleaner once we're on the north side of this ridgeline."

"Uhh, Mitch?" Marcus said. "We've got a problem."

"What?" Rapp said.

"I can't get a lock on the phone."

Rapp cursed, angry at himself more than Marcus. Had he been in the Iranian's place, Mitch would have pitched the phone, but he was hoping for a one-in-a-thousand chance that either Ruyintan had grown lazy or the number he'd given Mitch corresponded to his personal cell rather than a burner. Mitch should have known that someone who'd been in the game this long wouldn't have made such a stupid mistake.

"Okay, no problem," Mitch said. "Nash should already be uploading the contents from the five or so phones I recovered from the Iranians' plane. Their owners all work for the same bad guy, so they've probably called him. Grab any numbers common across the phones' call registries and check if those handsets ping the cell towers in the vicinity of Abbottabad, Pakistan. If so, give me a talk-on."

Rapp was no cyber warrior, but he'd been hunting high-value targets long enough to at least be familiar with what was possible in the realm of digital exploitation. What he'd just suggested would require more effort on Marcus's part, but the hacker was up for the task.

Assuming he had enough time.

"Sorry," Marcus said. "I wasn't clear before. The problem isn't with the number you gave me. It's with the cell phone towers. The ones servicing Abbottabad are intermittent. It's like someone is randomly turning them on and off."

Rapp could have kicked himself.

The cell towers looked as if someone was randomly turning them off and on because someone probably was. Someone located at NSA headquarters in Fort Meade, Maryland. An American strike package was about to hit a compound less than a mile from the Pakistani version of West Point. Even though it was just after midnight, the odds that two Black Hawks hovering over the city's outskirts would go unnoticed were zilch. America's premier keyboard warriors were undoubtedly doing what they could to stack the deck in the SEALs' favor. This included randomly interrupting cell service in preparation for what would probably be a total blackout while the frogmen hit the compound.

Which would happen in less than twenty minutes.

Shit.

"Thanks, Marcus," Rapp said. "We'll handle things from here."

"Wait," Marcus said, "I can give you something. I got a hit on the first number you referenced. The metadata is ninety minutes old, but I can interpolate the cell's direction of travel. The mobile was heading northeast on Highway M-15."

The most direct route from Islamabad to Abbottabad.

"That helps," Rapp said. "Anything else?"

"Sorry, no. I hope that's enough."

So did Rapp.

CHAPTER 91

"**T**IME to shit or get off the pot," Stan said. "How we doing this?"

While Rapp had been on the phone with Marcus, Hurley had been kitting up. The clandestine operative had strapped on a plate carrier and loaded the chest rig with magazines. His HK was resting across his lap with a magazine seated in the well. No doubt he'd also verified the optics and made minute adjustments to his equipment.

Fifty percent of Rapp's assault team was ready to go.

Now they just needed a target.

Rapp grabbed his own gear as he thought about how to answer.

The countryside below slid by in a blur, and a yellow ribbon of highway stretched out his left window. At this time of the night, the road was mostly empty of vehicular traffic.

Mostly, but not completely.

Headlights cut through the darkness in twos and threes. As with any metropolitan area, a handful of night owls still prowled the streets, but even a handful was too many. Contrary to Stan's earlier sarcasm, there would be no waving a pistol at the Iranian vehicle and asking them to cooperate. He and Stan had to hit the target hard and fast to make up for their disadvantage in manpower. There would be no quarter offered or accepted, which meant that Rapp had to be right or else innocent Pakistanis would die.

"That's N-35 at nine o'clock," Derek said, "and Abbottabad's at our one. Where're we going?"

Something about the aviator's question grabbed Rapp and wouldn't let go.

Where're we going?

Then he understood.

Rapp didn't need to find the Iranians.

Ruyintan would come to him.

Rapp grabbed one of the tactical tablets, activated the mapping feature, and zoomed in on Abbottabad. "We're headed for a compound in Bilal town. Follow N-35 until you see an intersection with a divided, four-lane road heading east. From that intersection, take up a northeasterly heading for about two and a half klicks. You should see a rectangular farmer's field orientated from southwest to northeast. The field is about three hundred meters long and fifty wide."

"I've got the intersection," Derek said, "and I think I've got the field as well."

The Army aviator was flying the helicopter with the transponder off and the position and collision lights blacked out. This low to the ground, running into another aircraft wasn't really a risk, but Derek had still appropriated one of the sets of Stan's night-vision goggles.

The pilot's foresight was now paying dividends.

"If it's the correct field, you should see the Pakistan Military Academy about five hundred meters to the northwest," Rapp said.

"Tally field and the academy," Derek said.

"Great," Rapp said, scrolling across the map as he thought. "The target compound is about one hundred and fifty meters southwest of the field's center point. Stay west of the field so we don't spook the target. There's a north–south running creek about four hundred meters from the western edge of the field. Don't proceed east of that creek."

"Got it," Derek said as he put the helicopter into a slow turn to the left. "I'm already well into my reserve fuel. We've got maybe ten minutes."

"Lay it on me," Hurley said.

"Ruyintan's on the clock too," Rapp said, fiddling with the tablet. "He'll take the most direct route to the compound. That means heading northeast on Kakul Road from N-35. He'll pick up the Bilal Town Road turnoff and follow it south to Nazim Street. From there it's a straight shot northeast to the compound. Three hundred meters, maybe less."

"If I was delivering a pizza, those would be great directions," Hurley said. "But I still don't see—"

"Ruyintan has two shoulder-fired missiles and at least four or five fighters," Rapp said. "Odds are they're in a van or truck. How many vans or trucks do you think we'll see cruising toward bin Laden's house this time of the night?"

"At least one," Derek said. "I've got a van driving northeast on Kakul Road. Three o'clock at about eight hundred meters. Is that them?"

CHAPTER 92

SINCE the helicopter was heading south and the potential target northeast, Rapp had the best view of the van.

It wasn't much of a view.

Unlike Stan and Derek, Rapp wasn't wearing night-vision goggles. Without optics, he could only see bits and pieces of the vehicle as it passed through the weak light cast by the occasional streetlamp. Brake lights glowed red as the vehicle approached the entrance to the Pakistan Military Academy.

A moment later, the vehicle vanished.

"Come around to the right," Rapp said. "Nice and slow in case anyone's watching. I lost the van as it was coming abeam the military academy. Stan—you've got the eye."

"Turning," Derek said. "The second fuel light just illuminated. We're down to five minutes. Maybe less."

Rapp shrugged into his plate carrier and fastened the straps, his fingers moving on autopilot. Fighting the harness as the helicopter banked, Rapp seated a magazine in the HK and switched on his optics.

A holographic crimson dot stared back at him.

"Got the little fucker," Hurley said. "He just turned south on Bilal Town Road. I want to take him at the northeastern corner of the field. Get me there, Derek."

"I'll take him," Rapp said.

"No can do," Hurley said. "One of us needs to stay with the bird. I'm as good in close as ever, but you're better with a long gun. I'm hitting the vehicle and you're providing overwatch. Set me down, Derek. Now."

Rapp wanted to argue.

He didn't.

Stan was right.

"Do it, Derek," Rapp said. "Stan—grab one of the low-profile ear-bud sets."

"Way ahead of you," Stan said, pointing to his ear.

Derek flared the helicopter and Stan jumped while the skids were still five feet above the tilled earth. Without missing a beat, the JetRanger thundered back skyward. Rapp popped one of the earbuds into his right ear so that he could still hear Derek through the aircraft's intercom via his left.

"You got me?"

Stan's voice came through crystal clear. It was not lost on Rapp that he and Stan were now using the low-profile communications kit Nash had forced on him during the FAIRBANKS hit what seemed like a life-time ago.

Maybe Nash had a future on the seventh floor after all.

"Loud and clear," Rapp said. "The van is two hundred meters to your north and closing. How do you want to play it?"

"I'm gonna set up on the west side of the road," Stan said, "right at the northwest corner of the field. There's a clump of trees I can hide in, and I'll be shooting toward the empty field instead of houses. I'll concentrate my fire on the front of the van, but I'll be on the driver's side. You start on the passenger's side and work your way back. I'll call 'cease fire.'"

Stan's heavy breathing echoed across the radio. From the sound of things, it had been a while since Hurley had incorporated wind sprints into his fitness regimen.

"Roger all," Rapp said to Stan before triggering his headset's mike. "Derek—is there a way to jettison the cabin door?"

"Yeah—should be cotter pins on the hinges. Pull them and then push out. The door will fall away. What's the plan?"

"Stan's gonna initiate once the vehicle's abeam him," Rapp grunted as he worked the rusty pins loose. "Once he starts shooting, I'll need you to keep us steady so I can help."

"Got it—what's the initiation signal?"

That was a very good question.

Rapp pulled the final cotter pin, and the door went nowhere. Unbuckling his restraint harness, Rapp rotated in his seat, placed his feet on the door, and pushed. The slipstream was working against him. After two fruitless attempts, his brain reengaged.

"Derek—give me a slight right bank."

Apparently, *slight* was in the eye of the beholder.

The helicopter rolled right, and the door tumbled into space.

Rapp nearly tumbled with it.

As his feet slid toward oblivion, Rapp's fingers found the restraint harness. He grabbed the nylon webbing with both hands and hung on as if his life depended on it.

It did.

After what seemed like an eternity, Derek banked the helicopter back to the left. Rapp buckled himself in, thankful he'd slung his rifle around his neck. Otherwise, the HK would have joined the cabin door.

"Derek," Rapp said once he had a hand free to trigger the intercom system, "does this bird have a spotlight?"

"A small one."

"Get ready to illuminate the van on my mark."

"Got it."

"Stan, we will initiate with the bird's spotlight. Call when ready."

"Execute, execute, execute."

This time Rapp didn't try to find the intercom switch. Instead, he reached forward and slapped Derek on the shoulder, hoping the pilot would get the hint.

He did.

The helicopter's taxi light lanced through the darkness, catching the van in a puddle of silver. In a stroke of genius, Derek spun the JetRanger on its axis, orientating the aircraft so the light blasted through the van's windshield. The vehicle slowed, probably as the driver instinctively braked in response to the ocular onslaught. Rapp held the EOTECH's crimson dot on the van's passenger's-side windshield, moved the selector switch from safe to single shot, and began squeezing the trigger.

He worked through the first magazine in a methodical fashion, trying to make each shot count. He didn't know what if anything he was hitting, but he and Stan were achieving target effect. The van slewed to the right and came to a stop as the front wheels left the pavement for the road's dirt shoulder. After reloading, Rapp switched the selector switch to sustained fire and hammered through two more magazines using short, controlled bursts.

He was on his third and final magazine when Stan's voice crackled through his earpiece.

"Cease fire, cease fire."

Rapp complied, placing the HK on safe.

For the first time, he took in the sum of the vehicle instead of just the section he'd been shooting. Even from this distance, it was easy to tell that the van was significantly worse for the wear. The windshield was a mass of splintered glass and at least one of the headlights had been shot out. Most importantly, nothing moved. No scrum of bodies came boiling out of the vehicle, and no driver attempted to steer the van clear of the ambush site.

They'd done it.

"I'm clearing the vehicle," Stan said.

"Negative," Rapp said. "Wait for me to get on the ground."

"No time."

Stan moved toward the van with his smooth amble. Rapp ground his teeth at his mentor's actions, but he was more irritated with himself than Stan. Hurley had been working as a covert operative since before Rapp was born. He didn't take orders.

From anyone.

Pausing in front of the vehicle, Stan punched the HK's barrel through an already half-shattered window and fired several times.

"Trouble?" Rapp said.

"Better safe than sorry."

Withdrawing the rifle, Stan opened the door and plunged his torso inside. For a long moment Rapp could do nothing but stare at Hurley's backside and cycle through all the potential ways this could go wrong.

Then, Stan's voice crackled in his ear.

"I was wrong—we do have trouble."

"What?" Rapp said.

"We're missing a missile."

Where had he heard that before?

CHAPTER 93

"**Y**ou sure?"

Rapp regretted the reflexive question the second the words left his lips.

Maybe Stan would forgive his slip.

"Of course I'm fucking sure. I've got a van full of dead Iranians and a single missile case. We're short one."

Nope.

"Is Ruyintan there?" Rapp said.

"Stand by."

A pulsing light drew Rapp's attention to his watch.

His five-minute alarm.

The flight of Black Hawks would now be at their release point turning south toward the compound. Thirty-odd American lives were on the line because he'd told Irene to trust him, and now he was short a missile.

Damn it.

"Negative," Stan said. "Ruyintan's not here."

What had they missed?

A second vehicle?

Another target?

Had the original missile count been wrong?

"If I don't pick a place to land in the next thirty seconds, the helicopter's going to pick one for me," Derek said.

"Stand by," Rapp said, trying to sort through the problem.

What had they missed?

The van had been on the way to bin Laden's compound, so Ruyintan had either intended to warn bin Laden about the Americans or give him the missiles.

Then why was one missing?

Because that wasn't all the Iranian intended.

"Head north," Rapp said. "Back toward the military academy. Now."

The helicopter's nose dipped, and the aircraft surged forward as if the JetRanger had been shot from a cannon.

"We're not going to make it," Derek said.

"Get me as close to the Bilal Town Road turnoff from Kaul Road as you can," Rapp said. "Look for a chunk of land with the widest view of the sky."

"Roger that," Derek said. "We'll glide farther with more altitude, but that will also make us easier to see."

The aviator didn't elaborate.

He didn't have to.

Easier to see meant easier for the missile team to see. So be it. If the presence of a blacked-out JetRanger spooked the Iranians, Rapp would chance eating a missile in order to save the SEALs. But judging by his past performance, Ruyintan wouldn't make things that easy.

"Where the hell are you going?"

With a start, Rapp realized Stan hadn't been able to hear his conversation with Derek. "We temporarily lost sight of the van before it turned south on Bilal Road, remember? If they dumped Ruyintan and the other missile, that's where he'll be."

"What if you're wrong?"

"Then a helicopter full of SEALs is gonna die. If that happens, I expect you to knock on bin Laden's door and shoot him in the face."

"On it."

Rapp was preparing to reply when another sound demanded his attention.

Or rather, a lack of sound.

A lack of sound coming from the engine.

CHAPTER 94

"Lock your harness," Derek said. "We're going down."

Rapp did not lock his harness.

Instead, he leaned over the aviator's shoulder, peering through the windshield. Without the aid of night-vision goggles, Rapp couldn't see much of anything. Then again, he supposed that between the two of them, Derek needed the NVGs more right about now.

"Did you find the missile team?" Rapp said.

"Trying to find somewhere to land."

"The missile team—do you see them?"

"For fuck's sake, I don't . . . wait . . . yes! There's a field just west of the military academy. Three figures . . . maybe a missile."

Maybe a missile.

Not exactly definitive proof, but beggars couldn't be choosers. "Land on them."

"They're to our north and we've got a twenty-knot tailwind. I need to turn into the wind—"

"Land this fucking helicopter on top of them."

Rapp heard a hiss through the intercom system, but the aviator didn't turn the aircraft. Hunching forward, Rapp thought he could see a clump of dark figures in a field just ahead.

Dark figures that were rapidly drawing closer.

"Hold on," Derek said. "This is gonna hurt."

A heartbeat later, steel met earth.

Rapp's restraint harness kept him mostly upright, but since the inertia latching mechanism wasn't locked, his limbs pinballed around the cabin. The crash sequence was loud. The fuselage groaned, the rotors shrieked, and men screamed. Rapp didn't black out, but the world did get a little hazy. When he came to his senses, he was struck by two overwhelming sensations: every inch of his body hurt, and the air smelled like shit.

Cow shit.

They'd crash-landed into a freshly manured field.

That seemed like an appropriate metaphor for this entire endeavor.

Turning the quick release on his restraint harness, Rapp fought clear of the entangling nylon straps and tumbled to the damp soil. In a testament to the aviator's ability to follow directions, Derek had in fact landed the helicopter on top of the missile team.

Or at least one of its members.

A torso and section of leg protruded from beneath the helicopter's right skid. The rest of the man was presumably somewhere beneath the twin tubular sections of steel, but the Iranian wasn't going anywhere. The same could not be said for the monster of a human being coming around the helicopter's nose.

A monster with a gun.

CHAPTER 95

T HE sight of the armed man prompted four quick realizations.

One, Rapp recognized him.

Or at least recognized the Iranian's flattened nose, heavy shoulders, and cauliflower ears. It was Ruyintan's bodyguard from the café.

The bodyguard with the scarred knuckles.

Two, Derek was slumped in the pilot's seat. Rapp couldn't see much beyond the dark rivulets dripping from Derek's scalp, but he knew the aviator was going to have one hell of a hangover when he woke up.

If he woke up.

Three, Rapp's HK was no longer slung around his neck. Rap had slipped the weapon's sling over his restraint harness, and the rifle must have come free during the crash sequence.

Fourth, and most important, Rapp saw a black figure just beyond the monster.

A figure with a long tube resting on his shoulder.

Rapp felt the bulge of the pistol that was holstered at the small of his back, but with the Iranian on top of him, it might as well have been in the helicopter's cabin with his HK. He'd never draw the Glock in time.

Instead, Rapp rushed forward, sweeping the monster's pistol offline with his right hand and firing a hook into the Iranian's side with his left.

At least that's what he'd intended to do.

Unfortunately for Rapp, this was not the Iranian's first scuffle.

Rapp had knocked the gunman's pistol off target, but his left hook found air instead of flesh. The Iranian crashed Rapp's strike, leading with his forehead. The headbutt caught Rapp square in the face. Rapp tucked his chin at the last second, saving his nose, but a constellation of stars went supernova thanks to the skull-to-skull contact. Rapp shook his head, trying to clear the cobwebs, and instinctively brought both elbows up to cover his face in anticipation of a follow-up hook.

The blow didn't come.

At least not to his face.

What felt like an aluminum bat exploded into his side, followed by a sledgehammer to his head. The Iranian had cinder blocks for fists. The body blow clipped Rapp's thick back muscles instead of his liver, but the haymaker to his head knocked him on his ass. The Iranian scooped up his pistol from where it had fallen and extended it toward Rapp.

Derek grunted, and the cockpit door slammed into the Iranian just as the pistol fired.

The bullet impact sprayed Rapp's face with manure. He snapped his leg into a straight kick, torquing his hips and driving his heel through the monster's knee. The Iranian howled, instinctively reaching for the fuselage to steady himself.

For an instant, the monster's pistol wavered as pain overrode his tactical sense.

Rotating to his side, Rapp drew the Glock, indexed the pistol on the monster's chest, and pressed the trigger.

The pistol barked.

The monster grunted.

Rapp fired once more into the crumbling man's torso, then panned the glowing front sight post toward the man with the missile. The warbling sound of a seeker head locking on to a target competed for Rapp's attention with a thundering from multiple helicopters.

The strike package was overhead.

Rapp's world shrank to three glowing tritium dots—one on the Glock's front sight post and two on the rear. He brought the floating green orbs into alignment and pressed the trigger.

The pistol discharged, and the sights drifted up and to the left.

Rapp brought the orbs back onto target and fired again.

The pistol's slide locked open.

Scrambling to his feet, Rapp grabbed the monster's pistol and sprinted toward the crumpled form. He fired twice more into the unmoving body and then pulled the missile away from the dead man's chest. The seeker's tone changed, indicating that the weapon had lost lock. Rapp was reaching for the missile when a pair of black forms scythed through the sky, drowning out the electronic warble. Rapp tracked the strike package's progress for a moment before squatting next to the missileer.

A faint pucker marred the man's right cheekbone.

A pucker made by an American Marine's 5.56mm round.

Ruyintan.

The missile warbled a final time before falling silent.

Rapp looked south toward bin Laden's compound and the two helicopters loaded with commandos. The world's most wanted terrorist was about to receive justice, but there were still plenty more shitbags who needed killing.

His work wasn't done.

Not by a long shot.

Rapp retrieved the missile from Ruyintan's body, balanced it on his shoulder, and started toward the crashed helicopter and Derek.

In spite of everything, he began to smile.

For once in his life, Stan Hurley had been wrong.

You *could* save the day with only a half-empty pistol.

EPILOGUE

IRENE Kennedy watched her son thunder across the lacrosse field.

Though he had a preteen's lanky awkward appearance, Tommy's performance wasn't that of a kid still in braces. While she was far from an aficionado, Irene's interest in lacrosse had increased in proportion to her son's. She wouldn't be offering coaching tips anytime soon, but Irene had sat through enough games to know that her son was something of a savant. If he kept up the effort, Tommy would probably be able to attend college on an athletic scholarship.

This was not a development she, or Tommy's academic father, had foreseen.

For a moment, Irene was lost in the cadence of the play as her focus narrowed to just her boy and the opposing goalie. Spinning around two defenders, Tommy broke free and opened up a line to the goal. His stick snapped and the ball rocketed toward the net. Irene found herself on her feet, screaming in a manner not commensurate with her position as director of the world's most important intelligence agency.

The rubber ball clanked off the post, and the moment was gone.

"Shit," Irene said. "Shit, shit, shit."

"You're starting to sound like a soccer mom."

Irene turned to see Rapp standing beside her. She offered her cheek to be kissed but kept her attention on the field.

The game wasn't over.

"Didn't your mother ever tell you it's not polite to sneak up on people?"

"I didn't sneak," Rapp said. "I checked in with your security detail and stomped my feet the whole way. You were too entranced watching Tommy take a shot on the goal to notice."

"Rack," Irene said. "It's called a cage or a rack."

"Very good," Rapp said with a laugh. "If I didn't know better, I'd think you were enjoying yourself."

"Of course I'm enjoying myself," Irene said. "My son's on the field."

"Better get used to that," Rapp said. "Tommy's got the gift."

Irene let Rapp's words wash over her, surprised at the feeling of warmth they engendered. But as tempting as it was to bask in the joy accompanying the summer day, Tommy's success, and Mitch's unexpected appearance, she tempered the feeling. The man standing next to her might be a close friend, but he was also one of her most valuable employees.

An employee who'd been incommunicado for the last six weeks.

"Haven't seen you around the office lately," Irene said.

If anyone else had said the same words, Rapp might have become defensive. Since she'd been the one to speak them, he just nodded, acknowledging the observation in the same spirit with which it had been offered.

"Been busy."

"I've noticed."

The entire Middle East had noticed.

Irene hadn't been overly surprised when FAIRBANKS had turned up dead. The financier had American blood on his hands, and his assassination had been officially sanctioned by the CIA and White

House. Rapp had never been one to let an authorized killing gather dust.

But other jihadis began to follow suit.

Lots of them.

Iranian Quds Force officers, Hezbollah operatives, even a couple of Iraqi Shia militia members. Though none of the killings bore the signature of an American-sponsored assassination, taken in toto, even a fool could discern the message behind the string of killings.

And the Iranians were not fools.

There was just one problem—she hadn't ordered the hits.

"Have the right people gotten the message?" Rapp said.

Irene thought about her answer.

Though they did their best to treat her otherwise, the parents of Tommy's teammates knew that Irene was not just another lacrosse mom. The men and women who worked and lived in the national capital region were perhaps less impressed with security details than their countrymen who populated the so-called flyover states, but Irene was not another minor cabinet member. She was the director of the Central Intelligence Agency and one of the administration's most recognizable faces. As such, her fellow lacrosse moms and dads tended to afford Irene a certain amount of space, especially when hard-looking men or women engaged her in hushed conversations.

Men like Rapp.

After verifying that no one was within earshot, Irene turned back to Mitch. "Moradi has followed in Ashani's footsteps by opening a diplomatic back channel with me. The specifications for the missiles' guidance system were part of the first batch of intelligence he provided. It's some sort of acoustic cuing system. I'm told the scientists at Redstone Arsenal are already hard at work engineering countermeasures."

"Did Moradi say what Ruyintan had been planning?"

Irene brushed an errant strand of hair from her eyes before replying. "Ruyintan's primary objective was to shoot down at least one plane carrying diplomatic attendees from the regional security conference as they departed Islamabad International Airport. Preferably *our* diplomatic attendees."

"Why?"

"To drive a wedge between America and Pakistan. The missiles the Iranians were helping the jihadis smuggle into Afghanistan were meant to target our helicopters, but that wasn't their only purpose. Ruyintan wanted us to establish a linkage between the HIG fighters in Afghanistan and the shootdown in Pakistan."

"HIG fighters that the ISI had a history of funding," Rapp said. "It would look like their attack dogs went rogue."

"Or that members of the ISI had sanctioned the Islamabad operation," Irene said. "Either way, our relationship with Pakistan would have been strained to the breaking point."

"Why didn't Ruyintan go through with it?"

"Disrupting the bin Laden operation was an even bigger opportunity. If you hadn't stopped him, Ruyintan would have destroyed two Black Hawks loaded with Navy SEALs, saved the world's most wanted terrorist from capture or death, and cast blame on the Pakistanis in the process."

"How did he know we were coming for bin Laden?" Rapp said.

Irene shrugged. "I'm not sure he did, at least not with one hundred percent certainty. After he learned Ashani was offering us bin Laden, maybe he put a call in to an asset in Abbottabad and realized we were manipulating the grid or that our safehouse was jamming the electronic spectrum near the compound. Or maybe someone breached operational security during the lead-up to the raid. Perhaps Ruyintan just took a gamble. He'd been in this business a long time. Long enough to know when to put all his chips on the table."

Rapp nodded. "Either way, Ashani saved us. Did you take care of his family?"

"Ashani's wife and daughters have been relocated to California. Moradi assures me that the regime has no further interest in them."

Rapp nodded again but didn't speak. For a time, Irene was content to sit in silence. Only when a buzzer signaled the end of the match did she turn back to Rapp. "You missed Noreen's ceremony."

"I know. If there was any way I could've made it back in time I would have."

Irene had lost officers under her command before, and it never got any easier. Watching the master stonemason chisel Noreen's star into the Memorial Wall's white Alabama marble had been gut-wrenching, but Irene had also felt a strange sense of dissonance. As all of America celebrated the successful bin Laden operation, a select few citizens were grieving the passing of a CIA officer. Noreen Ahmed had worked under non-official cover status so her contributions to the raid would probably never be made public.

That was the life of a clandestine operative.

A life Noreen had willingly chosen.

But Irene still felt the weight of the new star gracing the lobby of the CIA's Original Headquarters Building. Noreen would probably not be the last officer to die during Irene's tenure, but Irene was determined to ensure those deaths were not needless or in vain.

This was difficult to do when one of her officers decided to go off the reservation.

"Would you like to tell me what you've been up to?" Irene said.

Irene was a bit irritated that she had to be so direct. When it came to operational matters, there were no secrets between them. She'd covered for his unexplained absence with the president and run interference for the corpses piling up all over the Islamic Crescent. She'd expected Mitch to return the favor with candor rather than obfuscations.

"I know about the panic attacks," Rapp said.

On the other side of the field, Tommy was engaging in a bit of adolescent jubilation with his friends. Between the rancorous recap of each boy's role in the win and the obligatory postgame speech by the coach, Irene figured she had about ten minutes alone with Rapp.

That would not be long enough.

"What do you mean?" Irene said.

"I had them too. After Anna died." Rapp paused as he ran his hand over his freshly shaved jaw. "I failed her, Irene. Anna and our unborn daughter were murdered because I didn't protect them. After my family was killed, I started wondering who I would fail next. The racing heart, chest tightness, debilitating anxiety, and sleepless nights weren't far behind."

The part of Irene that regarded Rapp as a younger brother wanted to hug him. The part that was his boss was furious that she hadn't noticed the changes in her top counterterrorism operative. She placed a hand on his arm and felt his muscles tense. "Mitch, I—"

"I'm okay now, Irene. I really am. You will be too. I noticed, but no one else has. Talk to Dr. Lewis—he can help."

Irene never imagined she'd be on the receiving end of mental health advice from Mitch Rapp. At her insistence, Rapp had spent a good deal of time in Lewis's office, not because she'd thought he had a problem, but because she hadn't wanted him to develop one. Rapp hated the sessions and wouldn't speak of them unless pressed. Lewis was only slightly more enthusiastic about the forced talks. Even though he'd served as the CIA's therapist for countless clandestine operatives, when it came to tough patients, Lewis claimed that Rapp was in a league all his own.

Perhaps the doctor had accomplished more than he knew.

"Thank you, Mitch. Really."

Rapp nodded. "I can't help you process what you're feeling, Irene. That's just not my gift. But I can help in a different way."

Irene stared at Rapp, wondering if she really knew him at all.

But she did.

A little too well.

"The string of assassinations," Irene said, trying to keep the emotion from her voice. "You did that for me."

"Not just you," Rapp said. "The world needs to know that kidnapping and torturing the director of the Central Intelligence Agency is not conducive to a long or full life. But off the record, yeah. Anyone who planned, aided, abetted, or even looked the other way while it happened has paid for their sins. Talk to Lewis, take up yoga, try meditation, whatever. Do what you need to do to get over this, but know this: I will never fail you like I failed them, Irene. Never."

Irene swallowed, trying to get past the lump in her throat. Rapp squeezed her shoulder and walked away. As she watched his broad back disappear into the milling crowd, the knot of tension in her chest began to loosen.

"Mom—are you okay?"

Irene turned to see Tommy in front of her. Impulsively, she wrapped her arms around her son and he hugged her back.

"I'm fine, honey," she murmured into his sweaty hair. "Just fine."

She wasn't.

Not yet.

But she would be.

AUTHOR'S NOTE

W HILE this book draws upon some of the actual elements surrounding the raid to capture or kill Osama bin Laden, it is still a work of fiction. As such, I took certain artistic liberties with timelines and events. My meddling aside, this part remains true—on May 2, 2011, twenty-three Navy SEALs brought justice to the man responsible for the worst terrorist attacks on US soil in our nation's history.

As a grateful American, I wish to say this to the countless men and women who made Operation Neptune Spear possible:

Thank you.

ACKNOWLEDGMENTS

I AM eternally grateful to have been afforded the opportunity to tell stories in Vince's universe. The list of people to whom I owe a debt of gratitude for making this happen is long and distinguished. I cannot thank them all, but I will try.

This would not have happened without Lysa Flynn, Sloan Harris, and Emily Bestler. These three are the stewards of Vince's legacy, and the guardians of the world he created. Thank you all for welcoming me to the family.

My agent, Scott Miller, was also instrumental in pulling this deal together. I once confessed to Scott that writing Mitch Rapp stories would be my dream job. Rather than laugh along with me, Scott said that he would try to make that happen. He did and I am forever in his debt. Thank you, Scott.

Kyle Mills and his lovely wife, Kim, have been among my biggest supporters throughout the transition process. Like all Flynn fans, I'm beyond thankful that Kyle agreed to step in after Vince's untimely death and continue Mitch Rapp's adventures. Rather than just tread water, Kyle expanded the series and took the characters in new and exciting directions. During our overlap, Kyle could not have been more generous with his time. From responding to every single social media post to reassure fans that I was up to the job, to sharing his final book tour with me, to fielding countless emails, texts, and phone calls, Kyle has been the consummate professional. Thank you, Kyle and Kim.

Bringing a book to life truly takes a village, and the village at Emily Bestler Books is populated by rock stars. Thank you all for welcoming me to the Fox Den and for your tireless work on *Capture or Kill*. One of the many benefits of joining the greater Simon & Schuster team includes the opportunity to finally work with master publicist and marketer David Brown. Thank you, David, for shouting about this book from the rooftops.

As my wife will tell you, I'm not a terribly interesting person. Fortunately, I have friends who fit that bill, and many of them graciously lent their expertise, technical or otherwise, to this novel. Colonel Kelsey A. Smith, USA, Retired, has been my friend and fellow gunship pilot for more than twenty years. Aside from his cameo in this novel, Kelsey helped me with the finer points of conducting an aerial area reconnaissance in eastern Afghanistan. Thank you, Kels.

Commander Jack Stewart, USN, Retired, used the aviation knowledge he's garnered in the cockpits of commercial airliners and FA-18 fighter jets alike to guide me through some of my trickier aviation conundrums. In addition to being a graduate of the Navy's Top Gun fighter school, Jack is also one heck of a thriller writer. If you haven't already, check out his debut novel, *Unknown Rider*. Thank you, Jack.

Though he now pens his Matthew Redd books by day while managing the *Real Book Spy* website by night, Ryan Steck was once known as Ryan the Rappologist due to his exhaustive knowledge of the Vince Flynn universe. In this capacity, Ryan graciously lent me his expertise by answering more than a few vexing Mitch Rapp questions. Thank you, Ryan.

The thriller-writer community is incredibly supportive, and I owe a huge debt of gratitude to the following authors: Mark Greaney, Brad Taylor, Brad Thor, Connor Sullivan, David McCloskey, Simon Gervais,

Taylor Moore, Tosca Lee, May Cobb, Samantha Bailey, Nick Petrie, Bill Schweigart, Brian Andrews, Jeff Wilson, Chris Hauty, Jack Carr, Joshua Hood, and Tessa Wegert. Thank you, all.

As always, I need to thank my family for supporting me as I chase my writing dreams. Angela, Will, Faith, and Kelia—I love you dearly. Thank you.

Finally, I would like to thank my fellow Mitch Rapp fans. Your warm welcome to the Flynn Family and your palatable excitement about *Capture or Kill* were a source of constant encouragement to me. I hope you love this book.

Don